PRAISE FOR KHURRU...

'Thrilling and immersive …violence, love, humour and razor-sharp observation keep the pages turning'
Times and **Sunday Times Crime Club**

'A timely addition to the new breed of socially committed British thrillers' **Guardian**

'Told with striking panache. Announces the arrival of a fine, fresh new thriller writer' **Daily Mail**

'Combining humour and tragedy is one of the hardest literary challenges, but Khurrum Rahman succeeds' **TLS**

'A very funny but tense thriller…Think
Four Lions meets *Phone Shop*' **Red**

'As much a coming-of-age story as a full-on action thriller, *East of Hounslow* is thought-provoking and entirely gripping' **Guardian**

'Sweary, funny and, above all, an absolutely cracking thriller that you'll tear through, this is the anti-James Bond that the 21st century needs' **Emerald Street**

'*East of Hounslow*, in which a young Muslim finds himself forced to become an MI5 plant in a group of jihadists, is as British as Nelson's Colum. A superb and exciting debut novel' **Telegraph**

'Clipped dialogues, staccato sentences and the hilariously brilliant prose set the pace of this excellent unputdownable crime thriller. The climax will leave you breathless' **New Indian Express**

'A brilliant thriller. You'd be mad not to buy this'
Ben Aaronovitch

Born in Karachi, Pakistan in 1975 Khurrum Rahman moved to England when he was one. He is a west London boy and now lives in Berkshire with his wife and two sons.

Khurrum is currently working as a Senior IT Officer but his real love is writing. He has a screenplay which has been optioned by a Danish TV producer but is now concentrating on novels.

The first book in the Jay Qasim series, *East of Hounslow*, was shortlisted for the CrimeFest last-laugh award, the CWA John Creasey Debut Dagger award and the Theakston Crime Novel of the Year Award, and was his first novel.

Homegrown Hero

Khurrum Rahman

ONE PLACE. MANY STORIES

This novel is entirely a work of fiction. The names, characters and incidents portrayed in it are the work of the author's imagination. Any resemblance to actual persons, living or dead, events or localities is entirely coincidental.

HQ
An imprint of HarperCollins*Publishers* Ltd
1 London Bridge Street
London SE1 9GF

www.harpercollins.co.uk

HarperCollinsPublishers
1st Floor, Watermarque Building, Ringsend Road
Dublin 4, Ireland

This edition 2021

21 22 LSC 10 9 8 7 6 4 3 2 1
First published in Great Britain by
HQ, an imprint of HarperCollins*Publishers* Ltd 2018

ISBN: 9780008384685

Printed and bound in the United States of America
by LSC Communications

To my very own Mischief and Mayhem,
and the one I call Jaan.

Prologue

Parking my Beemer in my driveway, I killed the engine and took a deep breath. Leaning back, I sank into the driver's seat and closed my eyes, enjoying the cool evening breeze coming in through the car window.

In the distance, I heard the low growl of a diesel engine. At first barely perceptible, the sound moved closer, louder, the vehicle picking up speed then humming idly as it came to a standstill close by.

A car door opened, and closed.

I opened my eyes and turned.

He was standing beside me, smiling down through my open car window. Like seeing a ghost.

'Hello, old chum,' he said, 'I haven't seen you in ages.'

I barely had time to catch a glint of something before his arm snaked through my window and, in perfect silence, sliced my throat from ear to ear.

PART 1

TWO DAYS EARLIER

Fatwa: A pronouncement of death by a higher authority.

1

Imran Siddiqui (Imy)

I'd never before come across a person like Jack. I had him tightly strapped in the backseat as I drove him to the location. He knew just as well as I did, maybe better, that I only had a small window to extract the information out of him. Because once we'd reached our destination he'd be protected to the hilt and there wasn't a damn thing I could do about it. He just needed to hold tight. But he'd made a mistake. He didn't know about me, about my past. I'd get the information I needed from the devil if it was the last damn thing I did. I was confident of it. I had to be careful, though. I couldn't get physical. If he turned up with so much as a mark on him, it would be me that suffered.

'Jack... C'mon, mate,' I started with the soft approach. 'Where is it?'

'I've told you,' Jack glanced outside the window at the buses lit up within Hounslow Bus Garage. 'I'm not telling you.'

I inhaled through my nose and gripped the steering wheel tightly. Even if I drove slowly I had maybe five minutes left of the journey. I loosened the grip and dropped my shoulders. He was observant, and I did not want him to see me tense. I turned the volume up on the CD player. In an effort to break him I had been playing *Yellow Submarine* on repeat, a song that he hated and one that I loved. It hadn't worked though; I was beginning to despise it; I took a quick glance in the rear-view mirror and he was singing along.

'Put it higher. This is my jam!' Jack squealed, and I immediately killed the sound.

'Jack. Listen... J-just listen.' I stammered and realised that I was about to plead. I've never before bent over for anybody and I wasn't going to start now. I pulled up at a red light and slipped the gear into neutral. I closed my eyes and tried to gather my thoughts and focus on my training. It seemed like a lifetime ago. It was a lifetime ago. A blare from the car behind broke me out of my thoughts.

'It's green,' Jack said.

His tinny voice echoed in my ears and I found myself grinding my teeth so hard that my temples started to rhythmically pulse. I slipped into first and set off with a stutter. I slid the window down and allowed the cold evening air to hit me, to jolt me into action, but I was fast running out of time and ideas. Jack sneezed. Gotcha! I moved my hand over the control panel and slid down every window. I eyed him through the rear-view and I could see Jack physically curl up into a ball, his shoulders hunched and his chin down to his chest. His bottom lip quivered. I almost, *almost* felt for him but instead I turned the air conditioning onto cold.

'You okay in the back, Jack?' I said, and with his chin still dug into his chest he lifted his big blue eyes at me and sniffed.

'I'm fine.'

'Bet you wish you wore a jacket now.'

'I'm fine.' He said, his face getting paler, angry goose pimples appearing on his arm.

'You ready to tell me or do I go higher?' I said, my hand hovering over the AC control.

'Do what you like. Go higher.'

I could not believe it. Why was it so hard to break him? When had I become so terrible at this? All my training, all my discipline had left me. As always, at times of stress, my scalp started to itch, as though a thousand little spiders were dancing through my hair and it took all my will not to scratch the hell out of it.

'You're sweating,' Jack said. His chin was now raised and pointing at me in defiance. My hand was at my forehead wiping away the sheen of sweat. He smiled, goofy and mocking and I dropped my hand immediately to the gear stick and gripped it.

No more Mr Nice Guy. This ends now. I closed the windows and killed the air con.

'I'm going to count to ten and if you haven't told me where the remote is then I am pulling over and going to work on your fingers until you do tell me. Is that what you want, Jack? Do you want me to chop off your fingers?'

'Why would I want you to chop off my fingers?' He blinked lazily at me.

'Because, you're asking for it.'

'I don't remember asking to have my fingers chopped off.'

It was an empty threat, an ill-judged bluff, one that we both knew that I would never go through with. I could never harm a single hair on his dumb side parting. I had lost, convincingly. The night that I had waited so long for, ruined. All the planning, wasted.

I pulled my Prius up to the location a broken man. There she was, stepping out of her Golf, a stack of files balanced in her hands. She was wearing a fitted grey trouser suit with Adidas sneakers, her heels knocking around somewhere in the confines of her car. She kicked the door shut and turned to us just as I was getting out of my car. She smiled at me and as frustrated as I was I could not help but smile back at her. It held for a long second as our smiles had a silent conversation.

Her name is Stephanie Mills, and every part of me is in love with every part of her.

I opened the back door, my smile replaced with a snarl, and unstrapped Jack out of the car. I gripped the back of his neck and frogmarched him down the path. He shrugged his shoulders away from my grip and ran to her. His protector. His Mother.

'Mummy, Imy opened all the windows and then he put the cold air on and I wasn't even wearing a jacket and... And... And...' He spurted in one breath, as I took the stack of files from her. She kneeled down and embraced Jack whilst giving me *that* look from over his shoulder. 'And he said he's going to chop my fingers off, Mummy.'

The look I delivered to Stephanie insinuated that it was all true. She stood up and smoothed down her suit as Jack scuttled behind her legs in mock fear.

'I swear it's like having two kids. Why do you two always have to fight so much?'

'Ask him!'

'I'm asking you, you're the grown up.'

'He's hidden the remote control. El Classico is on tonight.'

'El what? Forget it, I don't want to know.'

'It's a silly football match, Mummy,' Jack said, poking his head around her legs. Stephanie shot a look at him and he retreated back.

'So you're not staying tonight?' Stephanie asked. 'You can watch it here.'

'You can give me a bath, too and a bedtime story,' Jack chipped in.

'I've made plans with Shaz tonight, kid.'

She placed the palm of her hands on my chest and patted it once, twice. Her hands lingered as she planted an overdue kiss on my lips and whispered. 'Tomorrow? I'll cook.'

'Definitely,' I whispered back, my voice catching. Nearly three years together and her touch still made me want to forget the world and follow her voice, her smell. 'Tomorrow.'

'Say hi to Shaz from me. And Imy...' Stephanie inclined her head towards Jack who was now sitting cross legged on the front lawn picking clumps out of the grass. I nodded at her and with a too quick peck she turned and walked into her house.

8

'Alright, kid.' I sat down opposite him, legs crossed, mirroring him.

'Can't you stay?' His eyes everywhere but on me.

'I would love to. But I've got things to do. I'll come early tomorrow, we'll have lunch together.'

'I'm at school tomorrow,' Jack said, whine creeping into his voice.

'How about I swing by after? Take you to the park or we can go on a bike ride. Your choice.'

'Both... Can we do both?'

'How about you ride your bike *to* the park. How's that sound, kid?'

His eyes finally met mine and he nodded excitedly. 'Are you doing sleepover tomorrow, too?'

'I'll bring my PJ's. Let's make a camp and sleep in there,' I said. 'Now come on, bring it in, give me the good stuff.' He stood as I got to my knees and gave me a hug that only a five-year-old could possibly give, nice and tightly fitting into my body. I kissed him on the head and hissed in his ear.

'Where's the damn remote?'

'I'm not telling you,' he replied, whilst his hand snaked into my shirt collar and released damp grass down my back before running off inside laughing manically.

I sat in my car and watched them for a moment. Stephanie in the kitchen, steaming mug in one hand – *coffee*, *one sugar*, *no milk*. In the other hand she held a Spiderman beaker – *hot chocolate*, *microwaved*, *one minute medium*. Jack stormed in and clumsily climbed up onto the stool in front of the breakfast bar.

I said a silent prayer. Warmth, health and happiness.

But I knew that as much as I loved them, inevitably it would be me that took all those things away.

2

Javid Qasim (Jay)

The phone rang again, chirpy and incessant, desperate to be held. I looked across at the two other operators sitting either side of me. To my left Dave, or Davey as he liked to be called, a middle aged man who dressed way too young and smelt like tangerines. To my right, Kelly, a cute, geeky girl, the type who turned up transformed to the school prom and surprised the hell out of everyone, and ended up sleeping with Jason, the captain of the swimming team. Probably, I don't know. I just wanted to go home.

Kelly and Dave were busy on calls and the phone was still screaming in my face. I sighed loudly, my irritation clear to Carol, the team leader from hell. She glanced over at me just as I glanced over at the clock. Two minutes to five. Two minutes before I could get the hell out of this place for a few hours before it all starts again. I knew if I answered the phone I'd be stuck here past five. I can *just* about make it to five, but keeping me here any longer is tantamount to taking the fucking piss, especially on a Monday. I locked eyes with Carol and ventured out a hopeful smile whilst inclining my head towards the clock, the smile wasn't reciprocated, instead she nodded down her long beak at the phone. I huffed and puffed a little, just enough to have made my point, and then I answered the phone.

'IT Helpdesk, how can I help you?'

*

On the short drive home, I mentally pictured the inside of my fridge, it didn't take long. I couldn't be arsed with a big shop, I could do that later on my iPad, from the comfort of my armchair, but I did need a quick fix for the night.

I ducked into the newsagents at the end of my road and browsed the ready meals, picking myself out a prawn curry and a litre of milk. At the till, my eyes fell on the *Daily Mail*. On the front page a painfully familiar image was staring back at me. One I had seen many times, an image fast on its way to becoming as iconic as the plane flying into the twin towers on 9/11 or the devastated London Bus with its top blown on 7/7. My neighbour, my friend, Parvez Ahmed, laid out on his back atop a police van. His eyes open and lifeless, a sawn-off AK47 hanging around his neck and a Glock 19 handgun gripped in his dead hands. I picked up the newspaper, knowing full well that it was going to spoil the rest of my evening.

I placed the prawn curry in the microwave and read the article at the worktop. I was expecting inaccuracies, and it didn't disappoint. It had been around three months since the failed attack and the media just would not let it fucking go. It's exactly this kind of journalism that prods and provokes and burns an imprint into the public's consciousness. Not letting them move on, not letting us move on. Not a spare thought for those who suffered, whose families suffered. Parvez, who had died for a belief that many would never even contemplate understanding. Now they celebrate his death, parade the images like a badge of fucking honour. A constant reminder of the victory for the West. British intelligence working for the people.

But I knew better. I knew the truth.

Nine jihadis, four holding points, Oxford Street. All armed with automatic rifles and handguns, the objective to block in thousands of shoppers on Boxing Day, one of the busiest days of the year, and shoot at will. Parvez was one of the nine jihadis.

I was another.

I had been drafted into the Secret Service to spy on those that looked like me. My job was to uncover a terror plot and to establish what I could about the terrorist cell,

Ghurfat-Al-Mudarris. My career had been short-lived. I was no longer part of MI5, I no longer wanted to be. They had taken my life and hung it upside down, and people that I cared about had tumbled out. I'd given them the intelligence to prevent an unthinkable level of carnage, and they fucking rinsed me, man. Bent me over and fucked me and left me in a collapsed heap on the floor, sucking my thumb and crying out for my Mum. I gave them my all, flew half way around the fucking globe to a hell hole training camp where they knew that a certain somebody would want to see me. That somebody being Abdullah Bin Jabbar, better known to MI5 as The Teacher. A man shrouded in such mystery and myth that MI5 had to resort to using *me* – a small-time nickel and dime dope dealer from the streets of Hounslow – to ascertain information pertinent to national security. I gave them a name, I gave them locations, I gave them a description and in the process I found out that this fucking Bin Jabbar character, with the stupid fucking moniker, was my fucking father, who, until then, I had never before met.

And what did they do with that information? Jack-shit. The Teacher was still bouncing around between caves and mountains and safe houses somewhere in Afghanistan or Pakistan or who gives a fuck. I'd done my part.

Fucking MI5 and their fucking half-arsed operation. They didn't achieve shit, though they happily took credit for narrowly avoiding an attack on Oxford Street – never once mentioning that it was a stroke of freak luck that one of the jihadis had a last-minute change of heart and put a spanner in what would have made the 7/7 attacks seem like a teddy bears' picnic.

I sound angry. I know. I am. *Fucking fuming.*

MI5 referred me to a shrink to help me understand my feelings and recognise that my actions helped with a big result.

So, how did you feel when your friend Parvez was shot in front of your eyes?

It felt like shit.

He was about to start shooting innocent members of the public? He was going to be responsible for hundreds of lives? Women? Children?

Still felt like shit.

Why?

Parvez was my friend.

He was a terrorist.

They didn't have to kill him.

Don't you feel it was necessary? We're fighting a war on terror.

At that point I laughed in her ignorant face. War on fucking terror! The hypocrisy was mind-bending. Instead of helping me understand my feelings, it just vexed me further.

It was around then, a couple of months after the attacks, that MI5 sent me packing. They made me sign a lot of confidentiality documents, swearing me to secrecy, as if I would want anybody to know that I was a part of that organisation. They patted me on the back as though I was a child and gave me a briefcase full of gold coins, you know, *services rendered*.

Then what? I tell you then what. I did what I never thought I would do, I got myself a nine to fiver. Yeah, man; a white shirt, itchy black trousers and a fucking tie that was out to kill me. Hounslow Council, Helpdesk Operator! I zombied in there five days a week and spent my time sitting on a chair that stopped twirling around the same time as Fred and Ginger, surfing the web and talking on the phone to people dumber than I am, and then I zombied my way out of there. I didn't have to do it, I had money thanks to my *shut the fuck up* pay off from MI5, but I had decided that my life finally needed structure.

I scoured the rest of the newspaper, my eyes darting from headline to headline. There wasn't any news on my father. I knew there wouldn't be as I'd already checked on-line earlier that morning. And then later that afternoon. I hated myself for doing so and resolved not to do it again, knowing full well that I have no fucking resolve. I folded the newspaper tightly and whacked it hard against my thigh to snap me out of an approaching slump. The microwave pinged but my appetite had skated and replaced with thirst. I opened the fridge and sipped straight from the carton of OJ as my eyes landed on a Qatar fridge magnet that my Mum had sent me. Underneath the magnet was an old flyer.

I'd been attending the Tuesday sessions for the last couple of months. Maybe after the attack I wanted to be around normal, moderate, modern Muslims and not those who had ideas of devastating the West. They held talks for young Muslims, ranging from those facing 'issues' in the current climate, to those struggling to gain employment, or those who just wanted an environment where they were able to vent without judgement.

I could gauge the opinion of Muslims up and down the country just by spending an hour or two in that room, bouncing from person to person, all of whom had justifiable reason to be full of anger, but had the good sense to just get on with it. Unlike that popular minority, these Muslims wanted a place to express, and not to take extreme action.

This wasn't about that.

We shared stories, drank masala tea and munched on Jaffa Cakes. Once in a while, normally after an atrocity, we would be riled up at the media coverage or the lack of it, at our *Brothers*, or at the two patrol cars taking turns in cruising up and down outside the hall, just in case we all balled out wearing suicide vests and waving rifles, shouting *Allah hu Akbar*!

My life, truth be told, wasn't great. But a crappy office job and the Community Centre gave me some purpose. I didn't have to report to MI5 anymore, I didn't have to play spy, a role that I was fucking blackmailed into, *coerced*, as those bastards would call it. The only good thing that came out of it was that a nasty motherfucker named Silas who I owed a lot of money to was tucked away safely in jail thanks to a statement that I had given. Ten G I owed him; instead he got ten years. I was aware that when he was eventually released he would come looking for me.

Until then, I couldn't be touched.

3

Burj Al Arab Hotel, Dubai

Sheikh Ali Ghulam had lived his whole life in the United Arab Emirates in the city of Abu Dhabi. He despised being away from home, refused to join any of his wives or eleven children when they vacationed in the most extreme exotic locations around the world. He had a constant nagging thought that it was only a matter of time, and not coincidence, before a lunatic gunman or a suicide bomber decided that today was the day to spoil his vacation. The Sheikh seldom set foot outside of his home. He lived with his wives and his children and his servants on a sprawling estate, with two guest lodges and a small shopping village within the compound.

It was only business that held the might to force him from his home. Sheikh Ghulam never had and never would conduct business from his home, not a meeting, a phone call or an email. Any communication would have to be hand-written on a note and delivered personally to him by only a select few. But business was now calling, and it was that very reason why he travelled the short journey to Dubai.

Ghulam, dressed, as ever, in a long white *thobe*, and white headdress, stood with his back to the luxurious hotel room and looked out of the huge curved window of the Royal Suite on the top floor of the Burj Al Arab Hotel. The sun dipped and the skyscrapers obscenely illuminated the skyline. Ghulam could not make out the scene below him, but he imagined with certain distaste the crowd and activity that was taking place. Shameless and barely dressed women displaying all that should be precious to them, and burnt, ruddy-faced drunken men looking for a wife for the night. Westerners with their Western ways and a blatant disregard for the laws of a Muslim country.

The door to the suite opened. Ghulam noticed in the reflection of the glass that Pathaan had entered.

'I trust our guests are satisfied with their accommodation,' Ghulam said.

Pathaan was aware that he was being watched in the reflection, so replied silently with a slight nod and sat down on the armchair closest to the gold-plated phone. He slipped off his sandals and placed his bare feet on the coffee table. Out of the top pocket of his crisp, half-sleeved white shirt he took out a well-worn, small tin container and pried open the lid and removed a ready-wrapped paan. He folded it in half and then half again and placed it on his tongue before vigorously chewing it as the taste exploded inside his mouth, coating his teeth in red salivation.

Ghulam eyed him momentarily in part fascination, part frustration. Aba Abassi, known only as Pathaan, was head of security and the only person on his payroll who did not afford him the respect that was demanded of a Sheikh. However, although belligerent at times, Pathaan was a necessity; a confidante and protector, one who was highly trained in many forms of combat, which he carried out with pleasure and if the mood took him.

Ghulam had requested Pathaan to organise this meeting. It had taken Pathaan six flights and three cities in three different countries to arrange. Out of the three esteemed guests invited only two had turned up with the obedience that was expected of them. The third had needed to be convinced onto the Lear Jet.

'Alright,' Ghulam said. 'Let us commence.'

Pathaan picked up the gold-plated phone and dialled. It rang three times before he got a response. He ran his tongue slowly over his teeth, relishing the taste of the paan.

'Three rings,' he said on answer, 'is not acceptable.' He waited for the apology before instructing, 'Send them up.'

*

Mullah Mohammed Ihsan and Mullah Muhammad Talal entered the hotel room. Sheikh Ali Ghulam stood at the head of the table. Something in his face made the two Mullahs hesitate about greeting the Sheikh as etiquette would usually dictate.

'Sit.' Pathaan made the decision for them.

At the far end of the table was placed a large wide-screen monitor, with a USB pen drive attached.

'This has come to my attention,' Ghulam said, quietly. He nodded towards Pathaan who, with the press of a button on the remote, executed a file.

The footage was clear but without sound and motion, as though shot by a security camera. The time stamp read 15.22 and the date 26/12/2017. It showed a young man sitting on the back step of an ambulance, a blanket wrapped tightly around him and tucked under his chin. Even from the distance that the footage was captured, it was plain to see from the way his shoulders rhythmically shuddered that he was crying, as he looked around, lost, at his surroundings.

'Who is this Brother?' Talal asked.

'He is no Brother of ours,' Ghulam glared, his eyes ablaze with fire. 'This man is a traitor.' Pathaan placed a thin manila folder on the table. Ihsan opened it and stared at the 7×5 photo. Bright eyes and a nervous smile looked back at them as though he had just been caught. Which he had. 'I received intelligence from one of our men on the ground in London. This is the man behind the betrayal of our leader. His name is Javid Qasim.'

Ihsan cleared his throat and although it was just one word, he spoke it with careful measure. 'How?'

'Qasim attended our training camp, by invite, in Khyber Pakhtunkhwa where he was able to ascertain important details of our operation.'

'How much did he find out?' Talal said, finding his voice again after being under Ghulam's glare.

'Enough!' Ghulam slapped his palm on the table. A small bowl of hummus upturned. He then began softly drumming his fingers.

Enough as in Javid Qasim found out enough? Or *Enough* as in I don't want to hear another word from you? Talal decided it was best to wait for Ghulam to continue in his own time.

'This man, this *Muslim*, cowardly hid under the guise of a soldier of Ghurfat-al-Mudarris,' Ghulam said, quietly. 'Crossing the border into Afghanistan to meet with Abdullah Bin Jabbar and reporting every detail to the British Secret Service.'

The silence that followed screamed a thousand questions.

'The one thing I despise more than a Kafir, is a *Munafiq*.' Ghulam spat the last word as if it burnt a hole on his tongue. The others in attendance were aware of the treatment reserved for such a Muslim. 'And it is for that reason that I hereby put forward a fatwa on Javid Qasim.'

4

Thames House

At 12 Millbank – Thames House, MI5's headquarters – Teddy Lawrence, a young MI5 officer, knocked and entered the minimalist office of John Robinson, Assistant Director of Counter Terrorism Operations. It was the first time they had met since the foiled terrorist attack on Oxford Street on Boxing Day.

Lawrence had climbed the ranks rapidly, due largely to their close working relationship. Robinson had seen in him a kindred spirit, whilst Lawrence saw opportunity.

Robinson had lost weight everywhere but on his stomach. His sweat-stained white shirt hung loose over his shoulders. Uneven growth on a face that managed to be both pale and ruddy red. Alcohol probably, stress definitely, reasoned Lawrence. Whatever it was, Robinson looked like shit and no longer like a leader of men.

Lawrence, despite what they were facing, had kept up appearances. Seven fitted suits for seven days. Monday was a charcoal grey three piece. He'd been in the office for nearly three minutes without Robinson having uttered a word. Lawrence watched him standing at the floor to ceiling window, staring out onto the stunning views of the Thames as though the answer would float to him in a message in a bottle. They had both received the same brief that morning.

The Teacher was no closer to being located.

After the London attack, The Teacher was quick to go under, hidden away in the vast wild lands, somewhere in Pakistan or Afghanistan, unable to lead the might of Ghurfat-al-Mudarris. Still, the attacks occurred across Europe; smaller in scale but with a frightening frequency. Despite The Teacher's absence, his work continued.

Robinson mumbled something, but Lawrence couldn't quite hear as Robinson still had his back to him. Lawrence hesitated before asking, 'Sir. Can you repeat that?'

'Javid Qasim,' Robinson said, 'is the key.'

Lawrence now understood why Robinson had his back to him. It would have been an embarrassment for him having to backtrack, and he probably didn't want it seen in his face. It had been Robinson who'd terminated Qasim's contract – a rash decision, considering what he'd achieved for them in such a short period of time. From Qasim's intelligence alone, they'd narrowly avoided a multiple gun attack in the heart of London. Just as vital, Qasim had revealed The Teacher's locations and hideouts, along with a detailed description of the man that the world's authorities had, previously, had no knowledge of. After that it had been out of Qasim's hands. It should have been enough. Yet they had still failed to locate and capture The Teacher.

Robinson concluded there were doubts about the legitimacy of the intelligence, and he'd been quick to voice his judgement. It didn't sit comfortably with him that Qasim clearly had mixed emotions in what was asked of him. Robinson refused to let anyone who was sympathetic to the beliefs of Ghurfat-al-Mudarris continue working for the Secret Service. It had muddied the waters further when Qasim's relationship with The Teacher came to light.

At the time, and despite advice, Robinson could only see one way, when he should have been seeing it the other way.

'Javid Qasim?' Lawrence questioned, though he had already formed the conversation in his head.

Robinson finally turned and locked eyes with Lawrence. 'We can still use him.'

Lawrence nodded. 'I'll talk to him. Get him back on board.'

From the drinks cabinet, Robinson poured himself a large whiskey and a smaller one for Lawrence. He strode across and handed the drink over and sat down opposite him. Robinson leant back, an arm draped across the Italian leather two-seater that he'd insisted on having in his office, and crossed his legs. The arrogance that had been missing, as they repeatedly failed to capture The Teacher, was returning.

'No,' Robinson said. 'That's not what I had in mind.'

5

Hounslow High Street

Dean Kramer leaned his bulk against the back of his rusty old Range Rover. Like him, it carried battle scars, and like him it was still strong. He slipped out a Greggs sausage roll from a paper bag and proceeded to cut it in half with the first bite. In front of him, Kramer looked out at the scene on Hounslow High Street. A group of forty or so Asian youths, shuffling feet, a bundle of nerves and anticipation, being held back by metal barriers and Police. Nothing had kicked off, it hardly ever does at these things, but they had to make their presence felt. Opposite them, outside what used to be Dixons, now a discount store, St George and Union Jack flags flew high above a fifty-strong gathering of white faces, mainly men, holding signs and placards that read *Taking back our country* or words to that effect. They were led by a red-headed woman who Kramer knew well. With her she had her weapons of choice: a microphone, and a voice she wasn't afraid to use.

This was the third time this week that Kramer had watched Eve Carver and the rest of the faces. First in Leytonstone and then in Slough, before moving onto Hounslow. All areas heavily populated with Muslims.

He watched Carver bring the microphone to her mouth and clear her throat. It came out loud and crisp through the large box speaker. One of the Asians shouted something unoriginally offensive at her. A copper shook his head at him and he quietened down. Kramer took the second and final bite out of his sausage roll as she started.

'I went to the supermarket today. I thought I'd do a little experiment. I counted thirty tills. Twenty-eight of them were manned by brown faces.' She paused. She smiled. She continued. 'Isn't that strange? It's strange to me. And it's not just our supermarkets. Step into any hospital and chances are you'll be treated by a brown doctor. Step into any school and chances are *your child* is being taught by a brown teacher. Have you asked yourself, *what are they teaching our children?*'

'What are *you* teaching our children?' an elderly Asian man, who had stopped to watch, countered. His small voice was lost in the commotion as his wife hurriedly ushered him away.

'Take a look at our council, our government. The Mayor of Hounslow is a Muslim. The Mayor of London is a Muslim. Every day, five times a day, I hear the Islamic cries for Prayers. They are not adhering to our laws. We are adhering to theirs. Believe me, Sharia Law is spreading like the sickest of diseases. Here. In our country. *In our England.*'

Kramer yawned, loud and wide. He'd heard this or a variation of this three times already this week, and a hundred times before. This little show would be filmed and plastered over Social Media. Their profile would increase. Their numbers would increase. If they were lucky, a fight may break out and they would find themselves in one of the local papers. National even. But ultimately not a thing will change. Kramer wasn't here for that.

He tuned out as Carver moved onto *All Muslims are complicit in Terrorism*, and scanned the crowd. The two young lads weren't difficult to find. Black bomber jackets, skinny black jeans and red Doctor Marten Boots. They were the reason that Kramer was there.

He placed a call to Terry Rose.

'Rose.' Kramer sat in his car to block out the noise. 'They're both here.'

'Course they are,' Rose replied. 'You talked to them, yet?'

'About to.' Kramer glanced in his rear-view mirror. The two lads were mouthing off at the Pakis, intent and anger burning brightly in their faces, hands balled into tight fists, ready to fly. There was a third with them, younger, dressed the same, but looking painfully out of place. He stood close by and tried to imitate them but Kramer could see that he did not hold the same passion. 'There's another with them.'

'Who?'

'Don't know. He's been hanging around them all week. Could be a friend.'

'Alright. Suss him out, and call it,' Rose said.

Kramer ended the call. Brushed the crumbs from the sausage roll off his face and stepped out of the car just as the demonstration was dying down. He approached one of the lads that he knew by name and reputation only.

Kramer stood beside him. 'Simon Carpenter.'

Simon, his thick arms crossed, his face set like flint, stared at what was left of the dwindling Asian group as they started to disperse, to his satisfaction.

'Look at them go,' Simon said, eyes forward. 'Off to plot. To plan. We're not careful, they'll bring this country down to its knees.' Simon turned to look at Kramer. 'Who the fuck are you?'

Kramer, a few inches over six foot, was taller and wider than Simon. But not by much. Simon was built like no other eighteen-year-old. The other lad joined them. Kramer knew him as Anthony Hanson. He was taller than his friend, but he didn't carry the bulk. Taut, wiry, and handy with his fists. Had a history of substance abuse. Kramer had done his homework.

'Anthony Hanson.' Kramer smiled, producing crooked teeth.

Anthony gave him the once-over and then looked across at Simon. 'Who the fuck is this guy?'

'I'd like a word,' Kramer said.

*

In the absence of a coffee shop close by, Kramer took them to a dessert lounge a few doors down from where the demonstration had taken place. He ordered three coffees and waited for them to arrive before starting.

'I've seen you both at the last few rallies,' Kramer said.

'Yeah, so?' Anthony said.

'I've seen you, too,' Simon said. 'From a distance. Never seen you join in, though.'

'Don't agree with it.' Kramer shook his head. 'It's not right.'

'We got a Paki-lover on our hands,' Anthony said, his attitude clearly bolstered by having his friend by his side 'Prime example of all that's wrong with our country. If we can't stick up for our own then –'

Kramer shot him a look, one that had shut down many in the past. He made a show of interlinking his meaty fingers and Anthony's eyes travelled down to the red St George's Cross tattoo on his middle finger, just above his knuckle.

'What do you want?' Simon slipped off his beanie hat to reveal a freshly-shaved head.

'You're wasting your time,' Kramer said. 'These rallies won't get you anywhere. Their beliefs sit side by side with my beliefs, but the objective is a political one.'

'It's something,' Simon said.

'It's not enough. And I think you know it's not enough.'

'That supposed to mean?' Anthony said.

'Last year. The attack on Sutton Mosque.' Kramer left it at that. He picked up his coffee and took a sip.

Anthony glanced at Simon. Simon quietly kept his eyes firmly on Kramer.

'How'd you know about that?' Anthony asked.

'The attack on the Mosque was celebrated across the country,' Kramer replied. 'I made it my business to find out who was responsible.'

Anthony looked around nervously. Kramer smiled behind his coffee as he took a sip, amused at how Simon held his gaze like an equal.

'Who are you?' Simon asked.

'I am one of many. And we're making a stand.'

'So are we?' Anthony shrugged.

'Don't be daft, son. You think a few fucking marches and rallies is making a stand. Talk is cheap, and ineffective.' Kramer leaned in and lowered his voice. 'After desecrating the Mosque, you hid when you should have built on its momentum. Instead you wear a hole in your Doc Martens, marching relentlessly, trying to spread the word.' Kramer straightened up, took his time looking them both in the eyes. 'I work with a small organisation whose members believe that...' he paused. 'Action speaks louder than words. A belief that you once shared.'

'We still do,' Anthony said, then looked across at Simon who slowly nodded his agreement.

'That sounds like words to me,' Kramer said. 'If I see that you are serious, if you are capable in making a difference, a *real* difference, then...'

'Then what?' Anthony asked.

'My partner, who runs operations, would like the two of you to join us.'

The door to the dessert lounge opened with a cheery chime. The third lad, who'd been hanging around with Simon and Anthony, walked in and tentatively approached the table, trying his hardest to avoid eye contact with Kramer.

'Where were you guys?' he said, softly. 'I was looking for you everywhere.'

Simon leaned over the table and locked eyes with Kramer. 'Tell your partner we'll show you both just how serious we can be. And...'

'And what?'

Simon glanced across at the boy who smiled unsurely at him. He turned back to Kramer.

'Tell him there's three of us.'

26

6

Imy

I never did find the remote control so, back at my flat, I had to go back in time and operate the television up close and personal. Channel set to Sky Sports, I settled in, a bowl of crisps, two glass tumblers next to a jug of water, a bowl of ice and an unopened bottle of Jameson on the coffee table in front of me.

Compact was the word I would have used to describe my flat to any potential clients; pokey would have been more apt. The rent was set quite low, but I paid even less, one of the few perks of being an estate agent. A touch of damp on the walls, questionable décor courtesy of the previous owner, and a carpet which electrocutes. It sat nicely above The Chicken Spot which some may find distasteful – especially as the smell of greasy food was a constant guest – but, geographically, I found it convenient.

It was far from perfect, but for now it was all I needed. I could have easily moved in with Stephanie and Jack into their comfortable home in Osterley, and that remained the eventual plan. I know that she would like that, and Jack would be absolutely thrilled to have me always there playing Dad. However, for the time being I was enjoying living on my own after having lived with my Khala for the last twenty years. She was my mother's elder sister. They were both originally from Pakistan, but while mother had moved to Afghanistan, my Khala had built a life in England. Both following their husbands in the name of marriage.

Khala brought me up with more love than I could ever have wished for. I owed her everything, but eventually I'd had to get out and do my own thing. Even though I'm thirty-six, she was horrified at the thought of me moving out.

'People will talk,' she had proclaimed when I finally found the courage to tell her. 'They will say that I kicked you out.'

I didn't patronise her, she was right. In our community, people did talk. The textbook thought process was: *Thirty-six. Not married. Not living at home with his parents. Something terrible must have happened!*

I had to go though. I had to find a way of making things work with Stephanie and Jack – and I couldn't do that living at home with my Khala. She wasn't happy when I left home, so God only knew what her reaction would be when she found out that I have a white girlfriend who has a son from a previous relationship. For now, that had to be my secret.

*

I glanced at the time on my phone, considered pouring myself a small shot but decided to wait for Shaz who had just texted his arrival. He was downstairs ordering a bucket of hot wings. I shifted along the the two-seater as I heard his footsteps approach my door, which was left on latch so I wouldn't have to get up.

'You know what I don't understand?' Shaz opened with, as we touched fists. I could tell from his eyes that he was already high. 'If you're gonna hit a deer, would you get out of your car to check if it's alright?'

'You got skins?' I asked, before he unloaded whatever was on his mind.

'It's a fucking deer,' he said, flinging a packet of king size silver Rizla and a small ziplock bag of skunk onto the coffee table. He placed the bucket of chicken on top of it and I knew that he would very soon be searching for the gear. 'And then, and *then*, he goes to the boot of his car and finds something to put the deer out of its misery, as his bird who, by the way, is wearing a posh frock, 'cos they're on the way to a dinner party in the middle of a fucking forest, looks on from the passenger seat. I mean what the fuck does he know about whether the deer is suffering? For all he knows, it could just have a sore fucking head, it could be right as rain in a bit. That shit is just wrong, taking a metal cross spanner to the deer's head and going to town on it, whilst he gets soaked in deer blood just to impress his girl!'

'The match is about to start in a minute, Shaz. Is there a point to all this?'

'Just this film I was watching. It won two Oscars! Shit, what was it called again? Whatever! The point is... what's my point?' He shuffled out of his puffa jacket and sat himself next to me.

'Why didn't he just run the deer over?' I know Shaz, I know how he thinks.

'Yes! Why didn't he just run the deer over? If he really wanted to put it out of its misery, drive back and forth over the fucker until it's finally dead. There was no need to bludgeon it to death! I swear they give out Oscars like penny sweets these days.'

I liked Shaz. He liked to talk and I liked to listen to him muse about the unimportant things in life. It was one of the reasons that I was desperate to find the remote control. Frequently I needed to pause live television so he could spill whatever random nonsense that popped into his head.

I first met Shaz – Shahzad Naqvi, when I started working at Kumar's Property Services. The first few months I was kept in the office carrying out basic admin as Kumar inducted me. Shaz had been there for almost a year and had graduated to viewings. He would check back to the office twice a day, and I'd smell the alcohol on him. I'd see the red in his eyes. It'd make me furious that a Muslim would behave in such a manner.

After my induction, Kumar sent me out to shadow and learn from Shaz. Every lunch time, Shaz would take me to The Rising Sun pub.

A pint for him... a lemonade for me.

I couldn't help myself, I couldn't let it be. I had to ask. 'Are you not a Muslim?'

'Course I'm a Muslim. Fuck, man! Kind of question is that?'

He took a sip of beer, wiped his mouth with the back of his sleeve, and before I could question the contradictory action, he beat me to it.

'I take it you don't drink, Imy. Sup to you, yeah. That's your business. I ain't hurting no-one. My parents bought me up right and correct, mate. I know the difference between good and bad. Everything else... Well, it's just noise.'

Shaz took another sip, waved his empty glass and winked at the barman.

'Why you lookin' at me like that?' He grinned. 'I pray too, yeah, before you ask. Every night, in bed, a direct line to the man upstairs. I say whatever's on my mind. A thanks, a wish, world fucking peace, whatever! That's how *I* pray. I ain't saying other Muslims are wrong, but personally I don't think that I was put on this Earth to bow down five times a day, reciting Arabic prayers that I don't quite understand and – with all due respect – most other Muslims don't understand either. Going through the same motion day in day out. You know what they're thinking as their heads are bowed? *What's on TV tonight? Where'd I leave my sunglasses? What time's the gym closing?* Tell me that ain't true. Look... It's like this, I know I ain't Muslim of the year and when I do go and God judges me, I probably won't get to sit at the top table with the *Mashallah* crew. I'll most likely be in the nosebleed seats, with a pillar blocking my view! But trust me, yeah, I ain't going to hell. Way I see it, we've been given the gift of life. Live it, man, you'll be alright. You hear me?'

I heard him. It was all I could think about. I managed to convince myself that if I picked up a glass, smoked a little weed, there was no way I'd ever be suspected. It was the perfect cover. But really, I wasn't convincing anybody.

I easily fell in love with the lifestyle. I easily fell in love with having a choice. I *easily* fell in love with a girl.

Soon after, when Shaz and I went to the pub it was;

A pint for him… and a pint for me.

Now Shaz was a regular feature, and he was also the funniest person that I knew – mostly unintentionally. He helped me find laughter that had been absent for years.

Like me, he was a Muslim, and like me he wasn't much of one.

He rested one foot up on the edge of the coffee table. 'Let's take a moment or two to admire my new desert boots.' He said. And in that instant… I was back there again.

*

Most of what I remembered from growing up in Afghanistan was my impatience to grow up. In fact, just before all it kicked off, my biggest concern was that I was done with being nine. I had been counting down the days until I hit the all-important double figures. In my village in Afghanistan, ten was a big deal; ten brought you a certain amount of respect, responsibility and power. Ten was being a man. Though, whichever way I chose to look at it, the truth was, at ten, I was still a child. And at that moment, when everything changed, I had never before felt more like a child.

I remember my father telling me to run. I remember my mother screaming at me to hide. I remember that being the last thing they ever said to me.

The sound of gunshots was not rare in our small village in Sharana. For us children who were in a hurry to grow up, the sound signalled one of adventure. The presence of the Taliban was not uncommon; they would ride in on their dusty jeeps or their dusty horses and once in a while shoot a hole into the sky just to make us aware of

31

their presence. We would surround them with respectful smiles and sometimes they would let us hold their rifles. My parents hated it but acquiesced, because really, what choice did they have?

The sound of these particular gunshots were different. Cleaner. Relentless. Getting closer. Moving from home to home until they were pounding down our door. From my hiding spot, under my bed, I hear a muffled question, a nervous reply. My mother's scream, my father's anguish. Heavy feet making their way through our home. My parents separated. My father taken to our small kitchen and asked the same question over and over again. My mother taken into the bedroom, screaming, and forced to perform what should only take place between a husband and a wife. I couldn't move, my shalwar wet and stained, my eyes closed painfully tight and my hands clamped over my ears but still unable to block out the sounds of the final two shots.

Then silence. No more gunshots, no more screams. I opened my eyes and from my position under my bed, I noticed two things; the smoking barrel of a Heckler and Koch machine gun and a pair of sandy coloured, British military-issue desert boots.

'Well,' Shaz said, rescuing me from my thoughts and placing me back to the present. 'Pretty sick, right?

'Yes,' I snatched my eyes away from his boots. 'They're nice.'

7

Burj Al Arab Hotel, Dubai

Sheikh Ali Ghulam invited his guests, Mullah Mohammed Ihsan and Mullah Muhammad Talal, to join him for an evening feast. A small team of three waiters piled the table with platters of assorted meats, rice and naan breads. They ate in silence at the dining table, digesting the food quickly, hoping to get back to their hotel room and further digest what had been told to them. The only sound that filled the room was Pathaan noisily sucking away at the bones of a half chicken from the comfort of his armchair.

Ihsan and Talal were grateful that a spread had been laid on for them in the highest of company; they were especially grateful that the Sheikh had chosen them to share the information with. But they could not understand *why* it was them that he had chosen. The attacks on Oxford Street had been not of their planning, therefore they were not accountable for the failure of it. Ihsan, based in Germany, had his own students, three of whom were currently being prepped to visit a training camp. As for Belgium-based Talal, after careful watch, he had recruited twelve students from the deprived Molenbeek neighbourhood of Brussels, who had seen their local Mosque closed down as its teachings were seen as radical. Talal had been given an eighteen-month window in which to train these angry young men, and plot an attack in the very heart of Brussels.

Sheikh Ghulam placed his cutlery down on the table and loudly expelled gas, muted slightly by his fist. Ihsan and Talal followed suit but did not allow themselves the luxury of belching. They waited patiently but the impatience within them was clear. They wanted desperately to leave, to be away from Ghulam's glare and Pathaan's menace and to carry on this discussion in private quarters, to try to establish the possible reason why they might have been flown out to this meeting.

Ghulam had not seemed to address it. But they could not possibly question him.

Talal cleared his throat to speak. Ihsan shot him a look and discreetly shook his head. Talal went ahead anyway. 'Who was responsible for Qasim? With all due respect we carry out intensive checks with every one of our students.'

Ghulam nodded at Pathaan, one that could possibly have meant anything. Pathaan stood up and Talal braced himself, as though he was about to receive a blow to the back of his head. Pathaan smiled at the reaction and disappeared into the master bedroom.

'Imam Adeel-al-Bhukara,' Ghulam said, and Talal physically relaxed. 'He was also invited to join us. However, the Brother did not demonstrate the same sense of duty as you both.'

'So, he did not make it?' Ihsan asked.

'Pathaan can be quite persuasive,' Ghulam replied, as the bedroom door opened and Pathaan walked out dragging behind him a large metal suitcase on wheels. He laid it down flat, unzipped and flipped open the case. Inside Adeel-al-Bhukara was curled up in the foetal position, his walking stick laid across his body. Pathaan picked it up and poked him in the ribs with it. Al-Bhukara wheezed weakly and his eyes opened to slits.

'Please, join us,' Ghulam requested, and al-Bukhara's eyes widened in recognition.

Placing first one hand and then the other on the thick black Persian rug, he slowly crawled out of the suitcase before collapsing with exhaustion face down on the floor. His humiliation, far from complete, was furthered in the knowledge that his peers, his *Brothers*, could smell that he had urinated and see that, through the light cotton of his shalwar, he had defecated.

Al-Bhukara managed to lift his head towards Ghulam and mouthed *water*. His wish was granted as Pathaan, from a metal jug, poured water and ice cubes over his head. They watched as he managed to sum up enough energy to rise to his knees with his mouth wide open, and drink what he could from the waterfall. Whatever missed his mouth he collected in his hands.

Ihsan and Talal were up on their feet at the treatment of the much-respected Imam. The very same Imam who had a close friendship and unbridled trust with Abdullah Bin Jabbar, the honourable leader of their group, Ghurfat-Al-Mudarris.

'Would you like us to leave?' Ihsan asked.

'*Sit!*' Pathaan asserted, his arm outstretched and his finger pointing at them as if it could spit bullets.

'Look at me,' Ghulam said.

Al-Bhukara met his eyes, but kept his head bowed. 'Please,' he pleaded. 'I did what I was told. I did what I believed was right.'

'Javid Qasim was one of your students.'

'I did what I was told,' Al-Bhukara repeated.

'He was a *traitor*,' Ghulam raised his hand sharply. Al-Bhukara flinched. 'He was Secret Service.'

Al-Bhukara lifted his chin, the sudden fire in his eyes matching that of Ghulam.

'He was the *son* of Abdullah Bin Jabbar,' he hissed at the Sheikh and then the fire went out as quickly as it had arrived.

Ghulam took an involuntary step back. Ihsan and Talal glanced at one another, hoping that the other would tell them that they had misheard.

'We waited patiently for the boy to become a man,' Al-Bhukara continued. 'He started to move in the right circles, he started to take his Deen seriously. When word reached Bin Jabbar, he insisted that we should take him on. Fast track his education. I was but the facilitator. He was his father.' He took a breath, it came out as a low whistle. 'It was what he wanted.'

Ghulam regained his composure. 'Abdullah Bin Jabbar... who has evaded capture for so many years, is now on the run. Is *that* what he had wanted?'

Al-Bhukara said nothing.

'They are now aware of his description, his hideouts and his training facilities. I ask you again: is *that* what he wanted?'

A single tear slowly escaped Al-Bhukara's eye.

'Our cell has been compromised. Decades of hard work and planning, wasted. *Is that what he wanted?*'

Ghulam sat down on the chair, his outburst had tired him. He leant forward and with his finger lifted Al-Bhukara's chin and said softly. 'I do not care if Qasim is his bastard son. It is your role to thoroughly look at his background regardless of who he is. Good men died, men better than Qasim, and the Kafir now laugh at us, in their newspapers, on their televisions. I will not allow you to lay the blame at the feet of the great Bin Jabbar. As far as I am concerned, Javid Qasim was your responsibility.'

Al-Bhukara closed his eyes tightly. Sweat ran down his forehead and tears raced freely down his face. His body racked and shuddered as he clenched as hard as he could to stop himself adding to his already soiled shalwar.

Ghulam sat back in his chair and stared up at the ceiling. In his heart he understood that Al-Bhukara had no choice. When an order comes from the very top, no question, it has to be obeyed. Bin Jabbar had always run Ghurfat-al-Mudarris with heart and emotion, loved and adored by his vast army as he walked, lived and broke bread amongst them. Now he was impoverished, moving from barely-furnished safe houses to barren caves hidden in high mountains.

It was not how a leader should lead.

Bin Jabbar was no longer in the position to give further orders; the remainder of his days were to be lived out, running and hiding as the net around him tightened. Ghulam saw himself as the natural successor. Change had been forced upon them, but it was a change that was required. The teachings of Al-Mudarris were dated, his attacks planned meticulously so his men lived to fight again when thousands of men would be willing to give their lives for The Cause. His love for his people had clouded his judgement, blinded him to the truth that there is no higher sacrifice to Allah than the sacrifice of life.

'Pathaan,' Ghulam said, turning to him. 'Do we have any sleepers in the vicinity?'

'We have one. Based in West London, a few kilometres from Heathrow Airport,' Pathaan replied. 'In close proximity to Qasim.'

'Is he capable?'

Pathaans blinked. A vision of a scared child, held tight in his arms, flashed behind his eyelids.

'Qasim is the son of Abdullah bin Jabbar,' Ghulam continued. 'Regardless of his treachery he deserves the respect of a clean death… By our hands.'

'He is capable,' Pathaan said.

'It is time our sleeper went active. Make contact and inform him of the fatwa.'

Al-Bhukara was still shuddering, his sobs coming in quick staccato beats. Ghulam's intention was not one of forgiveness, there would be no second chances, but the knowledge that al-Bhukara had been acting directly under the orders of their leader troubled him. Could he punish a man for that?

Ghulam's eyes landed on Ihsan and Talal who had inched closer to the door, wearing expressions as though they had been caught peeping through a keyhole. He remembered why he had invited them. It was to illustrate to them that a mistake like this could never happen again.

'Pathaan,' he said, finally coming to a decision. 'Please, show al-Bhukara the respect that he deserves.'

Al-Bhukara lifted his head and exhaled a sharp breath of relief. Still crying hysterically, he opened his mouth and searched for words suitable for the huge gratitude he'd felt towards the Sheikh. From the corner of his eye he could see Pathaan rise from his armchair. Al-Bhukara turned his head towards him, just in time to see him cut the distance between them in two long strides and then raise his gun, shooting him point blank in the side of the head.

8

Imy

'Two of the greatest teams the world has ever seen,' Shaz said, knocking back the last of his drink. 'With an abundance of attack and creativity at their disposal, and it ends up being a soulless, goalless draw.'

Shaz and I had spent the best part of the night cursing the so-called spectacle that it was billed to be. Between us we'd cleaned a litre bottle of Jameson, coupled with a few joints, and then went one-on-one in my living room with a plastic football.

A little past midnight and one broken lamp later, we bumped fists as Shaz, who still lived with his parents, went home. I did not envy him one bit, knowing what he was about to go through. The journey home after a heavy night was never straightforward. I knew this as I'd been in the very same situation on many occasions when I lived with Khala.

First, it used to involve a detour to Heston Services to use their facilities and scrub my face clean. Then I'd spend five pounds on strong mints, bottled water and eye drops. Two in each eye, ten minutes to take effect. Knocking back the bottled water to help sober up, and popping mint after mint until I arrived at my front door.

Then the hard part.

Trying to re-enter my own home, hoping I didn't wake Khala. Slowly taking one tiptoed step at a time upstairs, then creeping past her bedroom, a quick glance to make sure she's asleep. Edging closer to my own room, avoiding the squeaky hot spots on the plastic carpet protector, before finally pushing my bedroom door open, tantalisingly close to my single bed. Fifty percent of the time I would succeed, the other fifty…

'*Imran.*'

Silence. Don't move. Don't breathe. Hope that it passes.

'Imran, is that you?'

The jig is up. Double back, lean against her bedroom door frame to stop from wobbling. On would come the lamp, then would come the questions. Her words, as always, running into each other at pace, her English better than ever before but still broken in places.

'Where were you?'

'Khala, sorry I'm late. Go back to sleep.'

'Sleep? You think I sleep? I wait for you. Why your eyes red?'

'I was on my phone most of the night.'

'*Astaghfirulah.*' She would always say *Astaghfirulah* when she was annoyed. Similar to how Christians use *Jesus*, but with more drama. 'You and your phone. You're going to ruin your eyes, how many times I tell you? You want to go blind, Imran? Do you? Well, do you? Because you know what is going to happen? You're going to go blind!'

'Yes, Khala.'

'It is two in the morning, you not have work tomorrow? You know how difficult it was to ask Kumar to give you job? You humiliate family name.'

'It's fine. My first viewing is at ten.'

'Why do I smell smoke? You smoke, Imran?'

'No, it was Shaz, he was smoking around me.'

'He is a stupid boy. I do not like him.'

'Goodnight, Khala.'

'Shall I make something to eat?'

'Goodnight, Khala.'

She sounds like a ball breaker. She isn't. She is the sweetest person I have ever known. She took me in at sixteen, and a damaged sixteen at that, and knocked the damage right out of me with her overbearing brand of love. It didn't matter that I was now in my mid-thirties, I was fine with her treating me like I was still that sixteen-year-old. Now that I was away from her, in my own place, she was very much still part of my daily life. One phone-call a day, numerous texts and three visits per week, minimum.

It was fine.

After the death of my parents I'd spent the remainder of my childhood in Afghanistan as a man. One with order, discipline and responsibilities. A way of life drilled into me from the age of ten until the age of sixteen when I was sent to London, to Hounslow, to live with my Khala. Now I'm of age, the hardness has softened, but it's still within me and I pray that it doesn't see the light of day. My life, if I'm honest, is easy. I feel love for and loved by those close to me. All I want is to live carefree for a little longer before I settle down with Stephanie and Jack.

I realise, though, that my destiny is not in my hands. One day, somebody may come calling and try to turn me back into that violent, angry boy. Dangling revenge as my motivation, reminding me who I really am and what I owe.

9

Jay

It was a little strange having a day off from work, as opposed to *always* being able to do as I pleased. In keeping with my new, straight-edged life I had to structure my day to ensure that things got taken care of. It felt good knowing that I could function like a responsible adult, but at the same time it was boring the life out of me.

My first task today was to pick up plane tickets from Shaan Travels in Southall. You can keep all your online deals; nobody touches Shaan when it comes to budget flights. He went down from £470 to £390 before I even had a chance to finish the complimentary crusty samosa and microwaved masala chai that he had laid out in front of me. I paid in cash and pocketed the ticket before moving onto Hounslow and its legendary Treaty Centre for a spot of holiday shopping.

In keeping with the rest of the Treaty dossers, I adjusted my walk as soon as I entered. A little more bounce, a little more swagger. It had been a while since I had been to Treaty and the memories embraced me warmly and I couldn't help but smile at the much-changed but same-old shithole. I think I was around twelve when it first opened its doors, and at the time it felt like a shift in direction. Hounslow High Street was ready to join the likes of its glossy neighbours Richmond and Chiswick. Problem was, there were just too many fucking Asians, loitering or on the pull or just getting up to mischief. Idris and I used to chill there most days after school, sat at a table right by the escalators, books laid out in front of us as a guise so the mall cops wouldn't ask questions, passing judgement on the girls from Green School as they sauntered by. Yeah, Treaty was the only place to be. A couple of quid in your pocket saved from skipping lunch, to be spent on penny sweets, fizzy drinks and the *Daily Sport*.

A few years later, to add to the Asian invasion, the Somalis arrived, and a few years after that, the Poles invaded the Treaty. Small cliques were formed, the odd fight broke out. It lost some of its charm. Now every second person in the high street is from a different background, chats a different language, wears a different colour. But they are all after the same fucking thing.

A bargain!

That's why I was there too. A holiday on the horizon, I was ready to spend some money – but not too much! I ducked into some fashion boutiques where even the mannequins looked embarrassed, and bought myself some travel essentials. Lairy Hawaiian shirts, luminous shorts, flip flops, and a panama hat which I was never going to wear apart from in the odd novelty photo.

Qatar, here I come.

Mum had recently moved to Qatar with her boyfriend Andrew – her *white* boyfriend Andrew. She didn't give a fuck about the gossip, and I certainly didn't either. Good on you, Mum, do whatever makes you happy. She had tried being a good Muslim wife. Didn't work out, Dad was more interested in playing terrorist.

Holiday haul complete, it was time to get some chores done around the house. So I popped into the cornerstone of the Treaty Centre, a delightful little place called Wilko – quality products at ridiculously low prices – for some cleaning products. I was stood in the queue, my basket filled with all sorts of hocus-pocus sprays and detergents which guaranteed sparkling results in seconds. I couldn't see how long the queue was as the person in front of me was well over six foot, wide as a motherfucker and black as the night. There is only one person I know with such a frame and he *really* doesn't like me... So, rather than stay and confirm my suspicions, I decided it was time I bounced.

I took a tentative step back, right onto the foot of a pensioner. He let out a raspy yelp. I threw my hand up in apology but it was too late, the mini commotion had got the attention of the man mountain in front.

Staples, right hand man to Silas, the man that I'd helped put behind bars.

'Alright,' I smiled brightly, as if I'd just bumped into a Facebook friend.

'Jay,' he said. 'Still knocking about, I see.'

The fuck's that supposed to mean?

'Yeah, you know.' I shrugged. 'Where'd you think I'd be?'

'We were just talking about you the other night. Wondering what you're up to. If you're in good health.' Staples smiled long enough for me to admire his latest gold tooth.

'I thought I could feel my ears burning.' I was trying to play it cool. I think it was working, even though every instinct in me wanted to spin on my heels and get the hell outta there. 'You know what they say when you talk about someone and then they unexpectedly show up?'

'Why don't you go ahead and enlighten me, Jay?'

'It gives the recipient long life,' I said, wondering if I had used *recipient* in the right context.

'Yeah?' he said. 'You may well be the exception to that rule, Jay.'

Yeah, it was a threat and yeah I was shitting myself, but I knew he couldn't do anything. With Silas tucked away in jail, Staples knew that the eyes of the law were on the rest of the crew. Besides, what the fuck could he possibly do in the middle of Wilko, in the middle of the fucking Treaty Centre?

I looked down at Staples' basket. He had Radox bubble bath, candles and shampoo, which was odd as his head was as shiny as a snooker ball. He didn't seem so tough after all, with his pampering products. I smiled up at him knowingly, refusing to take the bait.

'Say hi to Silas from me next time you go visit him in jail.' I couldn't help myself, I had to get a dig in. I placed my basket on the floor and left my place in the queue and walked away, pleased with myself for delivering the parting shot.

'Jay,' Staples said, and I ignored him, kept walking. '*Jay*,' a little louder. 'You haven't heard?'

That slowed me in my tracks. I wanted to turn around and ask him what he meant but I just knew whatever knowledge he wanted to impart would only play on my mind, and that was the very last thing I needed before my trip. I shook my head clear and walked out of the shop.

On my drive home his words kept creeping back, I tried to figure out what Staples could possibly have meant. It wasn't in my nature to sweat the small stuff, but where that psychopath Silas is concerned, I couldn't take it lightly.

You haven't heard?

The day had started off so well. I'd been getting shit done, but the run-in with Staples had knocked me sideways. So instead of donning my marigolds and going on a cleaning expedition around the house, as planned, I spent the afternoon watching crappy daytime TV whilst throwing a few choice expletives at Staples from a safe distance.

Frustrated, I decided that I needed to be amongst people. I killed the television and got cleaned up. It was Tuesday. Paki night at Heston Hall.

10
Imy

Like always, Khala announced her latest plans in a particular way. Not a request, not a question. She was simply telling me that it had to be so. Knowing that nothing could ever come of what she was setting me up for, I should have battled it, made my excuses. She was wasting her time and mine, and she was definitely wasting the time of the family who were looking to make a Relationship, a *Rishta*.

But, again like always, I couldn't bring myself to fight it. Reluctantly, I agreed and ended the call. A minute later, Khala messaged me a photo of the girl that I had to meet tonight. I could see Shaz curiously peering at me from behind his computer.

We were in the office. It had been a quiet morning. Two of my clients had cancelled viewings and Shaz's next client was due late afternoon. So we had set about carrying out some rare admin. Kumar's Property Services was a small set up. Two branches, one located in Cranford and the other, our one, in the parade of cheap shops in Hounslow West. The office had two rooms. A separate office for Kumar to lock himself in, and the main room which Shaz and I operated from, our desks situated opposite each other, separated by a seated waiting area against the back wall which the clients never used.

'What're you looking at?' Shaz enquired.

'Khala just sent me a photo.' I sighed. 'I've got a Rishta tonight.'

'Another one?' He smirked. 'Just go with it. Shit man, you never know. She might be the one.'

'Come on, Shaz.' I said, rubbing my face. 'I have Steph and Jack.'

'*Ooh*, *Steph and Jack*,' he imitated. 'You're not going to marry Steph, mate. You know that, right? It's not even possible. Khala will throw a fucking fit!'

'I'll find a way.'

'Course you will! I can see it now. *Khala, I'm seeing a white chick called Stephanie.* Slap! *She's a divorcee.* Slap! *Oh, and she's got a kid from a previous marriage.*' Shaz mimicked loading a shotgun. 'You get the picture: Khala stood over you with a sawn-off; you, lying on the floor with a hole in your chest, wishing *why-oh-why did I not do the simple thing and marry a Muslim girl.*'

'Alright, Shaz. You've made your point.' I busied myself with work, looking for a way out of the conversation. But Shaz had other ideas.

'Show me the picture of this girl, then,' Shaz said.

'No,' I said.

'C'mon, man,' Shaz pleaded. 'Just show it.'

'There's no point.'

'Of course there's a point.'

'What? What is the point?'

'I want to see it!'

'That's not a valid point.'

'It's what mates do,' Shaz said.

'I swear,' I said, as I unlocked my phone and located the picture. 'You're such a child.'

'Am not!'

I faced the phone in his direction.

'Here,' I said. 'Happy?'

'Hang on, let me call NASA, see if they can lend me their telescope!' Shaz said, from behind his desk. 'Fucking hell, Imy. Bring it over here.'

'You want to see it, you can come to my desk.'

'I'm your senior.'

'Why don't you start acting like it?'

I had hoped his lazy nature would win out, but his perverted nature prevailed. He approached my desk with his hand out. I reluctantly handed my phone over.

'Oh my,' he said, softly as he took his time making eyes at the photo. 'And you're going to say *no?*'

'I'm going to say no.'

Shaz bit down on his fist.

'Imy... Imy... *Imy*!'

'I'm not in the mood, Shaz. Here, give it back.' He stepped back before I had a chance to swipe it from him.

'I don't mean any disrespect, Imy. I want to make that clear.'

I scratched my head, it was either that or pin him to the ground, wrench my phone away and smack him over the head with it.

'Steph is fit, yeah. But this girl is next level. I'd give both my kidneys just to deliver her mail.'

'I don't even know what that means, Shaz. Give me my phone back.'

Shaz watched it all the way as he handed it back to me, as though he was trying to commit her to memory. I hit the home button and the image disappeared.

'You definitely going to say no?' Shaz asked carefully.

'Don't say it,' I said.

'Say what?'

'Just don't.'

Shaz blinked and stayed stood at my desk, and I just knew that he was going to ask anyway.

'Maybe you could give me her number?'

'No, Shaz. The hell is wrong with you!? Just go back to your desk.'

Shaz liked to paint himself as quite the ladies' man, but his tales of sexual escapades were like those created in the mind of a teenage boy. I'd never met any of his so-called conquests. He would constantly tell me that once he found somebody he was serious about, he'd introduce her. I knew him and I indulged him, but Shaz was well and truly cemented in the lonely hearts club. His heavy consumption of weed had turned him into a wreck when it came to the opposite sex.

'At least send me her photo.'

I couldn't help but laugh as he sheepishly trudged back to his desk.

'What're you going to tell your Khala? What fault are you going to find with this one? That she's just too beautiful?' He shook his head in disappointment. 'You need to man up, Imy. Tell Khala the score and then deal with whatever she throws at you.'

For once, Shaz was right. Khala deserved to know the truth and I had to be a man about it and deal with the consequences. But I wasn't ready. As always, the time wasn't right.

*

I signed off from work early with a list of viewings for the next day, and went back to the flat to get ready. I didn't overdo it with the outfit. If it was up to Khala she would have had me turn up in a suit. As it was, I opted for smart casual dark denim jeans, a navy blue shirt and Chelsea boots. I drove the short distance to Khala's and pulled up outside her modest home. I was about to hit the horn when I noticed her waiting impatiently at the kitchen window, even though I was ten minutes early.

I got out and opened the passenger side door for her as she walked down the path, wearing a parrot-green Indian suit that I hadn't seen before. Khala eyed me up and down before deciding *it'll do*, then planted a kiss on my cheek. She handed me the address. It was an East London post code. I cursed under my breath as I entered it into Google Maps. I was going to be so late for Stephanie and Jack.

I indicated and pulled out, as she filled me in at customary breakneck speed.

'Both parents retired but still involved in running an Indian fashion boutique on Green Street. I can't remember the name. You would have seen the advert on Star Plus.'

'I don't watch Star Plus, Khala.'

'You don't watch Bollywood films anymore?' She seemed shocked. We had spent many nights together eating our way through a three hour song-and-dance fest.

'Anyway, you were saying?'

'They have lot of money, I saw picture on Facebook, they have gold fence around their big house.'

'Okay,' I rolled my eyes discreetly.

'They have two sons, Nadeem and Kareem, one is accountant and one is lecturer. They both live at home with their parents.' I could sense her eyes lasering into me. I kept mine straight ahead on the road, praying for the traffic to open up.

'Are you going to tell me about the girl or...?'

'Her name is Rukhsana. She is graduate!'

'What subject?'

'Don't know. Just know she is graduate.'

'Okay, graduate, got it.' I thought I could just ask Rukhsana directly in the name of small talk. 'Anything else?'

'I told them that you still live at home with me.' She said it straight faced.

'Why couldn't you just tell them the truth?' I asked, redundantly.

'*Astaghfirulah.* That you live in a chicken shop.'

'Above a chicken shop.'

'Sometimes it is better to tell small lie than to lose face,' Khala said, in fortune cookie wisdom.

'I'm thirty-six, Khala. I can't live with you forever.' She didn't reply. Stony-faced silence. I understood. You don't leave home until you are married. 'Anything else?'

'I told them that your parents died of natural causes.'

I could see her looking at me, checking like a mother would that I was okay. She placed her hand on mine. I just nodded to no one and nothing in particular. She couldn't exactly tell them that my father was beaten and my mother raped, before both being shot dead in their home by British soldiers.

Khala was right. Sometimes it was better to tell a small lie.

*

The gold fence around the house was as tacky as a gold fence around a house, but behind it, the house was spectacular. They had set the security light to constant, probably for our benefit so we could fully appreciate just how rich that they were. The grounds were beautifully manicured with a double garage, no doubt home to a couple of luxury motors. We approached the door coolly, without acting like this was the first nice house that we had ever been invited to. Either side of the door sat a lion statue.

'Plant pots would be better,' Khala whispered loudly, as I pressed the doorbell.

The door was opened by four beaming faces who had gathered around the large hallway. The men heartily shook hands and the women embraced. Aslamalykum's bounced from one to another as quick introductions were made. The sheer excitement as to what could potentially be was apparent. The two sons, Nadeem and Kareem, sized me up from behind their wide judging smiles and cardigans. Mr Bashir, Rukhsana's father, carried an air of contentment, a man of pride, happy with the cards that life had dealt him. He snaked his arm around my shoulders and escorted me to the living room. Mrs Bashir seemed like one of those modern Aunty-Ji's; she was wearing a sari, with a good portion of her stomach showing through the sheer drape of the fabric. She slipped her arm into Khala's as if they were old friends and they followed behind us.

In the dining area within the stylishly-decorated living room, I wasn't surprised to see the food on display. The Bashir's didn't seem like the kind of people who would dream of getting away with shop-bought samosas and watered-down chutney. They indulged us with fish pakoray, sizzling seekh kebabs on skewers, papdi chaat, and a carrot salad that both Khala and I avoided.

As we sat around the dining table they casually bombarded me with questions, a hair's breadth away from an all-out interrogation. They tried to make it sound casual, a friendly getting-to-know-each-other conversation, but everything was covered. Childhood, education, hobbies, occupation, all of which Khala answered on my behalf – *Imran is in the property market*, sounded a damn sight better than *estate agent*. I wasn't taken aback by the sheer intensity of the social dynamic; I'd been to plenty of Rishta's before, so I expected the examination. Fair play, they had to think about their daughter. It was, after all, her future in question. But they did expel a touch of arrogance, as though they were above us. Little gestures, I noticed. An amused glance amongst themselves as Khala used her hands to eat the crumbly fish pakora, rather than the fine cutlery laid out. The way Mrs Bashir addressed her, speaking in crisp English – the exact opposite of Khala's diction – and using unnecessary words to highlight their superior grasp of the language.

After the questions and the food, the men moved into the living area with our cups of masala chai, whilst Khala was led away by Mrs Bashir for a tour around the house. As soon as she was out of sight, the men of the family seemed to visibly relax. Nadeem switched on the television and Kareem turned his attention to his phone. Mr Bashir started to comment on whatever cricket match was being shown. It was clear that Mrs Bashir pulled the strings of the household. I wondered what that would have meant for me if I was here with genuine intention. Would she be the kind to interfere in her daughter's marriage? Yes, almost certainly. I didn't give it too much thought as my phone vibrated in my pocket.

It was a picture message from Stephanie. Jack had built a small camp in his bedroom. A single mattress on the floor and a few plastic chairs acting as walls with a large bed sheet thrown over as a makeshift ceiling. Jack's favourite book, *Dear Zoo*, sat by the lamp, waiting to be read to him. By me.

They were both sat on the mattress looking rather pleased with themselves. He looked as cute as a lost button waiting to be found, and Stephanie looked as though she had spent time at the hairdressers. She had gone all out to make an effort, and here I was, the other side of London, with potentially my future in-laws, waiting for potentially my future wife.

As I thought about what lie to reply with, Khala walked back into the living room. Her eyes were bigger than I had ever seen before, as she tried her hardest to suppress her smile. She took a seat adjacent to mine and reached across and squeezed my hand. She was trying to communicate something with her eyes, but before I could work it out Mrs Bashir walked in. Her smile was tighter, as though she was about to unveil something that she wasn't yet sure we deserved to see. She moved to one side to reveal her daughter, Rukhsana.

She was quite possibly the most beautiful girl that I had ever laid eyes on.

11
Jay

My attitude towards Somalis was probably similar to the attitude towards Asians back in the day. We kind of got in the way. Took your spot on the bus, took away your jobs, we even took away your benefits. That's how I felt about Somalis for a while. In the early nineties they seemingly turned up out of nowhere and planted themselves in our schools, libraries, and parks – all the regular haunts. The only good thing was that Asians up and down the country breathed a collective sigh of relief as a new target had been firmly established for the bigots and skinheads to direct their hatred towards.

At Heston Hall Community Centre, a third of the number was made up by Somalis. When I started to attend these evenings, I naturally gravitated towards the Paki Muslims. No offense intended, I just felt more comfortable amongst those who looked like me. *Fuck*! That sounds racist. But once I got to know the Somalis, they were alright, you know, they were just like me. *Fuck*! That sounds racist, too. They were just trying to get by, but it was harder for them.

That was the topic of the conversation we were having as a group, sat in a small circle, towards the last half hour of the meet. Most had gone home after the guest speaker. Just four of us remained, with one notable exception. I didn't mind that the fifth member of the group hadn't showed. He did my head in.

The guest speaker – Trevor Carter, middle aged, white, with shiny pointy shoes and a gelled quiff which had a bigger personality than he did – had spent the best part of an hour trying to convince us that we have the same opportunities as every other walk of life. He was trying to recruit for his expanding double glazing firm, and he was very generously offering jobs. Telephone sales jobs, minimum wage.

'Have to give the man credit for trying though.' Zafar tucked a business card into his top pocket. 'I might give him a bell.'

'Brother, you have a Masters degree, Mashallah,' said Tahir, a family man, a little older than the rest of us and the man responsible for organising these meets. 'Do you not think you're a little over-qualified for this role?'

'Temporary role though, innit,' Zafar replied.

'Look at their website,' Tahir faced his phone towards us. 'Job section. They have senior roles, Brother. Accountant positions, senior salesman! Don't you find it strange that he didn't mention that?'

Ira snorted. She was a tiny little thing with one of the biggest voices. A proper little firecracker, approaching twenty but looking a decade older. Life's cards had not been kind to her, and as a result she saw things through undiluted eyes. Ira was a second generation Somali who wore her hijab like a hoody; her laser-like eyes powered through from beneath it. She'd changed her name recently. It used to be Isis. It wasn't that long ago that Isis had been nothing more than a sweet-sounding Muslim girls' name. Though with shit being the way it was, she felt she had no choice but to change her name. It would have been nice though if somebody had advised her not to change it from an Islamic Terrorist group to an Irish Terrorist group.

'Did you notice how he didn't once look at any of the Somalis?' Ira asked with a smile.

I was slouched down in my chair, engrossed in my phone, tuning in and out of the discussion as I popped from one social media site to another. But when Ira opened her mouth, it made you want to sit up and listen.

'Sister, do not take it personally,' Tahir replied.

'Save it,' Ira said, holding up a weathered hand. 'You jokers think that you're too good for a job like that, I'd kill for that opportunity.'

'So go for it, what's stopping you,' Zafar said.

'Please,' Ira purred. 'Are you thick? Why do you think Somalis have the highest unemployment figures in the country?'

'Cos it's easier to claim benefit, that's why.' Zafar threw up both hands to indicate that he was playing.

'That's a bit harsh, man,' I said, coming to the rescue of somebody who did not require rescuing.

'Leave it, yeah, Jay,' Ira said, finger firmly in my face. 'D'you think you're funny, Zafar? You wanna know what's really funny? That the only job we're considered for is waitressing or security guard or *here's a mop and a bucket* and *there's the floor*. As soon we manage to get an interview for a half-decent job, the interviewer sees the *not-quite-black* interviewee sitting opposite them. Trust me, yeah, they've made up their mind before a word has even been spoken. You wanna think about that for a minute before you start making jokes, boy.'

Zafar attempted an apology. 'I was only –'

'Shut up, I haven't finished yet,' Ira spat. 'Jay, let me ask you a question.' *Fuck's sake, don't get me involved.* 'You've got a half decent job at the Council, tell me how many Somalis you work with.'

'Uh, in my section... Or in the building... Including outstations?'

'Quit stalling, Jay. We all know the answer. So what's our alternative? We start our own business – plumbing, handyman, some shit like that? Wrong, nobody is going to hire us. Twenty or so years we've been rubbing shoulders with society and still we're treated like outcasts. Look at the Poles, five minutes they've been here and they walk into jobs, start their own successful business. Why the hell are they not looked down on?' Ira looked from face to face. 'Anyone want to venture a guess? No? Okay, I'll tell you. It's because they have nice light milky skin.'

Nobody dared add that the Poles, part of the EU, came here specifically to make a living. The Somalis came here to escape from a civil war.

'Would you like a drink of water, Sister?' Tahir offered.

'You trying to shut me up, Tahir?' Ira said, her smile less alive than usual.

Zafar stood up from his chair and approached Ira. He didn't attempt another apology. He just nodded knowingly and awkwardly rubbed her arm. The two of them always bickered on any number of subjects, but I could see that Zafar genuinely cared for her.

This was exactly why I came to these sessions. It was *the* perfect place to throw a tantrum, have a good old rant at the world. Most of these guys had given up. Zafar, a Masters degree in his pocket from a top London university, had hopes of strolling into a job to suit his vast skill-set, now he's considering taking on a sales role for a fucking double glazing firm. Or Ira, pushing a mop night after night in a basement kitchen of a hotel, when it was clear that, given the chance, she had the intelligence and confidence to achieve whatever she set her mind to.

Everyone had their own issues. God knows I had mine, but I was happy to listen rather than divulge. It helped. They were a good group of guys, genuine. They seemed to like me, which wasn't much of a surprise; I'm pretty likeable! But, I wouldn't let them get too close to me. They were forever inviting me out, outside of this environment, but I always had an excuse ready. As harsh as it sounds, they just weren't my type of people.

Tahir came back with a cup of water for Ira and a fresh pack of Jaffa Cakes for the massive. Like scavengers, all hands reached out and cleared the packet of its contents. We enjoyed the silence as we munched on the biscuits, and shared optimistic glances at each other – a look that said everything probably won't be alright, but as long as we have Jaffa Cakes then it can't be all that bad.

I caught Ira looking at the entrance, not for the first time that evening.

'Have you messaged Naaim?' I asked. Naaim was the missing fifth member and also the youngest. Ira was pretty protective towards him, in that way girls are when they sense damage. Naaim was pretty fucking damaged. His mother was wheelchair-bound. His father an abusive alcoholic. Yeah, pretty fucked up, full of that teenage angst that I keep hearing about. *Me against the world* kind of character. Probably why he and Ira connected.

'Yeah, Jay,' she said, 'messaged him, called him. He ain't come back to me.' Her voice drifted. 'Not heard from him in a couple of days.'

'Is he still seeing that bird?' Zafar asked.

'You wanna try asking me that again?' Ira threw him a look.

'Layla,' Zafar smiled nervously. 'Is he still seeing Layla?'

'Yeah. Getting serious, too.'

'Has young Naaim been introduced to Layla's father, yet?' Tahir asked.

'They're just kids!' I said. 'What's the rush?'

'It's better that he knows that Naaim has no untoward intentions towards his daughter,' Tahir said. 'If he was to find out another way...' Tahir shook his head. 'He should know, that's all.'

I was getting bored with this conversation. I shrugged, glancing at the time on my phone. There's worse things happening around the world than *boy meets girl, parents don't understand* drama, and we'd heard all about this particular saga in recent weeks. I'd never met Layla, but the way that Naaim harped on about her, I felt like I could write a dissertation on her.

Layla Shah, I now knew, was a homely Pakistani girl, as halal as a cucumber. I've known plenty of girls like that – strictly Muslim at home, but as soon as they step out of that environment, they transform into Beyoncé. And I'm talking about *Crazy in Love* Beyoncé!

But I don't think Layla was like that.

Her Mum had been out of the picture since a while back, so it fell to Layla, from a very early age, to take on the household responsibilities – pandering to the needs of her strict father and over protective brother, whilst balancing her studies and her dedication to Islam. The last thing she needed in her life was complication. But complication came, in the form of Naaim.

They'd met at school, both studying for the same papers – Naaim's a year older but he had spectacularly failed his exams the year before. She started to help him study, every day in the romantic setting of the school library – knees touching under the desk, you get the picture. Anyway, shit happens, and they got close, like proper close. Their relationship moved fast, they talked marriage, even went as far as to discuss what they would name their kids. Fuck, man, they're only teenagers!

On top of which, Naaim is Bangladeshi, and Layla, Pakistani.

Paki relationships which haven't been sanctioned by parents are, at best, a fucking minefield. Throw another colour, creed or religion into the mix and it's just asking for a slap.

Yeah, there wasn't going to be a happy ending to this story.

I yawned. I didn't even attempt to hold back, it came out like the roar of a lion who desperately wanted to Netflix and Chill.

'I'm beat. I'm gonna call it a night,' I said.

But before I could bounce, the door behind me creaked open and Naaim stepped through and stood at the door looking suitably intense and lovesick – and I sighed under my breath and decided to stick around long enough to say *wha's up* and then be on my way before he unloaded with another episode of the ongoing saga.

Naaim crossed the short distance, as Tahir greeted him with a Salaam and a smile, and pulled a chair into the circle. Naaim sat down heavily and looked passively into the distance.

I swear to God, the fucking drama!

'Naaim,' Ira said, 'been calling you for time. Everything alright?'

'Yeah, you all good, Bruv?' Zafar asked.

'Brother, can I get you a cup of tea? We're all out of biscuits, I'm afraid,' Tahir added.

Unlike me, whose relationship with this lot began and ended within the four walls of the centre, the four of them were tight. They'd met here but looked out for each other outside of Heston Hall Community Centre. I'd go as far as to say they were friends, with Tahir, older, been and seen thirty, playing the mentor figure.

'I'm going to shoot,' I said, getting to my feet. 'Catch you all next week.'

'Naaim?' Ira said, ignoring me. 'What's happened?'

Tahir, sensing all was not well, said, 'Take your time, Brother. There's no rush.' Not what I would have said considering the hour.

Naaim closed his eyes tightly and we all watched as a tear escaped and slowly rolled down his face. His shoulders shook and shuddered and then it was open season as Naaim exploded into tears.

I knew then that I wasn't getting home any time soon. Just to feel useful, I fetched a glass of water and a box of Kleenex and placed it by his chair. Ira had knelt down in front of him, holding his hand. Zafar was standing close by, at a loss, not quite knowing what to do. I sat back down and waited patiently in my seat for Naaim to tell us about the next brick wall that he and Layla had no doubt walked into. The seriousness of what he was about to reveal started to dawn on me when I noticed his quivering hand reach for the glass of water.

'Let's give the man some space,' Tahir said. Zafar sat back down, his eyes caught mine and we shrugged in tandem. Ira, who was still kneeling down in front of him, straightened up, pulled a chair close to Naaim, and sat down. She reached across and took his hand in hers.

Naaim nodded at the floor, took a deep breath, and shared a story of happiness that had been doomed from the start.

12
Jay

'It was our first time meeting outside of school,' Naaim said, tear-soaked, balled-up tissues on the floor around his feet. 'We'd just sat our final exams and I... I suggested that we should celebrate. It was my fault.'

His voice was soft. The others leaned in, apart from me. I kept my distance. My finger tap, tap, tapping away like a jackhammer on the seat of my chair, hoping that I could write off whatever was to come as kids play.

Ira squeezed his hand and smiled at him to continue.

'Her father and her brother had made plans for her to celebrate the end of exams. When she told them that she wanted to go out and celebrate with her classmates, they said no. The first chance she had, she simply walked out knowing exactly what the consequences would be.

'She'd told me that if she was able to make it, she'd be upstairs on the one-eleven bus. I waited at the stop, outside Chilli Chips like I said I would, and scanned the top deck as bus after bus came and went. And then there she was. Looking down at me. I was so happy... and so nervous. She smiled, and from her small smile... I knew, I just knew that she had gone against her father and brother's wishes. Layla never broke the rules, but she did that... She did that for me.'

Ira jumped in, quick to give him meaningless advice, clichés. *You'll see, Layla's father will come around... Just have to take it slow... It'll all be all right...* Zafar being Zafar said something very Zafar-like, *she's going to be dumped* on the first flight to Pakistan and forced to marry her cousin. Tahir stayed quiet, a look on his face that wasn't far from *I told you so*.

I kept my opinions to myself – only because I hadn't formed any – and watched Naaim, head down, facing the floor, knowing that he wasn't yet finished.

'You don't understand,' Naaim lifted his eyes, bringing the room to silence. 'I got on the bus and sat down beside Layla, not knowing what to say to her, not knowing what was waiting for her when she got home. She leaned her head against my shoulder and took my hand and I thought... I thought that together we could take on anything and anyone.

'We were alone on the top deck, our plan was to... well we didn't have a plan. We couldn't risk being seen out on the streets. We were just going to ride the bus to the end and back again... But when the bus stopped at Lampton Corner, I noticed three pairs of cherry red Dr Martens moving down the aisle. They sat directly behind us, on the back row. They were loud, brash, drunk. I could feel Layla squeezing my hand.

'One of them tapped Layla on the shoulder. She turned, and he blew her a kiss. She turned back quickly to me, and they started to laugh behind us. I didn't know what to do. The way she looked at me, did she want me to say something? Do something?

'They had a newspaper – they were rustling it loudly on purpose and I could feel it skimming the back of my head. I know that they were trying to provoke me but I didn't let them. They started to talk about the headline, and I knew at that moment I should have taken Layla's hand and walked away the minute they got on the bus.

'"*Did you read the paper today? Front page news, check it out. One in every five Muzlims sympathise with Jihadi's.*"

'"*That's so fucked up. One in every five Paki's? Wankers!*"

'"*It says here in black and fucking white. They did a survey. Look, the whole report is here on pages one, two, three, four, five, six and seven.*"

'Layla called my name... I smiled at her, as if it was all fine. I wanted her to feel safe with me, I wanted her to know that I would never let anything happen to her.

'They split up. One of them stayed behind, another sat on the other side of the aisle across from us, and the third sat directly in front, turning so that he was facing us. He held up the newspaper with the headlines emblazoned on the front, big and bold, as though the words could not possibly be anything but the truth.

'"*So are you one of those five?*" He said, I smiled at him as if I was in on the joke, "*Nah, he ain't no fuckin' Jihadi, look at the fear in the Paki's eyes.*" Across the aisle one of them was pointing a camera at us. "*What about your girlfriend? Is she one of those jihadi brides I keep hearing about?*"

'I tried to take control, I told him that we were both born here, raised here, that we don't sympathise with what is going on. I said it coolly, as though I wasn't fucking petrified. From behind, one of their arms slipped between us and rested on my shoulder – he was holding a beer can.

'"*Go on, mate, have some. Call yourself English? Prove it.*"

'He pulled the ring of the can. I flinched as speckles splashed on my face, the smell of beer was everywhere. Layla pinched her nose, she'd never before been that close to alcohol.

'And that's all it took; that instinctive gesture, the disgust on her face.

'That's all it fucking took.

'It happened so fast. Someone screamed "*This Paki bitch thinks she's better than us.*" From behind, Layla's head was wrenched back and her hijab was ripped off and thrown on the floor. Before I could do anything, beer was poured over her head. She let go of my hand and tried to stand but she was forced down by her shoulders and then he... he... he forced his tongue in her mouth and then... they just left. And I just sat there.'

Naaim stopped talking. He craned his neck back and stared up at the flickering tube light on the ceiling. The tears had started again, running freely down the sides of his face.

'Motherfuckers,' Ira spat, shooting to her feet. She was always going to be the first to react. Her face set tight as though she was ready to explode. I gently shook my head at Ira and she sat back down biting back her response. She took Naaim's hand.

Zafar was leant forward, head in hands. Tahir had his hands out in front of him as he silently whispered a prayer.

'Layla. Is she all right?' I asked.

Naaim continued, still staring up at the tube light. 'She was on the floor, crumpled in the footwell. She had her back to me as if she was ashamed. As if it were her fault. I picked up her hijab and handed it to her. It was drenched in beer. Her hands were shaking as she tied it back on and then... and then she turned to me and she gave me this look, as though... I hadn't been there for her... I wanted to hold her in my arms but I knew I had lost the right to ever touch her again.

'She slowly got to her feet and walked away from me using the back of each seat for support. At the next stop she got off the bus and walked back in the direction of her home.'

'Have you seen her since?' I asked before silence consumed the room.

'I don't know if that's a good idea,' Tahir said. 'Her family will help her get through it.'

'You could drop her a text?' Zafar suggested.

'I went to see her this morning.' Naaim closed his eyes tightly, stopping the tears from escaping. 'I knocked on her door. Her brother opened it. He must have worked out that it was because of me that Ira had walked out the night before and come back late. He was fuming. Their dad appeared behind him, demanding to know what I had done, said that she hadn't come out of her room all morning, had locked herself in and wouldn't answer her

63

door. He was waving a key in his hand, said he's going to let himself in and find out for himself.'

Naaim dropped his head, his eyes still squeezed shut. He placed his hands on the sides of his head and applied pressure, causing his features to scrunch up in the middle of his face.

'He went upstairs and... I heard him scream... loud... so fucking loud, deep, guttural. I'll never forget it. Her brother slammed the door in my face and I could hear his footsteps rushing up the stairs. I walked across the road and stared up at Layla's window.

'Through the curtain I could see her hanging from the ceiling. Her body swaying from side to side. Her father and her brother had been too late to save her.'

13

Heathrow Airport: Arrivals

'Remove your sunglasses.' The short, rotund, smug bastard Kafir at Passport Control rudely instructed.

'Excuse me?' Pathaan said peering down at him, as he slowly ran a hand through his oil-slicked hair. He was fully aware that he would be asked to remove his sunglasses. He was also aware that he should be keeping a low profile, especially travelling with a fake passport. But it was the instigator in him that liked to push just that little bit. Especially with Westerners and their lack of manners.

The Immigration Officer cleared his throat, forced a smile. 'Would you mind removing your sunglasses, please?'

Pathaan slowly ran his tongue over his teeth, enjoying the remnants of the last paan that he had devoured on the plane, smiled and then removed his sunglasses. After a long look at the passport and the Hindu name, the Immigration Officer handed it back to him.

'Enjoy your stay, Mr Arav.'

Pathaan bristled at being called that, but it was necessity. He had already seen a family hauled in for questioning, most likely because at least one of them was called Mohammed. He took back his passport and smiled warmly at the Immigration Officer, fantasizing about how he would look with a plastic bag wrapped tightly around his fat head, gasping, praying for mercy as he died painfully at Pathaan's feet.

Pathaan placed his sunglasses back on, picked up his black leather holdall, and walked through Terminal 3 arrivals at London's Heathrow Airport. Final destination: Hounslow.

14

Imy

I had some making up to do. *Damn*, I had some making up to do. Jack was a sensitive soul; it happens when you grow up without your old man. It was the kind of thing that could make you feel like the whole world was against you; the kind of thing that could make you hard as steel. I knew a little something about that.

I was already beyond late when I pulled up outside Khala's house. So I left the engine running and hoped for a swift extraction.

'Crazy boy racer, what is wrong with you?' Khala exclaimed. 'Did you leave gas on? Is your house burning down?'

'Sorry, Khala. I have to be somewhere.' I kept my foot firmly on the brake and slipped the gear into first.

'Switch the car off, you are wasting petrol.'

'Khala... Really, I have to go.'

'What is more important than your future? I am sure Shahzad can wait five minutes more. We need to talk.'

'I'm not seeing Shaz, Khala.'

'Then?'

Rather than explain, I stuck the car into neutral and switched off the engine. 'Okay, Khala,' I sighed, scratching the hell out of the back of my head.

'Are you using the coconut oil that I gave you for your hair? It will stop all this itching. You look like a homeless person when you scratch your head like that. Have you seen Doctor? You could have nits.'

I couldn't help but smile. Yes, she was frustrating the hell out of me and yes, she was overprotective, even for an Asian parent, but all her annoying qualities were full of love. I dropped my hands and forced them to stay on my lap.

'So,' she said, her eyes sparkling. 'What did you think?'

'She was alright,' I said.

'Just alright?'

Rukhsana may possibly have been the most perfect girl that I had ever met. Her baby pink embroidered kameez hid her modesty, but it also revealed a little untouched paradise. Her lips were full and red and when she broke out of playing the shy Muslim girl and met my eyes, they were full of mischief and promise. With a silvery tone, she spoke well, able to hold her own in a variety of subjects. She moved us with her considered view on the recent Paris attack and made us howl with laughter with a joke about a Pakistani politician that I'd never heard before. The way she moved across the room made me want –

Damn! I was so late.

'Yes, she was... She was cool,' I said, as precious seconds ticked away.

'I know what *cool* means, Beta. Your Khala knows!' She wobbled her head from side to side. 'She *is* cool. Okay I will tell them. You like her, yes.'

'She seems nice, but it's early days,' I sighed, loudly. 'Just don't go buying any gold sets yet, okay.'

Khala smiled at me as though she had heard something altogether different to what I had told her. I didn't have the time or the heart to tell her it could never happen. That was a different conversation for a different day. She put her hand on mine, wobbled her head again and finally left.

*

Jack probably didn't know that his mum was at her bedroom window waiting for me. Stephanie probably didn't know that her son was at his bedroom window, waiting for me.

I killed the engine as I parked in the driveway. Jack beamed down at me and left his station at the window. I got out of the car and waved up at Stephanie, but her smile wasn't as bright. I could hear the scrape of a chair being dragged and I knew Jack was pulling it to the front door to give him height so he could remove the safety chain. The door flung open and he flew at me, head down, arms pumping, bare feet against the cold paving, I swept him up in my arms and peppered him with kisses.

Over his shoulder, Stephanie was leaning against the door frame. In the photo that she had sent me of them both in the makeshift camp, her dark hair was curled, and she was wearing a turquoise dress. Her hair was now tied back, the dress replaced with jeans and a faded Stone Roses T-shirt.

'How much trouble am I in?' I whispered to Jack, my eyes trained on Stephanie.

'Mummy went to the hairdressers today and her hair was curly-wurly.'

'Wow, that much, huh?'

I carried him inside and kissed Stephanie, she turned her head away and my lips grazed her cheek.

'It's past his bedtime,' she said.

'Do you mind if I...?' I asked, and she nodded.

*

I had just finished reading *Dear Zoo* under the lamp light in Jack's camp. He was too in and out of sleep throughout to enjoy it, and I cursed myself for making him wait so long for me. I lifted the duvet up to his chest and held him from behind, waiting for his breathing to settle.

'Imy?' he whispered.

'Jack,' I replied, pleased in a way that he was still awake.

'You know Sammy Murphy from Year two, he's in Mrs Stevens' class?'

'Sure, what about Sammy Murphy?' I waited for a response. It seemed as though he was weighing up how to say what was on his mind.

68

'His dad never plays with him.'

'Oh, I see.' My heart fell, I could already feel what was coming next. Jack never ever talked about his own father, but on occasion he would use a proxy to discuss how he was feeling.

'He's always late home and then one day he didn't come home at all.'

I held him a little tighter, my face touched the back of his head, and smelt the wave of innocence coming off him. I struggled for a response. He fidgeted a bit and then shifted his body around so he was facing me, our noses nearly touching.

'Do you think that Sammy Murphy's dad doesn't love him?'

'I don't know, Jack,' I answered truthfully. 'But you know *I* love *you*, right? To infinity and beyond, and I'll always be here for you.'

That was the whole truth. I'd fallen in love hard with Stephanie, but I loved Jack with a ferocity that frightened me.

'I love you too,' he said and then scrunched his nose. 'You smell of Indian food.'

'Yeah, I, um... I may have had a kebab or two.'

'Is that why you were late?'

'Yes. I'm sorry.'

'Don't be late again.'

I watched him sleep for a moment and left him with a kiss on his cheek before crawling out of the camp. The kid had tried not to show it, but he was disappointed in me for messing up his plans and it damn near broke my heart. I didn't want to be *that* person. He'd been through enough heartache with his father.

It was time to buck up my ideas. I'd been happy enough to be smothered by Khala, picking up freshly cooked meals that would last me the week, having my clothes washed and pressed, whilst living it up in that crummy flat that a student would have been ashamed of, blowing my not-that-great income on getting wasted with Shaz. And now I had to play the arranged marriage game, keep Rukhsana sweet, keep Khala sweet, keep dodging the consequences of telling them the truth. Making my life more complicated than necessary.

When really, all I needed was right here.

*

Stephanie was watching a reality TV show, sat on one end of the sofa, perched forward with both feet planted on the floor as if she had just sat down and not yet got comfortable. I knew that she would've been at the bottom of the stairs listening in on my conversation with Jack. Checking to see how I handled him. I positioned the foot stool in front of her and lifted her legs on to it. I stretched out on the sofa and placed my head on her lap. I looked up at her. She was beautiful at any angle.

'Let me guess,' she said. 'Your Khala?'

I smiled tightly. She ran her hand through my hair and waited for me to explain. I did, the lie coming easy to me. 'Her arthritis was bad today. Actually it's been like that for a while now. So I offered to do the weekly shop for her. I did text you.'

'No,' she said, confidently, as though she'd checked her phone a thousand times. 'You didn't.'

I slipped out my phone and scrolled to the text message that I had prepared earlier whilst I was at the Rishta. I frowned at it.

'What is it?' she asked of my troubled expression. I showed her the message. 'You didn't press send.'

I exhaled as I pressed my forehead and I laid it on, lie after lie. 'I'm so sorry, Steph, I was off my feet. After the grocery shop, she had me disassemble and take some old furniture up to the loft. Then she made me dinner afterwards and I couldn't not stay. Seriously Steph, I thought I texted you.'

We sat in silence for a moment, her eyes fixed on the television.

'Imy,' she said.

70

'Hmm,' I said, searching for holes in my lie.

'You have to tell her.'

'I know,' I said. 'I will.'

She stood up abruptly and my head slipped off her lap and bounced harmlessly on the seat. I sat up as Stephanie stood over me and I waited for her to let loose.

'Imy, believe me, I don't want to be the kind of girlfriend that questions your every action. I refuse to be one of those women. I fully understand that you have to think about your Khala, I know she's like a mother to you. And, trust me, I *know* about your culture. But you can't hide this, *us*, from her any longer. She doesn't deserve that, Imy. We don't deserve it. We're not your dirty little secret!'

I opened my mouth, she lifted a finger before I could counter.

'I need to know where this is going. You can't just pick and choose to play the big family man whenever it suits you. It's not fair on Jack.'

'That's not fair, Steph. You know how much I love –'

'*I know*,' she said, her voice loud and abrupt. Her eyes travelled up to the ceiling, beyond which Jack slept. She waited for the inevitable.

'*Mummy.*' Jack's muffled voice came back at her through the baby monitor that she still insisted on using.

'When are you going to understand?' she said, softly. 'Love is not enough.'

I heard her tired footsteps padding up the stairs. I looked up at the ceiling and I could just picture her, holding Jack in her arms, running her fingers down either side of his spine, rocking him gently back to sleep.

I inhaled deeply and held it, then exhaled. I didn't know how I could prove to Stephanie just how much she and Jack meant to me. They needed more; I needed to give them more. I needed to commit and show Stephanie what she and Jack truly meant to me.

My eyes moved around the room until they landed on a small ball of play-dough.

I went upstairs and entered Jack's room. Through the sheets that made up the walls of the camp, I could see their joint silhouette. I crouched down and crawled through the makeshift cushioned entrance. Jack smiled at me over Stephanie's shoulder.

'Room for one more?' I said, knocking my shoulder on a chair leg and almost bringing down the whole structure. Jack separated himself from his Mum and we all sat, legs crossed, in a tight triangle within the camp.

I nodded at them both, grinning stupidly. They both looked at me with curiosity, and then at each other. It wasn't exactly Paris, but I could not care less. The romantic setting of the Eifel Tower had nothing on this beautifully crafted kid's camp, splattered with toys and comic books, put together by a five-year-old.

It was the perfect setting.

I winked at Jack and then I took hold of Stephanie's hand. I dug into the top pocket of my shirt and pulled out a play-dough ring.

'Stephanie,' I said. 'Will you marry me?'

That night we all moved out of camp and into Stephanie's bedroom and, with Jack in the middle, we spent the night there. It was, quite possibly, the happiest I had ever been.

From downstairs, as I was drifting off to sleep, I heard my phone alerting me to a notification.

15

Derelict Building Site, South London

Kramer stopped at the entrance of the Portakabin on the old construction site, the fluorescent light from the room in front of him blazing into the night. He leaned his bulk against the doorframe and watched silently as two coppers spoke with his partner.

Dean Kramer and Terry 'The Cherry' Rose, as he was affectionately known, had run together since their days with the Millwall Bushwackers, a football hooligan firm who'd been particularly nasty at the height of their powers in the eighties. Dishing out some of the worst ultra-violence during and after matches. Kramer was especially fond of the Millwall Brick, a weapon fashioned from newspaper sheets tightly wrapped around coins and soaked in liquid to add weight. A string was attached at the bottom to enable the swing of the Brick, and a large nail attached to the top to enable sickening damage.

Kramer was the force, whereas Rose had the intelligence – enough to realise that the road they were on would only see them in jail or in a box. So he convinced Kramer to move away and join a movement which shared their beliefs. They were the English Defence League and their primary focus was opposition to what it considered the spread of Islamism in the United Kingdom. They finally had a place in a society that breathed and believed like they did.

It was only when a young off-duty British soldier was murdered in 2013, by two Muslims in the streets of South London – in fucking broad daylight – that their association with the EDL had come to an abrupt end. Kramer wanted revenge, quick and painful; he wanted to start a riot in the heart of the Muslim Community in Luton and take them down, every last one of them.

EDL had planned sixty demonstrations across the country. A lot of noise and not enough action. They had become too big, too political, *too* fucking correct. And the result of their demonstrations? Nothing more than a few scuffles against anti-fascist groups. They got their names in the newspapers, their numbers soared, but not one Muslim paid in blood.

Again, Kramer and Rose walked away and started their own group, recruiting particularly nasty players from their Bushwacker days, as well as like-minded members of rival firms. Rose ran the organisation, Kramer recruited. It wasn't the size of the English Defence League, but then with size came exposure.

A young girl wearing a hijab was pushed onto a train track as a tube pulled in at Piccadilly Circus Station. The push was mistimed and her face connected with the side of the moving train, leaving her needing facial reconstruction.

At an outdoor five-a-side football pitch in Islington, two Muslim community football teams were set upon by two Pit Bull Terriers and a Rottweiler. Four men were savagely mauled.

A grandfather was attacked walking his seven-year-old grandson home from the Mosque after evening Prayers. He was struck on the head with a blunt object as the assailant sped by on a bicycle. That didn't kill him. But the fall to the ground, the impact of his head against pavement, did.

They called themselves The Second Defence.

Kramer decided the time had come to make himself seen.

'Everything alright?' Kramer asked Rose, stepping into the Portakabin. The two coppers turned briefly to look at him.

'Dean Kramer,' nodded PC Mohammed or Mahmoud or who gives a fuck. The same Paki copper they sent every time there was a hint of a skirmish involving *his* people.

Kramer frowned at him, taking in the pristine fucking uniform that he should have never been allowed to wear. Kramer didn't mind though, because ever-present with him was the delectable WPC Jenkins. She could wear the uniform for him any time she wanted to.

'I tell you what,' Rose said. 'Why don't you leave the video behind and I'll see what I can find out.'

'I can't do that,' PC Mahmoud said. 'Do you or don't you know the identity of the three assailants? It's a simple question.'

'When did this take place?' Rose asked.

'Yesterday evening,' WPC Jenkins replied. 'Between six and eight.'

'CCTV?'

'Vandalised,' PC Mahmoud said, growing frustrated. 'Do you recognise them, Rose?'

'Hard to tell,' Rose pointed at the laptop screen. The faces had cartoon characters superimposed on them. 'How'd they do that? It's pretty clever, eh?' Rose smiled.

'You think that *you're* pretty clever, don't you Rose?' PC Mahmoud took a step closer. 'An innocent girl took her own life after an unprovoked attack.'

Kramer felt his blood spike when WPC Jenkins put a placatory hand on the Paki's arm.

He couldn't bear it if they were fucking.

'Rose, this belongs to us,' WPC Jenkins said, slipping the flash drive out of the laptop. 'But if you want to view it again, see if it jogs your memory, you can easily find it. It's plastered all over the internet.'

'Where'd you say this happened?'

'Hounslow.'

Kramer and Rose glanced at each other and quickly away again. Rose scrunched his nose.

'I don't know anyone in that part of town. But, you know, I'll put the word out.'

'The girl was only sixteen,' Jenkins reasoned. 'Call us if you find anything, Rose.'

'Sure,' Rose replied. 'Your number still 999?'

*

Kramer guided the officers out of the Portakabin which served as an office, and watched them drive out of the old construction site and into the night.

'Did you speak with those lads?' Rose asked from behind his desk.

'Yeah, at the rally yesterday, in Hounslow.'

Rose rubbed his chin. 'Come round.' Kramer walked around the desk and watched Rose over his shoulder as he fired open a search engine.

'What happened?'

'Some girl topped herself,' he said, as he typed into the search bar *Bus - Attack - Muslim*.

'Paki?' Kramer asked.

'Yeah, Paki.'

He got a hit immediately. The video had been removed from the first three links, but the fourth had it available in full high definition glory. They both watched the short footage in silence.

'Is it them?' Rose said, as it came to an end.

'Can't be certain with their faces covered liked that. But, yeah, judging by the size and the way they're dressed, that could well be Simon Carpenter and Anthony Hanson. This happen last night?'

Rose nodded.

'Fuck! They don't hang about. That must have been a few hours after I saw them at the rally,' Kramer said. 'I broke their balls about fucking about at these marches. I think maybe they went too far trying to prove a point.'

'They certainly did that. There was a third person with them – whoever filmed it.'

'Yeah,' Kramer nodded. 'I think I know who that could be.'

Rose closed the lid of the laptop and drummed his fingers lightly.

'Go find them, Kramer. I want the three of them in my office.'

16

Jay

After Heston Hall, after hearing Naaim's story, I couldn't go home, not with it ringing around my head. I'd wrongly assumed it was going to be a soppy, mixed-relationship-parents-don't-approve tale. I'd heard many of those before and crap like that did not impress me, especially with all the *real* crap taking place around the world. I was cynical. I had become cynical. The last twelve months had hardened me, my experience jolted me awake to the serious threat that Muslims faced every minute of every day.

'Before you ask, the answer's no,' Idris said, trawling around in my mind. It was alright, though, I had known Idris long enough to grant him a little room in my head. We were shooting pool in an empty bar in Chiswick and I'd just finished telling him about Layla.

'No what?' I said, bent over the pool table, lining up a spectacular double on the black ball when other easier options were available. It was the showman in me.

'C'mon, Jay. You want me to find out about the investigation.'

I shrugged and swung my cue, clumsily slicing the white ball and sending it straight into the pocket.

'Shit, Jay,' Idris spluttered into his Sprite, then pulled off the shot that I had just royally screwed up. I dug into my pocket and paid him his dues, a two-pound coin.

'Just ask around, is all I'm saying.'

'It's not my department, Jay. But, yeah, there'll be an inquest into the suicide, and if I hear anything, I'll let you know. Seriously though, don't make it your business.'

'I'm not,' I said, and I wasn't. And I don't know why I asked him in the first place.

'C'mon, that's enough pool for the night, grab a seat, I'll get 'em in.' He grinned, showing me in the palm of his hand the ten quid in coins that he had liberated from me.

I slumped down on a stool at the bar and rested my elbows on a drenched bar runner. I swore under my breath as a day's worth of spilt beer seeped through my sleeves and touched my skin. It was the first fucking time in a long fucking time that I had been that close to alcohol, and it was tempting to upgrade my soft drink to something a little harder.

'Here,' Idris absent-mindedly plonked down a Fanta in front of me, his eyes taking in the barmaid. She smiled easily at him. If he wasn't my best mate, I swear I would hate him.

'Oi, Pakistani Ryan Gosling,' I said, 'Drink up, I wanna get out of here and hit the pillow. I'm shattered.'

'Didn't you have a day off from work today? Don't give me that exhausted crap, Jay. I've been up since before dawn,' he said. I sighed and waited for one of his never ending supply of cop tales. 'We raided a family home today in Feltham, three young children under the age of four, including a baby girl only six months old. The nursery upstairs, where she slept, was a fucking treasure trove of Class A drugs. Check this out, the sick fuck had… You know what *Aptamil* is? It's powdered formula that's used to make milk for babies, right. He had about a dozen of these Aptamil containers all laid out neatly on a shelf. Inside half of them were exactly that, powdered milk, but the other half…'

'Coke.'

'Yes, Jay, fucking cocaine.'

I may have had a day off from work, but I did have a scary little run-in in the queue at Wilko's, and then I'd heard Naaim recount a pretty traumatic story. I had a right to be exhausted too. God bless Idris, but he could be patronising, his cop stories always seemingly aimed at me because of my own drug-dealing past. I love him like a brother, but he didn't half love to straddle that high horse as though he was the only one making a difference.

I once made a difference, too, but he could never know that. I could never tell him. It would change our friendship into something else, and at that moment I just needed a friend.

'The fucked up thing was,' he continued, 'what separated the coke from the formula powder was a *tiny* black dot on the bottom left hand corner of the container. His wife, the baby's mother – who, may I add, was high at the time of the raid – can you imagine if she'd scooped out a couple spoonsful of coke instead of Aptamil? And fed it to –'

'Yeah, alright Idris. I get it.' I knocked back my Fanta. 'I don't do that shit anymore.'

'I know, I know, I know,' he said. 'I know you don't.'

'I'm just trying to get by, that's all.'

'I know.'

'Just seems like these stories are always aimed at me. I was never like that, I was small time, yeah, just a little skunk.'

'I know.' He sighed.

'And I do have the right to be exhausted too, you haven't got a monopoly on being tired.' I shrugged my jacket on aggressively, just to make a point, and walked out of the pool hall and into the car park, where I waited for him in my Beemer. I let the purr of the engine cradle me to sleep, only to wake up a few minutes later when the door opened and Idris slid into the passenger seat grinning; he was holding up a piece of paper with a phone number.

'Good for you! Shut the fucking door, you're letting the cold in.'

'No high five?' Idris said, his hand held high. I slipped the car into first gear and manoeuvred out. 'You used to be a lot more fun, Jay,' he said, and for some reason, I wanted to cry. 'This has really affected you... what's her name again? Lyla?'

'Layla! Fuck, Idris. Did you not listen to a word I was saying?'

'Alright mate, keep your topi on! And what's his name?'

'Naaim,' I sighed.

'Listen, Jay.' Idris took his time, choosing his words carefully. 'This is going to sound harsh, but it's not your problem.'

'Did I say it was my fucking problem?' I spat, choosing my words without the same care.

Idris gave me a look and shook his know-it-all head at me. He was right, annoyingly he was always right. But I couldn't get Naaim's weepy face out of my head. What he told us was disturbing enough, but it was that look in his eyes. I had seen it before, a look of anger and determination. A man hell-bent on retribution. Once upon time, not long ago, my friend Parvez carried a similar look. It didn't end well for him. Nor, I had to remember, did it end well for me.

I would not allow myself to get involved.

17

Isleworth and Syon School

'Lewis? Lewis...? Daniel Lewis!'

'Here... sir,' Daniel gazed through the window. He'd been watching the groundsman on his ride-on lawn mower who was spending his morning lazily cutting the grass, not methodically as he should, instead making random turns. He should have been going in a straight line to the end of the field, a neat turn and a straight line in the opposite direction. It bothered Daniel. At home, when he mowed the grass in the back garden, that's how he did it. Straight lines, up and down. He even made the same effort for Mr Wilmott, his elderly neighbour.

'It looks very much like you want to be anywhere but here, Daniel,' said Mr Brick, the science teacher, as he glanced out of the window to see what was taking Daniel's attention. 'Continue as you are, and you'll soon be cutting grass for a living too.'

The rest of the class sniggered, a mocking sound that filled the room. They had been waiting, wanting to see him taken down a peg or two. Daniel wasn't liked, but the dislike wasn't harsh. There was no bullying or cruel remarks. It was worse than that. They just simply ignored him. They didn't like that he didn't have to make an effort to make them all look intellectually inferior. They didn't like that he dressed as though he was from another time. Steel cap boots, bomber jacket, shaved head.

Daniel drifted easily through double science, and then ate on his own in the canteen. He was a few months in at Isleworth & Syon School. His father had moved him away from St Marks. He saw potential, the teachers at St Marks saw potential, but the company that he kept outside of school saw an altogether different potential. His grades slipped from A's to B's to C's, around the same time that he started to skip class, instead spending time getting drunk on the cheap down Lampton Park with Simon Carpenter and Anthony Hanson, who were both a few years older.

Daniel's father had suffered greatly the last year, losing his wife in a senseless car accident. Daniel had suffered more. He had been close to his mother, a friend-like quality they shared, the result of being an only child. His father tried desperately to replace that closeness, but it was inevitable that Daniel, at sixteen, would react. And react he did. The regular phone calls from school, the truancy. The odd visit to the police station for the odd shoplifting spree, all whilst preparing for – as had been drilled into him – the most important exams to date.

People fear intelligence, his mother had repeatedly told him. It hadn't made him feel any better. He was desperate to be liked, to be a member of a group, or a crew.

These days, he was a member of a gang.

They even had a uniform. Bomber jackets, black jeans and cherry Dr. Marten boots.

Just because his father had moved him to a different school, it didn't stop him from seeing his only friends.

Simon and Anthony liked him, genuinely liked him. They said he was funny, and around them he *was* funny. It was no secret that Daniel's new friends did not like the colour brown. Especially if that colour brown happened to be a Muslim. The word Paki was spoken frequently. It had made him uncomfortable at first, but he soon realised that Pakis were doing a lot fucking worse than name calling. His friends made him realise that this was *their* country, that this was *their* England, and if *others* wanted to live here, then they'd better fucking abide by *their* rules.

They made valid points, Simon and Anthony, and were able to argue them with a deep passion and intensity. What they lacked in academic intelligence, they made up in street smarts. He was learning from them.

Daniel fitted in easily, no longer scared to skip the odd class and stroll on down to Lampton Park, where Simon and Anthony spent most of their days. He would join them, drink and share a joint, as they dissected and discussed the latest stories in the red-top newspapers – whether it was on the importance of a sharp exit from the EU, or coverage of the terror attacks that seemed to be a permanent tabloid fixture.

Sometimes they would rile each other up.

Sometimes they went too far.

Like when they'd ripped the head scarf off that girl's head and poured beer all over her.

Daniel needed to be involved, needed to be part of the brotherhood. So he shot the whole thing on his camera phone. But even as he was filming, even as he was laughing, even when he edited it, obscured the faces of his friends, and uploaded it to YouTube, Daniel knew that he'd made a huge mistake.

18

Imy

I was the first up. Still basking in the high of the woman I loved agreeing to be my wife, and careful not to wake up Stephanie and Jack, I quietly slipped out of bed. Breakfast in bed was the order of the day. I picked up my phone from the living room, before heading to the kitchen. The battery had died so I put it on charge and placed it on the worktop as I went about cooking a breakfast fit for my family. As I chopped tomatoes, I thought about how this decision was going to force my hand. I would have no choice but to tell Khala the truth and hope that she would accept it. There would be no more Rukhsana, nor any other girls for Khala to line up for marriage.

I glanced at my phone, it had charged enough for me to check the message that I dimly remembered receiving last night.

*

Fifteen minutes later, hash browns, fish fingers and tomatoes sat burning in the grill as I sat slumped on the floor with my back against the kitchen cabinet, phone in one hand, head in the other, trying to steady my breathing.

Above my head, the smoke alarm began to beep. Jolted from my trance, thinking of Stephanie and Jack sleeping upstairs, I leapt up and waved a tea towel under the alarm, switching off the grill with my other hand. The beeping stopped and, slowly, I retrieved the three slices of toast from the toaster, buttered two and dropped the third into the bin.

I placed the breakfast neatly onto two plates and then onto a tray. The third plate went back into the cupboard. I trudged up the stairs, the steps seeming steeper, and walls narrower than before. I placed the tray on the side table and watched them. I wondered if that night we had all shared the same dream, that of laughter and unity and bedtime stories and of three becoming one. A fantasy that I was selfish enough to present to them, knowing with certainty that I would never be allowed to become that person.

Jack was gently shivering, I lifted the duvet, tucking it under his chin, and kissed him softly on the cheek. I walked around to the other side of the bed and kneeled down in front of Stephanie. Her eyes flickered momentarily and she smiled lazily at me. I whispered that I had to go work. She nodded, before sleep found her again. I had to breathe hard to stop the tears; I inhaled deeply in staccato bursts before kissing her gently on the forehead and walking away from them knowing that not only my life, but the lives of those that I loved, had changed.

Peel back several layers of me, past the carefree life that I lived, past a loving son to a loving Khala, past a friendship with Shaz, and past the love and devotion that I held deeply for Stephanie and Jack, and the truth of me is revealed.

I am a jihadist, and I had just been activated.

19
Imy

I sat in my car with my phone in my hand and the message that I had once longed for stared back at me, every word piercing a hole in the life that I had carefully created.

Package ready for collection
65 Parkland Avenue, BB3 2RF

I was expected to drop everything for the sake of revenge, for the sake of a war that I was no longer part of. I glanced up at Jack's bedroom window, and recalled the excitement on his face when I arrived the night before, and the disappointment on Stephanie's at my being late because I was busy living another life, *another* lie.

I leaned my head back against the headrest of my seat, and then again, harder, hoping against hope that it would somehow knock me out of this nightmare. Determined to figure a way out, I started the car, slipped it into reverse and glanced in the rear-view mirror. Past my red stained eyes, a man was standing across the road. He was wearing a sky-blue shalwar, kameez and skullcap, and he seemed to be staring directly at me. I narrowed my eyes as he checked his watch before walking away. I had been trained to identify a threat – and this sure as hell looked like one. Something inside my head tripped, and I found myself a target to take out my frustration on. I flung open the door and stepped out of my car, forgetting that it was still in reverse. It jerked back before the engine cut out. The sound of the jolt made him turn his head back towards me just as I strode across the road. I don't know what hell he saw in my face but his eyes widened and he picked up his pace before realising that wouldn't cut it. He broke into a run.

I hadn't run in a while, my body not tuned as it had once been, and the action felt stompy. But very quickly I found my feet barely hitting the ground and my arms pumped hard as I quickly cut the distance between us by half. He scrambled out his car keys from his kameez pocket and screeched to a halt next to a Honda. The car beeped and its lights flashed, indicating that it was unlocked, and he opened the door and placed one leg in. I crouched low and picked up speed and slammed my shoulder into the car door trapping and instantly breaking his leg below his knee.

His howl was harsh on my ears at that hour of the morning, I cut it short by clamping my hand over his mouth with my right and punched him on the side of the temple with my weaker left and bundled him across into the passenger seat as I got into the driver's.

My eyes furtive, first on the rear-view mirror and then quickly across both wing mirrors. Satisfied that nobody had seen or heard the commotion I turned my attention to him. He had a slight cut on his eyebrow from where my fist had connected, but more urgently his leg looked as though somebody had slammed a car door against it. He closed his eyes tightly and bit down on his open hand as he realised that a hint of bone was sticking out and his shalwar sopping in blood.

For all I knew he could have been an innocent bystander, who'd been in the wrong place at the wrong time and ended up on the end of an attack that I hadn't thought I was still capable of. I had become that person that they'd raised.

An apology was on my lips, but the way he was dressed and the way he'd been watching me, I had a feeling he had something to do with the message I'd received.

'What's your name?' I asked.

'Yousuf Ejaz,' he said, removing his hand from his mouth and smiling through his pain. 'Mashallah, Brother, it is good to see that you are still strong.'

'Tell me who you are, who you work for?'

'I have already told you who I am. As for my employer, He is the Almighty, the All-powerful.'

'How long have you been following me?' It was my third direct question. I had more lined up, but I could see that his skullcap was drenched with sweat, which was also pooling above his eyebrows. He was fighting to stay awake and I realised that he was going into shock. 'Give me the car keys,' I held out my hand, 'I'll drive you to the hospital.'

Instead of handing me the keys, Yousuf put a clammy hand in mine and squeezed it weakly. 'I haven't been following you. I have been keeping an eye on you since you were a young man. I have got to know you well, albeit from a distance, Brother. You have done a remarkable job, Imran, keeping your head under the radar, away from prying eyes. I am so... so...' He closed his eyes. His body shook as it came to terms with the shock it had absorbed. He needed treatment immediately. I reached across and tried to pry out the car keys from his hand, but he held on tightly.

'Go, Brother,' he said, fighting to keep his eyelids open. 'You have been called upon. You should have left last night when the message arrived. Allah will forgive. Just go.'

'I have to take you to the hospital.'

'*No*,' he said sharply. '*Now!*'

*

I'd called for an ambulance for Yousuf, using his phone, and left him in a semi-conscious state. Before I set off on my trip north I had to make a quick detour. I glanced at the clock on the dash and decided to pick up Shaz, as per routine. I needed him to keep an eye on things while I was away. If they'd been watching me, they may also be watching those close to me.

I pulled up outside Shaz's house and alerted him with a short sharp beep of the horn. The front door opened and he walked lazily down the path as he clumsily negotiated his arms into his blazer. The last thing I needed was for Shaz to be high.

'You know, Gareth, yeah, from Cranford branch?' he started as he always does without any greeting or preamble as he put his seatbelt on. 'He called me this morning, like ten minutes ago, check this out, he's taking a few days off and he wants me to cover his viewings. I was like, *fuck that*. Then he goes, no joke, yeah, that he's calling from the fucking hospital, says he's gone and tore a tendon in his shoulder.'

I moved out and headed towards work. I let him chat away as my thoughts bumped into each other.

'So I said, how'd you do that? And he tells me that –' Shaz laughed. He had an infectious laugh, and if the situation wasn't as it had been, I would have laughed along with him. 'He tells me that, no word of a lie, that he was doing his weekly yoga class with his missus and they were in the, I don't know, the fucking lotus position or something, and next thing you know, he's rolling around on the floor holding his shoulder, screaming. What kind of man injures himself doing *yoga?* Shit! You've seen Gareth, right? Big cunt! Plays rugby. I was like, *mate*, word of advice, keep that shit to yourself.'

'Shaz,' I asked. 'Are you high?'

'Mum dragged Dad to an early Tesco spree. I had the yard to myself, so I smoked a little something before breakfast.' He looked me up and down. 'Why aren't you in your suit, Imy? Kumar's going to have a fit if you turn up in jeans.'

'I need a favour, Shaz.'

'I'm all out of favours, mate.' He winked at me. 'Nah, go on, spit it out.'

'In between viewings I need you to swing by Steph's. She's working from home today.'

'Yeah, alright,' He said, then, 'Why?'

'There's been a spate of break-ins recently. I thought I saw somebody hanging around Steph's place. Probably nothing, but, you know."

'You think he was casing the joint?'

'Possibly.'

'You want me to fuck him up?'

'No, Shaz. Just call me.'

'I'll swing by around lunchtime. Do you reckon Steph will have made anything? I'm already hungry.'

I parked the car a few metres before the office, out of sight. The last thing I needed was Kumar to question me. 'Thanks, Shaz. As I said it's probably nothing but just keep your eyes peeled.'

'Yeah. Undercover, innit. Don't worry, I got this,' he said confidently, as he opened the car door into a lamppost.

20

Jay

By the time I'd dropped Idris off and got home, it was past one. It would have been sooner but I swear some fucker was trying to put the frighteners up me. Stuck to my bumper for a mile or so, xenon lights so bright I couldn't see him through my rear-view. I took a detour via Osterley as I didn't really want to lead them to my doorstep. The car overtook me at the lights, and I let him, tempted as I was to put my foot down and show him the difference between my Beemer and his Lexus. As it sped away, I made a mental note of the number plate but I swear it changed each time I ran it through my head. Probably some wet behind the ears teenager trying to impress his mates in his Mum's car. Still, it had freaked me out.

By the time I did hit my pillow, sleep had been replaced by adrenaline and I stayed awake with Naaim's story still knocking around my head.

My Batman alarm went off at half seven, but unlike the Caped Crusader I wasn't feeling so heroic. After a night tossing and turning, I didn't have it in me to go to work and sit at my desk and make soothing sounds over the phone to customers who couldn't work out why they couldn't print, scan or save. I called Carol, my team leader, and coughed and spluttered my way through an excuse. She didn't buy it, but I couldn't care less. She told me to get a Doctor's note, and I said that I was losing phone signal and cut her off. She'd be fuming, but it was my last day before my trip to Qatar and by my return, she'd have softened.

I stayed in bed for the best part of the morning and watched TV with one eye on my phone, checking news sources for any updates on my father. There was nothing new. I thought briefly about reaching out to Naaim, but I didn't have his number, and I didn't know his surname so I couldn't Google him or check out his Facebook profile. Anyway, maybe he didn't need reaching out to, not from me anyway. Seriously, when did I become such a fucking saint? Helping people whose surnames I don't even know! Whoever heard of such a thing? Besides, the last time I acted all saintly I'd got in well over my head and had to watch those I cared about suffer. *Had to watch them die.*

Let him be, I concluded. *I got my own problems, sunshine.* On top of everything else, Staples' words were still knocking around somewhere in my head. I shook my head clear of it, filed it away in a section of my brain entitled *Oh fuck!* and decided to make the most of my impromptu day off.

Tomorrow was my surprise visit to Mum in Qatar, and I still had a few things to do. Buying her a gift was one of them, but that could wait. First I planned to have a dirty, greasy, comforting lunch. It couldn't be local, though – I couldn't risk being seen by somebody from the office during work hours. So I decided Slough was the safest destination. Nobody goes to Slough; it makes Hounslow look like Venice.

I rolled out of bed and started my day. I wanted to avoid anything that involved effort so I skipped showering and, between you and me, I skipped washing my face and brushing my teeth too. It's not like I was due to meet anybody.

Bright eyed I wasn't, and bushy tailed could fuck off too.

*

Ah yes, Slough. The black sheep of Berkshire. I inhaled and smelt my surroundings. It seemed like I wasn't the only one who'd left the house without cleansing. Slough wasn't as multicultural as Hounslow – yeah, there was the odd black and white and yellow, but they were drowning in a sea of brown. As such, it was a place where I could easily get lost and, at that particular moment, as I glanced, not for the first time, over my shoulder, getting lost was exactly what I was looking to do. Because if I wasn't mistaken, I was being followed. First that Lexus had attached itself to me the night before, and now *this* fucking clown. My training in Islamabad hadn't taught me much – I'd been too preoccupied sending cryptic messages home to MI5 – but it *had* taught me that there are some nasty fuckers in the world, so you want to keep your eyes open. The guy behind me was wearing a deerstalker hat pulled down low over his eyebrows and a scarf pulled up high over his mouth with a dark overcoat over a dark suit. His outfit of choice was not one normally associated with the shoppers around these ways. Too smart, too suave. He was a fair way behind me but he moved quickly. Nothing suspicious there, he wouldn't be the first to be in a hurry to leave Slough. But in that small gap between his scarf and hat, his gaze seemed steady on me.

In my mind I flicked through those who had a bone to pick with me. There were many, but my first thought was Silas. In between doing push-ups and getting royally shafted in prison, he could have orchestrated a hit on me.

My heart raced, but I didn't. I continued to stroll. If I could just get round the corner at Sam's 99p Store ahead of this guy, then I would have the thirty-metre run towards the side exit of Queensmere Shopping Centre, and onto the parade, where I could easily lose him. As I turned the corner I side glanced back towards him; he was a lot fucking closer than he had been a moment ago. Once out of sight I broke into a run and cleared the thirty metres at speed, flew through the glass doors and out onto the parade. I looked back through the doors. Deerstalker wasn't anywhere to be seen.

Half an hour later, I was busy devouring a beef and melted cheese sub in The Meat Spot, Slough's greasiest joint, when I clocked Deerstalker through the front window. He was stood outside, stamping his feet to keep away the cold, and was holding his phone to his ear. This time I didn't give in to fear, instead letting logic take over. Maybe he was hungry, too. Maybe behind the stylish coat and the sharp suit there lived a meat-craving slob.

I couldn't make out his features as the day was bright, and the cold sun was hampering my view, but there was no question: he had his intentions set on me. The fear crept back in, but unlike last time when I scarpered, I kept it in check.

I took a noisy sip of my Pepsi, giving the impression of a man without a care in the world, as I worked out my next move. I got up calmly, thanked the grumpy-looking waiter, who looked like he wasn't used to gratitude, and made my way into the bathroom. There was a single pane window above the middle urinal. I looked down at my new hi-tops and grimaced as I placed one foot on the lip of the urinal, trying and failing to avoid the pooling yellow liquid. I hoisted myself up using the rusty copper pipe, and climbed up onto the window ledge. I palmed the window open and dropped out, landing flush in my Nike Air Jordan's. I took a second to gather my bearings, then ran along the back of the shops, past the rubbish skips and the employees out back having a smoke. I took the first gap that appeared between the shops and peeked my head around onto the High Street. From a distance I looked back towards The Meat Spot.

He was still there. I watched as he pressed his face up against the shop window and, realising he couldn't see me, stormed in. Once he was safely inside, I stepped out from between the shops and headed back towards Queensmere Shopping Centre, aiming to get to the car park, into my car, and the hell outta Slough.

As I approached the entrance to Queensmere, I turned back and risked another glance towards The Meat Spot. Almost immediately, Deerstalker came bursting out, no doubt pissed that I had given him the slip. I entered the shopping centre at a run – the car park payment machine was at the far end, but I reached there in good time.

There was just one person in front of me, but she was old and the technology was beating her. I stood impatiently behind her hopping from one foot to the other.

Come on, lady. Work it out!

She pressed the assistant button on the pay-machine and it beeped seven times before a lazy voice answered, and they got into a back and forth that I really did not have time for.

To my left there was a Debenhams department store. Four floors to get lost in. I shuffled towards it and stopped outside, using the shop display as a reflection to spot Deerstalker. It's not as easy as they make out in the movies; I couldn't see a thing past my own reflection and the mannequin holding a quite fetching leather man-bag.

I hustled inside the store and then scaled the escalators two steps at a time to the men's section on the third floor. My plan was simple. Deerstalker had seen what I was wearing; I had to change my appearance. Time was of the essence and I didn't have the luxury of browsing. I moved stealthily and purposefully towards the jacket section, and hooked a dark parka coat off the hanger and slipped it on without breaking stride. I did it so smoothly that I felt an old rush returning, something that been missing from my life. Next I moved to the accessories section and picked up and put on the first hat and scarf that I could lay my hands on.

At the cash desk, I insisted that the lady, much to her annoyance, scan my items whilst I was still wearing them. I couldn't risk dropping the disguise.

'Excuse me, sir.' Behind me was a security guard, hand on my shoulder, hot breath in my ear. 'Do you mind coming with me?'

'What for?' I said, holding up my Visa in his face. 'I'm just about to pay.'

'I'm afraid you're going to have to come with me,' he said.

I took in his name badge – Greg – there was a complaint in here somewhere – and stepped out of the queue. Greg, the in-shop cop, ushered me across the shop floor.

He led me to the back of the store and into a pokey video surveillance room. A second bored-looking security guard, open crisp packet in hand, swivelled around in his chair.

'Alright, Greg?' He checked me out. 'Is that him?' he asked.

'This is him,' Greg said. 'You got any crisps left in there, Jim? I missed lunch.'

'He don't look like much to me,' Jim said, emptying the packet directly into his mouth. 'Don't see the big deal.'

I tried to figure out why I had been hauled in. Was it because I was being difficult with the shop assistant? Doubt it. Could it be that I was running around the shop floor picking out random items and wearing them around the store like a mentalist? Nah, there's no law against that. Or could it be that they didn't like the colour of my skin? A thought which, at one point in my life, would never have entered my mind. But I had seen things that had changed my way of thinking. It didn't matter, anyway, because as long as they had me in this room I would be safely away from the smartly-dressed assassin.

My eyes wandered over to the bank of small monitors, nine in total, in rows of three. I scanned each one and, there it was, on the middle screen. The Deerstalker's hat.

'Call the police,' I said.

'What's that, boy?'

'The police.' I frantically dug around the pockets of the parka that I had hooked, searching redundantly for my phone. 'Call the fucking police,' I cried.

'Police!' Jim snorted. 'Around here, son, we are the police.' The two guards grinned and bumped fists. I moved closer to the screen, the static tickling my nose. I watched Deerstalker, his walk measured, eyes on the camera as though looking directly at me. He stepped onto the escalator and disappeared out of view.

'Where'd he go?' My eyes flitting to each monitor. 'The *fuck* did he go?'

'I'm going to have to ask you watch your language. That's your second profanity.'

I took a step closer to the desk, my hand reaching for the joystick on the control console.

'*Oi!* You can't touch that,' one of them barked, but I had it tight in my grip and I was moving the camera in different directions. Rough hands grabbed the scruff of the neck and pushed my face down hard onto the control console, the other pinned both my arms behind my back.

'Please, I'm in danger, call the police.'

'Keep still or we will have to use force.'

Fucking toy cops! The side of my face was squashed against the console, I managed to twist it so that I had a view of the screen and there he fucking was. In menswear. On this floor! He seemed to be asking a sales assistant for directions and she seemed to be pointing towards this very room.

Clearly, I could not depend on these two bumpkins to help me, so I lifted my leg and brought my right Air Jordan down hard. It met satisfyingly with a foot and a yelp. My arms were now free so I swung my elbow back blindly and it connected nicely with a ribcage.

With escape on my mind I moved towards the door. The handle turned even though I hadn't touched it. I took a step back just as Greg and Jim tackled me to the ground. I used my hands to break my fall before it broke my face. Once again my arms were pinned behind me, a knee in my spine for good measure, and a hand forcing my face down into the dirty threadbare carpet.

The door opened.

From my vantage point on the floor, I managed to look up, my chin painfully scraping the carpet. I cursed under my breath as he lowered his scarf and removed the deerstalker, and smiled at me like an old friend. Which he definitely was not.

'Javid Qasim.' He grinned. 'Making friends, I see.'

I spat out a mouthful of carpet. Raising my head, I looked my old MI5 colleague Teddy Lawrence straight in the eye.

'Jay… Call me Jay.'

21

Imy

So many times I had lain in bed, unable to sleep, fantasising about this very moment. I'd pictured it. My reaction. Felt it. Felt the adrenaline run through me until I was sweating through my clothes and onto my bed. Knowing that the time was close when I could drop the facade and play a small but significant part in the war that had taken away my family. But somewhere along the way, the enemies *became* my family. The façade became who I really was.

I had to find a way out of this.

Google Maps told me it was a four-and-a-half-hour journey north. I was going to make it in under four, touching a hundred when I could and slipping onto the hard shoulder if I had to. My mind raced as fast as my car, picturing myself in different scenarios, each with an unhappy and violent ending.

I was a junction from my exit when my phone rang. I took the call and switched it to loud speaker.

'Shaz,' I answered, my heart skipping. 'Everything okay?'

'Sweet as.' Shaz's voice came through clear, as though he was sitting next to me. I wish he had been.

'You didn't see anybody hanging around?'

'Nah, all good in the hood. Back in the car now, just outside Steph's place. Check this, Kumar lent me his Merc for viewings today, but there's this strange knocking sound coming from the engine. Hope he doesn't blame...'

Shaz trailed off mid sentence.

'Shaz. You there?' I asked as his voice drifted.

'Hang on.'

'Shaz?'

'Hold on a minute.' Shaz kept me waiting as he muttered to himself.

'Shaz! What is it?'

'Don't know. When I arrived earlier I clocked a man on a motorbike across the road from Steph's, but he left as soon as I pulled into the drive. Didn't think much of it... But –'

'What?' I wiped my palms on my jeans. 'But what, Shaz?'

'He's back.'

I slowed drastically from seventy to thirty and pulled over onto the hard shoulder without indicating. An HGV blared its horn as it sped past me, rattling my Prius.

'What does he look like?'

'Can't tell. He's wearing a helmet. Top to toe in leathers.'

'What is he doing?'

'I think he's looking at me. Why the fuck is he looking at me, Imy?' Shaz's voice was tight. 'Should I say something?' he said uncertainly.

'No, just... just let me think.' I was two hundred miles away.

'He's going. He's gone,' Shaz said. I heard the growl of a high-powered bike. Shaz exhaled loudly and then laughed nervously. 'I would have fucked him up.'

'It's probably nothing.' I tried to convince him, convince myself, but the wheels were in motion and spinning quickly. My past hadn't just caught up with me, it had caught up with the people I loved. Whatever it was I had to do, I had to do now.

*

I'd lived in Hounslow for many years, and watched the epic rise in integration and multiculturalism, but this place was the extreme opposite. I drove slowly down Parkland Avenue looking for number sixty-five, but it was difficult to focus as my eyes were glued to the sheer number of

Muslims. In Hounslow, it was not uncommon to see a woman in a Burka, but here they were all adorned from head to toe in black. In the space of minutes, and on the same road, I drove past two mosques and four halal butchers. I looked hard for a white face, a black, a turban, or a skirt. It was as though I had landed in another state, in another country. The segregation loud and proud, a community which thrived on a separatist environment.

I carried out a hasty five-point-turn on the narrow road as I realised that in my daze I had passed number sixty-five. The house on my left was number two-two-seven but I had already started to look for a spot to park as both sides of the road were rammed, cars parked bumper to bumper, so I drove at walking pace in the hope that somebody would pull out. I wasn't paying attention to what was in front of me and I had to slam on the brakes as a child was standing in front of me in the middle of the road. He wore a black kurta with black jeans and expensive-looking white trainers. On his head was a Pashtun hat, purposefully tilted to one side, lending the kid a thuggish appearance. He couldn't have been more than ten years old. He walked around to my side of the car and twirled his finger at me to slide the window down.

'Whas your name, Blud?'

'Excuse me?' Who he was or what he wanted, I did not know, but I wasn't about to give my name to him that easily.

He did that thing with his tongue, slurped it or kissed it, making that wet, bubbly sound to illustrate his annoyance. 'Your name, Blud! You got one, yeah, what is it?'

'Why don't you tell me your name, little man?' I said. He liked that; liked being called a man. He casually rested his elbows on the car window sill.

'They call me Rocket, yeah,' He smiled. 'Cos I go bang, you get me.'

'Rocket?'

'Yeah, Blud, aks me again and I tell you the same,' he said, his Lancashire accent starting to grind on me. 'So, who are ya, then?'

'Sorry, Rocket. That's none of your business.'

'But I told you *mine*,' he whined, and for the first time he looked and sounded like a ten year old. He moved away from the car, dejected, his hard-man image taking a blow. Through the windscreen I saw a man walking towards my car. This sparked the kid back to life and he was back in my face again. 'Who'd you think you are, Blud, driving that shit car down my manor? When I aks you a question, you answer it or you get jook up, yeah?'

It wouldn't have taken me much effort to just flick him away but my eyes were on this other guy. He had similar features to Rocket, so I assumed they were related. Not old enough to be his father, so I assumed brother.

'Rafi,' he shouted as he got closer. 'Is that him?'

'Don't know, he's not telling me his name, is he?' Rafi said, giving me his best hard-man stare. 'He don't look all that to me.'

The man approached the car and nudged Rafi to one side. He kneeled down and eyed me curiously and then asked me, 'What have we learnt, Brother?'

To anybody else it would have sounded like an obscure question, but to me, and to those who had studied the learnings of The Teacher, it was an easy answer. A lesson that we were taught above all others. We were not suicide bombers, we were fighters. Any attack carried out by the soldiers of Ghurfat-al-Mudarris never sacrificed life. Taking your own life in the name of religion, of jihad, was haram.

'Life is a gift,' I said, softly. 'Leave no man behind.'

'Mashallah, Brother.' He patted me on the shoulder. 'Rafi, go tell Mr Tamir to shift his motor. We have a guest.' Turning back to me he smiled. 'My name is Asif. Our Father will be home soon, he is expecting you.'

22
Jay

'We've got him, Sir,' Greg said, in his best Bruce Willis voice. 'He was a little tricky but we managed to detain him.'

'We'd been watching him, anyway, even before the call came in. He was acting erratically,' Jim added.

Lawrence nodded, trying his best to conceal a smile.

'Lawrence, do you want to get these toy cops off me?' I said, face still buried in the carpet, knee still in my back.

'So what are you, some kind of Special Forces?' Jim asked.

'More to the point, who is *he*? They said on the phone that it's a matter of national security,' Greg said.

'They like to exaggerate,' Lawrence said. 'It's not quite a matter of national security, but it's good to know that we have men like you on our side.'

They shared a shit-eating grin. I let out a squeal as they pulled my arms tighter behind my back in order to impress Lawrence, as though he had the power to help transform them from stupid cross-eyed security guards to Secret Service agents.

'*Lawrence!*'

'Okay, that's enough. Let him up,' Lawrence said. 'That's no way to treat a hero.'

'Err, hero?'

I felt hands move away but I stayed down for a minute. The meat sub from earlier was threatening to make an appearance.

*

After sheepish apologies and twenty quid in Debenhams vouchers as compensation, Lawrence and I walked out of the Queensmere Centre and found a Costa Coffee on the high street.

'What would you like, Jay? I'm buying.'

'Damn right you're buying. Cappucino... *Massimo*! And an almond croissant.'

Lawrence went to the counter to order and I moved around the coffee shop, looking for a table which would give me sight of the front and side doors, so I was able to see who was coming and going. I checked myself. Silas was behind bars, his operation ceased. His crew on high alert, feeling the heat on their collar. Only Teddy Lawrence was interested in me, and I wouldn't have a problem getting rid of *him*. So, fuck it, I sat down at the nearest table with my back to the entrance.

I may not be worried about him, but I had no idea why Lawrence was back in my life. We had gone our separate ways, his ruthless ambition made him a name at MI5 whilst I settled for some much-needed normality and structure. I wasn't concerned about his sudden appearance, but I was pretty pissed off at the way he went about it. So, when he placed the tray on the table, and sat down opposite me, it was the first thing I asked him.

'The hell was that all about?' I clocked the plain croissant in front of me. 'And what the hell is *this*?' I said, poking at the crusty looking croissant. 'Where are the almonds?'

'That's all they had,' he said, biting into his picture-perfect *pain au chocolat*.

'I can't eat this, it looks like old stock. How long's it been sitting out there?'

'I didn't ask,' he said. 'How you been, Jay?'

'I'm getting by. You going to tell me what just happened?'

'Just wanted to say hello.' That smug smile that I was once so familiar with, and irritated by, made its first appearance.

'Lawrence, do not waste my time, I will stand up right this second and walk out of here, I swear to God.' I stood up, just to prove how serious I was, but really, ain't no-one walking away from a free drink. 'There is nothing keeping me here. I'm through with MI5.'

'Shall I get you a megaphone? Not sure if everyone in Slough heard you. Sit down.'

I stood my ground for a moment and then sat down. Point made.

'Why were you shadowing me, Lawrence? You've ruined my day off from work.'

'Firstly,' he said, lifting a finger, 'it's not your day off, you pulled a sickie.'

'Oh, wow. Am I supposed to be impressed that you know that?' I said, secretly impressed that he knew that.

'Secondly, I wasn't shadowing you. I was trying to catch up with you, but you were scarpering around like a man demented.'

'Bullshit! I saw you outside The Meat Spot. You could easily have caught up with me in there.'

'Jay.' He smirked, and I knew pretty much what he was going to say. 'This suit set me back four figures. It's bad enough that I have to wear it around Slough, do you really expect me to walk into a stinking meat shop?'

'But you did though, didn't you?'

He nodded. 'Window above the urinal, right?'

It was my turn to smirk as he sniffed the arm of his fancy suit and grimaced.

'How'd you find me, then?' I asked, and then answered. 'You're tracking my phone.'

'I wasn't about to run around bloody Debenhams, so I arranged for security to pick you up.'

'The racist fuckers proper roughed me up,' I said, smoothing down my shirt.

'Get a grip, Jay. They were not racist.'

'They thought I was a terrorist.'

'Okay, Jay. I apologise.'

'Twenty quid of vouchers!'

'Jay, will you shut up for just a bloody minute?'

I sat back and crossed my arms.

'We need to talk.'

'The answer's no.'

'Hear me out.'

I shrugged at him, it was a small shrug but one which clearly said that my mind would not be changed. The last time that I had the *we need to talk* conversation, I was looking at jail time for dealing and assault. They told me that if I gave them a statement giving up Silas, and joined MI5 as the token Paki to spy on other Pakis, then they would make it all go away.

So I did. I sang. I joined. I fucked up.

In the process I helped save many lives, but I *still* don't know if I made the right decision.

'We still haven't caught him,' Lawrence said, his eyes on mine.

Him… Him… Fucking him!

'The Teacher,' he said, solemnly, as if I didn't know. 'Your Father.'

I could feel my face forming an expression and I wasn't sure what it was. I certainly wasn't glad that he was still on the run, but a part of me was glad that he hadn't been killed. Though, to be honest, he did deserve nothing short of an excruciatingly painful death.

I brought the coffee up to my lips, hoping that it would mask my face, stop me from revealing my feelings. I waited for him to stop trying to read me and continue.

'You did well, Jay,' he said, softly, which did not suit him. It was overly sincere to the point of bullshit. 'Due to your efforts we have his description, his real name and the name of a number of locations he operates from.'

Usually, I had a shrug for every occasion. Why waste your breath when a good shrug speaks volumes? But I found I couldn't produce it, as though somebody was forcing my shoulders down. I didn't open my mouth either, anxious that my voice might break and tears would follow. I just blinked at him and felt the first touch of moisture forming between my eyelashes.

'He's aware that we are onto him, and subsequently he's gone under. It's only a matter of time before we capture him. But sooner, rather than later.'

I pictured Saddam poking his head out of a hole in the ground. I pictured Osama getting shot in his fucking underwear. I pictured my Dad and blinked it away before I could picture anything else.

'If we can get him to show his face…' Lawrence said, carefully. *Very* carefully. Leaving me room to respond. Which I did.

'The answer is no.'

'*Jay!*' High pitched, frustrated. The *fuck* did he expect? He sat back and crossed his arms, mirroring me and held my gaze. I looked away. I wasn't playing that game. I picked up the butter knife on my plate and drilled it into the middle of the croissant. It stood proudly upright before the weight of it sent it clattering down onto the plate. 'You know better than anyone what he is capable of,' Lawrence continued, his voice returning to the pre-rehearsed soft. 'If it wasn't for your actions, hundreds of innocents would have died. Families, Jay, children. Look, just hear me out, okay. Ever since he went into hiding, GCHQ haven't picked up any chatter. All the websites hero-worshipping him as a means of recruitment are systematically getting shut down, and not by us! *They're* doing it, they are getting rid of any mention of him. It's like he never existed! But his work continues. Three weeks ago in Prague, a man walked into a café with a goddamn razor blade, and sliced the first person he set eyes on across the chest, a woman, celebrating her 80th birthday. Then he jumped over the counter and went to work on the face of a female Barista, before some customers intervened and detained him.' Lawrence watched for my reaction. I didn't give him one. 'A pizza parlour in Copenhagen, a popular student hangout, a small explosive built into a laptop goes off, three students died.'

I glanced out of the window, searching for something visual to stop my mind from picturing it.

'The men responsible for these attacks have both been captured. Both cleanskins. Not on any watchlist, no priors and no history of any suspect travel. But... when questioned they both uttered the same phrase. One that you're familiar with.'

Yeah, I was very aware of that phrase, it was one that had been hammered into me when I played jihadi amongst the mountains of Khyber Pakhtunkhwa. The Teacher did not believe in the act of taking one's own life. They never used suicide bombers; instead it was by means of guns, IEDs, car bombs and other tools of death and carnage. A soldier that fought for The Cause wearing a suicide vest would contradict the teaching of Ghurfat-al-Mudarris.

Life is a gift. Leave no man behind.

Lawrence took a sip of his coffee and eyed me over the rim. He'd played his hand without actually telling me what he wanted from me, but, in spite of what my school report card had alluded to, I ain't stupid. Lawrence believed that The Teacher would resurface for one reason only.

That reason being me. His son.

Should I go back, just so he could pop his head out, just for it be taken clean off by a sneaky fucking shot?

It's probably what my father deserved.

'Robinson,' I said. 'He sent you?'

John Robinson, Counter Terrorism, ruthless fucker. He who had sent me packing despite what I had given them. He'd never liked me, couldn't suss me out. It didn't matter. I didn't like him either.

'Robinson doesn't know I'm here.' Lawrence leaned in. 'He has his own ideas which I don't entirely agree with. But if you agree to this I can go over his head.'

I stood up calmly and for the third and final time, I said, 'The answer is no.'

23

Imy

I waited for the bemused neighbour, Mr Tamir, to vacate the parking spot. He clearly wasn't happy at being ordered to move his car, especially as there were no obvious spaces, but he agreed without voicing his annoyance. Whilst I waited, Rocket Rafi let himself into the passenger's seat and messed with the volume on my stereo.

'Your speakers are weak, Blud!' Rafi said, as he turned the sound right the way up.

'Leave it.' I clicked off the stereo. I could see his head turned towards me, taking my measure.

'It's gonna be sick, yeah?' he said.

I glanced through the windscreen, Mr Tamir was slowly shifting his car back and forth trying to manoeuvre out.

'The attack, innit,' Rafi continued. 'It's gonna be sick. One day I'm going to do something, yeah. Like you.'

I turned towards him, his eyes were wide and wild, as though he was counting down the days until he would be unleashed. It saddened me. I wondered if, like me, that passion would one day be replaced by something else.

Mr Tamir moved away and I finally managed to reverse park into the tight spot with Asif guiding me and whacking his hand on the roof every time my car got too close to another.

I removed my shoes in the porch and walked into their house. I followed Asif through the gloomy hallway. Islamic art hung above a rusty radiator, which I recognised as the

Ayut-al-Kursi. It was a prayer that I had once committed to heart, but now would struggle to recite. The Arabic was written beautifully in swirling calligraphy and engraved in wood. I stopped to read it.

I felt Saheed Kabir's stomach in the small of my back before I felt his hand clap heavily on my shoulder.

'*There is no God but He – the Living, the Self-subsisting, Eternal,*' Kabir translated. '*His are all things in the heavens and on earth. Who is there that can intercede in His presence?*'

Kabir nodded respectfully at the prayer, then held up a small see-through plastic bag spotted from the inside with blood. He smiled. 'Best lamb chops in Blackburn, Brother.'

He introduced himself to me as we shook hands, and he ushered me into the living room. Two women immediately shot up from the sofa and rushed away.

Kabir was a big man, frighteningly obese. He lowered his frame onto the middle of the sofa and motioned for me to sit adjacent to him on the armchair. Rafi came bursting into the room and at speed leapt into Kabir's lap, his stomach comfortably taking the brunt of the impact. Their laugh echoed around the room. 'This is my youngest, Rafi.'

'Yes, sir,' I said, keeping in line with the respect that is afforded to elders. 'We've met.'

'Abu, did you buy me the football cards?' Rafi asked, his voice sickly sweet, at odds with the caricature that I had earlier met.

'I knew I had forgotten something, Beta,' Kabir said.

Rafi frowned. 'It's okay, Abu.'

Kabir smiled and nodded towards the top pocket of his kameez. Rafi's face lit up as he snaked a hand into his father's pocket and emerged with two packets of Match Attack Cards. *Rocket*, as he liked to be called, peppered his father with kisses before dismounting from his lap.

'I'm going upstairs to do my homework now, Abu,' he cooed.

'Prayers first, Rafi,' Kabir playfully chided.

Rafi skipped out of the living room, looking far removed from the hard-man image he'd desperately tried to portray to me.

'You were late, Brother Imran.' Kabir turned his attention back to me. 'I believe the message was sent to you yesterday.' He smiled brightly as he said it, I could tell that he was a good father, the kind of man that was everybody's favourite uncle.

'I'm sorry, sir. I only received it this morning and I came straight away,' I said, as my mind raced back to proposing to Stephanie. *Was that only last night?* I cleared my throat. 'May I ask who gave the order?'

It wasn't a question that he would have been asked before.

He held my gaze for a moment. 'You ask this question, why?'

'I have to speak with them.' I forced my hands to stay placed on the arms of the chair when the nape of my neck was begging to be scratched. 'Can you put me in touch?'

'Many times the package changes hands before it arrives at my doorstep. I wouldn't know who has given the order and, young Brother, I don't need to know. I am blind to The Cause. As should you be.' He paused. 'I will ask you this only once: is there a problem?'

I should have realised that Kabir was a middle man. He couldn't help me. 'No.' I said. 'No problem.'

'Very well.' Kabir nodded slowly and his smile returned. 'But I can say this: you won't be alone.'

'Meaning?'

'You missed our other guest. He too picked up his package.' His smile wavered. 'Strange character, if I may be so bold. Not much for socialising.' He rubbed his chin. 'Very unsettling individual.'

I felt myself sinking into the armchair, as a shiver swept through my body. I had an idea who Kabir was referring to. Somebody who I had huge love and respect for. He had turned a lost angry boy into a man. A jihadi. Giving my life a purpose before sending me out on my own to a strange land. I remember clearly his last words to me:

Be patient, Imran. Keep your emotion and your anger buried deep within you. Your time will come, Inshallah.

And I had. Buried my anger so deep that it was no longer anywhere to be found. I wondered if whether, when we crossed paths again, he would notice that the fight in my eyes had disappeared.

He was the one that I had to talk to. He was also the one that would never understand.

'Brother, your package is waiting,' Kabir said, and nodded at Asif who had entered the room. 'This is my eldest, Asif. One day, Inshallah, he too shall do something worthy for The Cause.'

'I'll be ready when the time comes, Abu,' Asif declared.

'Mashallah. For now, he will take you to pick up your package.'

I stood up. Kabir stood up too but it took him a while longer and pride made him wave away help from his son. He walked me out of the house with a heavy arm across my shoulder.

'It is not my business what is inside the package, our duty is to keep it safe until it is collected,' Kabir said. 'Whatever it is that you are going to do, do it with Allah in your heart and Inshallah, Brother, you can only succeed.' He kissed me on both cheeks and whispered the *Ayut-al-Kursi* in my ear.

*

The package wasn't far so we walked. Asif bopped and bounced, stopping to say a respectful Salaam to an elder, a fist bump to a youth, or a polite nod to any Burka-wearing women. He was the man around these ways, and he was enjoying showing just that.

'See this newsagents, right here.' He pointed, as we walked past a parade of shops. 'Owned by a Kafir. The *only* Kafir on the street, trust me, Fam. He's been here for time! Gotta respect him though. We tried everything to get shot of him, even smashed that place up a couple of times. He's been threatened too, by some hard-hitting Brothers. We poisoned his dog once,' he laughed, 'but the little bitch was as tough as his owner.'

111

I glanced into the shop as we walked past it. A short, white, balding man with round spectacles sat proudly behind the counter in an empty shop.

'Yeah,' Asif smiled. 'Boycotted that fucker, too.'

We passed two halal butchers, located directly next to each other, both packed, and then a large Mosque. It should have looked alien, situated between a row of terraced houses on either side, but it fit, standing high above everything else, the minaret shining between tall slender towers.

'This is the main Mosque, but it's not our kind of place, you get me, Fam.' He side-smiled at me. 'C'mon, let's cross over.' He stepped out onto the road without checking for oncoming traffic, his hand out indicating priority, and swanned across the street as if he owned it. We stopped at a shoddy, brick-built, double-fronted building.

'Time back, this used to be a pub,' Asif said, sweeping his hand over it. If it wasn't for all the Muslims milling about, talking in hushed tones, peering blatantly at the new face amongst them, it would have still looked like a pub. 'We gutted it out, took one of those high pressured jet washers and rinsed the hell out of it. Took weeks to dry, but it got rid of the smell of booze and Kafirs.'

We removed our shoes and Asif led me inside the hastily-converted Masjid. There were no bookshelves, nor any Islamic literature. The lighting above was out. Instead the light was provided by floor lamps, whose yellow glare lent the room a sinister feel. The floor was without prayer carpets, in their place was random patterned bed sheets and throws. A crudely-drawn arrow on the far side of the wall indicated the direction to Mecca.

'It needs work,' he whispered over my shoulder, ensuring that he didn't disturb the few that were praying. 'We're raising money but it's difficult. Most Brothers are dedicated to the bigger Mosque across the road, and any money we do raise goes towards The Cause.'

Asif sat down and motioned for me to follow. He took out his phone and silenced it and then typed out a text message. A minute or two later a tall, well-built man with a wild, straggly beard entered the prayer area. He stood to one side and waited for those few who were praying to finish, and then one by one whispered in their ears and they all left the room without question, until only the three of us remained.

'Zahid,' Asif said. 'Lock up.'

Zahid walked out and I could hear the always-open doors of a Mosque being closed and locked. It was clear from the off that this wasn't a normal Masjid, and the worshippers were not your typical peaceful, religion-abiding citizens. The whole set up was geared for and towards The Cause; it had all the concealed markings of Ghurfat-al-Mudarris sympathisers.

'Is it ready?' Asif asked. Zahid glanced at me before nodding. 'I'll be back in a minute.'

Left alone, sat on the cold hard floor, I checked my phone. It had registered a couple of missed calls from Kumar, and a recent innocuous text from Stephanie which put my mind a little at rest. I slipped my phone away as Asif came back into the room. He was carrying a black briefcase, formed of hard, ribbed plastic. He placed it in front of me.

'Mashallah, Brother Imran,' he said with a change of tone, now righteous. 'I am privileged to be a small part of your jihad. Inshallah, I too will soon be in a position to carry out Allah's work.'

I looked down at the briefcase, unable to bring myself to touch it. I could feel his eyes on me, waiting for a reaction. I smiled; it was forced.

'Whatever is in there, Brother, may it bring us success.' He glanced at the wall clock. 'Let us pray.'

Asif took position facing Mecca. I stood up and joined him. On the floor beside me lay the case. Without having had a chance to investigate it, I knew that it had thick, reinforced walls and high-density pick and pluck foam interior. Externally, four heavy duty hinges and six dual stage latches, with a gripped extendable carry handle and travel wheels.

A case designed to carry a high powered handgun.

I snatched my eyes away from it and for the first time in twenty years I bowed my head and I prayed to Allah, whose help I now craved.

24

Jay

Honestly, I didn't care if I'd thrown a spanner in MI5's plans. My life was on track and chugging away gently through the boring countryside, with nothing to see. The last thing I needed was for it to derail.

Teddy Lawrence was a piece of work. I hadn't seen him since the Boxing Day disaster and in he swans, la-di-fucking-da, back into my life with a smile on his face and the balls to ask me back into the fold. As far as I was concerned I had gone above and beyond the call of duty, did what I was told to do, and did a fucking good job of it too. It was no longer my problem that they still hadn't captured Bin Jabbar. All the intelligence in the world at their disposal and they want *me* to entice him out.

There's no fucking way I'm playing bait, regardless of the prize.

I drove away, leaving both Slough and Lawrence in my rear-view mirror. I still had the afternoon to kill, and now more than ever I craved normality. I headed home, only stopping at the corner shop to pick up some over-priced cleaning products. Once I got started I found myself moving swiftly but meticulously from room to room. My mind focused solely on the job ahead. I vacuumed, dusted, polished, vanished and banished all signs of a lazily-led life. The house hadn't sparkled like this since Mum had moved out. I took pictures so I could show her that I'd become a domestic God.

I was on a roll and feeling good. My Beemer was due a service, so feeling pretty pleased with my work rate, I decided that I may as well get that done too. I wheeled it into Southall, left it with my trusty mechanic and went shopping for a gift for Mum. The spring in my step was back, my mind clear, my senses full of the colourful smell of food, the incessant chatter and the barrage of cars honking down Southall Broadway, as I dipped in and out of the many fabric shops, eventually settling on a beautiful maroon silk shawl. I picked up my Beemer from the garage and then treated it to an inside & out car wash.

Not once did I let the bad stuff cross my mind.

Idris called, asked me if I was in the area, hoping to scrounge a ride home. It was early evening and I was exhausted, but eager to keep the day going, so I said I'd swing by and pick him up from the station after his shift.

'Five-a-side tonight,' he said, as we headed towards his house. 'Don't forget.'

'I can't tonight,' I said,

'I expect you to pick me up at quarter to eight. Don't be late,' he said, ignoring me.

'Why am I always picking your ass up and dropping your ass home?' I said, as I pulled up outside his house and killed the engine.

'Cos you got the motor,' he said, gesticulating his hands around my car like a magician. 'Don't be late!'

'Seriously, I can't play tonight. I've got a flight to catch tomorrow.'

'Oh shit, Qatar! Is that tomorrow? Make sure you give your Mum a kiss from me.'

'I'll tell her you said hello,' I said, making a face.

'When are you back?'

'Fourteen nights and fifteen days.'

'Why couldn't you just say two weeks?'

I shrugged, reached into the back seat and brought forward a plastic bag. I pulled out the maroon silk shawl.

'I got this for Mum. What do you think?

'Yeah, very nice. Will you tell her it's from both of us?'

'No.'

He let himself out of the car. I started the engine. He knocked on the passenger side window. I slid it down.

'What now?' I said. I could tell from the expression on his face that he wanted to say something soppy and meaningful like *after all you've been through*, *you deserve a holiday*. But he knew better.

'Send me a postcard.'

'Not going to happen.'

'I'm gonna miss you.' He grinned.

'Fuck off!'

'Call me the moment you land otherwise I won't be able to sleep.'

I slid the window up hoping to catch his head in the frame, he moved his head back and gave me the finger.

I drove off smiling.

I took the long route home as I was enjoying the smoothness of my car after its service earlier. It had been the perfect afternoon and evening, nothing out of the ordinary and nothing exciting. A timely middle finger to Lawrence and MI5 as to how I chose to live my life.

I pulled up into my driveway. Somewhere behind me the sound of a car door opening and closing. By the time I had a chance to clock him in my rear-view mirror, he was there, standing at my open window.

'Hello, old chum,' Silas said, beaming, 'I haven't seen you in ages.'

I caught a glint of something.

25

Imy

On the return journey, I called Khala. She was pissed at me for not going into work, but otherwise she seemed fine. I called Shaz, who laughed at the episode outside Stephanie's house earlier on, not quite grasping the enormity.

Finally I called Stephanie. Jack was getting ready for bed. Her voice had a floaty quality to it, the marriage proposal, which may as well have happened in another lifetime, still fresh in her mind. I tried desperately to match her enthusiasm.

Satisfied that they were all out of harm's way, I pulled into a service station an hour into my journey home, curiosity getting the better of me. Thankfully the case had an extendable handle and travel wheels which made the otherwise intimidating bag look a little more ordinary. I wheeled it straight into a disabled toilet, figuring that I would require the space. I locked the door, placed the case on the floor, and kneeled down on my haunches in front of it.

Even though I had a fair idea of its contents I had not yet determined how I would be expected to use them. I assumed that it was going to be a gun attack. At what, I didn't know. At how many? I shuddered to think. I unfastened the six latches slowly one at a time; they snapped and sprang and the sound reverberated around the cubicle. I took a breath and lifted the lid.

I ran the tip of my finger against the cold muzzle of a Glock .40-calibre handgun. Light, easy to conceal, heavy on impact. Next to it was an Osprey pistol suppressor. Aligned neatly next to these were three magazines, which I saw were fully loaded with ammunition. Clipped into the top of the case was a manila envelope.

I opened it carefully and took out a document. Hand written in Arabic, I read and understood it to be the official issue of a fatwa. It momentarily threw me. I was expecting a date, a location. A mass target. I slipped another document out of the envelope. It was an enlarged image of a young, Asian male, trying his hardest not to laugh, to adhere to the strict rules of having his passport photo taken. Despite everything, it made me smile.

He looked familiar and it took a moment to come to me. I flipped over the photograph. Written on the back was his name and address.

Javid Qasim based in Hounslow.

I knew him as Jay.

I'd accompanied Shaz on many occasions when he had picked up from Jay. What wrong could a small-time drug dealer from the suburbs of Hounslow have committed, in order to deserve a death sentence from Ghurfat-al-Mudarris?

I picked up the Glock, pulled back the slide release and checked the chamber was clear, quietly amazed at how instinctively the movements came back to me. I picked up a clip, slid it home. I made sure the safety was on, before tucking the pistol into my jacket pocket. Then I clicked the briefcase closed, and headed back to my car.

*

After a dazed drive home, I'd arrived back in Hounslow early that evening, and I now found myself driving down Jay's road. My body impulsively making decisions, my mind not quite catching up. I was moving on instinct. Without realising it, I'd come to a realisation, one that would haunt me until my last day. As sick as it made me, I could do this. It was just one target.

Just one kill.

There was no alternative. It was my life or his.

When I received the message that morning, every type of attack had instantly run through my head. The bloodshed, the devastation. Not the question of whether I was capable; it was in me. I had the physical skill to cause destruction, to take a lot of lives and disappear without a trace. However, I would forever be on the run. The world would be looking for me. I'd never again see the faces of all those that I cared for. My life as I knew and loved it would cease to exist.

But one kill? One kill would be easier, cleaner. Quick in-and-out, a double tap to the chest, leaving no trace behind. Nobody would ever know I was there. I could carry out my duty and repay my debt to The Cause, then get on with the life I was meant to lead. My life with Stephanie and Jack.

I pulled up outside Qasim's house. The lights were off and the driveway empty. I had told Stephanie that I'd be spending the night at the flat, so I had nowhere to be but here. I decided to wait.

I closed my eyes, and I could visualise it clearly. Qasim stepping out of the car. I'd be on him, Glock trained on his lower back. Forcing him into his home. Pulling the trigger. Dropping him. Retracing my steps carefully out of his house and slipping away. Mission accomplished. By the end of the week I would be packing my bags and moving out of my flat and into the arms of a new life.

I slipped my hand into my jacket pocket and felt the cold steel of the Glock. As cold as the act of a kill. It felt familiar, a part of me for so long.

I heard the hard and heavy bass-line before I saw the car. A black BMW swung head-first into the driveway. I removed the Glock from my jacket, from another pocket I removed the suppressor. As I attached it, I watched a black Lexus pull up and park across his drive. I couldn't see inside the Lexus as the windows were blacked out, but the back door opened and out stepped a pin-thin man. Even though the weather was fine he was wearing an anorak with the hood up. I managed to catch a glimpse of his face. I didn't know him personally, but I knew who he was.

Silas was a man who came with a reputation.

He approached the driver's side of the BMW. A quick word exchanged and then I noticed his arm reach in and then back out through the window before swiftly walking back to his car and driving off. It looked very much like the quick exchange of a drug deal.

I waited a moment for the Lexus to reach the end of the road and turn off. Then, after disabling the interior light I stepped out, keeping the Glock low by the side of my leg, my dark denim helping to disguise it. I only got as far as taking a couple of steps towards the house when the reverse lights of the BMW flashed on.

The wheels screeched noisily on the spot before it hurtled out of the drive towards me. I dived out of the way as the BMW smashed into a lamppost at speed.

I slipped the gun into the back of my jeans and ran over. Peering inside the car, I saw that the side of Javid Qasim's head was resting against the steering wheel. There was blood down his front, pooling in his lap. His throat had been slashed.

He looked at me with barely open eyes, and smiled lazily.

I opened the door and gently lifted Qasim out of his car. I placed him on the floor in an upright position and I sat behind him and held him, letting his head rest on my chest. His clothes were soaked in blood. His eyes closed, as though for the last time. His breathing slow, shallow, barely there. Qasim was dying in my arms.

My work could have been done then and there. I knew I should just let him go.

The hammer of the Glock pressed into my lower back, a painful reminder of my jihad. Every instinct screamed at me to let him bleed out and die.

It was at that very moment that I realised what I was capable of.

I reached for my phone, and called for an ambulance.

PART 2

This is where you left me...

26

Jay

I was in and out of consciousness throughout the journey to the hospital, unable to fully sleep as the sheer amount of blood I was losing was stopping me from breathing, from swallowing. I blinked, and I was in the hospital, with a distant memory of being gently lowered onto a gurney. I tried to position myself onto my side, lift my knees to my chest and curl up like a ball. Clean hands pinned me down onto my back. I was silently outraged – clearly, on my side is my favoured position of sleep, so why wouldn't they let me lie there in peace? Obviously they were determined to keep me awake. They even slapped me a few times, which given my state I thought a little unnecessary. I tried, I fucking tried, face up towards the ceiling as the lights whizzed past me, bright and offensive.

My throat felt heavy, as though it was covered with, I don't know, a cloth or a dressing or something, and a hundred heavy hands were putting pressure on it. There were rushed voices around me – they said I was in an *aggressive state*, they said I was *not cooperating*, somebody said the words *exposed vocal cords*, as though I couldn't fucking hear them, it made me vomit down the sides of my mouth and onto my face and into my ears.

I blinked again, and was in another location, under another bright light, but this one wasn't moving. It hovered, stationary, like a huge space ship above me, threatening to land on me. Lots of covered faces peering over me, *that's right, mate, enjoy the show*. More words, long words, words I thankfully couldn't fucking understand. *Regional anaesthesia, bilateral block of the hypoglossal nerve, preparing for emergency tracheostomy.*

An anaesthetic face mask gently placed around my nose and mouth. All that effort trying to slap me awake, and now, they decided, was the time for me to sleep.

27

Imy

Covered head to toe in Qasim's blood, I arrived at my flat a little after midnight. I kept the Glock tucked into my jeans, the cold barrel skimming the skin on my lower back. I had debated hard whether or not to keep it on me, but the way events were turning I sided with caution.

It was a decision that was vindicated as soon as I unlocked my front door. On the floor, parked neatly next to the door, was a pair of weathered men's sandals.

My hand moved without instruction, shifting the tail of my shirt and wrapping my fingers around the grip of the Glock. I brought it smoothly forward, my other hand joining to steady the piece.

I moved quietly but quickly through the small living room which doubled up as bedroom and stood by the entrance to the kitchen, hidden from view. The kitchen, and the bathroom which lay beyond it, were the only other places to clear. I took in a breath and held it as I moved my head quickly around the door frame and back again.

In that snap movement I saw that my fridge door was open. Under the door I saw a flash of dark bare feet. I hadn't seen his face as the rest of the intruder was hidden by the door. But he hadn't seen mine either. I slowly moved my head back through the entrance, the Glock pointing safely at the ceiling but ready to snap down and aim.

I could hear him rattling around in my fridge as though he owned the place. I stepped into the kitchen. He cleared his throat, heavy and raspy. I flicked the safety off and pointed the gun at the fridge door as I risked a scope around the room. A black leather jacket was neatly hung over the back of a chair and a black motorcycle helmet was sitting on the small kitchen table. Past the fridge, past the intruder, at the back of the kitchen, the bathroom door was wide open, revealing that he did not have an accomplice.

I turned my attention back to the only part I could see of him. His feet from under the fridge.

The nail on the big toe of his right foot was black.

I released my breath, flicked the safety back on, and placed the gun on the table, next to the helmet.

*

After my parents had been killed, and after the soldiers had left, I had stayed under my bed. Though the crackle and hiss of a growing fire threatened to consume me, I was too frightened to move.

Through the smoke, I eventually saw a pair of open leather sandals moving around my bedroom. The nail on the toe of the right foot was black. The bed was lifted easily over me and in an instant a hand was taking mine and pulling me up to my feet. He had a black and white chequered ghutrah scarf tied tightly over his face to stop him from inhaling the smoke. He picked me up, my legs straddling his waist, my arms tight around his neck. He pushed my head down so my face was in the crook of his shoulder and neck, away from the smoke. As one we walked out of my burning home and into my burning village.

I lifted my eyes and watched over his shoulder as, with every step, my home grew smaller and smaller in the distance. He tried to place me into the back of a large, open-bed truck with some other children from my village, but my legs tightened around his waist, and my arms around his neck, refusing to let him go.

He whispered in my ear, 'Mashallah. You are a strong one.'

It made me relax my grasp, and he gently placed me on the bed of the truck. I felt the engine start beneath me. I looked up at him and he pulled the scarf away from his face and smiled at me.

His teeth were coated in red.

For six years I was worked over. From the age of ten, all I knew was replaced by what they wanted me to know. I was taught with children from my village, children that I had grown up and played cricket with. Like myself, their homes had been destroyed, their parents slaughtered. We were moved to a small working town deep within Gardez, which was located close to the Afghanistan/Pakistan border. We fed off each other's misery. Our mourning rang out as a cry for help. We were housed, cleansed and fed and sent out to work. They watched our every movement, and the strong amongst us, the good workers, were noticed. The lazy, the weak, those still pining for their parents, were moved along without explanation.

For the rest of us, our education began. Intently we listened, we learnt, we trained, each day our bodies growing stronger, our minds focused and our anger controlled. I put my mind to whatever they asked of me. Never once did I say *I can't, I won't*. My body became capable of doing things that I never thought possible. Hand to hand combat with blades and bars and bare fists. Every part of me took a beating, but so powerful was the will within me that I never once went down. On every opponent I saw the uniform of the enemy and I would not, at any cost, allow them to stand over me again.

At ten, I had wanted to kill those British soldiers responsible for the vicious deaths of my parents.

At sixteen, I wanted to kill everybody and anybody who sided, voted, affiliated themselves with the West.

With one bag in hand, I had landed at Heathrow Airport and then arrived at the door of my Khala. Her husband, my Khalu, had just passed away after losing a short battle with cancer. She was all alone. I was too.

She recognised me before I even had a chance to knock on her door. In the kitchen, washing the dishes, absentmindedly staring out onto the road, she spotted me stepping out of a taxi. Before I had the chance to pay the driver, she was standing out on the porch, washing gloves still over her hands, squinting, trying to confirm the connection. It was when I turned towards her that her eyes opened, and then her mouth opened and then she was rushing to me with her arms open. It was an embrace that had been desperately missing from my life. It was my Mother's embrace.

Khala had assumed that I had died, along with my parents. I told her that I had been living with another family until I could save enough money to travel and be with my own. Together, we relived the grief of my parents' death all over again, but it was different, softer and more compassionate. We laughed as she told me stories about my Mother, her Sister.

That first night, as I pretended to sleep, she entered my room, lifted the duvet up to my chest and kissed me on the forehead. It was a familiar touch and a familiar love that I hadn't felt in six years. She left the room and I spent the night crying.

I never understood Khala's fondness for the Royal family. Almost every room had a commemorative plate, a Union Jack cushion, a Lady Diana serving tray. It used to drive me crazy that she was celebrating everything that I wanted to destroy. But I played along, smiled at the silly sentiments. Here, I wasn't a jihadi hell-bent on revenge. I had to play the game, had to stay under the radar, away from suspicion. So, desperate to keep my cover, I took it to the extreme.

Not once did I enter a Mosque. In fact I stopped praying altogether. My parents had led by example and taught me about my Farz as a Muslim. Even after they passed, I didn't lose my religion, instead I embraced it further with a ferocity that came easily to me. I started to interpret Islam in a way that it was never meant to be interpreted, the teachings of Al-Mudarris blending effortlessly with the teachings of the Holy Quran.

I'd always had time for Allah, made time for Allah. So to just stop was one of the most difficult things I ever had to do. But, I had to get out of that mind-set. If I was going to succeed in my jihad I had to stay away from prying eyes, and to achieve that I could no longer move in those circles.

I kept my head down and waited patiently until the day the message reached me, until the man who had lifted me out of the carnage gave me my instruction to violently descend on all the Kafirs around me.

But life has a way about it.

*

'Allah has brought us together again, Brother,' Pathaan said, shutting the fridge door. I stood for a fraction of a second taking in that familiar face. It had grown old, but the eyes had not lost any of their intensity. Then I was on him, my arms around him. The last time our chests collided he was taking me away to a new life. I had grown taller but I still dropped my head into his shoulder, his shirt bunched in my fist as he gently rubbed my back.

I released the grip on his shirt and we separated.

He looked me straight in the eyes. I tried to hold his gaze, the way he taught me a man should. He nodded as though I had passed my first test and patted me hard on the shoulder. His eyes travelled down at my clothes, soaked and stained in Javid Qasim's blood. And then he echoed the words that he had said when we had first met.

'Mashallah. You are a strong one.'

129

28
Jay

Can somebody please tell me if I'm fucking dead?

I mean, I don't actually feel dead, but some confirmation would be nice. Either show me a doctor or show me heaven or hell. In the event that I am dead, should I not be seeing a white light and experiencing a sensation of floating through a long tunnel? I read something like that once in one of those glossy women's magazines whilst I was in the waiting room at the Dentist's. Instead, everything was black and my body felt light. The fantastic pain that I was feeling in my neck seemed to have vanished all too quickly. Had my soul done a runner and left my body? Maybe, just maybe, those annoying Atheists were onto something; maybe this was death. Once you die, you *don't* move onto a higher plane, you don't get to meet your maker. A feeling of nothing, just left alone with your own thoughts for company for all eternity.

Could one-point-six billion Muslims have been so wrong about the after-life?

Come on eyes. *Open*. Fingers, *flex*. Toes, *wiggle*. Heart, *beat*.

Fucking nothing.

Coma! I'm in a coma. I hadn't considered that option. Mum and Idris are probably sat with me right now. Holding my hand, telling me stories, hopefully somebody is regularly shaving my face. Coma or no coma, I've got to keep up appearances. I wondered how often they would visit me; every day, once a week, once a month, then on birthdays and then just phoning in to see if old Jay has stirred.

I'll wake up one day, soon. *Please* be soon. I don't want to emerge from my coma and find that everything has passed me by. Mum's married to Andrew, the war on Islam has come to a peaceful end – *wishful thinking* – technology has moved on and away from me.

I really don't want to be that guy who has the lamest mobile phone on the block.

My body violently shuddered, breaking me out of my musings. It felt like somebody had taken a mallet to my chest. *Motherfu–!* Then immediately another. An electric jolt dancing through my body. My eyelids flew open and I saw two white pads hovering above me.

Stop it. Stop fucking doing that!

I'm awake.

*

The doctor stood above me, his tone intense and suitably dramatic. The medical terms, with more syllables than necessary, flying over my head. I got the gist of it though: my windpipe was cut, blood pooled in my lungs and as a result I had a pretty decent infection. But my carotid and other major blood vessels weren't severed, otherwise it would have been *adios*, *Jay*. Doctor Jones, who had none of the charm of *the* Dr Jones, told me I was a very lucky young man. At that moment I didn't feel lucky, or young. But I knew, in time, it would hit me like a long-time slap in the face: how close I came to death.

The guy in the bed next to me snored through the night. The incessant beeping of machines. The regular trill of a phone. A nurse noisily carrying out her rounds every ninety minutes, pushing a creaky trolley, all adding to the soundtrack of my night, keeping me awake.

But it was okay. I was alive.

I made a mental note to buy a box of chocolates and flowers for each of the doctors, nurses and surgeons who had fixed me and stitched me. I should also get something for the paramedics who arrived at the scene. I added up approximately how much it was going to set me back and then decided that one big fat Thank You card, *to all staff*, would suffice. The one person that I really had a debt of gratitude to was the man who had pulled me out of my car.

I didn't get his name, but before near death had found me, I did see his face. A face that I was not about to forget. I closed my eyes and there he was.

It wasn't the first time I had set eyes on him. He was definitely a Hounslow boy, one I had seen on many occasions, especially when I was dealing. He drove around in one of those hybrid numbers. He used to pull up at my old stomping ground at the Homebase car park in Isleworth, always with the same guy. Shaz, I think his name was.

Shaz would jump in my car or slip past the driver's window for a quick exchange, whilst my saviour would stay put in his car. I remembered Shaz well enough, as he always bought substantial sizes – and I remembered *him* too. We'd acknowledge each other, through our cars with a slight nod, never with words. I would occasionally glance at him as Shaz weighed up and appraised the skunk. He didn't look like your run-of-the-mill Hounslow bod. Something about him, the way he would viciously scratch his head as though he was fighting against some inner demon, his eyes reflective and unsure, not quite fitting the scenario. Yeah, his eyes. That same look he gave me, unsure, uncertain, as he'd pulled me out of my car.

I let my head sink into the pillow, a warm feeling washed over me as the first stirrings of sleep found me. I said a silent prayer, a silent thanks, and closed my eyes.

I saw Silas' vengeful face smiling down at me. The blade in his hand. Then my fucking blood, *everywhere*, as he opened me up from ear to ear.

My eyes shot open. Sleep wasn't coming anytime soon.

I knew that when Silas found out I was still alive, he was going to try to kill me again.

29

Imy

There was only one room to sleep in. The pull of a lever transformed the sofa into a bed and the living room into a bedroom. Out of respect, I offered Pathaan the bed. I took the floor, so tired was I that I could have slept comfortably on rocks.

There was no talking, and catching up could wait. I showered hard, before I slept, removing all traces of blood, and when I returned he was already asleep on the sofa-bed.

I woke up first and made him breakfast, the same as I had done every morning for six years. Masala tea and bread broken into small pieces soaking in a bowl of hot milk, with three sugars sprinkled over. I placed it on the kitchen table, next to his motorbike helmet and keys. As I waited for him to rise, I looked out of the kitchen window. Across the road sat a black two wheeled cruiser.

'2011 MV Agusta.'

Pathaan was leaning against the same door frame where, just a few hours previously, I was standing with a Glock in my hand. 'It's a bit showy for me. I much prefer my '85 Kawasaki. But this is what was waiting for me when I arrived.'

I remembered his Kawasaki, a real no-nonsense motorbike, red engine covered in red earth. It was a mode of transport for me on many occasions. As a passenger, sitting at the back, arms around his waist and then, as I got a little older, sitting precariously at the front, hunched over the handlebars, my fingers tight around the hot steel, helping him manoeuvre the bike through the long and twisty Karmashy Village Road.

'Do you still have it?'

'I still have it,' he said and sat down to his breakfast. Sip of tea first before launching into his bowl. No gratitude, I didn't expect it, but it still felt cutting. It was what I'd gotten used to, living in a civilised country for the last twenty years. Pathaan looked at my bloodied clothes peeking out of the top of a full wash basket in the corner of the kitchen. 'Tell me.'

'Yesterday morning, I drove to the pick-up point and collected the package,' I said. Pathaan put a spoonful of milk-drenched bread into his mouth, his jaw moved systematically breaking down the bread into near-nothing before swallowing. 'I arrived back in Hounslow early evening, determined to carry out my jihad.'

'You were impatient, Imran. A mistake could be costly.'

'Twenty years, Pathaan Bhai. I waited. Every night I dreamt of the moment that I would receive the message. Maybe I was impatient, but I was ready.'

Pathaan's calculating eyes were on mine. After a moment he nodded towards the table. 'Under my helmet.'

I lifted his motorbike helmet. Under the helmet sat a small tin, rustier than I recalled, which instantly invoked long-forgotten memories. I pried it open and in silence did what I'd done for him countless times. My hands and fingers were now more used to wrapping a tight joint, and it showed as I handed him a loosely-wrapped paan. Pathaan studied it with a smile playing on his lips. He folded the paan, opened his mouth wide, and placed it on his tongue. I watched him move it around his mouth before sinking his teeth into it.

'You broke Brother Yousuf's leg,' he said. 'Is that any way to treat an old friend, Imran?'

It took me a moment to recall what he was talking about, even though breaking someone's leg with a car door wasn't something to easily forget.

'It was a misunderstanding. I called for an ambulance immediately. Is the Brother alright?'

Pathaan didn't answer, instead he pulled out of his top pocket a metal toothpick and proceeded to pick out bits of the leaf and tobacco from his teeth. So I asked him, 'What do you mean by old friend?'

'Yousuf was your neighbour, in Sharana, you both grew up together, and you both lost your parents together.' He placed the toothpick back in his top pocket and ran his tongue over his teeth and then bared his clamped teeth at me for inspection. Apart from the red coating, I nodded that they were clean. I was aware what he was doing. Small familiar acts pushing me back into a place that I did not want to be in.

'He has been watching you for a long time, Imran,' Pathaan continued. 'Everything is reported back to me. You have exceeded all expectations. Living a life which wasn't natural to you. I know, Brother, I know. The drugs and the alcohol and the carefree living. The best part...' He slapped the edge of the table hard as his laugh echoed around the small kitchen. 'You are with a Kafir, what is her name? *Stephanie?* Tell me, Imran. Did you impregnate her yet?'

I was that child again, eager to please him. Frightened to anger him. I lowered my eyes and focused on a drop of spilt milk on the table between us.

'Allah will forgive you for your sins.'

'I did what I had to do, Brother,' I said. 'This country is not safe for a Muslim unless you are playing by the rules of a Kafir.'

Pathaan locked his eyes on mine as though he was stealing my soul. I noticed his jaw clench very briefly before his face relaxed and he smiled.

'It looks like my stay here is over, Imran.' Pathaan picked up his rolling tin and slipped it in his shirt pocket. He stood up and shrugged on his biker jacket. 'This... country. It fills me with disgust. Every whisper, every look, every white face judging, waiting, wanting for me to react. I wanted to, believe me, Imran, I wanted to hurt each and every one of them. Ghurfat-al-Mudarris has done so much but there's so much work left to do.'

'I'm glad you came.' I stood up and embraced him warmly. 'I missed you.' It was true. He was a man who'd brought me up and showed me a war so personal that I had no choice but to be a part of it. Easily justifying the hate and the thirst for revenge. I understood that. I did. I still do. Pathaan was only one man of thousands, trying to right what is, and remains to be, a huge injustice.

Ghurfat-al-Mudarris is not a religious movement, it's a political movement. They are not trying to sell propaganda with the belief that the apocalypse is coming. They are retaliating in kind to the thoughtless killing of innocents all over the world in Muslim countries. Theirs is not a war against non-Muslims, it's a war against the governments around the world who continue to devastate our lands. Pathaan still carried the hate that I had long let go.

I could no longer have him in my life. Our paths had taken us in different directions.

'I can go home now?' He said it as a question. I knew what my answer had to be.

'It's over,' I nodded, meeting his eyes and not knowing what I was seeing in them. 'I saw my opportunity to enact the fatwa, and I took it. Javid Qasim is dead.'

30
Jay

As is the Hounslow way, word spread quickly about the attempt on my life. During the first few days in hospital I had a couple of visits. At that stage, I couldn't talk, it hurt to just open my mouth. I lived the life of a mute, gesticulating, nodding and gurning like a fool. My eyebrows had never been so active. One of the nurses tried to convince me that body language makes up something like sixty per cent of all communication. I didn't think so.

From the Heston Hall Community Centre, Ira, Zafar and Tahir came to visit me early into my stint. They even brought flowers! I wouldn't say we were friends, but they had gotten to know me over the last few months and I'm not sure what part of me was giving out the impression that I was a flowers kind of guy.

Their presence irritated me. They seemed uneasy trying to communicate with me, eyes flitting towards the heavy stitching across my throat and then away again. I could see them growing increasingly uncomfortable, until they decided to talk amongst themselves as if I was wallpaper.

I tuned in and out as they discussed the weather and the latest episode of *Game of Thrones*, before inevitably moving onto Naaim.

'He's in a bad way,' Tahir said. 'Police aren't yet connecting her attack on the bus to her suicide.'

'Cops will suss it out,' Zafar said, with maybe a little too much nonchalance for Ira's taste.

'Why you always gotta say stupid shit for?'

'God, Ira, calm down, will you.'

'Maybe you should both calm down,' Tahir attempted to smile it away.

'Fuck that, Tahir. You keep out of this,' Ira spat. 'I wanna hear what Zafar's got to say.'

Tahir's cheeks turned a browny red. He looked away, not used to that tone from somebody half his age.

When Zafar didn't indulge her, she continued. 'Cops are either too dumb or too fucking lazy to work it out. They only pull their finger out if the victim is rich, middle class and white, then it's fucking front page news. So, don't talk shit, Zafar. Even if they do find those murderous bastards, it'll be their word against Naaim's. It's not like the whole thing was captured on CCTV.'

'Surely they can make a match, Ira. Give 'em some credit. Naaim's given a description and that video is plastered all over the internet.'

Video? What video? I looked at them in turn. Ira and Zafar were locked into each other and Tahir was still looking away, waiting for his face to return to its normal colour. *Excuse me, can someone notice me and tell me about this fucking video?* I felt around my bed and failed to find the pen and pad that the nurse had left me for communicating with my visitors.

'Description?' Ira shook her head, tiredly. 'What? Shaved heads and white. That could be anyone, Zafar. The video is useless.'

Zafar finally turned to me as though I had the answer. I didn't even know the question. I looked at him blankly, like I didn't know what the fuck they were talking about.

'The attack was filmed and posted online,' Tahir said. 'Edited to obscure the faces of the attackers.'

I nodded and blinked heavily.

'Just 'cos the cops can't do anything,' Ira said, 'doesn't mean something can't be done.'

I let my eyes rest and thought about Layla. *What had pushed her over the edge? What had made her take her own life?*

Was it the sickening attack? Or did she find out about the video online for the world to see, making her humiliation complete?

A feeling of injustice to Muslims, that I had buried deep inside in exchange for keeping my head down in the pursuit of normality, bubbled to the surface. I got it, I fucking got it. Ira had a point. But how far would she go to make it?

I heard a flirty giggle from one of the nurses and opened my eyes. I knew before I turned my head that Idris had arrived. As he approached my bed, I caught his eye and discreetly angled my head at the community crew. He understood immediately. A real friend. He would never buy me flowers.

'I'm afraid I am going to have to ask you to leave,' Idris said, flashing his copper's badge at them. 'I need to speak with Javid Qasim.'

As you do in the company of the police, they hustled quickly. I shook hands weakly with Tahir, a fist bump with Zafar, and Ira swept my hair to one side and smiled her goodbye, before giving Idris cut-eyes.

'Not a fan of the police, I take it,' Idris asked, taking a seat closest to the bed. 'Friends?'

I shook my head quickly and immediately felt like an idiot. As if decent, honest Muslims were not cool enough to hang with me.

'I like this quiet you. You're a lot less annoying,' he said. My voice may have deserted me, but my middle finger was fully functional.

Idris didn't come bearing gifts. No chocolates, magazines, not even fucking grapes, only cutting remarks. He picked up the clipboard from the foot of my bed and attempted to dissect my medical notes. It amused me, the way he acted nonchalant, as though his best friend hadn't just nearly died. It was all a front. I vaguely recalled that the night before, Idris had been here. I was hopped up on drugs and barely conscious but I was aware what was happening around me.

I'd been aware that, like a sap, Idris was by my bedside, holding my hand.

I was aware that he kissed me on the forehead and told me he loved me.

So, yeah, act as cool as you want, mate, I've got your number. As soon as I get my voice back I'll be ripping the piss out of you. I'll probably leave out the bit where I also, at that moment, felt an overwhelming love for him.

Fuck that. He don't need to know.

'Just a heads up, Jay,' he said, placing the clipboard back. 'Two of my colleagues from Hounslow nick are going to visit you at some point this afternoon. To take your statement.'

I covered my eyes with the tips of my fingers and shrugged at him, before dropping my hands back to my side.

'Shit, Jay, it's like communicating with Lassie. What's that supposed to mean?'

I sighed, rolled my eyes, and tried again.

'What…? You didn't see who it was?'

I nodded animatedly. Idris looked around and, satisfied that nobody was in ear shot, he dragged his chair forward and leant in.

'Regardless of whether you saw the attacker, we both know who's responsible.'

My eyebrows joined forces as I frowned at him.

'Silas,' he said, softly.

I didn't confirm, but denying wasn't an option. How Idris knew, I don't know. Last year only MI5 and Chief Superintendent Penelope Wakefield of Hounslow Met had knowledge about the deal I'd cut. All Idris knew was that I was on the police radar for dealing. He'd warned me about it on a number of occasions. Stressing that it was only a matter of time until the police came knocking on my door. So it wasn't a surprise that he'd sussed out that I had grassed to save my own skin only for Silas to pierce it.

I didn't want to get into it. I yawned, wide and fake, the effort felt like each stitch was popping. I hoped he'd take the hint and leave me to rest. But Idris had other ideas.

'Tired?' he said. 'You can sleep after I've gone.' His eyes landed on the floor and he picked up the pen and notepad that had slipped under the bed. He lobbed it onto my lap. 'I want to know everything.'

I sighed, knowing he wouldn't let me be, and jotted it down for him. Everything about Silas, him being out of jail, coming for me. Not quite *everything*, though. I couldn't tell him about my role with MI5.

Idris' lips moved silently as he read it, a habit that used to annoy me when we were at school together. On completion, he nodded and smiled, and then he started to tell me his plan.

31

South London

It was a thrill to see Simon and Anthony waiting for him at the side of the football pitch. Especially a thrill that his fellow students, who tended to ignore him, saw that he was part of something. Secure in the knowledge that eyes were on him, Daniel greeted them warmly.

'Get changed,' Simon said. 'We've got a meeting.'

Daniel quickly changed out of his football kit and into his *uniform*. Eager to join his friends he didn't shower or use the toilet. He walked out of the dressing room and spotted his friends standing by an old white Range Rover. In the driver's seat was Kramer, the man he had seen at the rally in Hounslow.

Anthony opened the back door and Daniel got in the car. With Anthony next to him and Simon in the front, he didn't question what they were doing or where they were going. Instead he smiled at his classmates who had gathered, watching curiously as the Range Rover pulled away.

Thirty minutes into the drive, he was squeezing his legs together, bursting to go. But he couldn't exactly ask permission. How would that look? He decided to grit his teeth and hold it in.

With traffic, the journey to Croydon was just short of the two-hour mark and it concerned him that he wouldn't get back home until late. Not that he had a curfew, but he did have an Economics exam first thing the next morning. He texted his father to let him know that he'd be revising in the school library and not to expect him home for supper. Simon in the front appeared calm. Anthony, next to him in the back, his head between the two front seats, was chatty. Daniel wondered if he'd taken a pill.

The Range Rover slowed and without indicating pulled off the main road into an opening between two tall metal gates. Judging from the rusted JCB diggers and random machinery spread around the grounds, it looked like an abandoned building site where the workers had downed tools long ago.

Kramer killed the lights and slipped the keys out of the ignition. Without the growl of the car engine, the silence was unnerving.

'Let's go,' Kramer said. 'Mind your step, there's crap everywhere.'

Three doors opened, Kramer, Simon and Anthony stepped out. Daniel debated whether to exit from his car door but decided against it as he didn't want to be standing on the same side of the car as Kramer with his friends all the way on the other side. So he scrambled across the back seat, stepped out from Anthony's door, and stood close by him. Anthony gave him a bemused look.

'Supposed to be a function hall.' Kramer pointed to a boxy concrete building in a state of disrepair. Daniel could just make out the imposing silhouette; he wondered if they had toilet facilities, but didn't voice it. 'The client ran over budget a couple years ago, so we set up base here. We still use the hall, it's perfectly safe, even though it don't look much. We have meets here every three months, and a jolly on St George's Day.'

To the left, adjacent to the hall, a dim light was emanating through the plastic window of a Portakabin. They headed towards it carefully through the dark and the dirt and the machinery and the tools.

Kramer knocked on the door and peered his head through.

'Got guests,' he said, then turned towards them. 'Come on lads, shake a leg.'

Simon, Anthony and Daniel walked up the few metal steps leading up to the Portakabin and stepped through. In the overly-heated room, Kramer introduced the man who was sitting behind the desk as Terry Rose. The name meant nothing to the three boys.

Daniel stood with his hands clasped behind his back, but it felt odd. So he crossed his arms under his chest, but that felt too assured, and he was feeling really very far from assured. He decided to jam his hands into the pockets of his jeans.

Behind Daniel, at the back of the Portakabin, Kramer was sitting on the only other seat available in the room, a worn puffy leather armchair. Anthony was bouncing around the room taking special notice of the Millwall scarf tacked to the wall just above the outline map of the United Kingdom with the red St George's Cross running through it. Simon was standing directly in front of the desk, imposing his representational position.

'We just gonna stand around making eyes at each other?' Simon started.

Terry looked past Simon and raised his eyebrows at Kramer. Daniel turned just in time to see Kramer grinning back.

'You must be Simon,' Rose said.

'Yeah. You wanna tell us what we're doing here?'

'I requested to see you lads because I recognise kindred spirits.'

'What's that mean?' Anthony looked horrified. 'We ain't no fags!'

'I didn't think you were.' Rose looked amused.

'So?' Anthony said. 'You wanna tell us the fuck is going on?'

'See to it that you watch your mouth, boy,' Kramer growled from the back of the room. 'And I'll see to it that I'll watch mine.'

Rose held up a hand to calm Kramer, just as Simon held up a hand to Anthony. The lines clearly drawn.

'Like yourselves, we represent a group of like-minded people who are shit-tired of seeing this country embarrass itself, embarrass its people,' Rose started. 'England is no longer about the English. We are no longer the priority. Laws are introduced to help those who want nothing more than to destroy this once-great country.'

'Too fucking right!' Simon spat, taking over the proceedings. 'Just today I walked past a group of four women covered head to toe in black. Fuck knows what they had on underneath. These *people* saunter around spitting at our culture, imposing their beliefs, dressing to intimidate and provoke. Placing the laws of their religion above the laws of the land. Let me tell you something; there are two thousand Mosques in England. Do you know how many Churches were shut last year? Nearly a thousand! Believe me, it's not long before we have more Mosques than Churches!'

Daniel noticed Anthony nodding in agreement and joined in.

Simon continued. 'Slowly these cunts are taking over town by town, until the whole country is nothing but the colour brown, all singing from the same Sharia hymn sheet. Hounslow, Slough, Ealing, Staines, *fucking* Chiswick! All brown as dirt. Don't even get me started about the shit that's happening up North.'

Daniel had heard this level of hatred many times, but this time it was different, as though Simon was trying his hardest to impress upon Rose exactly how kindred their spirits were.

'He isn't shy, is he?' Kramer said after a moment of silence. 'He'll be sitting where you are soon.'

'Not until they wise up,' Rose said. 'Let's talk about the girl on the bus.'

Daniel clenched tightly, his heart dropped into his stomach.

'What about her?' Simon asked, calmly.

'The boy that was with her has been speaking to the police.'

'I need to use the toilet,' Daniel blurted. '*Now*. I need to use the toilet now.'

'Outside,' Kramer said.

Daniel pushed opened the door and looked out into the darkness. 'Where?'

'Anywhere, boy.' Kramer said.

Daniel's fingers worked the zipper as he hurried down the steps. Finding himself a spot at the side of the Portakabin, he finally relieved himself, stepped away from the puddle that was travelling towards his cherry Dr Martens, and zipped up. He could just about make out the glint of the tall metal gates that they had driven through, and desperately wanted to run through them and all the way from South to West London until he was home. Daniel closed his eyes tightly in defeat, his thoughts bumping into each other. The mention of the girl had made him vomit in his mouth. The mention of the boy going to the police had nearly made him drop to his knees and sob like the child that he was.

Daniel opened his eyes and took out his phone. He noticed how it trembled in his hand as he stared at it for help. He had to call someone, he had to tell someone. But who could he call and what would he say? He tried to take a deep breath to clear his mind but it came in quick bursts. Pocketing his phone, he crouched to his haunches and lowered his head until his breathing evened out.

'*Boy!*' Kramer bellowed. 'Where are you?' Daniel appeared at the bottom on the steps. 'We're waiting for you.' Daniel stepped into the Portakabin and stood next to Anthony and Simon.

'It took Kramer a little more than no time to work it out,' Rose said. 'How long do you think it'll take the police to knock on your doors and give your old dears a fright?'

'We've got an alibi, mate,' Anthony said. 'My old man.'

From the back of the room, a nasal snort from Kramer. 'Peter Hanson. Pill dealer. That's your alibi? Not exactly a pillar of the community, your dad.'

'How'd you know my old man?' Anthony felt his face reddening.

'I make it my business to know,' Kramer said.

Daniel swallowed. Did they know his father, too?

'Your alibi isn't reliable,' Rose said. 'Way I see it, you lads have problems. Have a look at yourselves; the three of you stick out like a particularly sore fucking thumb. That boy described you all to a tee. Red Doc Martens, black jeans, black bomber jackets. Shaved heads.'

Anthony looked to Simon for guidance. Daniel looked nauseous. He covered his mouth with his hand. Simon remained expressionless.

'But...' Rose added, 'he failed to give an accurate description of your faces.'

Daniel let out a long-held, audible breath, as though he had just been saved from drowning. Anthony, looking relieved himself, clapped Daniel on his back.

'Kramer set you a challenge, to show us how serious you were. I have to say, I'm impressed. And I'd like you to join us.' Rose looked at Simon. 'Here at The Second Defence we look after our own.'

'So do we,' Simon put out his hand and they shook.

'Get yourselves some new clobber. I don't ever want to see what I'm seeing. Am I making myself clear?' Rose said. 'And for future reference, don't go filming yourselves. I don't care how clever you've been with disguising your faces. We do not need that exposure.'

Daniel cursed himself. Posting the video online, in an effort to impress his friends, was a mistake that could have cost him dearly. One that he would learn from and never make again.

He decided, at that moment, that regardless of what time he got home he was going to hit the books and cram all night until he was sat in front of the Economics exam paper. And after that, Daniel decided, he had no choice but to distance himself from his only friends.

'I'll brief my lawyer, just in case this thing escalates,' Rose said. 'Kramer?'

Kramer nodded. 'I'll put in a call.'

'Also, I think a *strong* word with the brown boy before he has a moment of clarity.' Rose addressed the lads. 'Keep it discreet but do whatever it takes.'

147

'How do we find him?' Anthony asked.

'I'll find him, shouldn't be too taxing. I'll let you know,' Kramer said. He stood up and spun his car keys around his finger. 'Welcome to The Second Defence,' he grinned.

Anthony rediscovered his bounce and Simon allowed himself a rare smile. Kramer held the door open for them and they turned to leave. Daniel stayed rooted. He had barely spoken, apart from asking permission to go to the toilet, but he had something say.

'What about the girl?' Daniel's mouth went dry. 'What if she speaks to the police?'

'You not heard?' Rose said.

Daniel shook his head.

'That night,' Rose said. 'She went home and committed suicide.'

Daniels hand once again flew to his mouth, and this time he was unable to stop the vomit from seeping through his fingers.

*

An old green Toyota hatchback parked across the road from the metal gates leading to the building site. The driver, fingers tightly gripped on the steering wheel, watched them leave the Portakabin and get into a white Range Rover.

'Is it them?' she asked, softly.

Naaim nodded.

Ira placed her hand on top of his.

32

Imy

Pathaan had seen my state, had seen Qasim's blood on my clothes, on my skin, and it shone off me with honour. I'd lied about killing Jay, as, these days it would seem, I always do. It was second nature to me. But I had no problem lying to Pathaan if it would help me to get my life back.

I had my life back.

We'd just finished an hour's session at the trampoline centre, Jump Giants, near Heathrow. For around twenty minutes it was such fun – after which, muscles that I had never used before screamed at me to act my age. I persevered, though, continued on regardless, as Jack was in his element, bouncing happily from one trampoline to another, daring me to catch him. I had never seen him so blissful, so content. His fantasy of having a father figure had been realised.

We stepped off, hot and sweaty, steam emanating from Jack's head, and walked up the stairs to the viewing balcony, where the contentment on Stephanie's face mirrored Jack's in every way. I sat down next to her as she handed out much needed bottles of water.

'Can I play the car game?' Jack asked me.

'Sure.' I handed him a few pound coins. 'But stay where we can see you,' I said, fitting into the father role with the same ease.

Stephanie leaned her head against my shoulder and took my hand in hers. Together we watched Jack go at it on the arcade machine.

'This is just perfect,' she said. 'May our bubble never burst.'

We had a wedding day provisionally pencilled in for the end of the year. She liked the idea of the warm feeling that a cold winter wedding brings. Stephanie was already scouting for locations and dragging me off to meet with caterers. I didn't have the heart to tell her that Khala would certainly want to get involved in almost every aspect of the wedding. That's if Khala would ever forgive me. I still had to come clean with her about Rukhsana. I still had to come clean with *Rukhsana* about Rukhsana.

She and I hadn't met since the introduction, but she had been calling and texting frequently, the insinuation clear; a friend who may become something more. She had been on at me to meet, to take our relationship further. I'd been careful to delete any trace of our conversation. If Stephanie saw it, well, I didn't even want to think about how that would play out.

Rukhsana deserved to know the truth. It couldn't be over the phone, I had to do it face-to-face. I owed her that.

Still, my priority had to be telling Khala about Stephanie. And Jack. I'd discussed it at length with Stephanie, and she had allowed me the time, knowing that it was cultural, something that I couldn't rush. Stephanie isn't the type to give an ultimatum or a deadline. But I didn't want to test her patience.

In the meantime, I was slowly distancing myself from my old life, one step at a time.

I had all but moved out of my studio flat. I still had the keys for a few more weeks, until I saw out the notice period, but my belongings now had a place at Steph's. The only thing that I'd left behind was the Glock, which I had never needed to use. I'd have to find a way of safely disposing of it.

I watched Jack crash and burn on his game, my hand already in my pocket, rooting around for a pound coin as he approached me.

'Can I have another go?' he asked, sweetly.

'There you go, kid.' I couldn't quite read his face as I placed a pound in his hand. Jack swallowed and looked nervously at Stephanie. She smiled encouragingly at him.

'Thanks, Dad,' Jack said, softly.

It was the very first time that he had called me Dad, and it filled my heart with happiness.

But before I could reply, something behind him caught my eye.

I glanced past his shoulder and over the viewing balcony. A man sat downstairs, at a table in the cafeteria. Rolling a paan. Looking up, eyes locked onto mine.

Jack looked down shyly at his feet, his body gently swaying, waiting for my reaction.

'Imy,' Stephanie's voice sounded muffled over my heart pounding in my ears. 'Imy?'

I caught the rejection on Jack's face as he sloped back to the arcade machine. I stood up.

'Imy,' Stephanie's hand on my arm.

'Somebody I know,' was all I could muster, her hand slipped away as I walked towards the stairs. I took the steps one at a time. Not trusting my legs, I held onto the bannister for support. I moved towards him. He was sitting dead centre of the large cafeteria. My walk felt unnatural, my arms stiff by my side. He watched me all the way, I dropped eye contact and took in the surroundings of the trampoline centre. None of it made sense. In that instant, my lives, which I had tried desperately to keep from colliding, collided.

'Pathaan Bhai,' I said. He nodded towards the chair opposite and I sat down.

'I thought, maybe, I should check one last time before leaving you, Imran. In case you have... what is that word? Overlooked anything.'

I swallowed, hard. It would have been noticed.

'I hold you in very high regard, Imran, I always have,' Pathaan continued. 'And I know that you are more capable then most to carry out your jihad.' He paused. 'So you can imagine my surprise when my source informed me that Qasim is still living, breathing.'

I watched him blankly as he placed the paan in his mouth, sinking his sharp teeth into it, and wiped his mouth with the back of his hand.

'I think I understand what's happened,' he said. 'But why don't you go ahead and explain it to me.'

To my right a young family of four. Kids eating cake. Parents drinking coffee. To my left proud grandparents cheering on their somersaulting grandson from the side-lines.

'I left him... for dead,' I said, finding my voice.

'How did you do it?'

'His throat. I cut his throat.'

'You didn't use the...' Pathaan made a gun with his hand, pointed it at me and pulled the trigger. 'It would have been quicker. Cleaner.'

I shook my head. 'No, I thought –'

'What, Imran. What did you think?' Pathaan tapped a finger rapidly on the table. He waited no time for me to respond. 'Maybe I tell you what I think. Somebody else got to Javid Qasim before you, and you chose to pass it off as your doing.'

I said nothing.

'Young Qasim has made some enemies it would seem.' He stopped tapping his finger on the table and it felt as though the whole room had silenced. 'Tell me, Imran. Did you wait for his last breath as you held him in your arms?'

With a jolt, the realisation hit me.

Pathaan had been there. Had seen it all.

'You lied to me, Imran.'

There was nothing, *nothing*, I could say.

'Did you think I wouldn't read it in your face? I battled to shut down every instinct telling me to tear you down where you stood. Where you lied to me... I let you be, Imran. I walked away from your betrayal. I needed time and space to think.' He dug his finger into the side of his head. I knew that above me, Stephanie was watching. It

152

took all my strength to not look up and smile at her that everything was alright.

But Pathaan did. He looked up at my family.

'This country has made you weak.'

'Pathaan Bhai...'

'These... people have made you weak.'

'Please, Pathaan Bhai.'

I hesitantly looked up. Stephanie was watching from the viewing balcony. Jack by her legs. I smiled at them. *Everything is alright.* Jack still carried rejection on his face. I met his eyes and he hid out of sight behind Stephanie.

'What do you want?' I turned away from them.

'The man who pulled the knife on Qasim. I need a name.'

Silas was well known around West London. Shaz and I had picked up and smoked his weed through many of his dealers, Jay being one of them.

'Silas Drakos,' I said.

'He will try again,' Pathaan said. 'I cannot allow that. It is of importance that Qasim is given his traitor's death by a soldier of Ghurfat-al-Mudarris. You will tell me where I can find this Silas.'

I nodded obediently, but I knew it wouldn't be my only contribution.

'Your failure is my failure. Allah will forgive. I may not be so generous.'

'What do you want?' I asked, again.

'You will wait until Qasim has recovered. You will wait until he is able to see the promise of life in front of him. Word will reach you when the time is right and then I want you to snatch that very life away from him.'

I closed my eyes and tried to even my breathing. I heard his chair slide and footsteps move away. When I opened my eyes, Pathaan was behind me over my shoulder, his sickly sweet paan breath my ear.

'You are not to fail me again, Imran,' he glanced up at the balcony. 'If you hesitate, I will give you all the motivation that you need, Brother.'

33

Jay

You ever wished for something so hard, so *fucking* hard, that it actually comes true?

I don't know what I was thinking agreeing to his plan, but Idris was convincing and, really, what were my options? He'd planted the seed in my head and I had spent my two week stint in hospital considering it and nothing else.

They kicked me out of hospital after a couple of weeks. I was healing nicely and my voice was getting stronger. I wasn't far off from being back to my annoying best. Idris picked me up in my car. I had given him the keys to my Nova as my Beemer was still somewhere in police lock-up, being treated as a crime scene.

'When do you think I'll get my Beemer back?' I asked, as I tried and failed to get the seatbelt on across my neck.

'I'll find out.' Idris pulled out of the hospital car park. 'As you're not willing to talk, I'm sure it'll be sooner rather than later... You sure you want to do this tonight?'

'Fuck, Idris, it was your idea, don't go bottling it now.'

'I'm not. You should get some rest first, is all I'm saying.'

'Well don't. Let's just get it over and done with.'

I looked out of the window. It was a bright and crisp evening. I slid down the window and closed my eyes, enjoying the cool polluted air on my face as we joined the A4 on the way to Hounslow High Street.

Idris' plan was a simple one. This whole episode with Silas started way back, before MI5, before Teddy Lawrence – when my car was stolen along with Silas' money and gear, and I found myself in debt to him for ten large. Today, I was going to pay it back, with a five grand cherry on top. It would put a dent in the *thanks but no thanks* money that I'd received from MI5, but I was earning now and willing to take the hit.

Idris would be by my side, in the capacity of the law, just so Silas knew that he was on their radar again. Would it be enough to pacify him? I really don't know. So as insurance, I'd written and signed a statement pointing at him as my attacker, and had given it to Idris to reveal in the event that there was another hit on me. I'd make that clear to Silas, and hope that a potential attempted murder charge hanging over his head would be enough for us to walk in opposite directions.

I stepped into my bank branch, well aware what I looked like and what I was asking for. Behind the glass, the lady bank teller lost all her professionalism when she saw my sewn up throat. When I asked for fifteen large, she looked at me in fear, as though I was going to hold the place up. After I provided identification, she set me up with a man in a suit, who whisked me away into a stuffy room and interrogated me for twenty minutes before allowing me to leave with my money. A hold up would have been quicker.

I walked the short distance to where Idris was waiting for me in the Treaty Centre car park, paranoid that I was carrying fifteen large in cash in a Tesco canvas bag. The thieves, the junkies, the hard hitters of Hounslow, would be able to smell money on me from a mile away.

'You got it?' Idris asked, as I reached him without incident.

My throat hurt and my voice was weak so I nodded.

Idris started the car and we headed for Kingston to make the drop to Silas.

*

I don't know much about motorbikes, but the one that whispered past us just after we parked across the road from

Silas' house was sick. Dull black, with a splash of blood red around the rims.

The biker parked his motorbike outside the gates to Silas' place, on the opposite kerb to my Nova, and for some reason Idris and I both slid down in our seats. We watched him dismount. He was dressed in black leather and he kept his black helmet planted on his head as he walked towards Silas' house.

'Do you know him?' Idris asked.

'No. Possibly one of his dealers... Let's wait 'til he leaves,' I said, a little relieved at the delay.

'Agreed,' said Idris, the relief also apparent in his voice.

34

Kingston, Southwest London

Pathaan parked his motorbike across the road from a dated Vauxhall Nova. Through the dark tint of his visor he discreetly scoped the wide suburban street. He felt confident that no-one would pay any attention to him on a quiet weekday afternoon. It was the kind of street that had never before experienced violence.

He dismounted and walked calmly to the large double-fronted house. Five cars were parked in a neat semi-circle around a tall stone water fountain.

A drug dealer with immaculate taste. Pathaan could appreciate that.

It hadn't been difficult for Imran to obtain Silas' address. Pathaan had it a few hours after he'd requested it, but he sat on it for a while as he casually spent that time scoping the house. He had been surprised not to see any police presence, and understood it to mean that Javid Qasim had not talked. It would have been ideal if Silas had been arrested for attempted murder, keeping the path clear for Imran to carry out the fatwa. There was no way that the son of Al-Mudarris should die at the hands of a drug-dealing Kafir. Qasim's death had to arrive at the hands of jihadi.

But not just yet.

Realising that no attempted murder charge was heading Silas' way, Pathaan had instructed Imran to wait.

The front door of the house opened and a well-built black male walked out. In one hand he held a bulky handheld radio transceiver, and in the other hand was a glass tumbler with a couple of fingers' worth of gold liquid. The black man noticed him immediately, but it didn't matter. Pathaan's intention was not to hide.

'The fuck are you?' the sentry said as Pathaan walked across the drive, passing high-end German manufactured cars and stopping at the door. 'what's with the helmet? Ain't nobody ordered a fucking pizza.'

Now up close, Pathaan sized him up. He was big. Hard black muscles straining through a T-shirt too small for such a physique. His radio crackled and a voice came through.

'Staples, who am I looking at?'

Pathaan glanced up at the camera brazenly pointing directly at him from above the front door. Staples lifted the radio to his mouth.

'I'm just about to find out.'

Hand to hand, Pathaan could have dropped him, but considering Staples' size, it would have taken a little time.

'Lose the helmet,' Staples instructed. 'Let's see if I agree with your face.'

Pathaan didn't know what that meant, nor did he care.

He reached a hand behind his back and his fingers moved across the handles of the seven knives that were tucked into his leathers. He slipped out a small push dagger and buried it into Staples' right shoulder, an inch behind the collar bone.

'*Motherfucker!*' Staples hissed and reached around with his left hand to remove the protruding blade but before he could, a second dagger was inflicting the same punishment to his left shoulder. Staples dropped to his knees. Pathaan didn't have much time. Silas would have seen the altercation and would be making suitable arrangements. He reached behind and pulled out an altogether larger knife, and tucked it under Staples' chin, just enough pressure to kiss and break skin. Pathaan gestured for him to get up onto his feet.

'Inside,' he said, as Staples spat out redundant threats, and pushed open the door.

Pathaan slipped the hunting knife back in its sheath. He stood close behind Staples, using his bulk as a shield. He wrapped his hands around the ivory handles of the daggers sticking out of Staples' shoulders.

'Move.'

'Fuck you,' Staples said. His voice came out hoarse, the sweat rolling down the back of his bald head as he stood his ground. Pathaan gripped the handles tighter and turned them so the blades moved a half an inch through the flesh.

Staples started to move slowly through the wide hallway.

'Take me to Silas.'

At the end of the large hallway there was a room on either side. Pathaan looked into the large room to his left. A beautifully kept library, a grand vinyl record player sitting neatly on top of an oak cabinet, crackling out Sinatra. A young woman wearing a red and white string bikini stared blankly up at the chandelier, seemingly willing it to drop. She turned her attention to them and, despite the blood dripping from Staples' shoulders, she smiled weakly. Pathaan cleared the room with his eyes, and when satisfied that, apart from the junkie, it was empty, turned his attention to the room to his right.

A scrawny white male with a tattooed face and a second, dreadlocked male, both wielding machetes. Beyond them, a man, nonchalant despite what was taking place around him, was sitting back comfortably on a sofa. His legs stretched out on a coffee table, fingers moving quickly over a games controller as the reflection of the seventy-inch television danced wildly in his eyes.

'I'd prefer it if they had guns,' Silas said, not taking his eyes off the screen. 'It just seems like you know what you are doing, and I'd feel a touch safer if they were packing. Problem is, we got raided. Those busy-body coppers took all my pieces, but they still couldn't keep me behind bars. I let somebody else suffer for that,' he laughed then swore under his breath as his avatar died a grisly death. He flung the games controller onto the coffee table. It landed noisily on a silver metal tray and made an indentation in the small mountain of cocaine. He turned his attention to Pathaan. 'So, would you like to tell me who you are and what the fuck you are doing in my home?'

Pathaan answered by ripping out the blades from the shoulders of a shrieking Staples. In the same fluid movement he dug them deep either side of Staples' waist, gliding them upwards and opening up his sides, up to his armpits. Staples dropped for the last time, his scream fading to a gurgle. Silas took in Pathaan from head to toe.

'I see you've met Staples,' he smiled. 'I'd like to introduce you to Aaron and Cassius.'

Tattoo-faced Aaron and dreadlocked Cassius exchanged smiles and walked side by side towards Pathaan, only splitting up on approach. They circled him until one stood in front and the other behind him, an arm's length away. Both moving briskly on the balls of their feet, slicing the air with their machetes with murderous intent, but, Pathaan thought, without the will. It was clear that they were waiting for him to make the first move.

So he did.

Pathaan placed one foot over the fallen Staples, and left his other foot standing in place as he bent low at the knees. He spread his arms out to the side, the small bloody blades of the push daggers catching the light in his hands. He flicked his wrists, so that his fists were facing down.

With his arms out to the side, his front and back were exposed. Aaron and Cassius saw an opportunity. Each took a step forward, machetes high above their shoulders, just as Pathaan knew they would. He spun ninety degrees on his heels, his waist and his arms moving with the same precise measurement. Both blades met with flesh, easily slicing a straight line across their lower abdomens. As their intestines began to spill, Pathaan finished them by slamming the daggers into the two men's hearts.

Silas watched in fascination as his men took their time dropping to the floor.

'Bravo,' he said, pointing a gold-plated Sig Sauer handgun at Silas. 'That was one hell of an interview. I can confidently

160

say that you have passed the physical.' He released the safety. 'Why don't you sit down so we can discuss how much I'm going to pay you?'

Pathaan looked at the gun.

'Oh this,' Silas said. 'The coppers didn't find this one.'

Pathaan reached back and felt his finger grip the hunting knife as he moved quickly towards Silas. The deafening sound of the gunshot offended him more than the bullet hitting his Kevlar vest and, red-teeth bared, he dug and twisted the knife into the side of Silas' neck.

35

Jay

A few minutes after seeing the biker disappear behind the tall gates to Silas' house, our brief reprieve was lifted as he walked back, mounted his bike and left. I wiped my clammy hands on my jeans, and glanced at Idris. He was looking back at me, mirroring my *I'm not quite ready* expression.

'Idris,' I said, as the biker disappeared out of view. 'I was thinking...'

'Now's not the time, Jay.'

'I think you should wait in the car. Let me do this.'

'Yeah,' Idris said. 'Let's not do that.'

'Hear me out. If it all kicks off, you could lose your job.'

'You walk in there alone, Jay,' Idris looked past me towards Silas' house. 'You're not coming back out.'

I nodded. He was right. I could have argued it, but it was pointless. I needed him there. He was an integral part of the plan. More importantly, I wanted my friend by my side.

'Don't go blaming me afterwards, then.'

'Course I'm going to blame you,' Idris smiled. 'Don't worry, the plan is tight. In and out, yeah?' He reached around to the back seat and grabbed the cash-filled Tesco bag and placed it on my lap.

'Money talks,' he said, his glass half full.

'Bullshit walks,' I said, mine half empty.

We stepped out onto the street and side by side we crossed the road, and walked through Silas' drive, past all of his killer motors. We stood at the door and pressed the doorbell. We waited a long minute before I decided to ring again.

Eventually... the door opened.

A scrawny girl dressed in a red and white string bikini was standing in front of us. Clearly off her head, she blinked lazily at us through glazed eyes.

'Is, uh, Silas around?' I asked.

She looked blankly at us.

'Staples?'

A hint of a smile played across her face. It was painfully clear that she'd once been a beautiful, vibrant girl, before she got involved with that drug-dealing scumbag. She leaned casually against the doorframe, that hint of a smile now in full bloom, she said, 'They're dead... They're all dead.'

I froze momentarily, unable to comprehend the words of this crackhead. Despite what he'd said about avoiding any trouble, the copper in Idris rushed past her into the house. The Jay in me remained standing at the door. I could see Idris at the end of the hallway peering into the living room. He turned to me and hissed, 'Jay. *Get in.* Shut the door behind you.' I stepped past the girl into the large hallway. 'Do not touch anything. In fact, hands in pockets at all times.'

I slid the canvas bag high over my shoulder, jammed my hands into the pockets of my jeans and walked through the hall. I joined Idris at the entrance to Silas' living room. We didn't dare take a step further.

His right hand man, and right fucking tough bastard, Staples, was face-down on the rug, in a pool of blood. He had two long slits on either side of his upper body, as though somebody had unzipped him. Nearby, two of Silas' henchmen had dropped, one either side of Staples. I recognised them both from my past visits. Both nasty pieces of work, who I had on occasion shared a joint with. Cassius was frozen, on his knees, his head dropped, chin resting on his chest, his unruly dreadlocks curtaining his face. Aaron, in the foetal positon, his hand on his stomach as if he'd tried desperately to tuck his internal organs back in. The tear-shaped tattoo under his left eye had never looked so fitting.

On the garish purple velvet sofa, the bright light emanating from the television reflected in Silas' dead eyes. A dark red hole in the side of his neck was slowly dripping blood and darkening his pale pink shirt.

We didn't touch anything, didn't say a word, as though our voices may have left behind a trace of evidence, and placed us at the scene of the crime. There would be no explaining away our presence, especially with the 15k weighing heavy on my shoulders. On top of which, I had a motive.

The girl, the junkie, brushed past me and calmly climbed onto the sofa next to Silas. She tucked her bare feet underneath herself and lifted Silas' arm so it rested around her shoulder. She rested her head on his chest, closed her eyes, and gently started to snore.

I turned to Idris just as he turned to face me. He inclined his head towards the front door. I nodded in agreement.

Yeah. Time to go.

36
Imy

Once again, I had two alternate visions for my future. One of bliss with Stephanie and Jack, marriage on the horizon, a family life that I'd longed for. The other, black, bleak, and violent. Running from a dream that I had once chased. No longer part of that life where all I'd wanted was hurt, to feel it and to deliver it to anybody who even resembled those who took away my mother and father.

Over the last couple of weeks, since I last saw Pathaan, I'd been phoning the hospital every other day to check on Qasim's progress. I wanted to hear *there's been complications*, I wanted to hear *I'm sorry, we couldn't save him*. The last time I called, they told me that he'd been discharged. I would be expected to carry out my duty. I had failed the first time. I couldn't fail again.

Jack was sitting next to me on the sofa negotiating a Cornetto, as he watched *Toy Story* for the second time that day, mouthing the lines and laughing to himself.

'Do we have to watch this again?' I said for no reason at all.

'It's my favourite film,' Jack said.

'Why don't you watch something else, do something else?' I sighed, my frustration, not for the first time, searching for an outlet. A few days before, I had snapped at Jack. *Play with me. Play with me.* On repeat. His voice grated at my nerves. I told him sharply that I was busy and I went up to the bedroom. Three minutes later, the guilt kicked in and I was back down, apologising and playing hide and seek.

'Let him watch it,' Stephanie looked at me over her iPad. She was browsing all things wedding related. She smiled passively at me, recognising my mood.

I picked up my phone just to keep my hands busy from scratching the hell out of my head. I browsed through the local news headlines. Silas Drakos' murder was being reported as gang related. I knew better. I moved onto various social media apps, and absentmindedly scrolled for something to catch my attention. I stopped at a *Missing Child* post.

Staring back at me was a small face, tilted towards the camera. I'd only met Rafi Kabir, *Rocket Rafi*, once, but he'd left an impression on me. A child with beliefs that no child should hold. A child like I once was. The photo staring back at me was at odds with the spirited kid that I had met; unsure, camera shy, eyes raised impatiently at the photographer rather than on the lens of the camera. There wasn't much information; ten years old, a contact phone number, and the date of his disappearance. Two days after my visit to Blackburn. Seemingly, his bags were packed and some of his clothes were missing, so kidnapping had been ruled out. Rafi had just upped and left.

'You okay, Imy?'

'Hmm.'

'Are you alright?' Stephanie asked again, her finger suspended over the iPad.

'I'm fine.' I locked my phone and placed it on the glass coffee table. It vibrated noisily and immediately. Stephanie's eyes moved to it and quickly away again as Rukhsana's name flashed on the screen.

'Work,' I said. Pathaan, Rafi, now Rukhsana, my phone full of secrets that Stephanie could never know about. I walked out of the room and took the call in the kitchen.

'Rukhsana,' I said. 'Hi.'

'Shouldn't it be *you* that should be calling *me*,' Rukhsana said, her tone flirtatious, revealing.

'I messaged you,' I said, leaning against the worktop.

'A call would have been better.'

166

'In this day and age, a call is the last option, wouldn't you say?' I said, easily slipping into my other life.

'Maybe I'm an old fashioned kind of girl.'

'We should meet. Are you available today, for coffee?' I said.

'Dinner would be better.'

'Another time.'

'Fine,' she sighed. 'I'm actually meeting some friends tonight in Chiswick, that's not far from you, right?'

'It's close,' I said, relieved that I wouldn't have to travel to east London and write off the whole night.

'There's a cute little coffee shop off the green. I'll text you the address. Shall we say six?'

'Okay, I'll see you shortly,' I said, just as Stephanie stepped into the kitchen. I disconnected the call, cutting Rukhsana short just as she was saying goodbye.

I cleared my throat, Stephanie watched me as if I had something to say.

'I have to pop into work later.'

'Is that who was on the phone? Kumar?'

'We've just had a new property come up on our books. Already four viewings booked for tomorrow. Kumar wants me to draw up and print the paperwork.'

'You're going to miss the party.'

I rubbed my face as Stephanie heavy-handedly wedged dishes into the already-packed dishwasher. I had genuinely forgotten that I was supposed to take Jack to Sienna's *Pirates and Princesses* themed birthday party.

'I'll speak with Jack,' I sighed. 'He'll understand.' I entered the living room to break the news to Jack, when I heard a text alert and realised I'd left my phone on the worktop. I doubled backed and rushed back into the kitchen. My phone was in Stephanie's hand. I looked down at it and I could see the notification on my home screen. It was from Rukhsana. The address for the coffee shop, the meeting time, followed by a single kiss. Stephanie's eyes were thankfully on me as she handed me the phone.

It was a close one, and it could have been a whole damn lot closer. It was time to put an end to my lies. One of them, at least.

*

Rukhsana was waiting outside the coffee shop. She was dressed in fitted blue jeans, and cream heels that offset her navy blue blazer. An effort not matched by me.

'Rukhsana. Hi.' I approached her with my hand out which she left hanging and stepped in for an embrace. 'I'm not late, am I?' I asked, extracting myself from her.

'If you were late, I wouldn't be here.' She smiled and hooked her arm in mine and we entered and found a booth at the back of the coffee shop. She eyed me as she removed her blazer to reveal a sleeveless white blouse.

'Are you growing a...' Rukhsana pointed at my face.

'Oh. No, I just haven't shaved in a few days.' I realised it was more like a week since I last shaved, and a couple of days since I'd showered. I leant back in my chair.

'You look better clean shaven,' she said.

I smiled and nodded knowing I looked like shit. I waved a waiter over and ordered a coffee, she ordered something a little fancier. Over her shoulder I spotted a man, vaguely familiar. He was sitting by himself, trying his hardest not to look at us. 'Is that –'

'Yes, that is my brother, Kareem.' Rukhsana smirked. 'I'll be thirty-two in two weeks. I work in the city, sometimes until late. But as soon as I have to meet a boy, my parents insist that I take a chaperone. In case your intentions are sinister... Are they?' Her smile upgraded to a giggle. 'I'll try to lose him, next time we meet.'

'Rukhsana,' I said, ready to tell her there wouldn't be a next time.

'Imran.' She smiled.

The waiter was on us, fussing, making small talk as he placed my coffee and her foamy number on the table. He left and the moment had passed. Frustrated, I waited for another as I agitatedly scratched my thigh under the table.

Rukhsana was switched on and proceeded to ask pertinent questions of me. She asked me if I had any property, my ambitions. How many children I would like. If I was planning to live at home with Khala after marriage or move out. She even put theoretical scenarios to me: if she was invited to a hen do, in Ibiza, how would I feel about it? Trying to gauge if I was the jealous type, the controlling type. Unable to keep up I stopped her abruptly in full flow.

'I'm seeing someone.'

She shifted slightly in her chair, for the first time losing a little cool. Her hand tightened around the mug.

'Sorry,' she pursed her lips. 'Can you repeat that?'

'I'm sorry.'

'Is it serious?'

'Yes... I'm sorry.'

The door to the coffee shop opened. I looked past Rukhsana, I looked past her brother who was lost to his phone and there he was, the cutest little pirate. Red eye patch, black bandana wrapped around his peanut head and a stuffed parrot on his shoulder. Behind him, stopped in her tracks, was Stephanie.

Rukhsana turned in her seat and locked eyes with Stephanie. Jack ran to our table and hopped onto my lap.

'When are you coming home, Dad?' he said, pulling playfully at my ear. 'Mummy said you were working.'

Stephanie slowly approached the table and took it all in. First disbelief in her eyes, and then simply a sadness that I'd never seen before.

'Steph,' I said, and I didn't know what else to say. My lies ran dry.

'Is this *her*?' Rukhsana said, taking great pleasure in my predicament 'Looks to me like you have yourself a ready-made family, Imran. Which begs the question, what *are* you doing here? With me?' She smiled. Sweetly.

Stephanie grabbed Jack by the arm and lifted him away from me. I shot to my feet. 'Steph... Wait,' I said brushing past a grinning Rukhsana and rushing after Stephanie as she purposefully strode towards the door. I reached for her arm.

'*Don't you dare!*' Stephanie screamed, silencing the room.

I released her arm and she walked out, with Jack looking back at me unsure if he'd ever see me again.

37
Jay

Home alone and with nothing to think about but the mess that is my life. Somebody had popped Silas; an angel with a blade. The cops weren't knocking on my door. The crackhead was the only one who could place Idris and me there, but you know... ain't no-one paying attention to a crackhead. I should have been happy, or somewhere close to it, but my life was moving in different directions than the one I wanted it to move in. External forces at work.

I still hadn't seen the attack on Layla. I'd found several links to it online but couldn't bring myself to watch it. Instead I dreamt it, interpreted it, my mind worked hard to piss me off. I'd wake up *furious* that a life could be snatched so easily, *resolute* that I would do something about it. But seriously, what could I do? Layla was just one of a million injustices.

I spent twenty minutes in front of the bathroom mirror, carrying out mouth and neck exercises that the physio had given me. My reflection looked a fucking mess. I'd lost weight due to my diet of soup and mush. My face gaunt, dark circles deepening under my eyes, and what was that? *A fucking grey hair.*

I looked old. Like my father would have, if he hadn't been covered in third degree burns all over his face and body, caused when he detonated an explosive vest outside the US Embassy in Madrid.

I stepped away from the mirror at the morbid thought, and made my way slowly downstairs, wondering what to do with the day. I slumped in my armchair and stared at the television, which was turned off, the remote out of reach. Next to the television was a great big Get Well Soon card that my work lot had sent me along with an even bigger bouquet of flowers, *know your audience*, *people*. I'd made the token effort and put them in a jug – couldn't find a vase – then watched them wilt and die in record time. I was so bored out of my skull that, get this, I actually wanted to go back to work just to be around people and their inane conversation. But I had officially been signed off and it went against all my natural instincts to work when I didn't have to.

I sighed loudly and unlocked my phone. I had a missed call from Zafar. I recalled vaguely exchanging numbers at Heston Hall. It's what you do when you get a little familiar with someone. It didn't mean he had to use it. I didn't think we had a chatting-on-the-phone relationship. It's an altered dynamic, like bumping into your hairdresser down the fruit and veg aisle. I dialled him back as I contemplated the poor metaphor.

'What's happening, Jay?' Zafar wasn't the *Aslamalykum* type. 'I was just texting you.'

'Zee. What's happening?' I'd never before called him Zee, nor heard anybody else refer to him that way. *Altered dynamics!* I could hear the awkwardness in the beat of silence. I cleared my throat; it still fucking hurt.

'Just checking in. How're you?' he said.

'Yeah, you know. Well.'

'Good! That's good... So Tahir and I are going for a bite to eat at that Lebanese place tonight... Shit, can't remember what it's called. Behind Treaty.'

'Mrwa.'

'That's it.'

'Ira, Naaim, they coming?'

'No,' Zafar said, 'Just the two of us and you, if you can make it.'

Paranoia set in. After Silas' attack, I wasn't taking any chances – even if he was dead, there were plenty of others who might be interested in me. In the space of a second before I replied, I tried to figure out the angle. The last year had affected me more than I cared to admit. I now saw threats in any situation that was even a little out of the ordinary. We had a relationship that was, and should be, limited to Heston Hall. None of this extra-curricular bullshit, and that includes their visit to the hospital. *Why'd they do that? Did they find out about my past, that I attended a training camp in North Pakistan? Was Heston Hall some sort of terrorist breeding ground?* And why the fuck did they not invite Naaim and Ira? *Had they proven themselves to be unworthy, untrustworthy?* It didn't add up and it fed my fucking paranoia. It wouldn't be the first time that I'd been put under the microscope by a bunch of *Brothers* looking to exploit me.

'Jay?'

'Yeah.'

'Only if you're feeling up-to-it. Haven't seen you at the meetings recently, obviously, with your... you know, injury. Be nice to catch up.'

Meetings. Something sinister about the way he said it.

Was this my life now, looking for intonation, for a meaning that wasn't there? Stop it, Jay. *Fuck!*

'Go on, then,' I said, after battling with myself and emerging the victor.

*

The spy in me turned up fifteen minutes early. I cruised slowly past Mrwa. It was empty, save a young couple in the far corner. She was romantically being spoon fed the creamy foam from the top of a tall drink. No danger there, I ascertained.

I parked my car on a single yellow and walked the short distance. Opposite, Tahir and Zafar were approaching the restaurant. We met outside and I carried out a respectful handshake and a *Salaam* with Tahir, and a fist bump and '*sup* with Zafar.

'Shall we,' Tahir held open the door.

I walked in first and the waiter directed us to a table for four. I made sure that I sat facing the entrance. Tahir sat opposite with Zafar next to me. We nodded, smiled, made a little crap talk as we browsed the menu. They asked me how I was healing. I wasn't close enough with them to answer in the form of a shrug, so I told them about my diet, the daily physiotherapy and medication. It was a snore-fest; I was boring myself.

It didn't go unnoticed that they were exchanging discreet glances. They were pacing, waiting for the right moment to break it to me. Letting me talk shit as they took my measure. *I've been here before. I know the game.* Had they sensed my frustration at the meetings and decided that I could be, *what's the fucking word? Groomed.*

'Anyway,' I said, cutting myself short. 'What's the occasion?'

Tahir smiled at me. 'Do we need an occasion for friends to meet, Brother?'

'I guess not.' *Friends? I didn't sign up to be friends.*

'Though there is something that we would like to discuss with you.'

I shifted in my chair. Next to me, Zafar did a little shifting himself. The waiter was at our table. Jug in hand. Three pairs of eyes carefully watched the waiter slosh grey water into each glass. I used the time to work out my next move. *Give nothing away. Note every last detail. Entice whatever information you can from them and then give it all to Lawrence and MI5 to fuck it all up.*

'We, me and Zafar, want to speak with you about Ira,' Tahir said.

'Ira? This is about *Ira?*' Relief washed over me quickly followed by concern. 'What's happened? She alright?' I glanced to my side at Zafar. He said nothing.

'Ira is fine, Brother,' he said. 'We're just a little worried about her.'

'Worried? Why?'

'She's getting involved in something that isn't any of her business.' Zafar raised his voice a little. Tahir indicated,

174

with a placatory hand, that maybe he should be the one to explain but Zafar wasn't having any of it. 'With all due respect, Tahir, it was your idea. You said we should listen to him, support him. That's exactly what Ira's doing... We should have called the police. He's been acting crazy recently.'

'He? Who?' It hit me as soon as the words left my mouth. 'Naaim?'

'Yeah, Naaim.' Zafar stood up in a huff. 'I'm going out for a cigarette. You coming?' he asked me.

'I can't,' I said, pointing at my stitched neck.

Zafar opened the door. Before stepping out he held the door open for an Asian man. He stepped inside, bringing in the cold with him. I checked him out. Dark jeans, a crisp white half-sleeved shirt despite the weather, and Bata sandals. Typical freshy! Probably gets pulled by the fuzz daily, I thought, as my eyes travelled over him. I caught him looking back, not a glance either, gaze totally focused, maybe because he was aware that I was silently judging his dress sense. I offered him a canned smile and looked away.

'You'll have to forgive Zafar,' Tahir said.

'What's there to forgive? It's fine,' I said.

'He and Ira are very close. He's like a brother to her.'

'I know, man,' I nodded. I'd seen them bicker plenty, just as siblings would. 'How's this related to Naaim?'

'In your absence, Jay, Naaim's behaviour has become... erratic.'

'Yeah,' I wasn't surprised. Why wasn't I surprised? I just wasn't. I'd recognised that look in Naaim's eyes. One of loss, one of revenge.

'He found one of the three boys that attacked Layla.'

'How'd he manage that?'

'Every day he travelled that very same bus, that very same route. Waiting. One of them got on. Naaim sat directly behind him.' Tahir leaned in. 'He told us that he wanted to put his hands around his neck and strangle the life out of him.'

'But he didn't though, did he?'

'No, he didn't.'

I looked away as though there was nothing to worry about, as though alarm bells weren't ringing in my head. Freshy had taken a table in the corner of the restaurant. He'd slipped off his sandals and placed his dirty bare feet on the chair opposite, his eyes still boring into mine as he blindly wrapped a paan. Tahir followed my sight and turned to see what I was looking at.

'Salaam, Brother.' Tahir frowned at him. 'Do you mind taking your feet off the chair?'

'Tahir, leave it,' I said. The man folded then popped the tightly-wrapped paan into his mouth. I could see the black on the soles of his feet and his overgrown toenails from the gaps in between the slats of the chair.

'You are in a restaurant, Brother. Have some respect, Brother,' Tahir said.

You can *Brother* as much as you want, but *Brother* ain't shifting. Freshy didn't acknowledge Tahir, didn't even look his way, because he was still too busy fucking glaring at me. Anyone else, and I'm meeting their eyes and getting into it. But this guy, besides bad table manners, something didn't sit right with him.

'Do you know the Brother? Tahir asked.

I shook my head. No Brother of mine. Zafar walked back in, bringing with him the sweet smell of cigarettes, making me crave one. 'Ira just called me,' he said, taking his seat next to me. 'Wanted to know where I was.'

'What did you tell her?' Tahir asked.

'That we were here. She'll be down in ten.' Zafar shrugged. 'Thought, as we're all here, we can talk to her. Jay... Are you in?'

'*In?* In what? What're you talking about?'

'We're going to intervene.'

'Is this what this is? An *intervention*?' I snorted. 'Bit far-fetched, this! Look, Naaim is angry. Ira is angry. I am! He had a chance to retaliate, but didn't. Doesn't that show that whatever thoughts he's having, he's not exactly going to carry it out.' Even as I was saying it, I didn't quite believe it myself. I just wanted to distance myself from this conversation, this situation. 'Why doesn't he just tell the police?'

'Because Ira is right: he's a Muslim and they're three white kids! Do you know why he didn't do anything to that boy on the bus? He wants them all! He wants all three of them and he wants to hurt them. It's eating him up that he wasn't able to protect Layla when he had the chance. He feels like he failed her... And you know what, he did. He *failed* her.'

'That's not right, Brother,' Tahir interjected. 'You were not there.'

'If I was, we wouldn't be in this situation. He wimped out, and now he wants redemption.'

We hadn't touched our drinks, we hadn't ordered our meal, and I couldn't care less. I'd decided that as soon as the opportunity arose I was making my excuses and walking. To hell with this noise. I ain't taking on somebody else's war. Not again. My jaw rhythmically jutted out of my cheek as I ground my teeth, holding back the profanity that was never far from my lips. I hadn't dropped a *fuck*, out of respect to Tahir, it wasn't how I spoke in his company, but all I wanted to do was scream until I had exhausted every variation of that fucking word.

I leaned back in my chair and crossed my arms. 'What's any of this have to do with Ira?'

'She walks around with a chip on her shoulder,' Zafar sighed. 'Everything bad in her life, she puts down to the system. Now she's in his ear. Trust me, them together is asking for trouble.'

'We just want to talk with her,' Tahir said. 'Young Naaim listens to her. We must ensure that she uses her influence to guide him.'

I rubbed the shit out of both my eyes. *This has nothing to do with me.* Zafar looked genuinely disappointed as I realised I had said it out loud. I got to my feet and zipped up my jacket, that I hadn't got around to taking off. I had to get away. I had my own mess to sweep up.

The door opened and in walked Ira.

'I've just come from Naaim's place,' she said, softly. Zafar and I shared a look. 'His Mother suffered a heart attack today. She passed away a few hours ago.'

'I'm sorry to hear that,' I said. 'Look, I better get going, my throat's hurting a little. I'll catch up with you guys.'

Yeah, it was a cold reaction, but it wasn't like *her* Mother had died. If I stayed, I was sending out the wrong signals, like we were a tight knit group, like we can fucking depend on each other. I didn't ever want to be in that situation again.

I made my way out of the restaurant, past where Freshy had been sitting. I hadn't noticed him leave. I opened the door and the cold air slapped me in the face. I kept my head low as I passed the large restaurant window, knowing that they were all looking at me. I *fuck*, *fuck*, *fucked* under my breath, all the way to my car, knowing that I'd done the right thing but in the wrong way.

38

Imy

Stephanie would have needed the space and I gave it to her. I drove around aimlessly for a couple of hours before I went back home, searching for the perfect lie, but I knew that tonight she would only settle for the truth.

'Steph,' I called out. My head poking in the gap between the front door and the door frame. The flimsy safety chain stopping me from entering. 'Please... Hear me out.'

I waited a moment for her to appear. When she didn't I considered giving the door a nudge and breaking the chain, but Jack was a troubled sleeper and I couldn't risk waking him.

I closed the door and sat down on the stoop, just as I had two years ago.

This three-bedroom semi-detached house had been my first ever viewing, and the client had been late. I knew that if they didn't turn up soon Kumar would lay into me, especially since I'd left the client's contact details back at the office, so I'd sat on this very step and waited.

Thirty minutes in and I was ready to give up and face Kumar, when a silver Golf pulled haphazardly into the drive, stopping just inches away from me. The client stepped out of the car, her smart grey suit too creased for the time of the morning. She mouthed an apology to me as she turned to open the back door. I saw the tail of her white blouse not quite tucked into her trousers. She fumbled in the back seat. A small red and white sneaker fell out. She took out an owl rucksack and an orange beaker and placed it on the roof of the car. And then she brought out Jack. A breadstick in each hand. He was two years old at the time.

I picked up the fallen sneaker. 'Is this yours?' I smiled at him. He stretched his arms out and attempted to leap from his mother to me.

'Da-Da?' Jack babbled, to me.

'Sorry. He says that to every man who shows him a little attention... It's a long story,' Stephanie said, smiling away her sadness.

The viewing lasted longer than it should have. I don't know what it was. A stolen glance. A shared glance. A smile. Neither of us in a hurry to leave.

Afterwards, I gave her my contact details. 'If you'd like another viewing, call me,' I'd said, and then surprised myself by saying, 'Or you can call me anyway.'

*

The front door opened, the safety chain still dividing us. In between the gap, Stephanie appeared, the baby monitor that she still insisted on using gripped in her hand.

'Is she your wife?' she asked.

'Can I come in?' I said.

'I asked you a question.'

'No. She's not my wife.'

'Are you together?'

'No, Steph.'

'Don't lie to me, Imy!'

'I'm not. Not anymore... I went to break it off with her.'

'Break it off?' She took a step back and put her hand to her chest.

'You don't understand.' I rested my head against the door frame and closed my eyes. 'You'll never understand.'

'Make me understand,' she said, and when I opened my eyes, the chain was unhooked and she was standing closer to me. Just the threshold between us.

'Rukhsana wasn't the first. My Khala... She's been arranging them.' I expelled air. 'For marriage.'

'Marriage?' Stephanie said, her voice barely reaching me. 'We're engaged, Imy.'

'I know, Steph.'

'We're supposed to be getting married this year.'

'I know... I... I know. She... They... mean nothing to me. Each time I make my excuses, find a fault and turn them down, and resolve to tell Khala about us, but no sooner do I do that than another one is lined up. It's... it's incessant. Every time, the expectation, the hope on her face, never wavering.'

Stephanie stepped outside, closing the door gently behind her, and sat on the stoop. I sat down next to her. The baby monitor between us, the steady rhythm of Jack's nasal snoring filling in the silence.

'You were sat right here,' she said, 'when we first met.'

'I was just thinking about that,' I said. 'You nearly ran me over.'

'Imy... Make me understand.'

'My parents... After they died, Khala showered me with love. She was the mother that my own never had the chance to be. She turned her life upside down for me. I remember her taking on a second job. She would often say the first job was to feed us and the second was to pay for my wedding. Don't you see, Steph? She's set a path for me and I don't know how to step off. It would break her.'

I finally released a breath that I didn't realise that I was holding. All of a sudden, I felt so tired. The truth had exhausted me.

'I've told my parents about you,' she said. 'They weren't happy. *A Muslim*, was about all they could muster. That and shock. It took them a while to get used to it. But they saw how happy I was. Isn't that all a parent wants for their child?'

I shook my head. It wasn't the same. 'You don't understand.'

'You're right, Imy,' she said. 'I don't understand, and maybe I never will. But I know that you understand that what I hold most precious is sleeping upstairs, and it has

181

taken him a long time, Imy, to get to where he is today. No longer is he wetting the bed. No longer are his teachers calling me to tell me that he's not communicating, that he's just sitting in a corner by himself, silently, crying all day, every damn day. When his father walked, he took away a part of that boy. But now.... He's starting to smile, again. To laugh. Do you know who that's down to?'

I did.

'You're worried about upsetting your Khala, I get it. I know, Imy; I know how much it's stressing you out, more-so since you moved in with us. Since you proposed to me. You haven't shaved. You barely shower. You're not sleeping well, Imy. Last night I had to remove your hand from your head and hold it in mine, before you ripped your skin. Other times, your mouth is moving as though you're having a silent conversation.'

I had finally come clean about Rukhsana, about Khala, but how could I tell her that my sleep has been punctured with nightmares of Pathaan, smiling, baring his blood-coated teeth, his hands around the throat of my family, strangling the life out of them. That I was on edge because I was waiting to be given an instruction to kill.

'Jack adores you, Imy. He loves you. We both do. But I can't wait around wondering whether or not you are going to do the right thing by us. Me and you... we can't go on like this. I will not allow men like you, like Jack's father, to take Jack apart piece by piece.' Stephanie stood up and over me. 'I can't have this conversation with you again, Imy, and I can't decide for you.'

Stephanie walked back into the house leaving the door open.

39
Jay

I ain't much of a sleeper, though not out of choice. I compare it with what soldiers suffer after they return home from battle. Post-traumatic stress disorder. The horrific memory that stays in your head from when you carried your wounded friend over your shoulder to safety, in a war that killed your soul. I guess I was suffering from something like that. Maybe a milder version.

I've tried to stay positive, move forward, away from conflict. It wasn't even my conflict, it belonged to another. But yet as hard as I try to get back to a simpler life, one without noise and revenge and fucking conflict, I can feel myself getting dragged back as though it's my only purpose.

And now, a new face to freak me the fuck out. I'd never seen that freshy in the restaurant before, but he'd looked at me as though he wanted to kiss me or kill me. Hounslow has its fair share of idiots that like to give the stink-eye but this guy gave it some and more, as though I'd once wronged him.

I switched on my once-busy phone. Just one text message, from Tahir, informing me the details of Naaim's mother's funeral, and saying that they'd be going back to his place after, and that I *should* be there, too.

Can't these people take a fucking hint?

I sighed. Thought of a hundred reasons why I shouldn't be there. And then I got ready.

*

I don't quite know if it's religion or tradition, but Muslim funerals have to be arranged immediately after the time of death, with the burial taking place the next day. It made me wonder what I would want at my own funeral. I don't want to it be rushed. I don't want Mum on the phone to the florist as soon as I've taken my last breath. Take your time, shed a tear or two. Spend a couple of days talking amongst yourselves about just how great I was! I want a proper Elvis-style casket, not a nondescript wooden box. I want a wake – Muslims never have a wake – I want music, 'Pac spitting *Bury me a G*, through the speakers, as glasses of sweet lassi and cups of masala chai are raised in my name. I want the works.

Not like this.

Sat at the back of Sutton Mosque, amidst a handful of wailers. Naaim sat quietly beside the raised wooden casket. He wasn't crying, just rocking back and forth. Ira sat next to him. She wasn't crying, just rocking back and forth. There was a framed photo of his mother sitting on a small table by the coffin. She wore a sorrowful expression, as though she was watching her own funeral.

'Salaam Brother.' Tahir shook my hand and sat down on the floor next to me, followed by Zafar who nodded his greeting and sat on the other side of me. 'It will mean a lot to Naaim that you came.'

I highly doubt it, but nodded anyway.

'Are you coming to the Quabaristan, Jay?' Zafar asked.

I wasn't planning to go to the cemetery. Paying my respects at the Mosque was my only intention, but having seen the low turnout, I figured I should help make up the numbers, bearing in mind that in Islam, women are not allowed to visit graves.

The hearse led, the small convoy trailed. We headed towards Greenford Park Cemetery, leaving Ira and all the other women behind at the Mosque. The burial was impersonal, as a bunch of strange men, drafted in by the Imam, stood around the casket. Naaim, the only relation, was quiet and unapproachable as Tahir found out. The casket was lowered into the ground and we took turns covering it with earth until the JCB took over. A Prayer carried out by the Imam was observed in respectful silence and the small crowd quickly dissipated, leaving just a few of us.

'What now?' Zafar asked.

I shrugged. I just wanted out of the cemetery. I was acutely aware of how close, very recently, I had come to death. I wondered how many would have attended my funeral. Idris, the Heston Hall crew, Mum. It would be like this: a bunch of well-meaning Muslim strangers from Sutton Mosque, unfamiliar hands lowering me into the ground. There was once a time when I thought I was the man around Hounslow, but it was the kind of popularity that being a drug dealer attracts. They weren't friends. They didn't care. They didn't visit me at the hospital. They certainly wouldn't come to say goodbye.

I think I was starting to get a bit depressed. I think it was a long time coming.

'It's okay, Brother.' Tahir put his arm around me, as I wiped a tear from my eye. 'Moments like this make a man question his own existence, his mortality.'

'Live life to the fullest.' Zafar added a perfectly timed cliché.

'Mashallah, Brother,' Tahir nodded. 'We must never fear death, but we should never forget that it is coming, without warning and without question. Live and love and laugh with those closest to you.'

That's it. *That is fucking it.* Tahir was right. He, Zafar, Ira, Naaim, they'd tried to get close to me and I'd pushed them away, rejecting them again and again. They weren't my kind of people; Heston Hall was the only place I'd allow myself to be near them. Why did I think I was better than them? Because I wear better trainers, and Tahir wears a cotton shalwar and kameez. Or because Ira wears a hijab. I thought I was too good to be around those whose appearance screamed Muslim. Zafar was a funny guy, mostly unintentionally. Tahir was the sensible head.

Ira, the feisty one and Naaim, the youngest, in desperate need of support.

I think I needed them as much as they needed me. More.

Naaim was on his haunches in front of his mother's grave, his fingers aimlessly combing the freshly laid soil.

'He's going to need our help,' I said, surprising them as much as myself. 'He's probably going through hell. Layla... and now his mum.' I moved away and approached Naaim, expecting my efforts to be rejected. I placed my hand on his shoulder. He turned to look up at me, his eyes dry and lifeless. We all react in a different way when facing death, but I hadn't seen him shed a tear throughout the funeral. I took my hand away from his shoulder and put it in front of him. He took it and I helped him to his feet.

'Look, I'm... I'm really sorry for your loss, man,' I said. It didn't feel right. I couldn't leave it like that, something about this kid filled me with a hope of redemption. 'I'll never understand what you're going through, but know this, we're here for you... I'm here for you.'

I stepped forward and took him in my arms. Naaim placed his head against my shoulder and shed his first tear.

*

In Naaim's living room, the curtains were drawn a good few hours before they needed to be. A dull, artificial light barely illuminated the room. The television was set to UK Gold. A classic but politically incorrect old sitcom. Simpler times.

We talked. Not about the funeral, not about Heston Hall, just bullshit small-talk. Naaim quiet at first, conversation respectful at first, but when Zafar couldn't stop himself from laughing, as Tahir misjudged a dunk and his custard cream plopped into his tea, the mood lifted.

'Here,' Ira said, 'Give it to me, I'll make you another.'

'No, Sister, it's fine.' Tahir took a sludgy sip and made a face.

Ira disappeared anyway and returned a moment later with a replacement tea for Tahir and took her place back on the sofa, next to Naaim.

'Milk's almost finished,' Ira said. 'I'll pick some up in a bit. I'll get some basics too, fridge is bare.'

'Mashallah,' Tahir said.

'You want us to chip in, Ira?' Zafar stood up and dug around fruitlessly in his pocket.

'Sit down, yeah, Zafar,' Ira replied, 'We all know you ain't got a dime in there. You're more unemployed than I am.' Naaim snorted. It served as a moment for all us to join in and laugh at Zafar's expense. Or lack of it. 'Don't worry,' she continued. 'I've got plenty funds, yeah.'

'Struck gold, have we?' Zafar sat back down.

'Benefits kicked in.' Ira shrugged. 'I get by.' Zafar opened his mouth, but she was onto him, quick. 'You better keep that mouth of yours shut, yeah. If they won't pay us to work, they better pay us to survive.'

'I didn't say anything,' he replied, with a knowing smile.

'Yeah, you better not.'

'Can you pick up some sturdier biscuits, Sister?' Tahir joined in.

It was nice, considering that we'd just come back from a funeral. Natural, it felt very much as though this group of people, this Muslim motley crew, were going to be in my life for some time, if I let them.

'You know what's funny?' Naaim said, 'My father doesn't even know his wife has died.'

I looked over at Zafar. We both silently agreed that it actually wasn't that funny.

'He wasn't there for her when she was alive. Why should he be there when she's dead?' Naaim said.

'Screw him,' Ira exclaimed.

I could feel Zafar and Tahir both looking at me, I knew exactly what they were thinking. *This is what we were talking about.* They were right. Ira's influence was there for all to see. And if we weren't careful, it would get us all in trouble.

40

Maimana, Afghanistan

Before Abdullah Bin Jabbar was affectionately known as The Teacher.

Before he detonated his first explosive vest and suffered horrifying third-degree burns that resulted in blackened, charred skin all over his hands, face and body.

Before he created Ghurfat-Al-Mudarris, a terror cell that grew in numbers; men and women who shared his passion for life and his hatred for the West.

Before his legend grew and The Teacher became a mythical figure that could never be touched.

Before all of that, his name was Inzamam Qasim and he lived in Hounslow.

He worked as a chef in an Indian restaurant on Kensington High Street. His signature minted lamb chops drew admirers from afar. For three years he saved whatever money he could as he carefully studied the intricacies of running a successful London restaurant with the ambition of one day opening his very own place. It was his only dream at a time when dreams were achievable. Qasim wanted a partner by his side, not a business partner but a life partner. Somebody he could share this dream with as their family grew.

His parents showed him a photo of a girl. He liked it.

He met her once. He liked her.

Her name was Afeesa and they were married within a few months. Qasim's closest friend, Adeel-al-Bhukara, a Muslim scholar, was his best man. They honeymooned in

Marrakech. A few days in a small hotel with a few stars behind it. They spent the days browsing the souks, and visiting the Atlas Mountains. At night, when they weren't getting to know each other, they watched the small hotel television. Only the news channel worked.

The coverage of Operation Desert Storm, the Gulf War, was so very different to what he had seen and read on the news and newspapers back at home. The death and destruction of hundreds of thousands of men, women and children. *Babies*.

The easy deaths of innocents. The easy deaths of Muslims.

In the time that they had spent in Marrakech, watching the war unfold on the portable television, they witnessed reports of cluster bombs dropped at a truck stop. Open fire killing attendees at a wedding – a wedding just like theirs had been, a young couple celebrating the start of their lives together. Two missiles ripping through a busy bank. Another missile killing everybody on board a public bus. Twenty-three homes in an agricultural area hit with bombs in two separate attacks. All taking place within a period of three days.

And always the same result. No survivors.

When the newlyweds got back to England, to London, to Hounslow, it was a different story. The roles were reversed. Villains were heroes. A war justified. Sympathy for the Devil. The Allies consistent in their lies, just as they were consistent in their murder. It quickly became clear to Qasim that he had been told and sold a pack of lies.

He had always believed in helping the weak. He had always believed in an eye for an eye. He didn't know just how far that belief would take him.

He told Afeesa that he wanted to help. He told her he wanted to fight. She told him she was pregnant.

Inzamam left her with money that was once dedicated to a dream. He left her with a roof over her head and food on the table. He left her to fight for a cause bigger than him, than them, than their unborn child. His friend, Al-Bhukara, promised he would watch over them.

Inzamam Qasim changed his name to Abdullah Bin Jabbar. Soon, he was affectionately known as The Teacher or, in Arabic, al-Mudarris.

His son was born. He was named Javid.

Twenty-eight years later the war against Muslims still consumed the world. In that period, four million Muslims had died at the hands of the West. It was a war that The Teacher could not win, but he would die trying. His organisation, Ghurfat-al-Mudarris, which had grown quick and hard, had a direct hand in fifteen devastating retaliation attacks. Planned meticulously and carried out to shattering effect. He never once asked his men to sacrifice themselves in war. Those who were caught welcomed the questions, the torture. If they had to, they would die slowly and painfully before they gave his name.

From London, Adeel-al-Bhukara kept in communication with The Teacher. He told him his son had come of age. He told him that *Jay* wanted to fight for The Cause. Just like his father before him.

For nearly thirty years The Teacher walked amongst his people, through their villages, welcomed into their homes. They worshipped him and loved him for what he was desperately trying to achieve. Any one of them could have spoken out against him. Revealed his location, his identity. But they would not. They did not.

But his son would. His son did.

The one and only time that Abdullah Bin Jabbar met his son, he felt a certain pride. Even after all that he had achieved, it was a pride that he had never felt before. With visions of his son one day taking over from him, and leading the good men and women of Ghurfat-al-Mudarris into battle, he revealed too much to Javid.

Al-Bhukara was right. Jay wanted to fight for The Cause, but it was a different cause.

Javid Qasim was responsible for the failed attack on Oxford Street. He was responsible for revealing The Teacher's locations, description and the infrastructure of his cell. Javid, his own blood, had done something that his own men had never done. He had failed him.

The Teacher would spend the remainder of his days on the run. Ghurfat-al-Mudarris, the organisation that he had built from blood, sweat and tears, would never operate with the same ruthless efficiency with the eyes of the Kafir firmly on it.

The Teacher knew what was expected of him. A message had to be sent.

Javid Qasim had to die.

The thing was, Abdullah Bin Jabbar could never give that order, because something unexpected had happened.

He'd fallen in love with his son.

*

Intazaar was a small run-down restaurant located in a poor rural village in the Maimana region of Afghanistan, surrounded by broken, little-used roads. Behind it is a crop field used to grow wheat, maize, barley and rice.

In the basement of Intazaar is a small kitchen where Abdullah Bin Jabbar, fearless leader of Ghurfat-al-Mudarris, now worked as a chef.

These days, his legendary lamb chops, which once dazzled the taste buds of Londoners, and delighted the mother of his only son, now feed the hungry in a village left in a state of disrepair by a war that they didn't ask for.

In the corner sits a large, well-used Aga cooker. It would require three strong men to move it. Behind it is a masked, secure-coded panel, accessible only by Bin Jabbar. The panel, once removed, leads to a tight tunnel. On hands and knees, the tunnel runs a hundred metres and then meets four more underground tunnels that stretch two miles underneath the crop fields and out into four different neighbouring villages.

Four fully fuelled vans, each fitted with a hidden compartment, are stationed close by.

The lamb chops sizzled away to near-perfection on the Aga. A little longer was required for that slightly burnt, crispy taste. Bin Jabbar buttered the freshly made tandoori naan bread as he waited. His efforts were measured, his people were waiting to be fed, regardless of the disturbing news that he had heard. He waited patiently for confirmation. If it came, The Teacher would have to take a huge risk and come out of hiding. Preparations were already being put in place.

His dear friend, Latif, the only follower of Ghurfat-Al-Mudarris that he kept close, walked down the narrow stairs and into the kitchen basement.

'Al-Mudarris.' Latif swallowed.

Bin Jabbar carefully turned over the lamb chops one at a time. 'Latif.'

'Muhammad Talal is here at your request.'

He turned off the Aga and turned to see a man standing cautiously behind Latif. Bin Jabbar was accustomed to the awe and admiration that his people expressed for him. He was also aware that those who set eyes on him for the first time couldn't help but register disgust at the dark layer of seared skin that covered his face and hands. Though never once had he seen fear in the eyes of his men, as he had in Talal's.

He knew the meaning of it. But he had to hear the words from the mouth of the messenger.

'Al-Mudarris.' Talal lowered his eyes. 'It is by the grace of Allah that –'

Bin Jabbar held out a charred hand to cut him short. He gestured to a wooden chair at the small wooden table. Bin Jabbar poured Talal a glass of water and stood opposite, behind an empty chair. He leaned forward, resting his hands on the wooden rail of the chair.

'I would have come sooner, Al-Mudarris, but I was detained by the Belgian authorities. For two weeks they questioned me, repeatedly.' Talal put a hand to his heart. 'Wallahi, I didn't say anything.'

'It is okay.' Bin Jabbar kept his frustration in check, hands gripped the rail. 'Tell my why you are here.'

'I have news. Sheikh Ghulam has taken control of Ghurfat-al-Mudarris in your absence.'

Bin Jabbar nodded.

'I attended a meeting at the request of the Sheikh.' Talal cleared his throat. 'He has raised his first order.' Talal looked nervously at Latif.

'You may speak freely, Talal,' Bin Jabbar said.

'But Al-Mudarris...' Talal said.

'Please,' Bin Jabbar inhaled, his fingers tightening and whitening around the wooden rail of the chair. 'Continue.'

Talal picked up the glass of water and brought it to his lips, sipping generously. It spilled down his chin and onto the table. 'Sorry,' he said, as dabbed at the spilt water on the table.

The wooden rail collapsed underneath Bin Jabbar's grip, he flung the chair across the kitchen. Striding forward he upturned the wooded table and placed his hand around Talal's throat.

'*Speak, now.*'

'Javid Qasim.' Talal spoke quickly, the glass shaking in his hand. 'The Sheikh has placed a fatwa on your son.'

Bin Jabbar released his grip. He gently straightened out Talal's kurta and patted him lightly on the chest. Latif remained neutral in expression.

'Latif,' Bin Jabbar said. 'Please show our guest out.'

Latif helped Talal to his feet and escorted him out of the basement kitchen. Bin Jabbar stood at the Aga and ignited it. He needed to feel something, to feel pain. He slowly lowered his hand on the flame. It burnt and peeled away another layer of skin, yet he could not feel any sensation.

'Al-Mudarris.' Latif returned and silently watched Bin Jabbar's steady hand over the flame as the faint smell of burning skin reached him. 'Please,' he said, softly.

'Give me your phone, Latif.' Bin Jabbar removed his hand from the Aga.

Latif adjusted his glasses. 'I will arrange for a secure phone.'

'No.' Bin Jabbar held his hand out. 'Now.'

Latif placed his phone in Bin Jabbar's hand. He could clearly see the redness, swelling and blistering that had appeared on it. 'Javid,' Latif surmised.

Bin Jabbar nodded. 'I have to hear his voice.'

'Al-Mudarris, I must advise against it. They will be watching Javid, have alerts on his phone, precisely for this very reason. They will trace this location within seconds.'

'It does not matter,' Bin Jabbar said. 'I am not coming back.' He picked up the upturned wooden table and sat down, placing the phone in front of him. He stared pensively at it.

'If you travel, they will hunt you.'

'My people will carry me through, Latif.' Bin Jabbar smiled at his friend. 'It's the only way that the fatwa can be lifted. I must speak with Sheikh Ghulam.'

There was nothing that Latif could say to change his mind.

'Arrange for this food to be distributed, Latif. When they are fed and strong, send three men to move the Aga. Then I want you to ensure that each driver at each location is awaiting my arrival. Go, now.'

Bin Jabbar waited for Latif to leave the small basement kitchen. He picked up the phone from the wooden table and before he could see sense he dialled his son's number.

With each ring he heard his heart hammering against his chest, harder each time the ring went unanswered. His mind wandered into a darkness, each thought worse than the last. The call was eventually answered. Bin Jabbar gripped the phone tightly in his hand and pressed it to his ear. The first word that he heard trapped his breath and broke his heart.

'*Mum?*'

41
Jay

I was well into my sleep and not even close to facing the day when my mobile rang, rudely disturbing me. I squinted at the digital clock, it was just past seven. Fuck, I didn't wake up this early for work; I certainly didn't wake up at this hour on a day off.

There was no voicemail set up on my mobile to act as a middle-man, so either I answered or hoped that the caller took the hint. But the caller was insistent.

I spun my body around and shifted to the other side of the bed. I reached out to the side table and clumsily palmed around, knocking a bottle of water and vitamins to the floor before locating my phone. I slipped out the charger and held the phone in front of my face. I blinked at it a few times as my vision cleared. It was a strange formation of numbers. Numbers I did not recognise. Definitely not a UK number. I had Mum's Qatar contact details saved on my phone, so *MumQatar* would usually appear on my screen. I briefly thought about ignoring it, but maybe it was Mum, maybe she was calling me, for whatever reason, from another number. Whoever it was seemed desperate to speak to me. So I answered it.

'*Mum?*'

I heard a sharp intake of breath. It sounded familiar.

'Mum. Is that you? Can you hear me?' Fully awake and alert, I shifted myself up so that I was sitting up against the headboard. 'Call me back, yeah? This is a bad line. I'm hanging up. Call me back, Mum.'

I disconnected the call and sat staring at the phone, waiting for it to ring again. My finger hovered over the screen ready to swipe. I waited a few minutes and when she didn't call back I freaked a little. I'd clearly heard something, so fucking familiar it made my heart leap into my mouth. A short sharp breath, as though she wanted to call out to me but someone had clamped a hand over her mouth and suffocated her words. To hell with the charges, I returned the call, but it wouldn't connect. A recorded message in another language, Arabic, maybe. The national language of Qatar; the call had to have come from Mum. I quickly scrolled through my contacts list stopping at *MumQatar* and punched dial.

A male voice answered confirming my worst fears.

'The fuck is this?' I spat into the phone.

'Jay?' he said.

'Yeah. The fuck are you?'

'Jay, calm down. It's Andrew. Are you okay?'

Andrew..! Fuck, Jay, get your shit together.

'Andrew, where's Mum?'

'She's having a shower... What's happened? You're worrying me.'

'Did she just call me?'

'No. She's in the shower. Her phone is with me.'

'Can you put her on?'

'She's in –'

'I know! You said! Can you just put her on?'

He sighed. I could just picture him, Mr Mild Mannered, having to deal with the wayward son. What, did he think just because they'd moved to a foreign land that I would no longer be in her life? Think again, Andrew!

'Just one moment, Jay,' he said politely.

I cursed myself for being so rude.

I heard him padding around the room and then knocking on a door. A muffled reply. Then the sound of a high powered shower and snatches of conversation.

'Hang on,' he said to me.

The shower stopped. Some rustling around. More snatches of conversation, clearer now that the shower had stopped.

Everything alright.

I don't know. He seems agitated.

Okay. Give me the phone.

'Jay?' Her voice strained, worried. I caused that.

'Mum.'

'Are you alright?'

'Yeah,' I took a breath. 'I'm fine. Did you call me a few minutes ago?'

'No, I've been in the bathroom for the last fifteen.'

'More like thirty,' I heard Andrew say in the background.

'Oh, okay,' I said, biting back my overreaction. I tried to even out. 'So, how've you been, Mum?'

'You worried me. You worried Andrew. He was pale as a sheet.'

'A bit of sun will sort that right out.' Now that I'd heard her voice, the front was back. The wisecracks, the ill-timed wit.

'Jay?'

'Yeah, Mum?'

'I am really trying here.' Her voice softened, a door closed, a conversation between mother and son. 'Andrew's teaching job is going well and I'm enjoying the reception work. My life is close to where I want it to be. But I have to know that you are coping, because I will drop everything –'

'*Mum!*'

'Don't Mum me, let me finish. If I think that you're struggling, I will drop everything in a heartbeat and get on the first plane back. My priority, the single most important thing in my life, is you, Jay. That will never change regardless of where I am… Tell me that you understand.'

'You're overreacting, Mum.'

'You make a frantic phone call demanding to speak to me, and *I'm* overreacting. Now tell me Jay, do you understand?'

'Yeah, Mum,' I said. 'I understand.'

'Are you sure, Jay?' She sighed. 'Say the word and my bags are packed.'

'Sorry, Mum. I didn't mean to freak you out. I got a phone call this morning and I just had the strangest feeling that you were in trouble. I fu... I screwed up. It won't happen again.'

'Are you having night terrors, Jay?'

I laughed loudly into the phone. She returned it with a nasal chuckle. *Night terrors!* As though I was still five years old, and running into my mum's room to check that she was still there because I'd dreamt that, like my father, my mother had gone too.

'Nightmare, Mum. Don't say night terror. And no, I'm not,' I lied.

'So, you're okay?'

'Yeah, Mum.'

'I don't have to worry.'

'No, Mum.'

42

Imy

Stephanie could have ended it and I would have understood. But I think she wanted desperately to believe. For Jack, for herself, for us. She'd left the front door open, insinuation clear: step through it as a man.

I'd felt relieved that another part of another life had been revealed. The truth had exhausted me and I slept peacefully, albeit on the sofa. It would take further effort on my part before I shared intimate space with her.

'Did you sleep here?' Jack, his features scrunched together, stood over me, not quite knowing what it meant, but knowing that it meant something. 'Why?'

'I was watching TV last night until late. I must have fallen asleep,' I said, my first words of the day a necessary lie. Jack got inside the blanket and stretched out on the other side of the sofa.

'I'm not going school today,' he said, reaching for the remote. 'Insect day.'

'Inset day!' Stephanie walked into the room. I could tell by her tired eyes that she hadn't slept as well as I had.

I took her by the hand and gently pulled her towards me. 'Get in,' I said, knowing I was pushing my luck. She stood her ground until she noticed Jack glancing our way. 'There's no room.' She smiled tightly at me.

I sat up and moved into the middle. Jack, still stretched out, placed his feet on my lap. Stephanie sat down. Our shoulders touched, but didn't stay that way for long. We sat in silence, eyes on the television, thoughts elsewhere.

I side-glanced to my right, Jack gently chuckling to himself as Tom chased Jerry with a pitch fork. I glanced to my left at Stephanie, arms crossed under her hunched shoulders. The three of us under a warm blanket. There wasn't anywhere else I'd rather be.

'Today.' I leaned in towards Stephanie. 'I'll tell Khala the truth about everything. Today.'

She slipped her arm in mine and rested her head on my shoulder.

With my family next to me, I made a promise that I would never again hurt them.

And to do that, Javid Qasim had to die.

43

Jay

Mum left to start a new life in Qatar around the same time that MI5 chewed me up and spat me out. I thought I'd be able to handle it. She thought I'd be able to handle it. We were both wrong and I think we both knew it.

I was starting to despise being on my fucking own. To despise the unwanted thoughts and unwanted memories. I tried to keep busy, keep my mind busy, but as soon as something a little out of the ordinary happened, my head was a fucking mess again.

That fucking phone call, man, it was still bugging me.

I had to stay positive. I had to keep occupied.

Idris was busy as a crime-busting bee, working all sorts of unsociable hours. I saw him occasionally; we shot a bit of pool, discovered the body of a drug baron that wanted me dead, you know, that sort of thing. I was seriously fucking lacking in the friends department. It was time to fill my life with Zafar, Tahir, Ira and Naaim. A motley bunch with varied personalities and definitely varied appearances. I created a *WhatsApp* group on my phone and added them all apart from Naaim – I'd get his number when I saw him next. I gave the group the name 'Kaleidoscope', which I thought described us perfectly.

I opened up the conversation.

> Going to pop around Naaim's later in the day.
> Let me know if you guys want to join me. 11:19

Zafar

Nice group name!!! We need a profile picture. 11:21

Tahir

Jay. You surprise me Brother. I will be there after Asar Prayers. 11:24

Zafar

Tahir, can I catch a ride? 11:24

Tahir

Yes. If you join me at the Masjid. 11:25

Zafar

Um… 11:25

Ha! I'll catch you guys there. 11:25

Ira

Will be there all day anywayz. CU L8R 11:28

It wasn't quite lunch time, but I hadn't eaten anything all morning. I popped a couple of pieces of bread in the toaster and whilst they browned I collected my cigarettes and sunglasses from my bedroom and went into the back garden for a smoke.

The Doctor had advised me not to smoke until my throat had fully healed, and then he advised me not to smoke after that. But my throat was healing nicely, and I was feeling pretty good about myself and the changes that I was trying to make. It was cause for a small celebration. What better way to celebrate than to spark up?

I walked to the far end of the garden and let my body mould nicely into the sun lounger. I looked up into the sky, just in time to see the clouds part and the sun to shine warmly onto my face. I smiled. It seemed like today the universe was on my side. I slipped on my shades, slipped a cigarette between my lips and sparked up.

From my vantage point, I could just make out a helicopter in the sky. Black with a gold roof. The kind of helicopter I'd seen on many occasions around these ways. The fuzz. It wasn't unusual to see them hovering around once in a while, keeping an eye from the sky as joyriders led the cops on the ground a merry dance through the back streets of Hounslow.

I could only get through half of the cigarette, so I put it out and disposed of it in an empty plant pot, gave the cops a cheery wave and headed into the kitchen. I buttered my toast and placed the slices on a plate and walked into the living room. Through the front window I saw a police patrol car crawl past my house. I perched myself on the arm of a two-seater, which was positioned right by the front window, and watched through the net curtain. The patrol car had parked around thirty metres away to the right of my house. A brief moment later another, this time a police van, parked behind the patrol car.

Last year, I'd got arrested. Fucking cop car pulled up right to my front door. I was handcuffed in full view of my neighbours and taken away. I knew they'd all been watching and judging behind the twitching curtains. Today it was my turn to enjoy the show and pass judgement.

My money was on Chinese Ali. He lived across the road, not far from where the cops had parked. He dealt in high quality pirate DVDs, but since the explosion of Netflix and Kodi, he'd reverted to stealing and selling car stereos. Still. A bit of overkill though, with the helicopter. Must have been a slow day at the cop-shop. I took a chunk out of the toast and waited for the action to unfold. I didn't have to wait too long as, from a distance, a grey Volkswagen Passat screamed down my road.

I carry stress in my back, and at that moment it felt as though a circus midget was catching a ride on my shoulders. I placed my half-eaten toast on the plate because I didn't want my mouth full when I started spitting fury. Every fucking profanity, in every possible fucking combination! The Passat screeched past my house at speed, with no respect to the 20mph signpost. I didn't catch sight of the driver, but I knew who it was. I'd once sat in that fucking car.

It screeched to a halt next to the patrol car. A rushed conversation through open windows.

My ears burning red as, no doubt, my name was being bandied about.

Reverse lights on, the Passat on the move again, the reverse gear not designed for the speed it was moving. The shriek of tyres. The two cop vehicles. The fucking 'copter circling over my back garden. Why don't they just send an email out to all my fucking neighbours?

Please ensure you are all at home around 11 a.m. We're going to fuck with Jay again. It's going to be a hoot!

The Passat screeched onto the pavement right across my drive, effectively blocking in my Nova. And out he stepped.

Suit, fitted. Shoes, shiny. Face, fucking smackable.

I had just about had enough of them coming in and out of my life whenever they pleased and throwing it into chaos.

Furious, *fucking furious*, I opened the door before he knocked on it.

'Get inside,' I hissed at Teddy Lawrence, as I looked over his shoulder. Yeah, the curtain twitchers were out in force. I shut the door behind him and stomped into the living room.

'The fuck, man?'

'Hang on.' He held a finger out and put his phone to his ear.

'Come into *my* house and tell *me* to hang on!'

'Hang on, Jay,' he repeated, and into the phone he said, 'I'm with Qasim. He's secure.'

I looked out of the window. The police car and van moved away. I crossed the room, through the patio into the garden. 'Jay, stay where I can see you,' Lawrence said, as he finished the call.

I ignored him and walked to the end of my garden, where I'd just enjoyed a smoke and contemplated the positive changes to my life. I looked up to the sky and the police helicopter was also moving away. I'd given it a small wave earlier, now it was getting two fingers.

'Come inside, Jay,' Lawrence said, standing at the patio.

'Fuck off, Lawrence.'

'You want to have this conversation in the garden, within earshot of your neighbours? Come inside, Jay.'

I walked back inside, past him and his stupid face, which for once did not carry any sign of smugness, and sat heavily on the sofa. He pulled out a chair from the dining table and placed it in front of me.

'What do you want?' I asked, quietly. The fight leaving me, replaced by an almighty tiredness. 'The police cars, the helicopter. All for my benefit. Why?'

Lawrence rested his elbows on his knees, clasped his hands and leant forward, his face was close to mine, toothpaste close. 'In case you made a move.'

'Made a move,' I said, more to myself. 'I haven't got any fucking moves! All this cloak and dagger bullshit, if you want something just ask.' I sat back, claiming some distance and muttered, 'And I'll tell you where to fucking go.'

Lawrence allowed me a moment to simmer down. Then said,

'At 7.02 a.m. you received a phone call.'

That helpless feeling, when I thought I'd heard Mum's trapped breath, returned. Calling her back. Getting the recorded message. *Arabic.* Jumping to conclusions. Jumping to the wrong fucking conclusion.

'Was it... him?' I said, weakly.

'What are you saying, Jay? You didn't know?'

I shook my head. I couldn't trust my voice to hold out on me.

'We traced the call to North Afghanistan, the Faryab province. A place called Maimana... Mean anything to you?'

Another shake of the head. I took my eyes off him and they landed on my phone by my side. I glared at it, as if it was the phone's fault. The first chance I got, I was going to replace it. New line, new number. One that I would not be giving out to fucking MI5.

'A unit was dispatched to a small restaurant called Intazaar. The phone used to call you was located.'

'He wasn't there, was he?' I laughed, cold and mocking. Yeah, inappropriate, but I was through giving a shit. 'The hell is wrong with you? Find him, put him down, and leave me the fuck alone.'

'Jay, you have to understand our position.'

'How about you understand my position?' I shot up and moved away without a destination in mind. I found myself standing in the middle of the living room, wondering if I clicked the heels of my Air Jordans, might I be magically transported to fucking Kansas. Lawrence stayed seated. He turned his head slightly and spoke over his shoulder. His tone measured as if to hammer home his point.

'The Teacher is the most wanted man in the world, and you, Jay, are our only link to him. He's tried to contact you once. He will do it again. You can help us find him and detain him for what he's done – to you, to this country, to innocent people all around the world.'

'No,' I said. 'No! How many times do I have to say it.'

'What did he say to you?'

'What? You think I had a conversation with him? *Yeah, Dad, I'm fine. Life is just fucking grand. How about you? Still killing innocent people, you crazy motherfucker?*'

'Tell me what he said?'

I switched the TV on and channel hopped, not giving him the satisfaction.

'Look, Jay,' he said after a moment. 'Your departure from MI5... God knows it could have been handled better. If it was up to me, you'd still be with us. I truly believed that you had more to offer us.'

I shrugged. 'I wouldn't have stayed.'

'They couldn't figure you out. They were never quite sure if you would deviate from your mission.'

'They? At least have the decency to say his name.'

'Robinson.'

John Robinson, Assistant Director of Counter Terrorism and first rate bastard!

'Your friendship with the attackers, especially with Parvez Ahmed, and correct me if I'm wrong, was genuine. You bought into what they believed in.'

'I didn't buy into anything,' I said. 'But yeah... I understood.'

'So you can understand why we had to dispatch the police units. We didn't know what he said to you, or how you would react... Jay, I need you to tell me what The Teacher said.'

'You are out of your fucking skull, do you know that? MI-fucking-5!'

'Jay.'

'Nothing! That coward didn't say shit!'

'He didn't give you a clue where he may be heading?'

All that aggression, all that emotion, that fucking phone call that I was now replaying over in my mind had drained me. I sat back down opposite Lawrence; genuine concern was etched on his face and I couldn't work out why.

'No, Lawrence,' I said, softly. 'He didn't say a word.'

'Why do you think he called you?'

'I honestly don't know. I didn't even know it was him until you turned up.'

We sat in a moment of silence. I was no longer pissed at him. My anger had been misplaced.

'Jay,' he asked. 'Are you alright?'

I didn't think he was making small talk. The question was asked in earnest, so I replied with my most honest response. A small shrug.

'If you want,' he said carefully. 'We can arrange further counselling.'

'Lawrence... Please... You can't keep dragging me back into this. I went to hell and back for you. People I cared about died. I've nothing left. All I want is for you to leave me alone and let me live my life.'

He didn't respond; he didn't have to. I was aware that they would never stop tracking me. A change of phone number would not make a difference. I could move address, change my name, leave the country, but they still had the power to find me. The only way our association would end would be when they killed my father.

44

Hounslow Police Station

Daniel jammed his hands in the pockets of his faded blue denim jeans. Not black. On his feet he had on white Reebok Classics. Not cherry Doc Martens. He wore a lightweight navy blue parka which pleased his father, who'd had enough of seeing Daniel in that cheap black bomber jacket. He said it made him look like a thug.

He was worse than a thug. An innocent girl had taken her own life and Daniel had helped tie the noose. The guilt was like nothing he'd felt before.

It was why, late that morning, he had been standing across the road from Hounslow Police Station, trying to figure out how the last twelve months went from mourning for his mother to mourning for a girl that he'd had a hand in killing.

In his desperation to belong, he'd easily been led, his views and opinions no longer his own. Skipping class and heading to Lampton Park to get drunk with Simon and Anthony. Easily becoming immersed in their passion for their country. Their anger and frustration, collectively feeding off one another. Laws bent, policies renewed to treat the minorities – *that one particular minority* – with near impunity, regardless of the hatred they held towards the West.

But it was just talk, just venting. It was never supposed to be more than that. Not for Daniel.

On the bus that day. That lad. That girl. Head covered, flaunting Islam, on the top deck of a *London* bus, as if she owned it. It acted like a trigger for Simon and Anthony, Daniel could see it as soon as they'd set eyes on them.

It was one thing to dress the part, but they had to act the part, too, if they wanted to be accepted by people like Kramer.

But they went too far. God, even that thug Rose thought they had. However Daniel looked at it, tried to justify it, a girl had died as a direct consequence of their actions. His actions.

Now Rose had suggested that they find the boy on the bus and do *whatever it takes to keep him quiet*. It excited Simon and Anthony, more so that they had been given the green light from the leader of a far-right extremism group. As though permission from a grown-up.

No more, not for Daniel. He knew that he'd never fully escape his actions, and would have to carry it around with him for the rest of his life, but he wouldn't let it define him.

Daniel took a breath, his mind clear as to what he had to do, and crossed the road towards Hounslow Police Station. He had to come clean. Whatever it took to ease the guilt of an innocent girl's death hanging over him, even it if meant providing the names of his friends.

With one hand on the door handle to the police station, Daniel felt his phone vibrate. He slipped it out of his Parka. It was a text message from Simon.

Where are you?

Instantly paranoid, he dropped his hand away from the door handle, spun on his heels and walked away.

*

'Fucking buzzing, swear, just fucking buzzing,' Anthony exclaimed, enjoying the cocktail of a well-built joint and cheap vodka. He was hopping about, animated. Simon watched him with amusement from his spot, on the bench, at the back of Lampton Park.

'Here he comes,' Simon said, looking past Anthony.

Anthony turned around and saw Daniel cross the park.

Daniel watched them watch him. He tried to gauge their mood. The text message frightened him. As if a physical pull. They might as well have been standing at the police station, pulling him away. It had the same effect.

'What is up with that jacket?' Anthony laughed.

'You can talk,' Daniel replied. 'The fuck is that?' He exhaled through his nose, relieved that were treating him normally. There was no way they could have known where he had been or what he was planning to do, but the text message had set him on edge.

'What this?' Anthony pointed at his grass-green sweater. 'This is Farah, mate. Designer, yeah. Went down to TK Maxx, didn't I?'

Daniel nodded and turned his attention to a sober-looking Simon. 'Alright, Simon?'

'Alright, Daniel,' Simon said.

Anthony handed Daniel a joint and he pulled lightly on it, trying to act as natural as possible. It felt oddly comforting to see Anthony in bright green and Simon wearing a blue Timberland tracksuit. They looked younger. Actually they looked their age. When they donned their Doc Martens, the bomber jackets, it felt like a uniform. And with uniform came a hierarchy. It had never been said but it was clear that Simon was the leader, with Anthony Second-in-Command, whilst Daniel tried to climb the ladder. But at that moment, they looked for all the world like three kids hanging around a park bench.

'Anthony, let's sober up, eh?' Simon said, as Anthony reached for the near-finished bottle of vodka.

'Only a drop left.'

'Yeah, but still. Daniel, you too, have a couple of pulls and put the joint out. Got to keep our heads clear.'

'Why?' Daniel asked.

'Kramer just texted me an address,' Simon replied. 'We've got work to do.'

'Let's do it. Let's just fucking do it today,' Anthony exclaimed.

'Do what? Whose address?' Daniel felt the tremor in his voice.

'The Paki lad, who else? We've got to shut him up,' Anthony cried.

Simon read out the text message. '16 Fern Way. Heston.'

'What else does it say?' Daniel asked, as he made a mental note.

'There's a couple of kisses at the end of it! What the fuck else do you want it to say?' Anthony laughed as though they were on their way to play knock-down-ginger.

'I mean, do we know his name? Does he live alone? We can't just turn up at his door.'

'That's all it says,' Simon said. 'You alright, Daniel?'

'Yeah, I'm fine,' Daniel replied.

'Good.' Simon squeezed Daniel's shoulder, but it didn't relax him. 'Tonight, we'll do it tonight.'

Daniel nodded confidently at Simon before smiling across at Anthony. A single thought running through his head. He had to get to Naaim first.

45
Imy

Yousuf Ejaz had walked into the restaurant aided by crutches. He made sure to catch my eye as he was shown to his table. Despite the fact that I had smashed a car door against his leg, he smiled warmly at me. It wasn't unexpected that I was being watched; it would be this way until I had received word from Pathaan and carried out the fatwa.

'*Imy.*' Shaz clicked his fingers in my face. A little Nandos Extra Hot Sauce smeared on his left cheek. 'You listening to me?'

'Sure,' I said.

'What did I just say?' Shaz narrowed his eyes.

'That you've been using the same brand shampoo all your life,' I said, trying to muster appropriate enthusiasm when my mind was elsewhere.

'For a second I thought that your mind had drifted off to cushion covers and wallpaper samples.' Shaz fidgeted in his chair. 'Shit, Imy. I don't feel comfortable here. I mean it's alright, but I miss chilling in your flat, dipping into a bucket of chicken and skinning up a fat one.'

'Those days are gone, Shaz. I have to grow up, make things work with Steph.'

'Come on, Imy, one more night,' Shaz pleaded, a childlike quality to his voice.

'Maybe,' I said. 'Let's see how I get along with Khala first. I'm going to see her as soon as we're done here.'

'You're coming clean?'

'I'm coming clean.' I nodded.

'We definitely have to hook up after and celebrate.' He smiled.

'I'm going to wash my hands.' I sighed and stood up before my irritation became clear. It wasn't his fault, but Shaz was starting to frustrate me. He may not know about every damn thing that was happening in my life, but he did know that I was trying hard to move forward with Stephanie, Jack and Khala. I could no longer be as carefree as him.

I walked through the restaurant to the wash room. I passed Yousuf. He was sat by himself, watching me over the menu. I wanted to grab him by the lapels of his kameez and scream at him to stop following me. Instead I acknowledged him with a curt nod. He returned it with a warm smile.

46

Jay

'Hey. Yo. Jay!' Idris clicked his fingers in my face. 'Are you with me?'

'Yeah... I'm with you.' I glanced around and took in my surroundings, just to remind myself where I was. My eyes landed on the Nando's menu on the table in front of me. I picked it up and glanced over it, unable to make out the words let alone decide on my order.

'God, Jay. Have you clocked a mirror lately? You ain't looking your best. Looks like you're smuggling loot under your eyes! You not sleeping?'

'Sleeping's for wimps!' I said and then couldn't stop myself yawning. 'Just got a few things on my mind, that's all.'

'Did you hear that helicopter this morning?' he asked. 'It wasn't far from yours.'

'Yeah.' I blinked at him. 'I saw it.'

Idris looked over his shoulders, ensuring that we weren't overheard. We were alone up on the first floor of Nando's, apart from the woman at the far end of the floor, wrestling a baby onto her breast. Like us, she'd probably come up for some privacy.

'Straight away I assumed the worst,' he whispered.

'What d'you mean, worst?'

'Silas,' Idris mouthed.

I nodded. With all the drama in my life, Silas had taken a back seat, in a different car, driving in the opposite direction.

'Your boys made a breakthrough yet?'

'Put it this way, they're not pouring all their resources into it. But a minimum task force has been set up. I have a man on the inside,' Idris said, tapping the side of his nose. 'I've pulled him out of the fire a few times, so he owes me.'

'Yeah.' I cleared my throat, trying to muster appropriate interest, but my mind was on Lawrence, the phone call, my pain in the arse father.

'Did you know he had CCTV?' Idris said. 'Above his front door.'

'Hmm. Who?'

'*Jay!*' Idris raised his voice. 'Smell the fucking roses. Hell is wrong with you?'

'Silas?'

'Yes! Silas! CCTV! Above his front fucking door!' He tapped the side of his head. 'Where are you, Jay?'

'Alright. I'm here. Don't get loud.' The mother, who'd eventually managed to get her baby to latch on, glared at us as the baby removed itself from her breast to watch the commotion. I smiled an apology, catching flesh. She quickly covered her modesty. Idris sat back with his arms crossed, judging me. I allowed it. Even the great Detective Idris Zaidi couldn't work out the mess in my head. After a moment of his eyes boring into me, I said, 'The footage wasn't found, was it? We wouldn't be sitting here if it did.'

'The footage was uploaded directly onto an external hard drive.'

'It wasn't there when your boys turned up?'

Idris shook his head.

'What else did your inside man say?' I asked.

'From what he tells me, they're not exactly breaking their backs trying to find the killers. Between me and you, they're secretly celebrating Silas' demise.'

'Killers? Plural? You think there's more than one?'

'You tell me, Jay. You saw. Three bodies, sliced and gutted. Had to be more than one man, possibly a rival firm.'

'Silas didn't have any rivals,' I said. In my mind's eye I saw the man on the motorbike.

'It's not him,' Idris trawled through my mind again. 'Chances are he saw what happened and quickly got the fuck out of there.'

'He was in there a while, Idris,' I said,

'Well, if it was him, I wouldn't like to be on the wrong side of him. Either way, I can't exactly mention him, it would place us at the scene, and right now, Jay, as it stands, you and me were nowhere near there. So... You know, let's just keep our heads down and I think we'll be alright.'

Idris smiled at me. I didn't have it in me to mirror it. Man, I didn't even have it in me to shrug. I tried to feel relief but it just did not come. Fucking Idris and his fucking bright side of life, bless him. Chatting about *keep our heads down* and *we'll be alright*. Every time I try to keep my head down there's somebody waiting to yank it back up by my hair and make me face things that I just want to fucking forget.

Yeah, Idris would stroll through the rest of his life without breaking stride, but the future wasn't looking so rosy for me. Silas had been the least of my problems, but not the last of my problems. He may have been the meanest motherfucker in Hounslow, but the meanest motherfucker on earth is my Father, and I swear, at that moment I wished *him* dead over Silas.

'How's your...?' Idris slid a finger across his throat. It sent cold shivers down my spine.

'Fuck's sake, Idris. Have some sensitivity!'

'Sorry, Jay.' He grinned.

'It's alright. My voice is back to full strength and I'm able to eat pretty much anything. I even had a smoke earlier. So, yeah, you know...'

'Now that you're back to your irritating best, you should start thinking about getting back to work.'

'I have been.'

'Well... That's good. Try and forget the whole sorry episode. I might swing by later, after my shift.'

'Can't today. Got plans.'

'Remind me – with your right or left hand?'

'With this hand,' I showed him my middle finger.

'So what're you up to?'

'Seeing some mates.'

'Mates…' He raised one eyebrow, a trick I was never able to master. 'What mates?'

'From… Heston Community Centre,' I said cautiously, and then felt like a twat for saying it cautiously. So I overcompensated. 'Zafar, Tahir, Ira and Naaim.'

He nodded. 'Naaim?'

'Yeah, Naaim.'

Idris smiled. Lips pursed tight. It pissed me off. If you're going to smile, smile properly. I want to see teeth. I want to see wrinkles under the eyes. Not this bullshit, patronising, *we need to talk*, tight fucking smile. I immediately went on the defensive.

'What's that mean?' I asked.

'What does what mean?'

'That stupid look on your face.'

Idris looked away from me, figuring out if he should say what he wanted to say. I could read him like a fucking comic. His eyes landed back on me, and he said, 'Jay. We need to talk.'

And there we fucking have it.

'No, Idris, actually we don't.'

'I'm worried about you. Shit, Jay, I'm really worried about you! Why'd you have to get involved?'

'I'm gonna hit the toilet. Order for me.' I stood up, I had to get away from this conversation. I knew pretty much, word for word, what he wanted to say to me. I could have written out the script and slapped it on the table in front of him. I didn't need to hear it.

I walked downstairs and headed for the men's. A Paki-looking Paki looked up from his menu and stared my way. A couple of nights ago, the paan-chewing freshy also gave me a similar look, but I was hesitant to return it. Something in his eyes made me want to keep my distance and look away. But this guy? In his ill-fitting shalwar and kameez combo, and his crutches leaning against the table, I had no problem with. I returned his look with a well-practised Hounslow look of my own and he quickly looked away.

Yeah, back to your menu, mate. I ain't in the mood for this shit.

I entered the toilet and stood at the sink, looking down into the plug hole, trying to place him. I couldn't. First Freshy at the restaurant the other night, and now this fucking guy! Both glared at me as though I'd had a threesome with both their wives.

Fuck knows! It seemed like, these days, I don't even have to try and I make enemies.

With the absence of a better option, I shrugged it off. I turned the cold water on and splashed it in my eyes. I wrenched out a couple of paper towels and dried my face. The cubicle door opened and I glanced up into the sink mirror. A man whose face I could never forget stepped out. He stopped in his tracks and locked eyes with me through the reflection. My stomach performed an Olympian somersault. He approached and stood next to me at the sink, turned on the tap. I opened my mouth to speak, but those words that I had rehearsed so many times, those words of gratitude, just wouldn't come. He turned off the tap and dried his hands. I swallowed, cleared my throat.

'You... um...' *The words, the fucking words.* He concentrated on drying his hands as though he hadn't heard me. I started again. 'You were there. You saved my...' I didn't even get the chance to finish the sentence as he dropped the paper towels into the waste basket, turned his back on me and walked out as though I wasn't even fucking there.

For a long minute I stood perfectly still, in a stupor, as I ran through what had just taken place. I tried to work out his reaction, or lack of it. The way he had looked at me before ignoring the fuck out of me. I knew that he'd recognised me.

47

Imy

I had to walk away from Javid. I couldn't stay and watch him smiling nervously, shuffling uncertainly, as he struggled to find the words to express his damn gratitude. How could I look him in the eye in the knowledge that the day was fast approaching when I would not hesitate, not for a heartbeat, to shoot him dead.

I drove slowly to Khala's. Traffic allowed me time to untangle my thoughts, compartmentalize and put things in order. At the top was my family. I had to tell Khala the truth about Stephanie and Jack.

Khala never had a bad word to say against England or the English. The majority of her friends are Muslim, and she regularly attended Ealing Islamic Centre to listen to lectures and catch up for a chat and a gossip. But there was more to her than that. She loved living in London. She was immensely proud, to a fault, of the Royal Family. You just had to walk around her home to see that. Princess Diana, The Queen and The Queen Mother, all present in one form or another, all strong powerful females. Just like my Khala.

When I moved out from her home and into the flat, understandably she wasn't happy, but she didn't let it get her down for long. She joined an evening class at Hounslow College to help her with modern technology, so determined was she to keep in touch with me by messaging, email and Facetime – as well as the daily phone calls.

Khala has a way about her, an easy charm that naturally attracted people to her. In class she effortlessly made friends that weren't Muslim, that weren't brown. She would thrive on that, dropping names nonchalantly into conversation; Theresa and Penelope, or as Khala would call them, *Teeresa and Plenpee*. They had even visited her at her home on occasion, where she'd happily hosted and fed them and then boasted proudly about it at the Islamic Centre.

That was Khala. She adapted and integrated. But, bottom line, her Muslim values meant more to her than anything else. How she would react when I told her about Stephanie and Jack, I didn't know. I prepared myself for the worst as I pulled up outside Khala's house. A black E-Class Mercedes, private plates, was parking outside. I recognised the car and realised that the worst was just about to get even worse.

I watched from my rear-view mirror as the driver's door opened. Mr Bashir stepped out. He looked apprehensive, as though he would rather be anywhere else. He walked around and open the passenger door. Out stepped Mrs Bashir. Glammed-up in a dark blue Indian suit, she adjusted the dupatta on her shoulder and made a face of unbridled disgust, probably at having to step on a pavement, on a street, in a town, which was far beneath her. Out stepped Nadeem from the back, followed by Kareem. Finally, and inevitably, with oversized dark sunglasses shading her eyes, out stepped Rukhsana.

They walked the narrow path leading up to the house, and I knew two things for certain. One: Khala would have seen them; she spent a lot of time at the kitchen window and her eyes were always peeled for activity. Two: she'd be haphazardly placing any dishes from the sink into the dishwasher, out of sight, before rushing into the living room, de-cluttering and plumping the cushions. Finally, she'd dash upstairs to put on her favourite button-up sky-blue cardigan, that I'd bought for her on Mother's Day. She said it made her feel posh because it was from Next.

I stepped out of the car and jogged the short distance to the house, cutting the Bashirs off at the door. Mrs Bashir's features screwed up as soon as she set eyes on me. No question, they were there to pick a fight, to make my Khala feel small, and I could not have that. My first instinct was to fix her with a glare of my own and tell them to piss off back to their plastic life. But I couldn't make a scene, not on Khala's doorstep. So instead I said, 'Please. Don't.'

Before they could respond, the front door swung open and my Khala appeared, looking smaller than her five-foot frame, but making up for it with a huge smile.

'Aslamalykum!' Khala's voice strained, her breath a little ragged from running around cleaning the house.

To prepare for a visit from a family that may end up becoming a relation, takes a lot of organisation; it's a huge deal. For them to turn up unannounced had really set her on edge.

'What a lovely surprise. Please come in.'

They didn't return the greeting, and I noticed the corner of Khala's lip twitch, but her smile held. I stood to one side as one by one the Bashirs entered. Khala nodded and smiled to each member as they walked past her, lovingly rubbing Rukhsana's arm. She directed them into the living room, and asked them to make themselves comfortable. I stood in the hallway, trying to calm myself.

If any one of them tried to belittle my Khala, I swear to God, the mood I was in...

Khala motioned for me to come inside, her smile momentarily absent, her eyes wide as she looked questioningly at me. There wasn't an answer that I could articulate by just a look or a gesture, so I gave her a hug and kissed her on the head, before she ushered me into the living room.

The Bashirs watched me like prey, satisfied looks on their faces at what they were about to reveal. Mr and Mrs Bashir had taken the two armchairs either side of the sofa, where Nadeem and Kareem sat, with Rukhsana between them, playing to perfection the role of the overprotective big brothers. I placed two dining chairs, so we were sitting facing the Bashirs. Khala sat on the edge of the chair, wringing her hands on her lap.

On any other occasion, Khala's first reaction when she had guests was to offer food and drink, and then to bring food and drink regardless of whether they wanted it. However, she had read the mood correctly. This was not a social call. This was far from furthering the Rishta.

'Has he told you yet?' Mrs Bashir, straight into it.

Khala looked up at me, her eyes big and tired. I gave her the smallest of smiles and resisted the urge to reach across and squeeze her hand.

'You see,' Mrs Bashir continued, 'Imran has been living a second life. A very cosy second life, it would seem. One that he has neglected to inform you of.' She crossed her legs and rested her arms on the fabric of the armchair. Her moves measured, taking a twisted joy from showing us, even in our home, that she was in control.

'I'm afraid that Imran has not been straight with you,' Mr Bashir added, his tone a little more respectful, though his words equally harsh.

With her hand flat on the arm of the armchair, Mrs Bashir lifted a finger. Mr Bashir shifted uncomfortably in the other armchair. The message was clear and direct: leave it to her. Nadeem and Kareem continued to glare at me. Rukhsana, wide eyed and innocent, played the victim.

Khala remained quiet.

'You should know, your precious *Imran* has been lying to you,' Mrs Bashir said. 'Or maybe you were aware of it... Yes, now that I think about it, it makes perfect sense. What did you think was going to happen, that Imran was going to walk into my daughter's life, into *our* lives and continue to lie to us, too? It's lucky that we found out when we did.'

'Mrs Bashir,' I spoke up. It wasn't fair to leave it to Khala to defend me when she still wasn't sure what was going on. 'I was honest with Rukhsana.'

'*When* I address you, Imran, you will know about it.' Mrs Bashir's finger was back up, straight and stern. I wanted to pull it back and hear it break. 'How dare you talk to me about honesty? You brazenly walk into our house, with bad intentions towards my daughter. All the while you are living it up with a *gandi gori*.'

Dirty white girl.

I expected my Khala's head to whip towards me, and silently tear me to shreds. But her eyes weren't on me. Instead she was focused on a small tangle of hair on the cream rug.

Mrs Bashir followed Khala's gaze and she twitched her nose in obvious disapproval. They both lifted their eyes off the tangled hair and their gaze met. I think, out of all the dirt that Mrs Bashir was dishing out on me, it was that dirt on the cream rug that really pissed Khala off.

'Do you have problem with my home?' Khala said, her delivery slower than usual.

'It's not my problem,' Mrs Bashir sneered. 'Rest assured, my family and I will never set foot in this house ever again. I would like to know what you are going to do about Imran.'

'Do you think you are better than me?' Khala reached across and took my hand. 'That your home is better than mine.'

'I don't think you understand what I am trying to say. Would it be easier if I speak in Urdu?' Mrs Bashir said, condescendingly.

'I understand everything, Mrs Bashir.'

'Imran has –'

'I haven't finished talking. Do not dare int'rupt me in my home. Now I speak and you listen,' Khala snapped. It was a side to her that I had never seen before. 'My Imran has more 'tegrity than your whole family. You are not good enough for him, your daughter is not good enough for him. Whatever he has done, I will deal with. It is not your business. Who you think you are making faces in my home? Why did you not call before you came, rude person!'

'Khala,' I said.

'Wait, Imran. I not finished. This is my home. In fact...' Khala got to her feet and strode towards Mrs Bashir. 'Up,' Khala said, motioning with her finger. 'Up!'

'I beg your pardon,' Mrs Bashir said. Mr Bashir was already on his feet.

'What is the meaning of this?' he said, nervously.

'You shuttup!' Khala said and grabbed Mrs Bashir from under her arm and lifted her to her feet.

Nadeem shot up from the sofa. He was older and bigger than Kareem, who had sensibly stayed seated. He stepped towards Khala in an ill-advised defence of his mother. I was in his face before he had the chance to intervene.

'Back off,' I said, quietly. He stared at me, his teeth jutting through his jaw, his hands balled. A part of me, *that part of me*, wanted him to make a move. He must have seen it in my eyes. He backed off.

Khala took the armchair that Mrs Bashir had just been evicted from.

'This is my chair,' she said. 'Now, is there anything else you want to say about my Imran?'

'I have never been so insulted in my life,' Mrs Bashir huffed. 'I don't want anything to do with your family.'

'Good,' Khala said. 'Get out of my home.'

*

Led by Mrs Bashir, and without further word, they hurried out, awkwardly bumping into each other in the narrow hallway in an attempt to avoid another lashing from Khala. Mr Bashir seemed apologetic, but didn't have the courage to put it into words. I shut the door behind them and took a breath. It was my turn to face my Khala. The mood she was in, I didn't think she'd hold back.

I entered the living room.

I noticed the tangled ball of hair had been removed. Khala was sitting in her armchair. I pulled forward the dining chair and sat closer to her.

'Who is she?'

'Khala.' I wanted to explain in my own way.

'I ask you question.'

'Stephanie.'

'Are you married?'

'No, Khala.'

'Is she pregnant?'

'No, Khala.' I cleared my throat. 'But she does have a son. His name is Jack.'

'*Astaghfirulah!*' She closed her eyes and took a breath, before asking, 'Is he your son?'

Jack's goofy face popped into my head. Yes, he was my son.

'No, Khala. He's not my son, but we are very close. You'd like him, he's a great kid.'

'How old is... Jack?'

'He's five.'

'Where is father?'

'He's not a part of their lives anymore.'

'Tell me about this girl.'

'Khala,' I couldn't help it, my face lit up. 'Stephanie is everything I want from a partner. Intelligent. Caring. Strong. She's an amazing mother... Like you, Khala. She's just like you,' I said, realising how true that was.

She stayed quiet for a minute, but, not knowing if I had broken her heart, it felt longer.

When she eventually spoke, it was Khala who broke my heart.

'I am disappointed in you, Imran.'

'I know.' My head and my heart dropped.

'You don't know anything. I raised you better than this. You made a stupid choice.'

'Khala, I understand your position. Believe me, the last thing I ever wanted was to disappoint you... But I cannot walk away from them.'

'*Understand my position?* You silly boy. That is why I am disappointed? You think that I am so small-minded that I care about what my friends at the Islamic Centre will say?'

'I didn't want to embarrass you.'

'You know Mrs Hashmi, who runs the pharmacy on Vicarage Farm Road? Her son, Akthar... He is a gay.'

'Okay. I... I didn't know that.'

'But she still very proud of him. Akhtar's boyfriend is Muslim!'

I laughed. She tried to suppress it, but a smile escaped her.

'And you know Mrs Bhatt? She is teacher at Hounslow College.'

'Yes, a lecturer. What about her?'

'She married forty years, anniversary party last week. I went. I tell you something.'

'Okay. Tell me.'

'They both have lots of boyfriend and girlfriend.'

'*Really?* They're swingers?'

'Yes. They are both singers,' she said, with a head wobble. 'Mr Prizada was in jail last year, and not on business in Spain... Mrs Quereshi likes to have a glass of wine every night. Mrs Akeel from the corner shop sells holiday cigarettes.'

'Duty free cigarettes?' I made a mental note of that, it'd save Shaz a few quid.

'So, Imran, don't you ever think that you can embarrass me. I have been through too much and seen too much to worry what our comm'nuty are saying... But, I am very disappointed in you because you did not come to me.'

'I'm so sorry, Khala... I should have realised. I should have said.'

'I wasted so much time with all the Rishtay, met so many families, made so much food. And I tell you, Imran, not one of those girls were good enough for you.'

'Stephanie is,'

'Girlfriend-boyfriend no good. You should get married soon.'

I smiled and kneeled down in front of her. 'I just need your blessing, Khala.'

She placed her hand on top of my head and gave me the blessing that I craved.

'*Astaghfirulah.*' She said. 'Such a hard name to say. Stef'nie.'

'You'll get used it, Khala.'

'Get me the house phone. I have to tell *Teeresa and Plenpee.*'

48

Jay

Five minutes into dropping Idris home from Nando's and not a word passed between us. Silence had almost always sat comfortably with us, but this time, in the confines of my Nova, it felt suffocating. I heard a low growl. It could've been my hungry belly given that I'd rushed out of Nando's without eating, with Idris hot on my heels. My erratic actions only serving to prove his point, that I needed a good fucking talking to.

I could feel his side-glances, his search for an opening. Ignoring him I glanced in the rear-view mirror. The low growl was a few cars behind and gaining quickly. I followed its movement as it got closer, black leathers, black gloves and a black helmet, only slowing and matching my speed as it reached my side. I could've reached out of my window and touched his knee. I checked out his bike, dull black, with red around the rims. I'd seen it before. His head turned towards me, I caught a glimpse of myself in the tinted visor of his helmet before he gunned the engine and sped away.

I was pretty certain it was the same bike that I saw outside Silas' house the night he'd got his arse handed to him on a plate. Did I need to add him to the long list of people who wanted a piece of me? Was it even the same guy? Fuck, man, what do I know about motorbikes, there's probably a thousand of that model. But that glance as he passed me…

I opened my mouth to mention it to Idris and then closed it again. Silas was dead. According to Idris, the cops had concluded it was gang-related. Mentioning it would only muddy the already murky waters.

'What?' Idris said, still itching for an in. 'What were you going to say?'

'Nothing,' I said.

'What's happening with you, Jay?' He sighed. 'Do you not see it?'

Hold on to your hats. Here comes Idris.

'See what?' I said, bored already and approaching frustration.

'You've… you've…'

'I've… I've… Get on with it, Idris.'

'I'm going to be frank, Jay,' he said, serious tone.

'Okay,' I said, bouncing from one radio station to another. 'Who shall I be?'

'You can be quiet, is who you can be.' Idris killed the radio.

'Go on then,' I sighed, wishing that I had an ejector button so that I could send him flying, maybe get stuck in a tree. I laughed to myself.

'You're losing it, Jay. Ever since your Mum left, not even slowly, you've quickly lost the plot.'

I nodded. He was right, I'll give him that. I'd made some bad decisions.

'I mean, apart from all this business with Silas, I don't even know half the shit you're up to.'

I side-glanced at him and gave him something that I'd been working on. The one shoulder shrug.

'For instance, that crew from Sutton Mosque that you were hanging out with last year. You must have known at the time that their thinking was…'

'Was what?'

'Not ours.'

'Yeah,' I said. 'I did.'

'And look at them now. What's his name? The convert? Dead. *Shot dead.* That girl. Dead. *Shot dead!*'

229

He didn't mention my friend Parvez. I know he wanted to and maybe I needed to hear it.

'And Parvez,' I said, quietly.

Idris nodded. 'Yeah, and Parvez... Do you realise how fucked up that is? God, he grew up with us! From what I remember he was on you like a shadow when we were kids.'

Unable to trust my voice. I nodded.

'It shows, right, that anybody can be indoctrinated,' Idris said.

'I wasn't.'

'You could have been, Jay.'

'I wasn't.'

'You just as easily could have been caught up in that attack on Oxford Street.'

I stayed quiet as he judged me from up on his perch. It was a long time due and I know it was coming from a good place, but he was doing my head in. Idris didn't know the full story and it was something that he would never know, and by bringing it up he was trying to entice it out of me. *No fucking chance.*

The traffic opened up, and I put my foot down, wanting to drop him home and away from me as quickly as possible. Without indicating I slipped out of my lane and attempted to pass the car in front of me, but this wasn't my Beemer, and the pick-up wasn't the same. My Nova struggled and from the other side, high beams, a heavy hand on the horn, a Transit van head on and closing in fast. I jumped on the brake and retreated back into my lane as the horn echoed past.

'*Goddammit, Jay,*' Idris cried.

After the spell of awkward silence that one experiences after a dumb driving move, what he said next wound me the fuck up. 'And now this. The Heston Hall crew! Naaim! Have you not learnt your lesson, Jay?'

I gripped the steering wheel tightly with both hands and swung hard to the left. The car bumped and climbed the kerb and I put my foot down on the brake. I wrenched the

230

handbrake up, killed the engine and released my seatbelt, pulling it away from my body as though it was suffocating me, the metal buckle hitting my window with a satisfying clang.

Idris watched me silently as if each move served to validate his point. I reached across and dropped down his visor.

'Look!' I snapped at him. 'Go on, look in the mirror.'

'Jay.'

'Just look in the fucking mirror.'

'Alright,' he sighed. His eyes turned to the small mirror on the visor.

'Tell me what you see.'

'I get what you're trying to do, Jay. But it's not the same.'

'Tell me.'

'I'm not doing this.' He lifted the visor back into position. 'This is not about me.'

'You are doing this.' I flipped the visor back down. 'And this *is* about you.'

Idris looked at me. 'Bit dramatic all this.' Then he turned to the mirror. 'What? What do you want me to say?'

'Do you see a terrorist looking back at you?'

Idris laughed. It was forced. 'Hell no!'

'You're brown. You're Muslim. You live in Hounslow, a place full of Muslims. You're sitting in a car with another Muslim, one who was linked to a group who carried out a gun attack in the heart of London. By association alone, *you* are linked to those terrorists.'

'This is stupid.'

'Shut up. I ain't done yet. What? You think that because you're a copper, because you like the odd pint down the pub with your white colleagues, d'you think that makes you any less of a Muslim?'

Idris lifted the visor back into position. I didn't flip it back down but I wasn't finished.

'When you look in the mirror, you may see one thing, but believe me the world sees another. Deal with it Idris,

231

you're a *Paki*. The same as me, the same as Zafar, Tahir, Ira and Naaim. Just because they look a little different, think a little different, you decide to vilify them. Since when do you get to tell me that I shouldn't be hanging out with them?'

'I didn't say that.'

'Fuck you! You were thinking it,' I said. He didn't say anything. He was out.

Idris is my closest friend, I love him like a brother, but I was beyond disappointed in him. More so I was disappointed in myself. What he had said out loud was precisely what had been going through my mind. Every time they tried to get close to me, invite me out, I backed away. My involvement last year with Ghurfat-al Mudarris had rewired my brain, made me look twice, think twice about my own people. It disgusted me. I only started to attend Heston Hall because I desperately wanted to believe that there were moderate Muslims like me, but I was surrounded by hijabs, and shalwar and kameez, and skull caps, and people tagging *Mashallah* and *Inshallah* at the end of every sentence. It put me on edge. I wasn't sure what their motive was. I became the product of the media, looking for danger where danger did not exist. One harrowing experience and I was so quick to judge.

I now knew better and if they needed me then I'd be there for them.

*

It was two days after Naaim's mother had passed, and only one day since the funeral, but looking around his living room, it seemed as though Naaim had been without a responsible adult for some time. The curtains were still drawn shut and I was itching to pull them apart so the couple of hours left of daylight would seep in and maybe highlight the fantastic mess that the room was in. It was obvious where Naaim had spent the night, the blanket and pillow scrunched up on the sofa. Next to a half eaten banana, a black sock hung precariously

232

off the coffee table, looking to be reunited with its partner so they could make the journey to the wash basket. The beige carpet had a clear visible damp patch, the shape of France. It was faded brown, spilt hot chocolate I decided. There was a distinct smell of sweat and feet and something I couldn't put my finger on. Something fried. I stood just within his living room looking for the cleanest place to sit.

Ira had let me into the house, before she disappeared upstairs. I could hear her and Naaim talking in hushed voices, so I thought about switching the television on so it didn't feel like I was eavesdropping. I spotted the remote control, it was sitting in a bucket of chicken wing carcasses, which solved the mystery of the fried smell. I decided not to touch the remote. Instead I cleared my throat loudly and then felt overly conscious that I was trying to summon them down. To my relief the doorbell buzzed. I waited for either Ira, who seemed to have made herself at home, or Naaim, to come down and answer. They continued to converse in hushed tones. Great! I was already feeling like a spare part, now I had a dilemma to face too. Do I answer the door? It's not my house. It's not my door! What if it's Naaim's father, who he can't stand? I don't want that shit on me, I wouldn't even like to think about how that would play out.

It rang again, around thirty seconds after the first. A short sharp burst, as if the visitor didn't want to appear rude. I didn't think his father, from what I had heard, would be so polite, so I discounted him. It was probably Tahir or Zafar. I checked the time on my phone. It was approaching seven. Asar prayer would have finished by now, and Tahir did say he would come here afterwards.

I walked into the hallway and stood at the bottom of the stairs. I looked up, the hushed tones had now turned into hushed bickering. I looked at the front door, there was no glass pane or peep hole to determine who was on the other side.

I was over-thinking this. I opened the door.

It wasn't Tahir or Zafar. It wasn't Naaim's father. It wasn't what I was expecting.

233

He was white. I don't know why that would be strange, but it just was. He looked to be around Naaim's age, maybe a touch younger. His head shaved close, hands tucked tightly into his jean pockets and he was wearing a lightweight blue parka, zipped up to his chin.

We looked at each other for a moment before his eyes flitted to the door number and back to me as if he wasn't sure if he was in the right place.

'What's up, mate?' I smiled, only because I think he needed to see one.

'Is… Is…?'

Whilst I waited for him to get the words out, I looked over his shoulder to see who he was with. Maybe a parent had dropped him off at the wrong place. He noticed my gaze and whipped his head around pretty sharpish to see what I was looking at.

'You alright?' I asked him. He faced back to me, eyes wide with fright. 'Sure you're in the right place, mate?' His eyes glanced back at the door number and then he gave a quick nod of the head. 'Are you here to see Naaim?'

'Yes,' he said.

'You better come in then.'

I stepped out of the way and let him in. I guided him to the living room and told him to make himself comfortable. I left him there and walked into the hallway just as Ira and, behind her Naaim, reached the bottom of the stairs.

'Naaim, how are you?' I asked, shaking his hand. He was still wearing the same clothes that he wore to the funeral, heavily creased as if he had slept in them.

'Jay,' Naaim said. 'Thanks for coming.'

'It's nothing. The others will be here soon.'

'Nice one, Jay. It means a lot to him,' Ira said. 'It's important to have people around.'

'Speaking of which, I let somebody in. He's waiting in the living room.'

Naaim glanced at Ira. 'Who is it, Jay?' Ira asked me. 'It's not…'

'No. Just one of his school friends, I think, wanting to pay his respects. I don't think he was at the funeral yesterday.'

Rather than go in and greet the visitor, Naaim looked puzzled as though he didn't have anybody apart from us who cared enough to visit.

'Could it be somebody from Heston Hall?' Ira asked.

'I don't think so,' I replied. *He definitely ain't from Heston Hall.* 'Where's your toilet?'

'Upstairs, first door on your right,' Ira replied.

'Oh, okay.' I left them standing in the hallway, exchanging glances that I could not interpret, and as I got to the top of the stairs, they started talking in hushed tones again.

I don't know what was going on. They seemed closer than ever as though they were wallowing in each other's misery. I locked the toilet door behind me and pulled down the lid and sat on the pot. I didn't actually have the need to use the toilet, I just wanted to find out where Zafar and Tahir were. It would have been rude to pull out my phone downstairs, given the situation. I dropped them a text and hoped that they'd arrive soon. In no hurry to go back downstairs, I gave myself a moment or two, just to gather my thoughts and figure out what I could bring to the table.

I was trying to be a friend to Naaim. I knew what he would be going through, that feeling of loss was something that I had experienced when mum left me for a life in Qatar. Obviously it isn't the same thing; my mum was stepping into a new life whilst his mother was stepping into the afterlife. He was going to struggle. I struggled, and I'm older and a little more experienced, but that didn't stop me from going off the rails and being downright self-destructive. So, yeah, I'd be around, pop in from time to time, keep him from *losing the plot*, as Idris so poetically put it. Once things settled down, I'd take him down to the Treaty Centre and introduce him to Wilko. If he's going to run a house, he should learn to do it on the cheap!

Our friendship won't be one of going out for a drink, or trying our luck on the catwalk of Hounslow High Street. It would be more of a mentor role... No, that sounds shit! More like a big brother role... Ha! That sounds shit, too. All I knew was, if he'd let me, I'd be there for him.

I'd have to keep my eye on Ira, too. The last thing Naaim needed was her *blaming the world* attitude in his ear.

My phone buzzed. It was Zafar. He and Tahir were outside looking for a parking spot. I stood up and redundantly pressed the flush, washed my hands and made my way downstairs.

I could hear heavy breathing and muffled crying from the living room. I guessed Naaim and the boy I'd let in must have been pretty tight to draw that kind of reaction. I stood at the bottom of the stairs and debated whether to walk back into the room. I pictured them embracing, Naaim crying into his shoulder, and I didn't want to interrupt that, but the cries were high-pitched, remorseful, and it didn't sound like they were coming from Naaim. It would have been weird for one of them to walk out and see me eavesdropping, so I tentatively stood at the door and looked in.

Naaim was slumped down on the sofa, his breath coming in heavy and hard. Next to him, perched on the edge of the sofa, was Ira, she had an altogether different look on her face. One that I hadn't seen before. I was used to seeing the laser-beam eyes, the snarl and the angst. This expression looked very much like *victory*. The corner of her lips curled up very slightly, her eyes alive and focused on the floor. I took a step into the room and glanced around the door to see what her gaze was fixed on.

The boy. The one I'd let in. On the floor. Curled up in a ball. Body racking as he sobbed and dribbled blood onto the beige carpet.

'The fuck, Ira?' I screamed as I quickly got down on my knees and helped him up into a sitting position. 'Shit, you alright, mate... C'mon, on your feet, yeah... Ira, water.' She stayed rooted. I looked over at Naaim, in his hand he held tightly a Rubik's Cube, the yellow side complete and coated in blood. 'The fuck happened, Ira?!' I didn't get an answer. 'Naaim?' Nothing. Only the sound of sniffling echoed around the room. 'Let's get you out of here, mate.' I grabbed him by the arm and got him to his feet. On the floor was his mobile phone. I picked it up and walked him out of the living room. In between whimpering he kept repeating '*I'm sorry, I'm so sorry*,' over and over again, as though it had been him that had provoked the Rubik's Cube attack.

I took him out and sat him down on the stoop. 'Stay here, I'll get you a glass of water.' I ran back into the house, glancing into the living room as I passed it; Naaim's head resting on Ira's shoulder. I ran into the kitchen and searched the cabinets for a clean glass and filled it with water. I tore a few sheets of tissue from the kitchen roll and then, remembering the tears and the snot, not to mention the deep bloody gash across his upper lip, I picked up the whole roll and ran back outside.

He was gone.

Zafar and Tahir were walking down the path towards me, smiling and waving. I looked past them just as a H91 bus was leaving the bus stop. The boy was sat at the back. The side of his head was resting on the near-side window. We watched each other until the bus was out of sight.

It wouldn't be the last that I'd see of him. I still had his phone.

49

Imy

Stephanie opened the front door as I stepped out of the car. It's not like her, the impatience, the having to know. It was clear how much this meant to her. *How did Khala react? Did I even tell her*? Uncertainty was etched on her face, but only briefly as I answered it with a smile.

'*Really?*' she said, her bare feet meeting me halfway up the drive.

'She can't wait to meet you,' I said, and then she was on me, arms around me. 'She said that we should get married.' Her fingers gripped my shirt as her hold tightened, and I felt like the biggest fool for not being able to bring this joy so much earlier.

'Listen, Steph, Shaz wanted to meet tonight at the flat,' I said, feeling like a fool. 'But I can stay. We've a lot to talk about.'

'You've told Khala,' she said, stepping back into me, hands around my waist. I nodded into her eyes. 'It's all I need to know, Imy. Go, enjoy yourself. Besides,' she smiled, 'we've got you for the rest of our lives.'

I think, for the first time, she truly believed that. Once I get the message from Pathaan and fulfil my duty, I'll start to believe it too.

*

Like so many times before, and probably for the last time ever, Shaz and I were back in the flat. With our feet up on the coffee table, in front of us lay different forms of fried chicken dripping in Tabasco and garlic sauce, alongside two open bottles of San Miguel and some fancy tequila that Shaz had bought over from Mexico a few years back and was saving for a special occasion. And, of course, a slow-burning joint in Shaz's hand, with the promise of more judging by the potent smell of Skunk coming from his jacket pocket.

The only problem was that I just wasn't in the mood. Telling Khala was a huge step, but there was a long way to go.

'When's your curfew?' Shaz asked.

I rolled my eyes, knowing Shaz, he was going to run with the *ball and chain* joke all night.

'I'm staying the night here,' I shrugged. 'I bought a change of clothes for work tomorrow. Probably get home after that.'

'Hang on. Wait a *fucking* minute.' His tone incredulous. 'Not only did Steph give you permission to –'

'She didn't give me permission, Shaz,' I said.

'Not only did Steph give you *permission*,' Shaz said, sticking by his guns. 'She also said you can disappear for the whole night?'

'Yes,' I said, knowing that it would stop him trying to wind me up. I didn't tell him that Stephanie didn't want me stumbling back late and waking Jack up. 'That's not all. I told Khala.'

'No way! Never thought you'd go through with it. All good?'

'All good,' I said.

'Finally manned up.' He clinked my untouched glass.

'Cheers,' I picked it up and threw it back, savouring the burn, hoping that it might jolt me out of my mood.

Shaz filled the air with chatter as he told me how much he was going to embarrass me when he gave the best man's speech at my wedding. I smiled and nodded but I just wasn't there. I took a long pull and held it in, slouching down into the sofa and closing my eyes, letting the smoke swim slowly inside me. I mentally pictured delivering

Javid a quick painless death, and wondered if, in those last moments, would he see in my eyes that my hand was being forced.

'Cute,' Shaz declared, knocking me out of my thoughts. I opened my eyes. The television was set to Sky News and a photo of a pretty young Asian woman was on screen. She had an easy smile, as though her smile would carry her comfortably through life. A second photo appeared beside the first, it showed another woman in a hospital bed. One eye barely open, the other forced closed, a frown that looked unnatural. Her face carrying the fresh scars of a horrific facial injury. '*Fuck!* Is that…?'

'It's the same girl,' I said, sitting up.

A reporter was standing outside University Hospital Lewisham. I turned up the volume.

'What should have been a memorable day for Fiza Akram, as she set out to celebrate her 18th birthday, quickly turned into an unimaginable horror. Driving in her car, a present from her parents to commemorate the milestone, she came to a stop at the traffic lights. A moped carrying two men pulled up next to her and one of the men threw a liquid substance, assumed to be acid, through her open car window. Akram suffered severe burns to the body and neck, but none quite as evident as that on the face of this aspiring young model. Early reports suggest that she may be blinded in her right eye. The attackers have not yet been identified.'

The reporter placed a finger in his ear, listening to whatever was being said to him through his ear piece. He nodded gravely as he took in the information.

'Change the channel. It's like groundhog day,' Shaz said, pouring two neat tequila shots.

'Let it be for a minute.'

The reporter composed himself and continued. 'This is yet to be confirmed, but reports are coming in of two further acid attacks. A young couple sitting on a bench in Greenwich Park, and a separate attack through a car window on the junction of Arlow Street. The victim, an as-yet unidentified elderly man, is believed to have suffered a fatal heart attack as he waited at the scene for medics to arrive. Both locations are within a two-mile radius of the earlier attack on Fiza Akram, and witnesses are believed to have seen a moped carrying two men. There is no indica –'

'Shaz,' I yelled, as he changed the channel. 'Leave it on!'

'The fuck, Imy?' he groaned. 'This is depressing the hell out of me.'

'*Please*… Just leave it on.'

Shaz hesitated for a moment before changing it back to the news. 'This was supposed to be a celebration,' he muttered.

'It is,' I said. 'It will be. Let me just watch this for a moment.'

'Supposed to be the end of an era,' Shaz huffed.

I ignored him. If I'm honest it frustrated me that he could so easily brush off an attack on our people. I had to watch it, I had to let it wash over me. It was exactly attacks like this that could turn a good man into one filled with hatred, fuelling fantasies of revenge. It was a circle so vicious that the word *vicious* seemed too soft to describe it.

I sat watching in silence, allowing it easily to stress me out. I scratched the back of my head, then I felt something under my eye, so I scratched there. Then under my chin.

'Don't let it get to you, man,' Shaz said, as he lined a Rizla with weed.

With effort I forced my hands onto my lap. Even then my hands were balled up into fists. Shaz's presence and his nonchalant throwaway comments made me uneasy.

'It's the world we live in,' Shaz continued. He licked the sheet and wrapped a tight joint and waved it in front of my face. 'This'll make everything better… You seen my lighter?' He stood up and patted the pockets of his jeans before moving across the room to the front door where his jacket was hanging on the handle, and rooted through the pockets.

The news cut to the commercials. I sat back and focused on the clock above the television. The second hand had just started its descent, a minute away from eight o'clock. I watched it glide smoothly, and tried to relax my breathing. I wanted to shift myself back into the night. Smoke that joint, drink that drink. But I was so angry, more so with my friend than the attacks that had taken place. I couldn't understand how a Muslim, no matter how unobservant, could have such an indifferent attitude.

The second hand quickly reached the halfway mark, my anger melting into disappointment. Trying to convince myself that we're not all wired the same way. That Shaz hadn't been touched by tragedy as I had. I could see him from the corner of my eye, victoriously holding up his lighter. I stayed focused on the clock.

We'd sat here, in this very spot, on countless occasions, talking for hours about the unimportant. Laughing so loudly that tears would often fill my eyes as my neighbours pounded the wall. It was a simple joy that at one point in my life I had never dared to dream I would experience.

The second hand had completed its journey. I took one last deep breath, poured myself a generous shot of tequila and necked it quickly.

'She was so beautiful,' Shaz said, as the commercials finished and the victim's face flashed back on the screen. He was still standing by the front door, examining the joint, straightening out the creases.

'She still is.'

'With respect,' Shaz said, tearing the top of the joint. 'She ain't. Her face is fucked up, her life is ruined... You know who's to blame for this? Fucking... What's that group called? Mudarris something. And the guy who runs it. The Teacher.'

'Shaz... '

'I'm so fucking bored of switching on the TV and seeing yet another attack. Paris, Brussels, Manchester, *fucking* London. It was only a matter of time before some equally fucked up white boys took revenge.'

'You don't know what you're saying.'

'And I suppose you do,' Shaz said, lighting up the joint.

'I do,' I said, quietly.

242

'You don't know squat, Imy. Take my advice, keep your head down and get on with it. It's not your war.'

'They're my people.'

'Yeah, well…' he said, and I wish to God he had left it at that. Through a cloud of smoke, I heard him say, 'Easy to say from the comfort of your sofa. Tell me, Imy, if they really are your people, what the fuck are you going to do about it?'

I was on my feet and in his face. He took a step back, catching his heel against the front door. He smiled nervously, unsure, a smile new to me. I should have mirrored it, smiled back and let it go. But his words, still raw – *What the fuck you going to do about it?*

After so many years, that rage that I had buried inside, finally spilled out. I grabbed Shaz by his throat so hard his head whipped back and connected against the door.

'I'll *kill* them, you hear me? I'll kill every last one of them,' I screamed in his face. 'They touched my mother. They murdered my father. *Do you hear me?* I'll find them, I'll rape them, I'll rip them apart limb by limb and then I'll burn them alive. *That's* what I'm going to do about it.'

I felt his leg trembling against mine. The cloud of smoke dissipated, his eyes were wide, terrified. I couldn't work out how we had got there. I couldn't remember what I had just said or done. I moved my hand away from his throat and cupped his face gently. I placed my forehead gently against his.

'I'm sorry,' I said. It was never going to be enough. That small word, always on the tip of my tongue, knowing that I would forever be saying sorry to those who I have loved.

I took a step back as tears formed but did not escape from his eyes. I could see the bruising already appearing around his neck. I took my place on the sofa, certain he would never again join me. My face in my hands as I rubbed the temples with my fingertips. I could hear the rustling of Shaz picking up his jacket. I didn't have it in me to meet his eyes. I only removed my hands from my face when I heard the front door open and close again.

I stared at the door for a long time, unable to believe what had just taken place. Unable to believe that I had gripped the neck of my friend with such force that his head had whipped back so hard that it had left a smear of blood on the door.

50

Jay

I had to go and open the door! I thought he was a friend
from school, there to pay his respects. The fuck was I
supposed to know that I was letting this boy walk into
hostile territory. I didn't know their relationship, but it
was obvious that he and Naaim shared some dark history.
Whatever he had said or done to Naaim would have had to
be pretty extreme to warrant a reaction like that.

Tahir and Zafar, oblivious to what had taken place, were
in high spirits, and they greeted me warmly as they walked
into the house.

'Salaam, Brother.' Tahir smiled. 'How are you? How's
Naaim?'

I made a face, it didn't go noticed.

'What?' Zafar asked. 'What now?'

I opened my mouth to speak, not knowing how to
explain what had just taken place, when a smiling, smug
Ira walked into the hallway.

'Tahir, Zafar,' she said, louder than necessary, probably
to inform Naaim that it was friends who had arrived, rather
than somebody else to smack. 'Great timing. I was just
about to put the kettle on. Oh, and Tahir, I've got those
sturdier biscuits for you.' She laughed.

'Everything alright, Sister?' Tahir asked.

'Yeah, what happened, Ira?' Zafar asked.

'Nothing happened,' she replied. I caught her eye. She
lowered her voice. 'Naaim had an unwelcome visitor.

Things got a little heated. He's gone now.' She shrugged.
How dare she use a shrug so inappropriately?

'A little heated, how?' Zafar said.

And then it came to me. It took a moment, but, fuck, did it come to me.

'Layla?' I whispered.

'Layla!' Zafar exclaimed, making my whisper redundant.

'Keep your voice down, Zafar.' Ira shot him a look. 'Nobody mentions this, okay.'

'Was he on that bus?' I asked.

'Not now, Jay.' Ira held up a hand.

'Was who on the bus?' Zafar said, clearly lost and better off staying that way.

'*Ira.*' I locked eyes with her. 'Was *he* on that bus?'

'Yeah,' she whispered. 'He's the one who filmed it and posted it all over the fucking internet. He's lucky he only got a smack in the face.'

Tahir took a step back, as though trying to remove himself from this situation. He was older than us. A family man. A religious man. He had set up the community centre as a way of separating us from violence and violent thoughts. Confident that dialogue would resolve all. I could now see that confidence waning.

'You and I are going to have words later,' Zafar said to Ira.

'Alright, later, yeah. Just keep your mouth shut for the time being. His mother's just died! Come on, get inside. He'll be wondering what we're doing in the hallway all this time. I'll put the kettle on. And remember, not a word.'

Ira ushered us into the living room as she headed for the kitchen. Naaim was still sat on the sofa, the Rubik's Cube remained tightly in his hand, the remote control in the other. Zafar awkwardly patted him on the shoulder as a way of greeting, whereas Tahir completely avoided eye contact, mumbling *Salaam* under his breath and finding somewhere to sit.

Naaim's eyes were raw red, but it wasn't from crying. He looked at each of us, as if daring us to ask him why he had a blood-splattered kid's toy in his hand. I sat down and looked towards the television. Naaim switched it on.

That day, the television was not going to provide any solace.

Quietly we watched the news report of the attacks that had taken place that evening. But they weren't the type of attack that normally made the news, and it wasn't the type of coverage that we were used to.

'McVitie's Chocolate Digestives,' Ira announced, as she walked in balancing a tray loaded with tea and biscuits. 'Especially for you, Tahir. You'll have no problems dunking these bis… Has this just happened?' Her attention was on the news.

'Yeah,' I said. 'This evening.'

'Where?' She sat down next to Naaim and crossed her arms, as though to stop herself from exploding.

'A couple of places. A few. Around Greenwich,' Zafar said.

'Which is it, Zafar? A couple, or a few?' Ira said, sharply.

'Three locations, Sister,' Tahir said. 'Three separate acid attacks.'

We continued to watch in silence. I've seen too much, been through too much, to not know exactly how the whole fucking thing was going to play out in the media. The coverage was sketchy, pertinent details were yet to be established, *apparently*. The report moved in a predictable loop, starting with an image of Fiza Akram, a young Asian girl who'd been scarred beyond recognition. A young couple in Greenwich park, no names, no photos, and an old man who suffered from a fatal heart attack as he waited for an ambulance. Little was mentioned about the attackers.

'Can you believe this shit?' Ira was always going to be the first to react. 'I'll tell you what, yeah. How about I report! How about I'll tell you who the attackers were. They were *white*. I'll tell you who the victims were; they were *Muslim*. I'll tell you what just happened. A terrorist attack is what just *fucking* happened!'

247

'Sister,' Tahir said. 'We can't assume anything.'

'Do not, Tahir,' Ira spat and held out a finger.

Tahir bristled at being abruptly spoken to by somebody who was young enough to be his daughter. He was from a generation where respect towards elders is expected. He turned his attention back to the news, the glare from the television highlighting his flushed face.

'You wanna walk around with your eyes closed, be my guest, yeah. But not me. I see everything.' Ira was far from finished, on her feet now, gesturing at the television. 'If this happened the other way round, the journalists would be clamouring over each other, foaming at the mouth, wanting to be the first to say it was yet again Muslims responsible, that it was yet again another terrorist attack. Fucking media fucking whores. Are they going to tell us what colour these attackers were? Are you going to tell us what religion they were? Are they going to say it was a *terrorist attack?!*'

Every contrived word from the reporter was being drowned out by every truth flying from Ira's mouth. She was furious. It was understandable and uncontrollable. Tahir never had a chance of calming her down. I didn't either.

'Retaliation,' I said, quietly. 'That's how it'll be portrayed. Retaliation. Revenge attack. Insinuation clear. We started it. It's the world we live in. There'll be more attacks. It's inevitable. From them. From us. I don't know. But there'll be more.'

'At least we'll have a little respite from those illiterate keyboard warriors,' Zafar remarked. 'The sideways glances at the supermarket, muttering snide remarks under their breath. Right? Now they'll have to take a good look at themselves. This shows, it illustrates *perfectly*, that the actions of a few idiots does not represent a race or a religion.'

Zafar was right. Then he said something so wrong. 'I'm kinda glad it happened this way.'

248

'Are you joking, Zafar?' Ira said. She had reclaimed her place next to Naaim on the sofa after animatedly attacking the TV, her outburst over – another on its way.

'No,' Zafar said. 'Shit, Ira. Hear me out; you've had your say.'

'Go on then,' Ira crossed her arms. 'We're listening.'

All eyes turned to Zafar, who looked like he wished he'd never opened his mouth.

'Just, you know... That... You know, looking at the bigger picture... I'm just saying... I'm glad we weren't the ones to attack. Now it's happened to us, maybe the... the... *view* on Muslims will change.'

'Jay,' Ira turned to me. 'Did he just say that? Seriously. Sometimes I tie my hijab a little too tightly, it affects my hearing.'

'It's not what he meant,' I said. 'Leave it.'

Ira predictably ignored my advice.

'What'd they teach you at that University, Zafar? I thought you had a Master's degree! What was it you said...? Maybe the view on Muslims will *change*?'

'Oh piss off, Ira,' Zafar said. 'Why you have to pick holes in everything I say? It's exhausting.'

'If you think that's exhausting, you best get ready for bed, 'cos you're about to get educated. We're going through a lot worse than having acid thrown over us. Homes devastated. Families torn apart. Our women raped, our children murdered, on a mass fucking scale. Do you hear what I'm saying, Zafar? All at the hands of the West. It's been happening for decades. Just because you saw something on the news. Just because it's happening in your country, in your city, under your damn nose, you think, *what*? That these Kafirs will *sympathise?*'

'We don't use that word, Sister,' Tahir said.

'What word? *Kafir?* No, Tahir, you don't use that word. I've got no problems calling a spade a spade. Whether you like it or not, we're at war. We can't ignore that anymore. We need to stand up and make ourselves count.'

The tea was cold. The biscuits still in their packaging. A cold silence enveloped us. I had heard plenty of these conversations before, listened as we debated at the community centre. But it had never been like this. Ira's feisty, yeah, fucking feisty! But never had she spoken with such venom.

Without words, Tahir, Zafar and I decided it was time to call it a night. We all stood up in unison and approached Naaim to bid him good night. He had barely said a word all evening. It was supposed to be about him, but it quickly became about something else.

Naaim looked up at us, the Rubik's Cube still in his hand and said, 'Where'd they get that acid from?'

51

Heston, West London

Daniel could not possibly present himself in his current state to his father, so before heading home he decided to clean himself up. He stepped off the bus a couple of stops early and headed to the McDonald's just off Henlys roundabout. He walked in and ducked straight into the customer toilets.

The blue parka that Daniel had worn turned out to be a small blessing on a day when he needed all the blessings he could get. It was made of a type of fabric that was easy to wipe clean. He pulled out a handful of tissues and wet them under the sink, and then set about cleaning the blood-stained jacket.

Once satisfied, he put it back on and washed his hands in the sink. He looked at his sad reflection in the cracked mirror. There was dried snot matting the wispy hair above his lips, that he'd tried to pass off as a moustache, and a deep cut across his upper lip. He washed his face the best he could whilst his mind raced, trying to find a feasible excuse. But he was tired and all that he could think of was, *I walked into a door.* His father would never believe an excuse that lame. So once again the blue parka, which he'd once hated, came to his rescue. He zipped it all the way up so that the lower part of his face was hidden from view behind the collar. As long as he could make it to his bedroom without suspicion, then he had all night to think of an excuse.

Daniel walked the mile home as slowly as possible, turning the ten-minute walk to twenty. He hadn't even had a chance to speak with Naaim, to warn him that Simon and Anthony, with the might of The Second Defence behind them, were coming after him. As soon as Naaim had set eyes on him, *in his home*, there was only one way that it would play out.

As Daniel approached the front door, he made sure the parka was in place, zipped high, hiding his face. His father would not question the odd appearance; he understood teenagers and wouldn't make a thing of it. Daniel slipped out the house key but before he could insert it the door opened and his dad was there.

'Danny,' he said. 'I was just heading out.'

It should have been perfect. Daniel would have the whole house to himself for the night and not have to worry about hiding his face or explaining himself. Instead, upon seeing his dad he burst out into tears.

'Hey, hey, hey, Danny Boy.' His dad said, as he stepped through the door and took his son into his arms. 'What's got into you?'

Daniel said something into his dad's chest. It came out muffled. 'What is it, son?'

Daniel realised that the collar of his parka had slipped and that his split lip was exposed. But it was late, and it was dark, and his dad hadn't notice.

'It's nothing, Dad.' Daniel ran a hand across his face. 'I just miss Mum.'

'I do, too, son. I miss her every day.'

It nearly set Daniel off again. It wasn't often that he cried. Before tonight, the last time had been when his Mum had died – and then he'd cried for a month. They both did. He forced a smile. His dad mirrored it, and for just that moment his problems disappeared.

'Where you going, Dad?'

'I'm going to see Amber,' his dad said. Daniel had met Amber twice. She wasn't very bright, but he liked her.

'You smell nice.'

'I think I overdid it. I mixed some Paul Smith with some of your Joop.'

'Maybe a bit.' Daniel laughed.

'A couple of your friends came by.'

'Huh?'

'I didn't know when you'd be back but they said you were expecting them, so I let them wait. They seem like good kids.'

'They're here.'

'In the living room, watching TV. Anthony and...'

'Simon,' Daniel said, his eyes on the living window, light escaping from the narrow gap in the curtains. His friends waiting for him.

'Look, Danny. I don't have to go.'

'No, Dad. Go. Have a good time.'

'She'll never replace your mother, you realise that, right?'

'Who?' Daniel said, his gaze still at the window, his mind elsewhere.

'Amber.'

'Yeah. I know that.'

His dad nodded for a moment, kissed his son on the top of the head, smiled and walked away down the path to his car. As he opened the car door, he turned to Daniel.

'Try to stay indoors today.'

'Yeah, okay,' Daniel said. 'Why?'

'Better to be on the safe side. Have you not heard the news?'

*

Daniel stood at the door to the living room and peered in. Anthony, still wearing his green Farah sweater, was perched on the seat of the sofa. On the side table beside him was a glass of orange squash. Under it a coaster. His attention was focused on the TV. Daniel noticed that he had removed his shoes in accordance with the house rules.

Simon was sitting in Dad's armchair, he still had on his blue Timberland tracksuit. A glass of orange squash in his hand. He noticed Daniel at the door, looking out of place in his own home.

'Your old man left?' Simon asked.

'Yeah. He's gone.'

'Daniel!' Anthony turned in his seat. 'We've been trying to get hold of you for ages. Where were ya?'

Daniel patted down the pockets of his coat and jeans. 'My phone!' he said, wondering where he had left it, and then remembered with a start that he'd probably dropped it when he lay crying at Naaim's feet. 'I think I've lost it.'

'Yeah?' Simon said.

'Yeah,' Daniel replied, glad for once at not having to lie.

'Well, don't just stand there. Come in,' Simon said.

'Yeah, make yourself at home.' Anthony grinned, before turning his attention back to the television.

Daniel walked into the room and removed his parka, placed it on the arm of the sofa and sat down next to Anthony. He noticed that the news was on. He didn't pay much attention to it but he could hear little snippets of what was being said.

'Daniel,' Simon called. 'Look at me.'

Shit! Daniel was so preoccupied at having to explain the cut above his lip to his dad, it completely slipped his mind that Simon and Anthony would want to know. He couldn't exactly tell them that he'd gone pleading to Naaim's house.

Daniel turned and faced Simon.

'What happened?' Simon asked, as he pulled the lever on the side of the armchair and the footrest came up – a feature that Daniel's dad enjoyed on a daily basis, but one which made Simon seem even more menacing.

'Show me,' Anthony said, turning in his seat to get a better look. 'Oh, shit! Who fucked up your face?'

Daniel's eyes landed on the television, as if it could provide a spark that would ignite the lie that he would have to tell.

'I don't know,' Daniel said. 'Just a minute ago, walking home from McDonald's. I cut through Shelley Crescent and, I don't know, I just felt something connect with my face.'

'Who was it?' Anthony spat. 'We'll fuck him up!'

'I just said, I don't know,' Daniel said, confidently, warming to the lie. 'I had my head down, couple of guys were walking towards me, and *Blam!*' He carefully touched his upper lip and grimaced in pain. 'It fucking hurt. I dropped down to my knees with my face in my hands. They just carried on past me.'

'Fucking cowards,' Anthony said. 'That's a proper gash, mate. That ain't no knuckle. I reckon that's a ring or a lighter to cause that sort of damage.'

Daniel nodded. He had obviously convinced Anthony. He looked over at Simon who was sipping slowly on the orange squash. Feet up in his dad's chair. Eyes calculating. Daniel ran through the story in his head. The lie was simple, there were no holes in it.

'You alright?' Simon asked.

'Yeah,' Daniel smiled. 'Just a bit sore. Like Anthony said, *fucking cowards*. If you guys were there, we would've showed them.'

We would've showed them! Fighting talk never sounded natural coming from Daniel. He might as well have accompanied it with a waving fist. He decided to keep his mouth closed before he said anything else dumb.

Daniel turned away from Simon and towards the television. He could feel Simon's gaze on the back of his head. His palms were sweaty but he resisted the urge to wipe them on his jeans. He focused on the news. The newsreader was reporting three separate acid attacks that had taken place a little earlier in South London. Victims all Asian. *Muslims*, Daniel thought. The two attackers on the moped, unidentifiable as they wore helmets. *White*, Daniel thought.

'I know who it was,' Simon said, and Daniel wanted to run.

'Who what was?' Anthony asked.

'I know who attacked Daniel.'

'Go on, then. Who?'

'Isn't it obvious?' Simon nodded at the television.

Daniel nodded slowly. 'It has to be related.'

'What? You think it was some pissed off Pakis? On the back of what's happened?' Anthony exclaimed as he made the connection. Daniel's simple but well-constructed lie began taking on a life of its own. 'Wankers! Been fucking with us for years. They don't like it when the boot's on the other foot.'

'Listen, lads,' Simon said. 'This is what's going to happen. Hounslow is gonna be teeming with brown tonight. So we stay put, bide our time.'

'What about the Paki?' Anthony said. 'Thought we were gonna put the frighteners on him tonight?'

'With all the best intentions, if we were to walk out there, just the three of us, we'd be outnumbered.'

'You're having a fucking laugh,' Anthony said. 'Since when do we back away from trouble?'

'Calm it, Anthony. I'll never back away from a tear-up, but we need to pick our battles carefully. It's too risky to move on Naaim tonight. There are probably cops everywhere. Remember what Terry said. We've got to be clever.'

Daniel stayed silent. It wasn't the first time that Simon and Anthony had had a disagreement, and it wasn't the first time that Simon had had the last word. Daniel was just glad that he wouldn't have to face Naaim tonight.

'So, we just sit here?' Anthony said.

'Yeah,' Simon replied. 'We just sit here.'

Anthony sighed loudly. His irritation clear.

'It's happening, lads. The uprising. We are now part of something that's bigger than us. What we've witnessed tonight is just the start.' Simon smiled for the first time that evening and said, 'London is a battlefield. And England, a war zone.'

52
Jay

Idris phoned me. He was outside. I couldn't be arsed to get myself out of bed and make the long trip downstairs. He still had a key from when he'd stayed with me, so, still half-asleep, I mumbled that he should let himself in. I heard the door open and close, and with some effort I shuffled myself upright so I was sitting against the headboard.

'Coffee?' he shouted, from downstairs.

'Yeah,' I shouted back. 'Black and Strong.'

Idris shouted something back, a wisecrack about Mike Tyson I think.

I checked the time. It was a couple of digits past eight, too early for humour, so I ignored him. He chuckled to himself, his laugh travelled from the kitchen and into the hallway. I placed my phone back on the side table, and my eyes landed on the phone that I had pocketed yesterday. The events of the night before came rushing back at me. The acid attack. Ira's furious reaction. Naaim… Attacking that boy.

I picked up the phone and ran my finger over a crack on the screen. I wondered if it had occurred during last night's scuffle. I pressed the home button, and I was glad not to be confronted by a passcode. Instead I was looking at an image of the St George's flag. I wasn't about to jump to a half-arsed conclusion, even though the conclusion seemed to be jumping out at me.

Now I knew that he'd been on that bus, first thing I did was check out his gallery, hoping to find the original video without the faces obscured. There were many photos of him with his parents, I guess. They went back years, so I skimmed through them. The early ones at a theme park and at the zoo, and as he went through the ages, beach holidays and his parents cheering him on at school football matches. Curiously the last photo was dated just over a year ago. After that, nothing. No more photos, and no incriminating video either.

I scrolled through his apps, not quite sure what I was looking for. I had a little nose around on his Facebook. His name was Daniel Lewis. There wasn't much activity. I moved on to his text messages, again there wasn't much to see. Either he was deleting his messages, or he didn't have many friends. Just a couple of regular interactions with *Dad*, *Anthony* and a *Simon* who seemed eager to get in touch with him.

Apart from his name, and the lack of a social life, I didn't learn a great deal about him.

Idris appeared at my door

'I come in peace.' He smiled, our previous conversation obviously still on his mind.

It annoyed me how fresh he looked. Ready to seize the day. 'Morning,' I yawned at him.

'Are we still best friends forever?'

'Until I find a better option.'

'Seriously, though, Jay.' Idris locked eyes with me. 'I'm sorry.'

'Go on.' He wasn't getting away with it that easily.

'I had no right telling you who you can or can't hang out with. It was a shitty thing to say. But you know... I was just looking out for you.'

'Where's my coffee?' I said, accepting his apology.

'Downstairs.'

'Why didn't you bring it up?'

'I don't really want to be drinking coffee in your bedroom. It's weird.'

'Since when did you become so cultured?' I said, as I made the strange sound that accompanies stretching.

'I'll see you downstairs.' He made a face and disappeared.

I picked up the phone. The right thing to do was return the phone to its owner, which was good because, if I'm honest, I also wanted to talk to Daniel. I wanted to hear the full story. His involvement in the attack which had led to Layla taking her own life, and then his turning up at Naaim's. His crying. It didn't fit. Something just did not seem to connect. I'd had only one very brief meeting with Daniel, and he didn't seem the type to... Fuck, man! What do I know? I've seen vicious violence from those who I'd never considered capable of it.

I scrolled through the contacts list on Daniel's phone and dialled *Home*. It rang through to voicemail. I decided not to leave a message. He didn't really have many other contacts, so I dialled Anthony, alphabetically his name appeared first and they seemed to be in touch quite often, judging by the text exchanges. Possibly a friend. He could at least point me in the right direction.

'Hello,' I said.

'Who's this?' Anthony, I assumed. An attitude that I did not care for. Accusing, as though I had stolen his mate's phone.

'Is this... Anthony?'

'Yeah. The fuck is this? You got my boy's phone?'

'Yeah,' I said. 'I have it.'

'He wants it back.'

'I know that. It's why I called?' I said, and then had the urge to explain myself. 'I didn't steal it, if that's what you're thinking. I found it.'

'What time is it? Shit, it's early!' Anthony muttered to himself. 'Give it a few hours and meet us in... You know Lampton Park?'

'I do,' I said, trying to work out what he meant by *us*. Why would *us* need to attend to pick up one phone? Were they the same *us* that were also involved in the attack. If so, did I really want to be meeting them?

'I was thinking that you could maybe tell Daniel that I have his phone, and to call me.' *Why was I so nervous chatting to this guy?* I figured it was because I was still in bed, still in my Batman onesie. If I'd been wearing my Air Jordans, I'd give it back a bit.

'I ain't playing Chinese whispers, mate. You've told me. I'll sort it.'

'Will Daniel be there?'

'*Obviously!* Four-thirty. At Lampton Park.'

'Yeah,' I said. 'Lampton Park.'

I headed downstairs, the television was tuned to MTV. A loud, brash, colourful music video assaulted my senses as I stepped into the living room. Idris was sitting on the sofa bopping his head to the racket. He'd always had shit taste in music. I turned down the volume and flipped the channel to the calm of BBC1 *Breakfast*.

'We should go Ibiza this summer?' Idris said. 'Get out of Hounslow for a bit.'

'I'm not going Ibiza.' I picked up my coffee, murmured 'Thanks,' and sat down next to him. 'Besides, if I'm going anywhere, it'll be Qatar. To see Mum.'

'With that scar still across your throat? Are you sure? She'll pack her bags and move back in before you could say *Mum, it was just a misunderstanding!*'

I ran my fingertips over the scar. 'Well, I ain't going fucking Ibiza!'

'Suit yourself.'

'What are you doing here? Shouldn't you be –'

'Got the day off. Thought I'd chill with you today.'

'Crime rate is going go through the roof.'

'Yeah,' he laughed. 'Thought I'd give the bad guys a day off.'

'Like that film,' I said, easing into the morning. 'Where you're allowed to commit any crime just for one day.'

'Which film's that?'

'I can't remember.' I shrugged, not even attempting to recall. 'Wanna come down Lampton Park with me later?' I asked him. If Daniel did turn up with who I thought he would, then it might be handy to have some of that police training behind me.

'Lampton Park?' He arched an eyebrow. 'Yeah, I'm up for it. What's the occasion?'

'Found someone's phone. Just returning it.'

53

Imy

I woke up late. I got into the office late. I arrived at my first viewing late. Kumar bit into me about my timekeeping and my appearance, telling me he had a good mind to keep me hidden away in the office and give Shaz my viewings. But Shaz hadn't come in to work. Backache, apparently. Shaz often said backache was the cream of excuses. He once spent five days in Tenerife with backache.

I knew the real reason why he wasn't at work. I had hurt my friend and it was all I could think about.

'Well,' the prospective buyer said as I followed him blankly around the two-bed flat, 'how long?'

'The lease?' I said, tuning in.

'Yes.' He sighed. 'How long is the lease?'

'I'll find out.' I'd left the paperwork at the office.

'The boiler, is it a combi?' he asked as we stepped into the kitchen.

'I think, yes.' I scanned the boiler. 'No, actually it's not. Can I confirm?'

I took him from room to room, failing to satisfactorily answer any of his questions.

'I'd like to see this property again,' he said. 'If you don't mind, can somebody else show me?'

'Sure,' I nodded, as my phone rang. 'Excuse me, I have to take this.' He made his annoyance clear as I stepped outside onto the front porch. 'Stephanie.'

'Imy, where are you? Her voice sounded strained, setting me on edge.

'At work, what's happened, Steph?'

'The school called –'

'Jack!' My heart picked up. 'Is he alright?'

'No, he's not alright –'

My mind immediately shot to a dark place. I rushed onto the road towards my car, an oncoming van braked hard, its horn blaring through me, drowning out Stephanie.

'Stephanie,' I threw open the car door and started the engine. 'What's happened?' Tight in front of me was an SUV, tight behind me was a Jaguar. I was boxed in. I slipped it into reverse and put my foot down, forcing the Jaguar back a few feet.

'You were supposed to pick him up!' she said.

I glanced at the clock on the dash. Jack finished school at three. 'Steph, it's okay. It's only quarter past two.' I let out a long breath and looked in the wing mirror. My client was inspecting the damage to his Jaguar.

'Imy, it's the last day. School finished at two today. We had this conversation.'

'I'm on my way,' I said. 'Five minutes.'

She sighed and disconnected the call. I punched the steering wheel in frustration and manoeuvred out, leaving the front door of the flat open and my client gesturing angrily behind.

*

I parked my Prius and ran the short distance to Jack's school. There were still parents and children milling about as I entered the playground, and I could see Jack standing at the door with Miss Hollis, waving excitedly at me. I smiled an apology at his teacher.

'Dad!' Jack waved. Miss Hollis smiled knowingly at me, recognising our relationship for what it had become.

'Dad...' A voice repeated to my right, as he took his position next to me. Entering my world again. I didn't have to turn and face him. I didn't even have to hear his voice. Pathaan's presence alone was enough.

I watched Jack struggling to get his rucksack on, then he came flying out, a week off school written on his face as he launched himself into my arms. 'You were twenty minutes late, Dad!' I reluctantly placed him down and his hand found mine. He looked past me and asked, 'Who's that man?'

'He's...'

Pathaan knelt down in front of Jack, a dirty grin on his face. I gripped Jack's hand tightly. 'I am a very old friend of your dad,' he said. 'You must be Jack.'

Jack made the connection. 'You were at Jump Giants.'

'Yes I was. I was watching you,' Pathaan said, and with a quick glance at me, added, 'Look how white you are.'

Unable to comprehend, Jack looked up at me and even though my heart was hammering inside my chest, I smiled down at him and when he returned it, it near enough broke me.

'Shall we go?' I said.

We, the three of us, walked back to the car. Jack dictated the pace, which was slower than I would have liked. I wanted to run. I wanted to carry him, his arms around my neck, his face buried in the crook of my neck, so he wouldn't have to see my past. Just like Pathaan had carried me all those years ago away from my burning home.

'What did you learn at school today?' I switched to autopilot.

'Um... I can't remember,' Jack replied.

'You should always remember every lesson that is taught to you,' Pathaan said. 'Did you know that I once taught Imran?'

'*Really!*' Jack exclaimed. 'You were his teacher?'

'Yes. In many ways I was.'

I could see the Prius in the near distance. I slipped a hand into my trouser pocket, wrapped my fingers around the car fob, and repeatedly pressed the button, trying to unlock the car from twenty yards away.

'Is that true, Dad?' Every time he said that word in Pathaan's presence it made me want to vomit.

'Yes,' I said. 'A lifetime ago.'

'And you know something else, Jack?' Pathaan said. 'He was my best student.'

The Prius chirped, the indicator lights flashed. 'Why don't you go sit in the car, Jack?'

'But I want to know more about –'

'You can sit in the front seat.' I quickly threw in the distraction.

Without hesitation Jack happily ran the ten yards to the car. I watched him struggle with the car door handle for a moment before bundling into the front seat.

I stopped in my tracks, wanting to keep a distance from Jack. Pathaan didn't follow my lead and kept on moving towards the car.

'Pathaan Bhai,' I said, putting my hand on his shoulder, stopping him. He looked at my hand on his shoulder. I knew he would have seen that as a sign of disrespect. I dropped my hand. He quietly fixed me with a glare, amused slightly. Calculating. Calculated.

My two worlds had overlapped and I was at a loss at what role I was supposed to play. *The father figure*, *the man*. Moving heaven and earth to keep the ones I loved safe. Or *the jihadi*.

To be one, I had to be the other.

'Silas is out of the way,' Pathaan finally said.

I nodded, making it clear that news had reached me.

'I've been watching Javid,' he said. 'In a restaurant, with his friends. Not a care in the world. He has recovered well... He looks well.' Pathaan smiled. His teeth were only slightly stained, not his usual coat of red from the constant chewing of paan. He would have resisted the temptation, not wanting to bare his red teeth in a school playground, scaring the children and attracting the attention of the teachers. The rest of him looked incongruously smart; ironed pale-blue shirt tucked tightly into loose black trousers, with a mobile phone clipped onto his belt, finished off with polished pointed black boots. It was how he would have envisaged a parent on a school run.

'He looks like a man who has his whole life in front of him,' Pathaan said. 'But we know that is not true.'

I wanted to take my eyes off him and glance at the car, just to catch a glimpse or a movement of Jack's tiny head. But I knew that would be a mistake. I had to stay in the moment. Give nothing away. But it was impossible. This was not the broken streets of Gardez, Afghanistan, where hatred was channelled, fuelling an all-consuming hunger for violent bloody revenge. This was the suburbs of Hounslow.

And just to hammer home the notion, the universe further conspired against me. I heard rapid footsteps behind me and I turned to see Clara, Jack's classmate, skipping towards me, hand in hand with her mother. They joined us and my head started to swim. I could see Pathaan, I could touch him, but I still could not place him here. I couldn't alter my mind-set. It was the most bizarre feeling. If I could just scratch my head. If I could rattle my brain. If I could just close my eyes.

We stood in a tight triangle. Clara's mother, Pathaan and I, with Clara at waist-level looking up curiously at the strange man.

'We took Clara to Jump Giants. What a gem of a place!' she said, breaking the tension with the most mundane statement. 'It's a little hidden away, though. My Satnav got itself in a right tizzy trying to find it.'

I nodded, but so surreal was the situation, my head barely moved. So I nodded harder and it felt and probably looked unnatural.

'Did you keep those little green socks that they give you? Hold onto them for Clara's birthday, otherwise you'll have to pay three pounds for another pair,' Clara's Mum continued, whilst her daughter continued to look up at Pathaan. I had to move them along; the way Pathaan was hungrily looking down at Clara, I wouldn't put it past him to eat her up right there and then.

'We're thinking a week Saturday,' she said. 'I'll send out the invites soon.'

'Yes.' I said. 'The invites.' I had no idea what she was saying to me.

'Mummy, can we go now?' Clara's eyes were fixed on the monster.

'Okay, must dash. Teatime awaits.'

Pathaan and I stood in silence until they were almost out of sight, only stopping briefly to wave at Jack through the car window.

'The time has come, Imran. This time, I expect results. And not just me. The Sheikh is losing patience. Do not make me lose mine.'

'Sheikh Ali Ghulam?' I was thrown.

Pathaan nodded. 'Al-Mudarris is no longer in a position to lead. The Sheikh has assumed control.'

Sheikh Ali Ghulam was a highly successful and ruthless businessman. He lived his life almost as a recluse, located in the United Arab Emirates. It was common knowledge that he had been born into wealth, using that money to further cement his success with a string of luxury hotels in the Middle East. However, what wasn't common knowledge was that he had also been funding Ghurfat-Al-Mudarris' operations. But since the much-loved and much-respected founder and leader, Abdullah Bin Jabbar, was now a priority target for the world's authorities, it would have been, without question, a simple decision for the Sheikh to take over operations.

I never questioned why a fatwa had been issued on Jay – had been preoccupied with the task itself – but it was starting to make sense.

'This is all down to Javid... How?'

'You were always a bright one, Imran,' Pathaan said. 'As I said to *Jack*, you were my best student.'

The man I held in the highest regard, once. The man I loved, once. Now I wanted to rip his tongue out with a blunt blade. Saw at it until blood filled his mouth, so he could never again bring Jack's name to his lips.

'Javid Qasim has unstitched the very fabric of our organisation,' he said, addressing a question that I had

267

forgotten that I had asked. 'It is due to this *Munafiq* that our once great leader is running like a lamb hunted by wolves. There will be no questions, there will be no trial. History has shown us, like all the great leaders before him. If caught, al-Mudarris will be killed without hesitation.'

They say that the truth is in the eyes. I let him look into mine, as I said, 'Qasim must pay in blood.'

'He must, Imran, *Mashallah*, he must!' He patted me hard twice on my shoulder. 'Every time that I see him I want to kill him myself. I cannot stand to see him alive anymore. But the honour is with you, Imran, and as my student I will bask in your light. Today is Friday, I will be leaving this filthy country on Monday morning. Understand this: I want Qasim to have taken his last breath before I leave. I want it done quickly and without hesitation. Do not test my patience any longer.'

The truth is in the eyes.

Without thought my eyes moved away from him, towards my car, towards Jack. Pathaan gently cupped my face with his hands and brought me back to him.

'You are not to fail me again, Imran.' He smiled. There was sadness there.

A short sharp punch to the side immediately knocked the wind out of me. I tried to bend at the waist to recover, but he'd gripped me upright and pulled me closer to his chest, holding me in an embrace. His lips brushed my ear, and he whispered softly.

'Do not let the *Shaitan* control your emotion, Imran, or I will take away everything you hold dear.'

54

Jay

I hadn't thought this through. Lampton Park at four-thirty. The fuck was I thinking? Lampton Park was located *literally* next to the Civic Centre where I worked. I was supposed to be at home recovering, not hanging about at the park. And half four! My timing couldn't have been worse. Council workers are lazy fuckers. I know. *I am*. Unless they're on rota to work fixed hours, they're itching to leave in their droves between four and five. I was bound to get bagged.

I pulled into the Bulstrode pub car park, opposite Lampton Park, just as a couple of colleagues that I recognised from HR were heading into the Bully. I slid low in my seat.

'You haven't thought this through, have you?' Idris remarked from the passenger seat.

'Was just thinking the same thing. Have they gone?'

'No. They're approaching the car armed with a clipboard and pen. Oh god, one of them is taking pictures.'

I risked a look through the gap in the steering wheel, as they disappeared into the pub without a glance.

'Jay. Calm down. Ain't nobody going to pay attention to this shit-bucket.'

'Yeah, well.' I straightened up. 'It's better than your motor.'

'What motor?'

'That's right.' I pulled the door handle. 'What motor?' I stepped out of the car and quickly crossed the road towards the park, Idris keeping pace with me.

'When am I getting my Beemer back? Did you find out?'

'I forgot to tell you. It's been booked to be cleaned out later this week. A cleaning firm from Heathrow that we use from time to time for crime scenes.'

'The police are sorting it out?'

'Don't be daft! It's up to the victim or his family to pay for it. Or a friend.'

'*You sorted it?*'

'I did. Couldn't have you see it in that state. Didn't want you to have night terrors!' Idris smiled, barging his shoulder into mine as we set foot into Lampton Park.

Rather than express the gratitude that I was feeling, I replied, 'You spend enough time in it, you may as well contribute towards it.'

'Not been here in years.' Idris glanced around the park. 'K Cider, remember? Drop of blackcurrant.'

'Snakebite! Yeah, I remember,' I said. 'Looking for the saucepan constellation in the stars.'

'Good times.'

'Yeah, they were alright.'

They were more than alright. Knocking up for Idris, exchanging pleasantries with his old man. His mum filling up our bellies and then we'd make our excuses and leave. Destination, Lampton Park, armed with cheap cider in our rucksacks. Getting drunk without much effort and fucking around on the swings and slides until we were sick and laid out under the stars, making plans and talking shit until the early hours.

Yeah, it was good times. The fucking best. But we grew up. We were forced to open our eyes and face the fact that we live in a fucked up world. Back then racism was being called a Paki and the occasional dust up. Not like now.

Daniel's phone rang. The caller display flashed *Anthony*. I answered.

'Is that you by the pond?' Anthony asked.

'Yeah. Where are you?' I said.

'Who'd you bring with you?'

'He's a mate.' Idris narrowed his eyes, I shrugged at him.

270

'Alright, spin around,' he said. 'See the bench at the end of the park, by the hut?'

I turned around and saw three figures in the distance. 'Yeah, I see you,' I said and he ended the call.

'Does this feel weird to you, Jay?' Idris said. 'It feels weird to me.'

'Nah,' I said, casually.

'Feels like a... I don't know, like we're dropping off a ransom to a bunch of kidnappers.'

'Idris?'

'What?'

'When we get there, drop back and while I'm chatting to them, *discreetly* take a photo of all three of them.'

'Drop back? Take a photo? You wanna tell me what's going on?'

'Nothing. I'm just returning the phone.'

'Yeah, you're right,' Idris said. 'This is not weird at all.'

55

Lampton Park, Hounslow

The last time that Daniel had seen him was through blurred, wet eyes. Curled up like a ball on the floor, sobbing uncontrollably and apologising repeatedly to Naaim. He'd picked Daniel up off the floor and walked him out of the house, before rushing back inside to get him a glass of water.

When Anthony had told Daniel that his phone had been found, he was relieved, and then he was scared. Scared that it would all come out. That he had gone to Naaim's house. That he had apologised for his actions! That he'd got smacked in the face and fallen at his feet.

Daniel hoped for a quick handover. Thanks and walk away. He'd said to Anthony that there wasn't any need for them all to turn up. Anthony had replied that *the caller sounded like a Paki*, and after the acid attacks, *we got to stay in numbers*.

They waited at the bench at the back of Lampton Park. Simon was perched perfectly still on the top rail of the bench, feet on the seat. Daniel sat tense, bent forward at the edge of the seat.

Anthony stood in front of them, bouncing from one foot to the other, his energy not dimmed by the joint that he was smoking.

He squinted his eyes as they got closer. 'The fuck!?' Anthony mumbled under his breath. He turned to Simon. 'The taller one's a cop. I recognise him. He's a fucking cop.'

Simon, unmoved, his expression neutral, eyed the taller of the two. 'You sure?'

'Yeah, I'm sure.'

'Alright. Lose the joint.'

'Why would he bring the police?' Daniel asked, his voice small, barely reaching Simon and Anthony. He stood up. 'Simon?'

'I heard you, Daniel,' Simon said. 'I don't know why.'

Anthony frowned. 'You haven't got anything dodgy on your phone, have you?'

'No,' Daniel said. 'Like what?'

'The video,' Simon said, evenly.

'The video. The fucking video on the *bus*?' Anthony cried, nervously watching the two men still in the distance.

'I deleted it, I swear,' Daniel said. 'Could they have retrieved it?'

'We're so fucked.' Anthony ran a hand over his shaved head.

'Anthony. Straighten up,' Simon said.

'Simon –'

'Straighten up!' he repeated, voice firm. 'They don't know anything. If they did, it wouldn't go down like this. They'd pick us up from our houses, and it would be more than two of them. This is something else.'

'Like what?' Daniel asked.

'Maybe they're just returning your phone,' Simon said.

56
Jay

'Jay?' Idris said.

I heard him but my eyes were on Daniel and his two friends. One of them was sitting on the rail of the bench, his feet on the seat, as though he was the guardian of Lampton Park. Daniel and the other were in an animated discussion with him, and they kept turning back to cast quick glimpses at us.

'*Jay?*' Idris repeated.

'What?'

'Green top. I know him.'

'Yeah, I see him. Who is he?'

'Anthony Hanson.'

'I spoke to him on the phone. How'd you know him?'

'His dad, Peter Hanson, likes to supply pills outside nightclubs. Had him in a couple of times. Anthony was there when we arrested his old man at his house, shouting the odds. Lairy little shit.'

'That definitely him?' I said.

'It's him. Check this out, Hanson Senior also has ties with the EDL. Judging by Junior's shaved head, it looks like the apple didn't fall far from the tree. You wanna tell me what's going on, Jay?'

Ira had all but admitted that the reason for Naaim giving Daniel a fat lip was because he'd filmed the whole thing and posted it online. I still couldn't bring myself to watch the video of the attack, but from what I'd been told the other two on the bus both had shaved heads. Hardly conclusive proof. One was tall, Anthony Hanson was tall, again, not exactly compelling evidence, though I did have Idris in my ear telling me that Anthony's dad had ties to EDL. The other attacker was supposedly stocky as fuck. And the third, sitting royally on the rail of the bench, was built like a fucking vending machine.

Was I looking at those responsible for the sickening attack?

I waited to see how it played out.

'Drop back, Idris,' I said.

'I'll be close.'

'Alright,' I said. 'Give me a minute.'

Two pairs of eyes accosted me as I approached, looking as though they could happily do some damage without much motivation. Daniel looked down at his shoelaces. He looked out of place, like a child trying too hard to fit in with the big boys, but maybe I thought that because I'd seen a vulnerable side to him. Anthony approached me, the familiar smell of skunk coming off him.

'You got my boy's phone?'

'Yeah,' I said.

'Did you nosey through it?' Anthony asked.

'Only to ascertain the owner of the phone, that's all.'

Fucking ascertain! Talk about bringing a knife to a gunfight. 'Which one of you is Daniel?' I said, not wanting to give too much away.

Daniel moved forward, and stood next to Anthony, who was busy making eyes at Idris over my shoulder, confirming their shared history.

'You're Daniel?' I asked.

'Yeah,' he replied. 'Give my phone back?'

A little attitude. Forced. Trying too hard to impress. *I saw you, mate. On your knees, begging for forgiveness.* I slipped out his mobile phone from the back pocket of my jeans. As I tried to hand it to him, Anthony snatched it away, his fingers brushing mine. He brought his hand up to his mouth and made a show of blowing on them, before wiping them on his sweater, as though I had passed on brown disease to him.

'Where'd you find it?' Anthony said, holding up Daniel's phone.

I couldn't help it. I had to return the dig. 'At the mosque?'

'The fuck d'you say?' Anthony stepped into my face and eyeballed me. I had to look up to meet his eyes. He feigned a head butt at me, I half expected it so I didn't flinch, but my insides did.

Idris coolly slipped in between me and Anthony. 'We got a problem here?' Idris said, calmly.

'I fucking know you, pig,' Anthony spat.

Idris held firm. The third of their group, who hadn't been involved as yet, stepped off from his perch on the bench. He moved slowly like a Rottweiler on the prowl, rolling his thick shoulders. Just as Idris had taken my position, he did the same by shouldering Anthony out of the way and taking his place. Nose to Nose. Toe to Toe.

'Fuck him up, Simon,' Anthony cried.

I wondered, was it really the mosque comment, or were they looking for an excuse? I would have loved to have seen Idris get into it with this Simon character. Idris is in good shape, and he's had all that copper training, but on the flip side this guy didn't look like he would fight fair, and I noticed his hand gripping onto something. Also, if Simon did happen to get the better of Idris, then he'd turn his attention on me!

Yeah, it was time to put a stop to this.

'Idris,' I tugged at his arm. He held firm, making eyes at Simon. '*Idris.* Come on.' He gave one last hard-man stare at Simon and then backed away.

'Yeah,' Anthony screeched. 'Piss off, copper.'

'How's your old man, Anthony? Still selling pills to underage kids?' Idris threw back.

'What'd you say, pig?' Anthony, his face screwed up, made for Idris, only for Simon to drag him back by the scruff of his green jumper. It was time to get going before feeding time at the zoo.

57

Imy

On the short drive home from school, Jack was incessant. Pathaan had placed the seed in his head and now Jack wanted to know about my past. His questions came at me rapidly. I tried to change the subject, but he was adamant, so I responded to his quick-fire questions with short sharp answers and the occasional grunt, giving away nothing but the bare minimum. My past wasn't something that was discussed often with Stephanie, and certainly not with Jack. It was quite simply a part of my life, I told them, which was uneventful. They didn't need to know.

Another lie. But a necessary one. Stephanie was able to forgive me when she'd seen with me with Rukhsana. Despite my actions, ultimately she understood my reasons. Something like this, how could she understand?

As soon as I pulled the car into the drive, Jack unbuckled and scrambled out before I'd even had the chance to put it into neutral. Stephanie spotted him from the window and met him at the door. I collected my work files and Jack's rucksack as slowly as I could whilst he, no doubt, updated his mother.

'Tell her, Dad. Tell her,' said Jack.

'Tell her what, Jack?' I said, wearily.

'About that man!' Jack looked incredulous. 'From Ghanistan.'

'It's *Af*ghanistan, Jack.' Stephanie looked at me curiously but didn't press. 'Let's get you inside. Imy can tell me later.'

'How was your night in with Shaz?' Stephanie kissed me as I stepped inside.

I took a breath as the events of the night came rushing back at me.

'Great,' I lied. It came easy.

*

Jack buried his nose in his iPad. Stephanie fixed snacks in the kitchen. Upstairs, I took my time changing out of my work clothes. I slipped off my shirt and stood in front of the mirror. I patted my stomach. Belly would be more apt. I had been living an easy life for too long, not giving a thought to my body. The regular pub sessions, fried chicken, and all the trappings of a carefree life. I felt ashamed. I wasn't overweight, but all that carefully-built lean muscle, from hundreds of hours of training, had turned soft. One of the teachings of Al-Mudarris, that had been constantly drilled into us – *Allah gave you a tool, a vessel. It is your duty to keep it conditioned until it is required.* Now mine would, finally, be required. Before Monday.

I peered down at the red raw bruise, the size of a fist, that had appeared on my side. I gently touched it. It still felt sore. It would hurt more tomorrow morning. I slipped on a T-shirt and went to the toilet. I noticed blood mixed in with the urine. It didn't surprise me. A well-executed punch to the kidneys would do that.

'They had a cake sale at work today,' Stephanie said, as I walked into the living room. 'I bought lemon drizzle.'

'Do you mind if I don't, Steph? Need to shift this,' I said, rubbing my stomach.

'Stop it! There's nothing there!'

'I'll have it,' Jack said, head still buried in his iPad. I placed it in front of him. He picked it up and shoved whatever he could in his mouth, some smeared around his mouth and chin, the rest on the floor.

'Did you happen to catch the news last night?' Stephanie said.

I continued to watch Jack. He sneezed and a splatter of cake flew out of his mouth and landed on his iPad. He used the palm of his hands to clean the screen and then, using the same hand, he wiped the snot from his nose, smearing it in with the cake on his upper lip. Sensing that he was being watched, Jack looked up at me. Blue eyes that belonged to another, smiling at me. I blinked at him as though noticing his eyes for the first time.

Pathaan had sat himself in my head.

'Imy,' Stephanie repeated. 'Did you hear the news?' The altercation with Shaz flashed through my mind. 'Last night. There was a...' Not wanting Jack to hear, she mouthed '*Acid attack.*'

'I heard.' I took a sip of my tea and turned my attention to the television. It was tuned into one of the kids' channels that was constantly on throughout the day. The adventures of a talking cartoon pig. 'Is anybody even watching this?' I muttered under my breath.

'It's so worrying,' Stephanie continued, not yet catching onto my mood. 'They're saying London is the acid attack capital of Europe. I'm always driving with my windows open. Just the thought of it... Just horrifying!'

I let out a 'Pah!', a sound of disbelief.

'What's that supposed to mean, Imy?' she asked me, calmly placing her spoon next to the lemon drizzle, signalling that she was ready to go at it.

'You've got nothing to worry about, Steph. That's what it means.'

'Nothing to worry about? And why's that?'

'C'mon, let's not do this.'

'No. Let's.'

'Steph.'

'Is it because I'm not brown? Does that make me safe?'

'Yes, actually. Those targeted were all brown. If you want to be specific, all Muslim! So yes, I think you'll be just fine.'

'Oh, I see. So it's one-sided now, is it? Shall we turn a blind eye towards the random gun attacks, or the mowing down of men, women and children by vans? Yeah, Imy. I feel perfectly bloody safe.'

Maybe they had good reason. Maybe their actions are justified.

The hell do you know about what's happening outside of your cosy three bed semi-detached home?

All you know is all they want you to know.

I didn't say that to Stephanie. It would have changed everything in a heartbeat. She would never understand. How could she? I said no more on the matter and she looked at me as though her argument was unquestionable.

And I realised that the person that I wanted to spend my life with would always share the opinions of those who had killed my family.

58
Jay

Back in the relative safety of my Nova, and wheeling away from Lampton Park and away from those... Fuck it! I'm gonna say it: *Filthy motherfucking racist cunts!* A few minutes in their company and I had absolutely no doubt that they had a direct hand in Layla taking her own life.

'Calm down, Jay?' Idris said, buckling up his seatbelt, as I flew over a road bump towards a traffic light seconds away from turning red.

'I need a drink,' I said, even though I hadn't touched a drop in months.

'I can see that. Just slow down, yeah?'

I took the light just as it turned red and rounded the corner onto Bath Road, straight into three lanes of traffic for as far as I could see.

'Never thought I'd be relieved to see traffic,' Idris remarked, to no response.

I looked from lane to lane, figuring out if I could steal space. It was rush hour and everybody was rushing home from their crappy nine to five. I dropped it into neutral and lifted the handbrake.

'Look, Jay, I know you're pissed off,' Idris said. 'Don't be. I come across losers like that all the time. Even in colourful, multi-cultural Hounslow!' He shrugged. 'It's just the world we live in. Racism is alive and well.'

I wiped my palms on my jeans. 'Have you seen that video yet? Muslim couple on the bus?'

'The attack? Yeah, I've seen it. Wankers,' Idris mumbled under his breath.

'What do you know about it?'

'I've spoken to the senior investigation officer who's handling the case, and separately they're carrying out an inquest on the suicide. They looked into Layla's background. See if there were any history of depression or abuse, something that would have triggered it.'

'I think it's pretty fucking obvious what triggered it!'

'I know that, Jay. But she didn't leave a suicide note and they cannot rule out that the two incidents are isolated.'

'Isolated! It's related, Idris.'

'Yeah, I know that, but there's no evidence relating the attack to the suicide.'

'*Fucking evidence*!' I mumbled to myself. 'What else did you find out?'

Idris took a breath and continued softly. 'Layla Younis, sixteen years old. Lived with her father and brother, a loving unit by all accounts. Her home life was secure. A little sheltered, but no big surprise there, young Muslim girl living in a male-dominated house. It's to be expected. School life? Not many friends, but well liked. Super intelligent, according to her teachers. She'd just sat her exams, that very morning. Expected to walk into a top university of her choice.'

Idris looked out of the passenger side window, as though shielding his face from me. It wasn't a side of Idris that I saw very often. He rarely showed emotion.

'A girl like that, Jay, could have had the world in her hands. Instead…' He shrugged and turned back to me. 'When Layla got home that night, broken, she went straight to her bedroom. Not knowing at the time that whatever humiliation she'd endured was about to get a lot fucking worse.'

'The video,' I said.

'Just after ten p.m. that night she received the first of forty-one text messages informing her that a video of her was doing the rounds all over the internet.' Idris slowly rapped his knuckles three times on my dashboard. 'She was found dead by her father. Her phone on her bed, playing the video on a loop.'

The traffic was suffocating me. The beaming sun hitting the side of my head was suffocating me. The crappy air-con in my crappy Nova was blowing hot and cold and fucking suffocating me. I slid down the window, and much like a dog, I angled my head outside and closed my eyes, letting the gentle breeze stroke my forehead.

'Why did you bring it up?' Idris asked.

'Just...' I shrugged.

I had worked out every eventuality. Really there weren't many. I was so fucking certain that Anthony and Simon had been on that bus, but that wasn't *evidence* enough. I needed confirmation. The road opened up a little. I used the reprieve to turn off the Bath Road into a dead end road just to get out of the fucking traffic. I parked the car under a large tree for some much-needed shade.

'Jump out,' I said. 'I need some fresh air.'

I leaned against my car door. Idris walked around and leaned next to me as I sparked up.

'This your idea of fresh air,' he said, waving the smoke away.

'Your mate,' I said. 'He still investigating?'

'You mean the SIO?' Idris smiled. 'Yeah, it's still under investigation, but it's a dead duck. Our tech guys have enhanced the hell out of the video. The faces are obscured with dumb cartoon characters. They've sussed out height, build, even age approximation, but we need a face. Naaim was interviewed; poor bastard's been through it. Anyway, cut to the quick, he gave a description but honestly it could have been any white youth with a shaved head. He didn't remember any distinguishing features, apart from red Doc Martens. Wasn't much to go on. For the first week he was at the station every day, twice a day for an update. I think he gave up hope after that.'

'Aren't all buses fitted with CCTV?'

'Covered in a lick of graffiti.'

'What if you found them?' I said. 'What would happen to them?'

'Unless we have the original video, it's almost impossible.'

'Hypothetically. What would happen?'

'Jay... Something you want to tell me?'

'Just answer the question, Idris.'

'Well, they're looking at aggravated assault, add to that sexual assault. Also whoever was responsible for filming the whole thing and then putting it online would be prosecuted under the Obscene Publications Act. All three had a part to play...' Idris stopped mid-sentence and pushed himself off my car and slipped out his mobile phone. 'You are kidding me!' Idris cried, staring at the photo that I'd asked him to take.

'Yeah.' I nodded. Considering that he was a detective, he'd taken his sweet time working it out.

'*That was them?*'

'Yeah.'

'*Anthony Hanson?*'

'And Daniel. And Simon.'

'Are you sure?'

'I'm pretty sure. Daniel's our budding filmmaker. The other two fit perfectly the description of the attackers.'

'Not exactly evidence is it, though, Jay?'

'Get your guys to compare the photo to the video footage. Surely that's enough to at least bring them in and question them. Fuck, Idris, I can't do everything for you.'

Idris tapped his upper lip. 'Let me think how this would play out.'

I gave him a moment to think whilst I did a little thinking of my own. I doubted that it would be the first time that Simon and Anthony would have been under police questioning, and they'd probably repeat *no comment* as their mantra. But Daniel, well, he was a different prospect altogether. I had seen him at his most vulnerable. The guilt dripping desperately from him, craving forgiveness, as he repeatedly apologised at Naaim's feet for his part in the attack. Yeah, young Daniel would not fare well under interrogation.

59
Imy

There was the slightest of gaps between the bedroom curtains, the size and the shape of a penny. Unable to sleep I watched the orange glow from the street lamp peeking in. I watched it through tired, squinting eyes that never quite closed for long enough to find sleep. It held my focus for hours, changing shape the longer I stared at it, until in my mind I decided it was an all-powerful, all-seeing eye, looking over me, looking at me. Seeing me for what I am.

As crazy as it sounds, I communicated with it. I prayed to it. To Allah. I replayed all my sins. The drinking, the drugs, Stephanie, her blonde hair fanned out on the pillow, as she slept beside me. I'd hardly prayed in years, not giving Him the space and time that He demanded.

How would He judge me?

The glow grew bright as my thoughts turned dark. It was *He* who took away my mother, my father. My family.

But I could never be angry at Him. Because it was *He* who had blessed me with Khala, Stephanie and Jack. My family.

He who takes with one hand, provides with the other.

Allah would forgive me for my sins. I truly believed that. But would he forgive me for the biggest sin that I was ready to commit?

Would he forgive me for taking another man's life?

The glow eventually dimmed and was replaced by daylight. I waited, as I do every Saturday morning, for Jack to crawl into our bed. Pathaan had given me two days, but I knew he would want me to do it sooner rather than later.

Stephanie stirred next to me. There were strands of my hair scattered across my pillow and I knew I had spent the best part of the night viciously scratching my head. I brushed them off, just as Stephanie opened her eyes.

She smiled good morning at me. I returned it, my smile tightly wound, before I closed my eyes and pretended to sleep. I felt her hand softly running through my hair. My head moved without instruction towards her as her fingertips gently stroked every scratch, graze and scrape. I could feel the pressure that had built up slowly alleviate from my shoulders.

I opened my eyes and this time my smile came easily.

'Imy,' she said.

'Yes.'

'You didn't sleep.'

I said nothing.

'Who is he?'

I closed my eyes tightly. Pathaan's hand around Jack's neck, his other around Stephanie's. Lifting them off their feet. Choking the life out of my life. I inhaled. I exhaled. And the picture disappeared.

'Somebody... from my past.'

'Ever since you saw him. It's doing something to you.'

I opened my mouth. One of a long list of lies waiting to easily escape from my lips. But instead, looking into her blue eyes, our noses almost touching, I just nodded.

'Should I be worried, Imy?' She asked.

'He reminds me of a time that I want to forget.'

'He reminds you of your parents.'

I nodded. Stephanie removed her hand away from my hair and wiped away a tear that I hadn't realised I had shed. She reached under the covers and found my hand and unclenched my fist, placing her hand in mine.

60

Afghanistan-Pakistan Border

Travelling undercover wasn't a problem for The Teacher.

The eyes of the world's authorities were sharp, their billions of dollars worth of intelligence giving very little room to manoeuvre, let alone to roam. But roam is exactly what Bin Jabbar did.

There was a twenty-million-dollar reward on his head, but Bin Jabbar had a very high level of trust in his people. Not only the members of Ghurfat-al-Mudarris, but also the thousands of sympathisers in Afghanistan and Pakistan.

Crossing the border into Pakistan was the biggest obstacle. Afghanistan was a landlocked country, dependent on Pakistan for its overseas exports and imports, but as a result of recent terror attacks, security was tight. Aside from the Pakistani armed guards, there were a scattering of armed US soldiers watching very carefully.

Bin Jabbar had changed vehicles four times during the long drive from his hideout, in the small village in Maimana. Each van was fitted with a well hidden-panel in the back wall, where he stood rod straight for hours at a time, with only bottled water, dried fruit and a semi-automatic Desert Eagle handgun within reach. Within the panel, a small vent was located level with his head, to enable him to breathe and also to communicate with the driver. Next to the driver was a woman and a small child. Bin Jabbar insisted on a young family. Handsome, beautiful and cute. A family is less likely to be stopped. A beautiful family is less likely to be questioned.

They'd arrived at the border early in the morning, at the busiest time of the day, and joined the huge queue of heavy-duty trucks and lorries. They crawled until they reached the check-point. They were asked to lower their windows and show appropriate documents for the goods that they were taking across.

Looking in, the guards saw a shy wife, a child curiously asking questions about the guns the guards were carrying, and an easy smile from the driver as he handed over the documents.

What they didn't see was the world's most wanted man, tightly clutching a semi-automatic handgun, ready to unleash hell on anyone who stood in his way as he journeyed across borders to try to save his only son, before an assassin could carry out a fatwa.

They crossed the border, eyes no longer on them. With the right preparations, he could roam wherever he liked.

It really wasn't a problem.

PART 3

La ilaha illallah Muhammadur Rasulullah:

In the name of Allah, We praise Him,
seek His help and ask for His forgiveness.

Whoever Allah guides none can misguide,
and whoever He allows to fall astray,
none can guide them aright…

61

Heston, West London

Daniel Lewis had felt something shift as soon as he opened his eyes that morning. As though today was the last day of a life that he no longer wanted to be involved in. Tomorrow, he would be free of it. He was encouraged further when he switched his phone on and a text message from a number that he did not recognise was waiting for him. It read:

Do the right thing, Daniel. J x

He couldn't be sure who *J* was, but he guessed that it was the same person who had returned his phone. The same person who had picked him up off his knees. Daniel was certain that Naaim would have told *J* about his role in the attack, placing him on the bus.

The last time Daniel had tried to tell the police, he'd bottled it. Simon and Anthony would not take lightly to a grass. Kramer and Rose would definitely not take lightly to a grass. But the guilt was chewing him up from the inside.

Daniel could hear the buzz of the shower as he glanced at the time. It was just past six in the morning. He should have been dressed. For the past year, whilst most are asleep on a Sunday morning, Daniel and his dad set off to Western International Market, to set up their clothes stall. It was a role that Daniel had stepped into since his mum died. He hated it at first, preferring to stay at home in bed and grieve, but had slowly grown to love it. He enjoyed sharing a breakfast of hot mini-donuts out of a paper bag from a nearby stall. He enjoyed watching his dad, coffee in hand, easily charming the customers. It brought them closer together. It was the only time his mind wasn't occupied with truancy, exams, and the incessant talk of a better Britain.

The shower came to a stop and Daniel got out of bed and slipped on the green football-print dressing gown that he had long grown out of, but refused to let go. He stepped into the hallway just as his dad stepped out of the bathroom, a towel wrapped around his waist.

'You're not ready, yet?'

'I'm not feeling so well,' Daniel said.

'What's wrong, son?' His dad frowned.

Daniel felt a tear forming, he blinked it away and shrugged. His dad put a hand on Daniel's forehead. 'Hmm… I'm not sure what I'm looking for here. You don't seem to have a temperature.'

'Just tired, I guess.'

'Tired? At half six on a Sunday morning. *No!*' He smiled. 'Up to you, son. Morning fresh air might help perk you up.'

'Do you mind if I don't?'

'Course I don't mind. I'll get all the mini-donuts to myself.'

'Bring me back some.'

'Alright, now. You take it easy.' He surprised Daniel by taking him in his arms. Daniel's face softly made contact with bare skin, still moist from the shower.

From his bedroom window, he watched his dad load the car and drive out of their quiet road, just as a police car turned in. Daniel tracked it until it was parked across his driveway. He picked up his phone and reread the message again.

Do the right thing, Daniel. J x

He replied:

I will.

There was a knock at his front door.

62

Jay

I'd made a note of Daniel's number before I returned his phone, and I was pretty fucking tempted to call him and ask him why he was such a weak fuck! Why he'd allowed himself to get involved in something so ugly. *It's too late to be apologising, mate. Sorry won't fucking cut it*. It was time he stepped up and did the right thing.

I'd decided to text him instead.

I wasn't expecting a reply, but was encouraged when he texted back early the next morning. It looked like he was going to come clean.

Idris had told me that he'd spoken to his mate, the SIO. It took a little time to organise, but they were going to present Daniel with a deal. It was all falling into place. The first opportunity I had, I was going to give myself a good pat on the back. With those animals locked away and justice served, Naaim would have no choice but to down tools and abandon whatever dumb notion of revenge he had.

Eager to find out what was going on, I called Idris. It rang through to voicemail. I sent him a text to call me back, and then I jumped out of bed and into the shower, surprised by how much energy I had for a Sunday morning. I felt good. In fact I felt fucking amazing. By eight, I was showered, shaved and dressed. Ready to take on the day.

'It's early, man. It's Sunday!' Idris finally called back, his voice distant as if his phone was placed on his pillow and he was talking to it, not into it.

'Yeah, sorry,' I said, sounding anything but. 'So tell me, then. What's happened? They get picked up?'

'God, Jay! How long have you been up for? You sound hyper... It's Sunday, man.'

'Yeah, Sunday, you said that already. Did they get picked up?'

'They did.'

'Good, now throw away the fucking key.'

'Well... Let's see,' Idris said, not sounding as confident as I'd hoped. 'They'll be questioned first and then we take it from there.'

'Trust me. That kid, Daniel, he's going to talk.'

'I hope so, Jay.' He sighed. 'Look, I'm not working today, but I'll swing by the station later and see what I can find out.'

'Later when?' I said, impatiently.

He yawned loudly. I quietly questioned the authenticity of it. I knew when he was trying to get rid of me. 'Later,' he said. 'I'll bell you later.'

*

I contemplated sending a message out on the 'Kaleidoscope' Whatsapp group, to meet me at Naaim's place, but decided against it. It was clear that Tahir was feeling increasingly uncomfortable with the way things were going with Naaim. Also, I didn't want Ira present when I spoke with Naaim, she'd only cloud his reaction. Zafar, well, he was neither here or there. The last thing I needed was for him to say some stupid shit. So I decided to go on my own.

I swiped the keys to my Nova from the side table, glancing at the spare BMW fob on the keyring and smiled. It wouldn't be long before I'd be reunited with my Beemer. My smile widened further as I stepped outside into the beautiful sunshine.

Yeah, today was going to be alright.

63

Port Gwadar, Pakistan

Bin Jabbar travelled on busy roads at busy times, knowing that the Pakistani authorities would be too lazy to carry out gruelling checks under the gruelling sun, only stopping those that looked as if they could be easily bribed.

He had changed his vehicle three times en route to Port Gwadar. He had spent one night in Mr and Mrs Hanif's family home. They welcomed him with open arms and wide smiles, feeding him rich food that they would never normally serve. Though the Hanifs were staunch sympathisers to The Cause, behind their wide smiles and hospitality there was a sense of awful dread. Bin Jabbar's men had visited their home before his arrival and taken away their boy Musa, who was seven, and their baby girl Miriam, who had never spent a night away from her mother. They were looked after at an undisclosed location until Bin Jabbar had vacated their home, serving as insurance. One couldn't be too careful, after all.

The final vehicle that picked up Bin Jabbar from the Hanif family home was a long semi-trailer. It carried a twenty-foot shipping container filled with furniture. At the back of the container, against the back wall, was a similar hidden panel.

He arrived at Port Gwadar during a busy period. The container was given a cursory inspection, lifted off the semi-trailer and placed on a ship along with sixty other containers. Once he felt the ship set sail, Bin Jabbar stepped out from behind the panel and sat on a wooden rocking chair. He disassembled the Desert Eagle handgun and placed it piece by piece on the small table in front of him. He took out a handkerchief from the pocket of his kameez and cleaned each piece carefully.

Destination: Abu Dhabi.

64

Hounslow Police Station

Daniel was asked if he would like an attorney or a guardian present. He declined both. A camera mounted high up on the wall pointed down at him, and he imagined everyone in the building sitting around a large screen watching him. In the tight interview room, opposite Daniel, on the other side of the table, two police officers watched him carefully. A large tape recorder was sitting on the table, along with an iPad.

After introducing themselves, they asked Daniel to confirm his name and address. After that the Senior Investigating Officer said, 'For the benefit of the tape, we are going to show Daniel Lewis a video displaying the events that took place on the evening of March nineteenth, twenty seventeen.'

All eyes fell on the iPad. Daniel did not need nor want to see those disturbing images again. So, instead, he kept his eyes fixed on the impossibly slow timer at the bottom of the screen. Somehow, that was worse. The sound even more harrowing than the images. Anthony's voice, scornful, urging Simon on. The tinny sound of Layla's scream, as her head scarf was ripped off. The glug of beer being tipped over her head and her muffled wail as Simon entered her mouth with his tongue. Her haunted cries filled the small interview room.

But that wasn't the worst sound.

The worst sound was a cruel, mocking laugh. A laugh that Daniel didn't recognise, but knew came from him.

After a very long thirty seconds the video came to a stop.

'Did you recognise the video which we just showed you?' the SIO asked.

'Yes,' Daniel mouthed silently. He swallowed and repeated louder. 'Yes.'

'Layla Younis took her own life that very same night.'

Daniel dropped his head, aimlessly chipping away at the edge of the table with his fingernail, trying to ignore the tears that raced down his face.

'By size and height, we know that neither of the two perpetrators are you, Daniel,' the second officer said. Daniel couldn't remember his name. Just that he was a Detective Inspector, and that he had a kindly face that made Daniel want to confide in him. 'However, what we do believe is that you filmed the attack.'

It wasn't a question, just a damning statement. So Daniel said nothing. The DI continued.

'Were you also responsible for editing and uploading it online using the handle "Takebackourstreets" from an internet café in Cranford?'

Daniel took a breath. He wanted to tell the truth before it consumed him, but at the same time he could not stop thinking about Simon and Anthony. His only friends.

'What will happen to them?' Daniel asked.

'If I were you, I'd be more worried about what's going to happen to you.' The SIO was clearly frustrated.

'If you can provide the names of those behind the obscured faces, we may be in a position to help you, son,' the DI said, his tone conciliatory, more so than his superior.

Daniel nodded, knowing that he would never be free of the guilt, but at the very least he'd be free to rebuild his life.

'Daniel Lewis...' the SIO said. Daniel ran an arm across his face and wiped away the tears, a trail of elastic snot snapped between his arm and nose. 'Can you confirm that you were on the one hundred and eleven bus on March nineteenth between 7.30 and 8 p.m?'

If he confessed to being on that bus, that would be it, the rest would come tumbling out just as he had rehearsed it on so many sleepless nights. His lips parted, the SIO and the DI leaned forward. There were two hard raps on the door. A uniformed officer popped his head in.

'Daniel Lewis' solicitor has arrived.'

'Lewis has declined the right to an attorney,' said the SIO, clearly frustrated.

'Well, he's here. And he's demanding to speak with his client, right now.'

65
Jay

I knocked on Naaim's front door and waited all of two seconds before knocking again.

I stepped back from the front door and glanced up at each of his windows, searching for a twitch or a shadow to indicate that maybe he was simply just blanking me. If he didn't want to open the door, I got it; I hated being caught off-guard. I've curtain-twitched at my bedroom window plenty of times and watched with satisfaction as the unwelcome visitor finally gets the message and fucks off. Especially on a Sunday morning.

Yeah, I should've got back in my car and come back at a more convenient time, but I was desperate to tell him the news that Simon and Anthony had been picked up and Daniel would be turning witness. I knocked again. Lifting the brass knocker all the way up and letting it drop, nice and gratifyingly loud. I did that a few times. When that failed I dropped to my knees and pushed open the brass letterbox.

A strong, rancid smell instantly attacked my nostrils. Naaim had been too preoccupied recently to worry about domestic duties. His house was a mess and the smell of fried food was overwhelming. This, though, was something quite different. It smelt as though somebody had tried to cook out-of-date eggs on a diesel engine.

Last year, I had visited Hisarak, a small village in Afghanistan. It had been devastated by drone attacks. I would never forget the smell of death. My brain made the connection and raced.

'*Naaim,*' I screamed through the letterbox and instantly gagged as the smell entered my mouth. No response, I had to act quickly. I shot to my feet, gave another glance up at the windows. No movement. To the side of the house was a wooden gate leading to the back garden, a touch taller than me but manageable. I had a quick look around to make sure nobody was watching. There was an old lady with a red and blue tartan shopping trolley and a walking stick, sitting at the bus stop, eyeing me carefully. I did a pretty good job miming that I was locked out. My time spent as a mute after I'd had my throat slit was coming into good use. She continued to stare at me.

I gripped the top of the gate with both hands and lifted myself. My weight put some strain on the flimsy bolt lock and the gate moaned before slowly creaking open and taking me along for the ride. I stepped off, coolly giving the old lady a thumbs up. She surprised me by raising her walking stick as a nod to my success.

I walked quickly down the path leading to the garden. I tried the back door. Locked. I put my shoulder into it. Hard. It didn't budge and it fucking hurt enough to not try again. I stood stupidly in Naaim's back garden, rubbing my shoulder, when I noticed the kitchen window. It was one of those large old-school wooden sash windows, and it was very slightly raised. I prised my fingers underneath and lifted. It was heavy and I was struggling. I gritted my teeth and with my back foot pushing against the ground, I lifted as hard as I could, those three gym sessions last year coming to fruition as the frame shuddered noisily past the sticking point and then slid easily up.

I lifted myself up and crawled through the window head first. My hands fell into the sink, clattering amongst the tower of dirty dishes. The rancid smell, worse now, washed over me. One at a time, I tried to pull my legs in, but my knee knocked against the wooden frame, causing the lower sash to slide back down. I quickly got one leg in. The other didn't quite make it, and the sash came down heavily, trapping my ankle. *Shit! Fucking shit!* My right foot was still hovering in the garden whilst the rest of me was in the kitchen. I tried to angle it, and in doing so my shoe got caught and my right Air Jordan dropped onto the lawn. *Fuck! Fuck! Fuckin' fuck's sake!* I felt a

'What's up with your hand?' I asked, trying to make the connection with the Marigolds but not getting there. 'Looks burnt.'

'Hot kettle. I wasn't paying attention, it's nothing.' He swung open the front door and imposed himself at the entrance. I recognised the hint, but chose to ignore it and slipped past into the house. '*Jay!*'

'Shit, Naaim.' I clamped my hand over my nose and mouth. 'The fuck is that?'

'I haven't had a chance to clean up much lately. I'll open some windows. Look Jay, I've got a lot on. Do you mind if –'

'I think it's coming from upstairs.' I moved across the hallway and stood at the bottom of the stairs. The smell was drifting down and making my eyes sting. With one foot on the bottom step, I turned to Naaim and said, 'I'm gonna go check it out.'

'Jay,' he said weakly. Then out of nowhere he opened his lungs and screamed '*Ira!*'

Apart from scaring the living fuck out of me, it served to justify my suspicion. Breaking guest/host protocol I bolted up the stairs, arm snaked tightly around my mouth and nose, my Air Jordans easily bouncing off the steps and elevating me two, three steps at a time.

I reached the top just as a wide eyed Ira stormed out of the bathroom. I caught a quick glimpse of her – she was wearing a surgical face mask. I didn't give her the time or space as I ghosted past her. I could hear her muffled voice as she said something from behind the mask. It sounded a little like '*Fuck!*' I pushed open the bathroom door.

The burn on the back of Naaim's hand. The Marigold washing up gloves. That *fucking* acrid stench! All starting to fit horrifyingly into place. At school, along with most subjects, I'd failed chemistry, but I could guess that the foot deep of clear liquid inside the bathtub was some type of high strength, highly corrosive, revenge-is-a-dish-best-served-with-fucking-hot acid.

The seemingly innocuous but ill-timed comment Naaim had made.

Where'd they get that acid from?

It looked like he'd figured it the fuck out.

66

Hounslow Police Station

The solicitor's name was Sandy White. A short, overweight man with red ruddy cheeks in a smart three-piece-suit. He smelt a little of aftershave, a little of sweat, and he was a little out of breath, as though he had expelled energy rushing to the police station.

He spoke with Daniel without any of the police officers present. *No comment* was ultimately the advice that he imparted. *No more, no less. Simply: No comment.*

'They said they're going to help me,' Daniel said and regretted instantly. 'But I didn't say anything,' he quickly added, acutely aware that the solicitor had been sent to him by Terry Rose.

'How?' White said. 'Help you how?'

'They didn't say.'

'Did they offer you immunity?'

'I don't know what that is.'

'Understand this, Daniel. You had a part to play.' White spoke slowly. 'You were involved. The only person that can help you is you. From what I hear, you're a bright kid, got a sunny future in front of you. Say the wrong word and you could be sitting in prison, leaving your poor old dad to fend for himself... Is that what we want, Daniel?'

This was a whole new world to Daniel, but he knew a threat when he heard one.

'I wasn't going to say anything,' Daniel said. 'I swear.'

'Good, good,' White said, and then he produced a neighbourly smile. 'The only thing you need to say now, is...' Sandy White put his fingers to his lips.

'No comment,' Daniel said.

67
Jay

I was on a fucking mission, man. Too many people had got hurt doing stupid shit on my watch. The dark cloud that had followed me around since the death of my misguided idiot of a friend, Parvez, weighed heavy on me. I still wondered if I could have found the right words, been more of a friend, spotted the signs earlier that he was turning. Would it have saved him? No, I honestly don't think so. But it didn't stop me from feeling like a shit. Parvez was fighting for *religion*, embedded in a terrorist cell that shared the same beliefs as him. He was ready to wage war and take innocent lives, to make nothing more than a fucking point.

Naaim was different. For starters, he wasn't a fucking jihadi. Naaim was fighting a personal war. One fuelled by revenge; one that you couldn't fault him for. Layla, his girl, snatched away from him in agonising circumstances. Add into the mix an alcoholic father who had physically abused him, and a mother who had died from a broken heart.

His loved ones gone, Naaim's intentions were clear.

He had nothing to lose but himself.

I made it my number one fucking priority that I would not stand by and watch another life wasted.

I wrenched open the living room curtains and cracked open the windows. Let the light in, let the smell out. Naaim and Ira sat quietly, close to each other on the sofa. I sat down heavily opposite them on an armchair, the heel of my hands digging into my eyes, until dark colours swirled behind my eyelids. 'Jay!'

I heard Ira call, her tone sharp as though I had in-fucking-convenienced them, made me further vexed. I dropped my hands, shot to my feet and stood over them.

'Acid! Are you out of your fucking minds?' I screamed. 'Seriously, the *fuck* are you thinking?' Naaim dropped his head, as though I'd shone a light on his stupidity. Ira looked as if she wanted to rip my head off. 'I can't... I just cannot... *believe* how far you're willing to take this. The hell are you trying to achieve?'

'Who'd you think you are, *Jay*?' Ira said, all her features knocking into each other. If she wanted to go, I was ready to fucking go. 'Coming in here, chatting breeze... Stay in your fucking lane, yeah. This ain't none of your business.'

'I'm making this my business!' I replied, then wondered if I could have delivered a less obvious line. 'Naaim... *Naaim*, look at me!' He reluctantly met my eyes. There was nothing but loss in them. 'Let me make something crystal clear. You're going to get caught! I guarantee it, there's no two ways! And they won't treat you like a dumb criminal, they'll treat you like a Muslim. You hear me? Like a fucking *terrorist*!' I let that sink in, then counted on my fingers. 'No rights! No voice! No counsel! They won't give a fuck about your grievances, your so-called precious vengeance. You'll spend the rest of your days in a fucking hole licking the boots of those that you hate.'

'Yeah, well, we ain't getting caught,' Ira said.

'It doesn't matter.' Naaim broke his silence in a small voice. 'It doesn't matter if I do get caught. I have to avenge Layla.' A tear rolled down his cheek. Then another. Then it was umbrella season. He put his hand over his face as his shoulders started to dance.

I should have felt sorry for him. Put an arm around him. But he was winding me the fuck up. 'Idiot!' I said. 'You think you're doing this for Layla? Is that it? Some misguided notion of romance? Get. A. Fucking. Grip.'

'Dickhead!' Ira spat. She put an arm around Naaim. 'That's a shitty thing to say. Can't you see he's still mourning?'

306

'*Then mourn!* Go find a dark corner, rock back and forth and sob your fucking heart out like a normal person. You don't have to ruin your life. Let the cops deal with it.'

Ira snorted. 'I didn't have you down as naïve, Jay. You're starting to sound like Zafar. Cops haven't done *shit*, ain't gonna do *shit*. You want us to just sit on our hands and let those Kafirs dig holes for us. The attack in Greenwich! Layla! Can you not see what's going on? They won't stop. Something has to change, someone has to step up. This ain't just about those three anymore. It's about *them* against *us*.'

After seeing the acid in the bath tub, it'd all become too fucking real. I'd completely forgotten why I'd swung by here in the first place. I kneeled down in front of Naaim and gently removed his hands from his face.

'Naaim,' I said, softly. 'They've been arrested.' He met my eyes and then blinked tightly. 'Daniel... He's giving a statement right this minute.'

'*Daniel!*' Ira exclaimed. 'The same Daniel that filmed the whole thing? The same *Daniel* that stuck it online for the whole world to see? *That* Daniel?'

'Yeah,' I said. 'The same Daniel who turned up at Naaim's door, begging forgiveness.'

Ira stood up. She shuffled through the clutter on the coffee table and picked out a set of car keys.

'Where're you going?'

Ira adjusted her hijab. 'Fuck off, Jay.' She walked out of the house, slamming the door behind her.

Good! Her presence was nothing but noise and confusion. She was better off out of sight. Naaim didn't try to stop her, he just stared into nothing. I sat down, taking Ira's place and stared into the same nothing.

'He's a good kid,' I said, after a moment of silence. 'Daniel... He got mixed up in the wrong crowd, is all... He's trying, man. He's really fucking trying to make it right.'

From the corner of my eye, I noticed Naaim barely nod. I could have gone on but there wasn't much else to say.

307

I stood up. I was done. I bent low and surprised myself by kissing him on the head.

'It's over.'

I opened the front door, just as Naaim burst into a staccato cry. I considered going back, but it was time for him to let it all out and finally mourn in peace. He didn't need me. He certainly didn't need Ira. Her whole life she felt as though she'd been swallowed up and spat out by the system. Because she was black. Somali. Or just Muslim. Who knows? Naaim just happened to be an outlet for her to channel her anger. But now, as rare as it is, justice will be served; the system that worked against Ira her whole life was now working for Naaim.

I crossed the road, the hint of a spring in my step, and approached my car. I flipped down the visor and glanced in the mirror. I looked like shit, the last few weeks well and truly written on my face. But I was feeling pretty good about myself. I buckled up my seatbelt and started the car. I looked over at Naaim's house as I indicated and manoeuvred out. He'd come *this* close to destroying himself.

I pulled into my drive. Before getting out of my Nova, I looked out of the driver's side window, just to make sure there was no knife-wielding maniac from my past trying to slice me. I smiled as I got out.

68

Imy

It was Sunday. Two days since Pathaan had put it on the line. The Glock was cleaned, checked and loaded. I would carry it out methodically and without emotion, and I'd be back home with nothing to fear but the demons in my head.

I had to get through the day first, and the small matter of Khala meeting Stephanie and Jack for the first time. She had called me late yesterday evening. Typical Khala, typical last minute notice. She officially invited us all for a *Dawat*. A feast fit for her new family. I couldn't tell her no, especially since she'd been so understanding. Stephanie wasn't as understanding; she needed more time to prepare and fuss and organise. Hesitantly, she'd agreed, and then frantically taken off to Westfield London for some late-night dress shopping, leaving me at home to feed, bathe and put Jack to sleep, when I really should have been out killing Jay.

Pathaan would not be pleased that I had left it until Sunday, the day before he was due to fly home. He would definitely not be pleased that I had left it late because of a life that he despised me for.

But tonight it would all be over. I would finally have repaid my debt to him and Ghurfat-al-Mudarris.

*

Stephanie woke up unnaturally early for a Sunday, and spent most of the morning in the bathroom. Jack was ready in ten minutes flat, an hour before we had to leave, his hair overly waxed and abnormally styled. I sat down next to him and polished my leather boots.

'Touch my hair,' Jack said. I gently patted it with my hand. 'It's so hard and spiky.'

'You look good, kid,' I said.

'What's that word again?' Jack asked.

'Aslamalykum,' I enunciated.

'Aslam....*kum*?'

'Perfect!' I smiled down at him. It was Stephanie's idea to greet Khala with a Salaam. She wanted to make a good impression. I heard footsteps coming down the stairs. 'Make sure you tell your Mum how nice she looks.'

'*Oh*! Do I have to?'

'You have to.'

Stephanie stepped into the room and stood nervously in front of us.

'You look nice, Mum,' Jack mumbled.

'Thank you, Jack,' she said. 'Imy?'

Through my Khala's eyes, I saw that under her pale blue three-quarter length dress her legs were bare. When she sat, the skirt would rise further, possibly exposing her knees and thighs. The printed blouse was a little low cut. If she leaned forward, her bra would be visible.

I blinked and looked at her through my own eyes.

'Steph,' I said. 'You look stunning.'

*

The late notice of the Dawat meant that we hadn't really had a chance to discuss it. I caught Jack's eye through the rear-view mirror.

'You alright, kid?'

'I'm hungry,' Jack replied. 'Will she have food?'

I smiled. 'She'll have lots of food.' I turned to Stephanie. 'How about you, Steph? Are you okay?'

'Honestly... No.' She placed her hand on mine. 'But I think I will be.'

I pulled up to the house. Predictably Khala was at the front door, waving excitedly and mouthing something that was impossible to hear.

We stepped out of the car. Jack ran down the path in front of us, repeatedly shouting '*Aslam Kum*', and then surprised us all by warmly cuddling Khala, holding her tightly around the legs. Khala's smile, so wide, reminded me of the time when I landed on her doorstep all those years ago. Here I was now, introducing her to my fiancé and my son.

Jack detached himself from Khala and made his way into the house.

'Aslamalykum.' I kissed Khala on the cheek. 'This is Stephanie.'

'Aslamalykum,' Stephanie said, effortlessly, as though she hadn't been practising. 'It's so nice to meet you.'

'*Mashallah*.' Khala placed a hand heavily on her heart as if to stop it from bursting out of her chest.

'Shall I remove my shoes?' Stephanie asked, as we stepped inside.

'Oh no, Beti,' Khala replied. 'I shampooed the carpets clean last night and they are still a bit wet.'

I laughed. Stephanie sensibly held back.

'It's not funny!' Khala chided. 'Get inside.'

Khala held Stephanie's hand and they walked through the narrow hallway. Stephanie looked back at me over her shoulder and flashed me an easy smile as they disappeared out of sight into the living room. I took a breath, clearing my mind of everything but now, and followed them in.

Stephanie was sitting on the edge of the sofa, Khala next to her, knees touching, still clutching her hand and chatting happily away. Jack was on the other side of the room, a fairy cake in one hand and the remote control in the other, flipping through the cartoon channels. Making himself at home.

I could smell and almost taste the spread on the dining table before I even set eyes on it. Khala had gone all out, a mixture of Indian snacks – fish pakora, seekh kebab, papadi chaat – and then treats that she presumed Stephanie and Jack would be used to: fairy cakes, stuffed garlic mushrooms, prawn cocktail and salmon fish cakes. Plates from both cultures, mixed in with each other, deliberately I'm sure. Khala's way.

'Doesn't it look wonderful, Imy?' Stephanie said.

'That's just the starter,' Khala said. 'I have lamb biryani on the stove and shepherd pie in the oven.'

'You didn't have to go to so much trouble, Kala,' Stephanie said, missing an H, making it sound even sweeter.

'*Astaghfirulah!*' Khala cried. 'You listen to me, young lady. Nobody ever leaves my house hungry. You understand this?'

I pictured a vision of the future. Every Sunday, down to Khala's for lunch. Apart from the last Sunday of the month when Khala would come to ours and innocuously pick holes in Stephanie's cooking and general housekeeping skills. Christmases and Eid's and our wedding. Khala taking care of Jack as Stephanie and I went out the odd evening. I could see it so clearly. My heavy heart soared and danced as I looked at the coming together of the three of them, knowing that this future could be mine. But it would come at a cost.

'Imran,' Khala said. 'All this excitement I forgot to tell you.'

'Yes, Khala?' I said pulling up a chair next to Jack. 'Tell me what?'

'This morning, I had visitor. Your uncle.' She beamed. Stephanie looked up at me. I smiled it away. 'He said he raised you before you came to live with me. We talked for more than one hour. He wanted to hear everything about you.'

'Khala...' The smile frozen on my face. 'What did you tell him?'

'Strange man. He had so many questions! But as soon as I told him that you and Stef'nie were getting married, he left.'

69

Hounslow Police Station

Two words. *No comment.*

When Daniel had returned to the interview room, this time with his solicitor in tow, the SIO and DI knew they had lost him. They put forward the deal and, against Daniel's judgement and burning desire to spill all, he had said 'No comment' and braced himself for the onslaught. They didn't get angry, as Daniel had expected, nor did they look surprised. They looked beaten. Nevertheless, they continued with the questioning and each time Daniel would utter 'No comment', he would follow it with a weak 'sorry'.

Daniel walked quickly and in the straightest of lines out of the police station. He knew behind him the solicitor, Sandy White, was keeping pace, as his large shadow loomed over him. He'd already made his mind up that once he and White had parted ways, he would head straight back into the police station. Ready to talk. Not only about Simon and Anthony and the attack, but also how the solicitor had insinuated that his dad wouldn't be safe if he talked. Daniel would not hold back. Could not. It had gone too far. He would tell the police everything he knew about Dean Kramer, Terry Rose and The Second Defence.

'Okay, thanks,' Daniel said to White, as they stepped outside the police station.

White mumbled something, and dialled a number on his phone.

'I'm going to walk home.' Daniel stepped away. White placed a hand on his shoulder.

'It's done,' White said into the phone.

Daniel looked back through the entrance to the police station. The SIO was looking back at him. Daniel smiled weakly at him, when really he wanted to run to him.

'You're not going home just yet,' White said, looking out onto the road as a white Range Rover pulled up outside the police station.

Kramer stepped out. Daniel caught a glimpse of another man sitting in the passenger seat. White gently nudged Daniel towards the car.

Kramer waved brightly at Daniel. 'Alright, boy! In you pop.'

Daniel ran through all the possible options in his head. All involved him running and not getting very far. The passenger in the front seat inclined his head just enough for Daniel to recognise that he was again in the company of Terry Rose. Daniel obediently got into the back seat.

White approached the passenger side window and Rose slid it down.

'All good?' Rose asked.

'For now. The police have nothing.' White glanced at Daniel in the back before speaking. 'As long as they keep their mouths closed, it'll stay that way.'

Rose nodded.

'My advice,' White continued. 'Cut ties.'

Rose closed the window in White's face and watched him shake his head and walk away.

'Fuck his advice,' Kramer said. 'They're good kids.'

'Where are we going?' Daniel's small voice sounded out of place.

'Do you know what day it is today, boy?' Kramer asked.

'Sunday?'

Kramer extended his middle finger so that Daniel could see it in the rear-view mirror. He saw the red cross tattoo on Kramer's finger.

'St George's Day,' Daniel said.

'That's right, boy. And tonight we celebrate.'

A series of loud bangs at the window made Daniel jump out of his skin and dive onto his side across the seat.

Terrified, he looked back up at the window. Anthony was beaming at him, Simon behind his shoulder. They bundled into the back seat with Daniel.

'Happy fucking St George's Day!' Anthony screamed, shaking Daniel by the shoulders. 'That was a fucking trip. Double celebration, eh lads? I'm ready to party!'

'You alright, Daniel?' Simon asked, in the way that he always did.

'Yeah. That was close, right?' Daniel smiled. 'Happy St George's Day!'

Simon shook hands with Kramer and Rose, asserting his position.

'You did well,' Rose said. 'You all did. I'm proud of you lads.'

Daniel's smile was practised and he held it easily. It hadn't crossed his mind that Simon and Anthony would also be questioned. He'd been so close to selling his friends out, not knowing that they were so close by.

Kramer started the car and manoeuvred out. Heavy rock from the radio kicked in. Anthony threw shapes to the music. Daniel nodded to the beat, aware of Simon glancing his way. He looked out of the window and noticed a girl slowly crossing the road. She stopped in the middle of the road and faced the oncoming Range Rover. Kramer slammed on the brakes with both feet, the back end of the car swerved as his tyres screeched to a halt a few feet away from her.

The girl didn't flinch. She just stared at the screwed up faces staring back at her.

'Fucking dumb Somali bitch!' Kramer slid down his window and stuck his head out. 'Get the fuck out of the way.'

She didn't move, instead she gripped the sides of her hijab and pulled it forward so her dark face disappeared into it and all that they could see were the whites of her eyes. She smiled. A wicked smile lighting up her face from within her hijab.

Then she slowly ran a finger across her throat.

70

Imy

Khala was holding court, her voice quick and high and full of excitement. Stephanie, laughing, was trying to get a word in edgeways. Jack was eating his way through anything sweet. I excused myself and headed upstairs.

I stepped into the bathroom and as soon as the door was closed behind me, I scratched and scraped the hell out of my head. First little scratches and then when that itch kept calling, longer scratches, both hands, from the back of my neck through to the top of my head, repeating it until strands of my hair and specks of my scalp fell onto the tiles.

Pathaan would have been furious that Jay was still alive. I had felt his impatience and his frustration the last time we had met, and his presence at Khala's house was designed as a warning, a motivation.

He knew who I cared for, who I loved, and he would not think twice, would not even blink, as a bullet screamed its way out of his gun and into my life.

I had to take Javid Qasim out. I had to do it now and prove my allegiance to The Cause, and more importantly prove that I hadn't failed him.

I looked in the bathroom mirror. My hair stood in different directions. I ran the cold water and filled the sink and dipped my head into it. The cool sensation soothed the abrasions on my scalp. My phone sitting on the edge of the sink vibrated, moving itself closer to the edge. I placed a hand on it and lifted my head out of the sink. It was a withheld number. I felt my heart stop. Water dripped from my head, down my face and onto my phone as I accepted the call.

'Hello?'

'Imy.'

'*Shaz?*' I instantly recognised his voice. My heart started to beat again.

'Yeah,' he said, softly.

I should have called him. It should have been me who reached out to him. Apologised for hurting him. I could tell by his voice that he was still feeling it.

'I'm so sorry,' I said, matching his tone. 'I... I'm so sorry. I should never have laid my hands on you.' I wanted to make it alright. I wanted to erase what I had done and go back to normal. I desperately wanted him to delight in the details of whatever first world problems were bothering him.

'Have you killed him yet?' he said.

I gripped the phone as my mind raced. 'Shaz... Are you able to talk freely?'

I heard him rustling about, a muted dialogue exchanged and then he said, 'Yeah.'

'Are you at home?' I asked.

'Yeah.'

'Is he with you?'

'Yeah.' Shaz's voice cracked. 'He's sitting on my bed.'

'Can I speak to him?'

Silence for a moment. Then Shaz said, 'I am a Kafir.'

'Shaz...'

'I am a Kafir and I have brought disgrace to my *Deen*.'

'*Shaz.*'

'When I die, I will burn in hellfire for all eternity.'

'Shaz. Listen to me!' I could hear Khala at the bottom of the stairs calling my name.

'I don't want to die, Imy.'

'Let me speak to him,' I said. '*Pathaan Bhai.* Please. Talk to me.'

'You have to kill him now.'

'*Shaz... Shaz!*' I was talking to dead air.

I raced down the stairs and entered the living room. I picked up my car keys from the coffee table.

'There you are,' Stephanie said, her smile waning when she saw my damp hair.

'I have to go,' I said.

'What's happened?'

Khala walked into the living room. She balanced three mugs of masala chai and one glass of orange squash on her Princess Diana memorial tray. 'You spend a long time in the toilet. All okay?' she said. 'Don't worry, masala chai will sort out all your tummy problems.'

'Khala. I have to go.'

'Silly. You just got here.'

'Imy had an urgent call from work, Khala.' Stephanie stood up, her easy smile back in place as she took the tray from Khala. 'Here, let me.'

Khala, disappointed, fussed around with the plates, not able to say what was on her mind in front of guests. Stephanie followed me into the hallway as I opened the door. I turned to see questions on her lips that I could not answer. The next time I saw her, it would all be over.

71
Jay

My Beemer was due to be returned tomorrow. Despite nearly losing my life in it, I loved that car. We'd been through a lot and I could not wait to get behind the wheel and cruise until the wheels came off. Windows down as the finest G-Funk era hip-hop spilled out onto the streets of Hounslow.

In my bedroom, I was sound-checking a playlist that I'd just finished compiling to mark the return of my car. Cypress Hill had just finished declaring 'I ain't going out like that' and in the small gap before NWA took centre stage, I heard somebody pounding on my front door as though they'd been knocking for a while.

I popped my head out of the upstairs bedroom window and saw an irate Zafar looking up at me just as Dr Dre started to impart his street knowledge.

Sunday had been good to me. Shit was coming together. Maybe it was the music, maybe it was the Raiders baseball cap and dark sunglasses I was goofing around in, but I was feeling great. Fuck, man! I was feeling... *Gangsta*!

I acknowledged Zafar through the window and started to mouth the lyrics at him, whilst bopping my head and gesticulating hand movements fit for a rap video.

'Open the door?' Zafar screamed up at me.

I wasn't about to let anything spoil my mood. I bopped my way downstairs and opened the door with a flourish. Still with Raiders cap and dark shades in place, I said, ''*Sup*?'

He slipped past me, ignoring my proposed fist bump. I shut the door and followed him into the living room. He looked around for somewhere to sit and then decided to just stand in the middle of the living room and talk at a hundred miles per hour. I couldn't understand a word he was saying, and the music wasn't helping. I shut the living room door to drown it out.

'Slow down,' I said. 'Take a breath.'

'God. This is such a bloody mess,' Zafar said, shrugging my hand off his shoulder. 'You don't know Ira like I do.'

'Ira...' I sighed. 'Trust me. I'm getting to know her.'

'You don't know jack, Jay. Her whole life, ever since she set foot into this country, she's been made to feel like shit. From school, to employment. The system has let her down consistently.'

'I know that,' I said, gently. I removed my cap and sunglasses. Zafar had really killed the fucking mood.

'You don't know the half of it, man. She talks some dumb shit sometimes. Every time there's an attack, she always, *always*, sympathises with the jihadists. Check it out, she once told me that she was thinking about leaving the country and becoming a jihadi bride!'

I looked him in the eye. 'But she didn't.'

'No.' Zafar slumped down on my armchair. 'She didn't.'

'Can I get you a drink? Think I got some Ribena knocking about somewhere,' I said. He shook his head. I understood. You had to be in the right frame of mind to be sipping on Ribena.

'You know it was me who encouraged her to come to the weekly sessions at Heston Hall,' he said. 'I thought it was helping and it was! Then this whole thing with Naaim... She just had to get involved just like I bloody knew she would. And when the police couldn't do anything, all those destructive thoughts and feelings came flooding back.'

'Hang on,' I said. 'I haven't told you. They've been arrested. Daniel, he's turning witness. Ira knows this. I told her this morning.'

'No, Jay,' Zafar said.

'What do you mean *no*?'

'I called her. She told me that she rocked up at the cop shop! Told me that she watched all three of them as they were brought in for questioning. She was freakin' out, Jay. Saying some stupid shit. I'm worried she's about to do something –'

'Alright, chill man,' I cut in. 'I don't know what her problem is, but it's out of her hands. They're getting dealt with. I told you, Daniel is giving –'

'They walked, Jay.' Zafar ran a hand through his hair. 'Ira saw it. All three of them walked.'

*

Screeching round a corner, the loose buckle of the seatbelt knocked against my shoulder. The least of my problems was wearing a seatbelt; I was busy breaking all known traffic regulations. My Nova groaned as I pushed it to the limit.

'Keep trying,' I said to Zafar.

'She ain't picking up.'

'Have you got Naaim's number?'

'Switched off.'

'Fuck!'

I turned the corner in third only to find a learner in front of me. I slowed a touch, dropped it into second and put my foot down. The little engine of my little car roared as I slipped past the learner.

'Text her,' I said.

'I have already. Twice.'

'*Again*. Text her again!'

Zafar then kept insisting that we call the police. But the police called me instead. I put it on speaker.

'Where are you?' Idris yelled through the tinny speaker. I hesitated for a split second. 'Jay! The fuck are you?'

Idris' tone jolted me into telling him the truth. 'On my way to Naaim's.'

He muttered something unintelligible.

'I think he's about to do something stupid,' I said.

'He's already done something stupid. Stay away, Jay. His house is crawling with Counter Terrorism.'

'*Counter Terrorism?*' Zafar whipped his head towards me.

'Who're you with, Jay?' Idris asked.

'Zafar,' I said. I heard Idris sigh. It pissed me off. I knew what he was thinking.

'Take me off speaker!' Idris snapped.

I mouthed *sorry* at Zafar, and put the phone to my ear.

'Has Naaim been arrested?' I asked.

'He's not there. But the search is on. Jay, trust me, stay away from him. Naaim Sarkar is now officially a wanted man.'

'He hasn't done anything,' I said weakly, knowing what the police would have discovered.

'His neighbours reported a strong smell coming from the house, a couple of uniforms went to check it out. It was quickly established that he was storing some sort of highly corrosive substance. Then it all kicked off. His home was raided. They found signs of sulphuric acid in his bath tub, along with aluminium foil and drain cleaner.'

'Fuck! Fuck!' I turned down Naaim's road and was stopped immediately by two policemen. They signalled for me to turn the fuck around. Past them I could see Naaim's house, cordoned off with yellow tape and crawling with police. Some in white hazmat suits. I looked across at Zafar, he was craning his neck, looking up at the police helicopter in the sky. His face a picture of disbelief. '*Fuck!*'

'Fuck is about right, Jay,' Idris said. 'In his bedroom, they found an empty box of masonry nails and discarded plastic bottles.'

I didn't want to ask Idris. I didn't want to hear the words. But he said it anyway.

'Jay... It looks a lot like Naaim is planning an acid bomb attack.'

72

Imy

The front door to Shaz's house had been left wide open. Pathaan would have wanted me to enter freely.

'Shaz. It's Imy.' I stepped into the hallway. 'Shaz?'

I quickly checked the living room and kitchen and then ran up the stairs. I twisted the handle to his bedroom door. It was locked. 'Shaz. It's me.'

'Imy?' Shaz's muffled voice came back at me.

'Yes.' To say I was relieved to hear his voice would be something of an understatement. 'Are you okay?'

'He said he's going to kill me.'

I rested my forehead against the door and closed my eyes. 'I won't let that happen.'

A sniffle. A cough to cover it. And in a broken voice. 'Just go, Imy.'

'Open the door please,' I said. 'I want to see you.'

'I don't want to see you!' Shaz cried. 'You fucking hurt me, man.' With all that had happened with Pathaan, he was still upset about me hurting him.

I took a step back and looked at the poster on his bedroom door. A skull smoking a huge joint, emblazoned on a large green marijuana leaf. Pathaan would have seen it. I recalled the phone call. Shaz's voice, but not his words.

I am a Kafir and I have brought disgrace to my Deen. When I die, I will burn in hellfire for all eternity.

My temper rocketed. I counted ten in my head, and tried to breathe through my anger. I could only manage seven before I kicked the door and the delicate lock gave way and the door flung open. I didn't enter his room.

Shaz was sitting calmly on the edge of his bed. He had a woolly hat tight over his head, finishing just below his brow. At first glance, it didn't look like he'd just had an encounter with Pathaan, but I knew there was more to it than first glances.

His eyes flitted to the grey tracksuit bottoms sitting on top of the wash basket. They were stained wet. I clamped my teeth hard at the thought of how frightened he would have been in Pathaan's presence.

'Can I come in?'

Shaz nodded tiredly. I entered the room and sat next to him on the bed. The faint smell of urine mixed in with the strong smell of Lynx body spray. We sat in silence, only the sound of his jerky breathing for company. I wanted to put my arm around him. Both my arms around him. Hold him tightly and lie to him that everything was going to be alright.

'Where are your parents?' I asked.

'Coventry.'

'When are they back?'

Shaz dropped his head in his hands and rocked back and forth.

'Shaz. Tell me when are they back.'

'Wednesday evening,' he said through his hands. 'He's gonna fucking kill me, Imy!'

I kneeled down in front of him and tried to peel his fingers away from his face, but he held tight.

'Listen carefully,' I said. 'Pack a bag, call a cab and check yourself into a hotel. Nothing local. Do you understand?' He remained hidden behind his hands. I grabbed his wrist and forced it away from his face. 'Tell me you understand.'

'Fuck off,' he spat and wrenched his hand away from my grip. With a trembling hand he wiped away the tears. Anger momentarily taking over from fear. 'Who are you that I should listen to you? Seriously, who the *fuck* are you?'

'I'm your friend,' I said, truthfully.

Shaz snorted. 'This is all your fault. He said he's gonna cut my throat and make my mum watch as punishment for raising a bad Muslim.'

'I won't let that happen, Shaz.'

A small drop of blood trickled from under his woolly hat and pooled around his eyelid. Shaz stood up and walked to the mirror. Through the reflection he fixed me with a gaze and removed his woolly hat.

Carved on his forehead was the word:

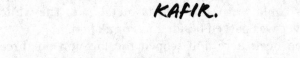

KAFIR.

73

Derelict Building Site, South London

Ira and Naaim were parked across the road a short distance from the old construction site. From their vantage point they could see past the rusty metal gate. The white Range Rover was parked beside the Portakabin.

They had been here and scoped the location on three separate occasions. They had established that it was the headquarters for a brutal right wing fascist group – The Second Defence. Ira determined that they were just as worthy of punishment as Daniel, Simon and Anthony.

It had been planned weeks ago. A St George's party to remember. Jay had almost ballsed the whole thing up. But, true to form, Daniel, that weasel, had buttoned up. He, along with his friends, along with the rest of the racist group, were going to pay a heavy price.

'I'm not afraid to die,' Naaim said.

'No one's dying, yeah,' Ira said.

'I want to be with Layla again.'

Ira flashed two passports at Naaim. 'You're going to be stuck with me for a while yet.'

Naaim leaned his head back against the headrest. 'I don't want to go Syria.'

'You rather go jail, Naaim?' Ira said.

Naaim said nothing.

Ira silenced her phone. She didn't bother checking the several text alerts or missed calls, but she had a good idea that it was Jay poking his nose where it didn't belong.

'A friend of mine will put us up for a bit, till the dust settles,' Ira said. 'Trust me, yeah, we'll be treated like royalty. After that, new names, new passports and... *Get down*!'

They both slid down in their seats as two cars pulled into the old construction site.

'The party will be starting soon,' Ira smiled.

74
Jay

The next stop was obvious. I drove as fast as I could to Golf Link Estates, Southall. But I had to slow down often as police cars were still screaming past us in the opposite direction towards Hounslow.

Ira lived on the sixteenth floor of a tower block. The lifts were characteristically out of order. We pegged it up the stairwell, adrenaline keeping exhaustion at bay. I thumped on Ira's door, changing fists for relief. Zafar was on his knees screaming Ira's name through the letterbox. A neighbour popped her head around her door. Through her inebriated state, she mumbled that Ira hadn't been home in weeks. We walked heavily down the sixteen floors, defeated, the exertion of the climb catching up with us. We approached my car in silence. I could sense Zafar glancing at me for answers.

'Now what?' he asked, as he sat in the passenger seat.

I started the car, but kept it in neutral. I opened up my messaging app. The 'Kaleidoscope' group that I had created had not lived up to expectations. It was designed to bring us closer together, somewhere we could take the piss and make plans and send silly GIFs. But apart from the opening conversation, there was only radio silence. I started typing. Zafar followed suit.

Ira! 19.09
Answer your damn phone. 19.09

Tahir
Salaam Brother. 19.09

Have you heard from Ira? 19.10

Tahir
Not today. Why? 19.10

Naaim? 19.10

Tahir
No. What's going on? 19.11

Fuck! 19.11
Sorry… 19.11
I have to get hold of them. 19.11

Zafar
Tahir. Can you keep trying Ira? 19.11
Ira. Call me!!! 19.11
Please. 19.11

Tahir
Zafar. What's happened???? 19.12

Zafar
I'm with Jay. Police are crawling all over Naaim's house. 19.12
We have to find them. 19.12
They found traces of sulphuric acid in his bath tub!!! 19.12
Think he's making an explosive 19.12

Tahir
La ilaha illallah Muhammadur Rasulullah. 19.13

Tahir has left the group.

We both stared at our screens and then at each other. The man had kids, a wife, and a job. He was most at home running the Community Centre, strong-willed enough to think that dialogue could and would solve all, but also aware enough to recognise a lost cause. I didn't blame Tahir for bailing.

'Now what?' Zafar asked again, as though I was running the fucking show. I had to get shot of him. He may have a few fancy letters behind his name from a top university, but he wasn't the quickest on his feet. 'Who are you calling?'

'Long shot,' I replied. Phone to my ear, I stepped out of the car.

75

Derelict Building Site, South London

There wasn't much room at the construction site to accommodate all the cars. Anthony had been tasked with moving the two JCB excavators to behind the function hall. It didn't matter that he didn't have a driver's licence. It didn't matter that he was two double shots down on Cîroc Vodka. He took on the task with glee.

Daniel's job was to direct the cars into the site and make sure that they were parked tightly. He was surprised to see old bangers mixed in with luxury cars mixed in with SUVs with baby seats in the back. Daniel struggled as the drivers grew frustrated with him. A line of cars impatiently waited on the main road trying to get in. Amidst car horns and profanities, Daniel glanced at Simon who was stood shoulder to shoulder with Rose, confidently greeting the guests and directing them into the function hall. He was fast becoming one of them.

'Jesus, boy,' Kramer laughed, slapping Daniel on the back. 'And I thought you were the bright one.'

'Yeah… Sorry.' Daniel's phone vibrated as he guided in another car, perilously close to getting its wing mirror knocked off.

'Go get yourself a drink, boy. You're verging on useless here.' Kramer winked at Daniel and took over. 'Go on. Fuck off!'

Daniel looked around. He didn't want to be near Simon whilst he was with Rose. He didn't want to mingle with the guests, who were stood around in small pockets outside the hall. Like the cars, the guests varied in appearance.

Well-groomed professionals in smart suits shared drinks and dialogue with skinheads in short bomber jackets and big metal toe-capped boots – an image that he'd once tried so hard to portray.

Daniel walked around the back of the hall, looking for Anthony. The JCBs had been clumsily parked, but Anthony wasn't to be seen. Daniel didn't want to head back just yet, so he sat himself in one of the diggers and took out his phone. He had a missed call from a number that looked vaguely familiar. Daniel stared at it, trying to figure out who it could be, when it rang again in his hand.

Daniel accepted the call without thought and then felt anxious, pulling it back away from his ear. He stared as a distant voice emanated from the speaker.

'Daniel... Daniel!' The voice said. 'Fuck's sake. *Daniel!*'

Daniel blinked at it a few times, and then, making sure nobody was in earshot, he put the phone to his ear.

'Yeah?'

'Daniel. Where are you?'

'*Jay?*'

'Yeah, Jay! I need to know where you are.'

'I'm sorry,' Daniel said, and then in one breath blurted out 'I messed up, they sent a lawyer, he told me to keep my mouth shut, they threatened me, said they would hurt my dad.'

'Alright. Okay. Shut up for a second. Tell me where you are.'

'I don't know,' Daniel said. 'At a St George's Day party, with my friends.'

'Friends? Anthony and Simon?'

'Yeah,' Daniel said as he heard Jay hiss *fuck* under his breath. 'What, what is it?'

'I need a location, Daniel.'

'It's at an old construction site. Croydon, I think. I saw signs for Croydon.'

'Shit! That's miles away! You need to get away from there, right now!'

'I can't.'

'Tell everyone they have to leave, right fucking now!'

'They won't listen to me,' Daniel said in a small voice.

'Daniel. I'm gonna need an address.'

'I really don't...' Daniel checked his 4G signal. 'Hold the line. I have an idea.'

He removed the phone from his ear but he could still hear Jay; '*Has he just put me on fucking hold!*' He opened up Maps, waited a second for the blue dot to find itself, then tapped it so that the street address and postcode popped up. He took a screenshot and sent it across to Jay, then put the phone to his ear.

'Clever fucker,' Jay said. 'Now listen to me very carefully. Call the police.'

'Police... Why?'

'Tell them there's a bomb threat.'

'*Bomb*,' Daniel mouthed. 'Jay... What's going on?'

'It's Naaim,' Jay said. 'He's coming for you, and he's fucking pissed off.'

76
Jay

It was the target. It had to be. Naaim and Ira had it all sussed out. Daniel, Anthony and Simon all in one place at a St George's party in South London.

'Any luck?' Zafar said. Another question. Not a solution.

'Possibly.' I sat back in the car and entered the postcode on the maps app. Estimated time one hour ten minutes. On a Sunday evening I figured I could clock it within forty-five.

'Where we going?'

'South London.' I inserted the key in the ignition and quarter turned it. '*Oh, c'mon!*' I cried and smacked the steering wheel with the palm of my hand.

'What?'

'It's not starting! We're gonna have to push start it. Do you mind?'

Zafar pulled his sleeves up and stepped out of the car. He walked around to my side and ducked down to my window. 'Clutch down, keep it in second,' he said, finally taking some semblance of control.

I looked up at him apologetically. 'Sorry, Zafar.' I turned the key fully and my Nova kicked into life. I slipped it into gear and put my foot down. Zafar yelped. I may have clipped his elbow with the wing mirror. I figured he'd be alright as I watched him shrink in my rear-view, his face puzzled, cradling his elbow.

Like Tahir, who had dramatically left the group chat, Zafar had a lot to live for. He was sitting on a Masters degree and I knew it was only a matter of time until he got himself a killer job, somewhere in the city probably, and led a full and rich life. I couldn't have him walk with me into fuck-knows-what and possibly not come out the other side.

Me? I had that MI5 training behind me. All five fucking minutes of it. I'd be alright.

I just hoped that Daniel had called the police. I couldn't do it myself. My phone battery was hovering in the red, and I needed whatever remaining juice to direct me to South fucking London.

77

Derelict Building Site, South London

From the boot of the car, the stench of sulphuric acid was growing stronger. Ira slid down her window. The music was just loud enough to spill out of the function hall and into the car. The whine of guitar and heavy drums. Ira could just picture them all dancing, drinking, rejoicing. Celebrating all that was wrong with this fucking country.

'Not one car has entered in the last thirty minutes,' Ira said. 'You noticed?'

Naaim wiped his clammy hands on his jeans. 'I'm ready.'

'Look at me.'

Naaim gave her a steely determined look, filled with hatred and revenge. 'I'm ready,' he repeated.

'You look it,' Ira smiled. '*Mashallah.*'

Both doors opened and they stepped out, meeting at the back of the car. Naaim popped the boot. Ira reached in and picked up the metal bar and a large, heavy-duty padlock. Naaim leant in and unzipped the main compartment of the rucksack. He stared at the ten plastic bottles, placed neatly and tightly inside. Satisfied, he zipped it back up then unzipped the side compartment. He wrapped his fingers around the wooden handle of the Bowie knife, the nine inch blade protected in its sheath. He attached it to the back of his belt and covered it with the tail of his shirt. Finally, he picked up the small detonator, trailed the wire through the inside of his shirt and tucked the loose end into his jeans.

They walked in silence towards the construction site, their strides matching and purposeful. They entered the metal gate, Ira parting to the left and Naaim to the right, then pushed the gates shut. Ira took out the padlock and locked it. Naaim glanced at the Portakabin. The lights were off. They set off, ducking low, using the cars as cover, and made their way towards the shoddy hall. They had done their homework. They knew that there were only two entrances. The main entrance and the stage entrance to the side of the hall.

The music faded out and they froze behind the bumper of a Bentley. The used the opportunity to scope the area through the back windscreen of the car. They watched as the door opened, and a man staggered out, an unlit cigarette between his lips. The dirty heavy guitars roared back to life. 'Fucking Sex Pistols,' the man cried and turned back to the hall, the room chiming along to the chorus: 'I am an anarchist!' The door shut behind him.

'Now!' Ira hissed.

Naaim was on his feet, and like a baton in a relay race, Ira slapped the metal bar in his hand. He ran the ten metres and wedged the metal bar in between the looped handles of the double doors. He signalled to Ira and she hurried to him at the entrance. She straightened her hijab and they slowly moved across the front of the hall and poked their heads around the corner. A man was standing facing the doors of the stage entrance. Naaim's hand reached around his back, his fingers gripped the hunting knife.

'Wait!' Ira placed her hand on Naaim's. 'Just wait.' Naaim replaced the knife in its sheath. The song faded out and the DJ made an announcement.

'Gentlemen! I give you our host; our dear friend and the leader of The Second Defence: Terry Rose.'

78

Derelict Building Site, South London

Daniel had called the police straight after speaking with Jay. He hadn't given any thought as to how he was going to explain it. He didn't quite understand it himself. He started with, 'I think there's a bomb threat.'

A *click* and a rapid transfer, and then the questions came at him calmly but quickly. Questions that he mostly had no answers to.

'What is your location?'

Daniel still had the address that he'd sent to Jay. 'Let me check.' He took the phone away from his ear and put it on speaker.

'Where exactly is the bomb right now?'

'It's not here.' Hearing that word – *bomb* – back, the enormity suddenly dawned on him. With his hand forcibly shaking, he scrolled through his phone looking for the address. The operator continued to question him.

'How did you come by this information?'

'I... I... Somebody phoned me.'

'What was the name of the caller?'

'Jay. I don't know his full name.' The app icons on his phone were blurring into each other as his eyes filled with tears.

'What form is the bomb in?'

'I don't know.'

'What is the current location of the bomb?'

'I don't know!'

Daniel's nerves were shot. He closed his eyes tightly and when he opened them, the apps became clear.

He remembered taking a screenshot of the address. He opened up the gallery app. All the photos were lined up in a neat grid of the life that he'd once had. One, in particular, called out to him. His finger gently stroked it and it filled the screen.

It was a time before Simon, before Anthony, when his mum was his only friend. At the fairground, they were squeezed together in a lime-green bumper car. A ten-year-old Daniel gripped the wheel, his face a picture of determination, whilst his mum placed a guiding hand over his, a smile as alive as she once was.

'Caller... Caller...'

Daniel's finger hovered over the image, unable to bring himself to minimise it.

'We need a location, caller...'

Anthony appeared, arms aloft, loudly singing the national anthem. Daniel minimised the photo as Anthony snatched the phone out of his hand.

'Mr Lewis, don't worry, I'll get Daniel home early,' Anthony slurred. 'Early in the morning!' He laughed and spluttered into the phone before disconnecting the call. He lobbed it back to Daniel. 'Come on, party's kicked off. Let's get wrecked!'

*

From the makeshift bar, which was just a long table, Daniel poured himself a third shot of vodka. The first was a double, which he'd knocked back just to keep up with Simon and Anthony, and the effects had relaxed him a little. The second helped clear his mind and he decided that he'd been massively overreacting.

Daniel looked around the hall, as he sipped on his drink, the music pounding in his ears. Nigh on a hundred guests singing and embracing and celebrating the occasion. Anthony enjoying making a fool of himself on the dance floor. Simon worked the room, firmly establishing himself with The Second Defence.

The group. The gang. *The terrorist cell...*

Daniel laughed at the thought. These were people, people like himself who just wanted what was best for their country. He was seeing it clearly now. Just the thought of Naaim turning up armed with a bomb sounded absurd. Did he really know this Jay guy well enough to trust him? He didn't. The more he thought about it, the more ludicrous it sounded. It was common knowledge that St George's Day was not celebrated as it should have been, for fear of offending the 'sensitive Muslims'. It was starting to sound more like a hoax, a ploy to get the party shut down. This was Daniel's day, a day to be proud of his country.

Daniel took out his phone and decided he'd call the police back and tell them it had been a misunderstanding. He stumbled his way to the exit, to get away from the noise, and attempted to pull the door open.

It wouldn't open.

Before Daniel could make sense of it, the music faded out and the DJ made an announcement. Slipping the phone back in his pocket he looked up just in time to see Terry Rose walk across the stage, microphone in hand, to thunderous applause followed by chants of 'Cherry... Cherry... Cherry.' Daniel joined in. It was fun.

Rose took his position on stage, ready to address his people. Behind him, to his right, was a six-foot Union Jack flag. To his left, the flag of England: the St George's Cross bleeding across the white background. Rose stood perfectly between the two. It was a powerful image. Some of the guests took photos on their phones.

So Daniel did, too.

'A great man once said,' Rose began, as the room dropped to silence. '"There is a forgotten, nay, almost forbidden word, which means more to me than any other."'

He took the microphone away from his mouth and held it by his side. He ran his eyes over the crowd, who seemed to lean forward in anticipation, knowing what was to come. Rose brought the microphone back to his mouth and said: '"That word is England."'

A hundred plastic cups were raised and a hundred lions roared 'England!' back at him.

From the back of the hall, Daniel noticed a small figure tentatively make his way towards Rose. Daniel blinked away the haze from his eyes and squinted at the figure. As his vision cleared, he felt his heart hammer in his chest.

Naaim had just casually walked onto the stage.

'Gentlemen, the evening's entertainment has arrived,' Rose mocked, taking the sudden appearance in his stride, to a ripple of laughter from the crowd. Daniel tried to open the door again, but it was still jammed, and it was starting to make sense why.

'What'd you want boy?' Rose asked, 'cos you really don't want to be here tonight.'

'He's probably delivering curry,' a voice shouted from the crowd, and a few others joined in with the slurs.

Daniel searched frantically around for his friends. Anthony was by the drinks table, enjoying the spectacle, happily screaming abuse at the boy. He hadn't registered what was happening, though it seemed that Simon had. Daniel watched him muscle through the crowd towards the stage and stand beside Kramer. Daniel called out to him from the back of the hall but his small voice was drowned out by the growing aggression.

79
Jay

My Vauxhall Nova was not built for the strain that I'd put on it. By the time I hit Croydon, black shit was smoking out of my exhaust. I reached the address that Daniel had sent me, but I couldn't work out the location. I drove up the street and then back down again looking for any signs of life, of a party, of police presence. But it was quiet.

I had my phone in my lap, and with one hand on the steering wheel, I redialled Daniel's number. The battery died before it could connect. My car charger was probably still covered in blood in my Beemer.

'Fuck!' I took my eyes off my phone and looked up at the road just as a dark figure flew past my car. '*Fuck!*' I swung to the right before straightening out. In the rear-view mirror I could see her looking back at me over her shoulder. Her eyes wide as cymbals, either at nearly being killed or because I'd turned up to put a hole in her demented fucking plans.

I flung open the door, jumped out and caught up with Ira. 'Where is he?' I screamed at her.

'The hell is your problem, Jay? You got some sort of hero complex or what?'

Ira tried to walk away from me. I gripped her arm and spun her back to me.

'Take your hands off me or I scream rape.'

'Do it! Get the cops down here.' I was so fucking vexed that I shook her hard. Her hijab shifted a little, and I felt guilty about it. 'Sorry.' I let go of her. She readjusted. 'Please, Ira.'

'It's too late.' Her quick glance over my shoulder was revealing. I spun to see a metal gate. Past it, a shit load of motors tightly squeezed in and beyond that, I could *just* make out muted voices coming from a building at the back.

Ira gripped my arm with surprising force, her nails digging into my flesh. 'This ain't none of your business, Jay,' she hissed through gritted teeth. I wrenched her hand away and sprinted across the road. The gate was at least ten-foot-high and secured with a padlock. There was nowhere to place my foot in order to climb it.

I ran back to my car and dropped it in reverse and with the door still open I backed it up until the bumper touched the gate. I scrambled out and climbed onto the hood and then up onto the roof. I had to stretch, and I felt my back clicking and adjusting as my fingers found purchase on the top of the flat metal rail. It didn't look pretty, but I managed to lift my bodyweight and throw a leg over the rail. I straightened out and sat on the flat rail. I looked out on the street, hoping to see police lights breaking the night with colour. I only saw the dark silhouette of Ira. I looked down at the ten-foot drop and swallowed.

Nike Air Jordans. 2017 Limited Edition. Don't let me down now.

80

Derelict Building Site, South London

By now the crowd was tight, shoulder to shoulder, hurling verbal abuse at Naaim. Daniel struggled but managed to get through the abusive crowd to join Simon and Kramer at the foot of the stage.

He wasn't surprised to see Simon standing perfectly still as it all kicked off around him. Cigarette lighters and plastic cups were launched at Naaim, drenching his clothes in alcohol. Daniel looked across at Kramer; his face looked as though he was ready to explode.

'You were told to take care of it,' Kramer snarled at Simon.

'I'll take care of it right now,' Simon said. He moved quickly towards the stage before Daniel could tell him about the bomb threat that Jay had warned him about.

'Wait.' Kramer grabbed Simon by the arm and pulled him back. Daniel noticed that the anger in Kramer's eyes had been replaced by something else. 'We have to go.'

Simon shrugged his arm away and watched in contempt as Kramer, all six foot four of him, started to back away. Rose, the legendary Terry Rose, leader of The Second Defence, had already sloped off the stage. The missiles being launched at Naaim slowed and then stopped. The guttural abuse directed at Naaim, slowed and then stopped. Replaced momentarily with an acknowledged pin-drop silence, followed immediately by a wall of screams and the screech of footsteps on the linoleum flooring quickly backing away from the stage and towards the exit.

Daniel turned his attention back to the stage, a picture forming in his head even before he saw it. Naaim was grasping something in his fist, his thumb running over the top of it and a wire trailing from below his grip. He had turned slightly to the side, and Daniel could now see the rucksack on his back.

'Simon,' Daniel cried. 'We have to go.'

Simon stood firm.

81

Derelict Building Site, South London

It was easy, Naaim thought. These were the same bastards who'd taken great joy in hurting and abusing people like Layla, without any thought of the consequences. Well, here's your fucking consequence. He knelt down and with his free hand he picked up one of the lighters that had been thrown at him. He turned to the two flags draped proudly behind him and lit them at the corners. He stepped away as they caught fire quickly, the flames rapidly running across the edges.

He slipped off his rucksack and placed it near his feet. With his right hand still aloft, gripping the detonator, he crouched down and unzipped the bag. One by one he neatly laid out ten plastic bottles in front of him on the lip of the stage. Over the top of his rucksack Naaim scanned the terrified faces in front of him. Where's your filth, now? Where's your supremacy? They were powerless... As once they'd made him feel.

His eyes stopped, in turn, at the three people that had tilted his world.

Anthony Hanson, who had mouthed off at Layla, taunting her and encouraging his friend to take away her modesty, was now hiding under the drinks table like a dirty cornered rat.

Daniel Lewis – Naaim had wanted to throttle him the day he'd walked into his house. And then he'd had his chance at redemption, of putting an end to it all. But like the weasel that he was, he had weaselled out of it.

Simon Carpenter, his dirty filthy hands all over Layla, his tongue inside her mouth. Ripping off her hijab and pouring alcohol over her head. When Naaim had revealed the detonator, Simon was the only one who hadn't run.

He will.

Naaim picked up the first plastic bottle and shook it. The satisfying sound of the masonry nails rattling and the hotter-than-hell corrosive acid swishing in rhythm. He counted five in his head and then with a feral roar that he didn't know he was capable of, Naaim launched the bottle as hard as he could. He watched it arc high and then drop perfectly in the middle of the desperate mob, clawing at the exit.

There wasn't a loud explosion. If there was one, he didn't hear it. But from the way they scattered and stumbled around in all directions, trampling over each other and clutching their faces, Naaim knew that the little improvised bombs he and Ira had created in his bathtub were working with devastating effect.

He smiled and picked up another bottle.

82
Jay

I twisted my ankle as I landed, the pain shooting up my leg. I stayed down on my haunches and put my hand to it. I didn't have the luxury of taking in my surroundings or working out a plan, as terrified screams ripped through the hall and across the car park.

'You're too late, Jay.' Ira rattled the gate from the other side.

Fuck you, I thought. I didn't have the time to say it. I got to my feet and ran, the pain in my ankle easing with every stride as I picked up speed. In front of me was a maze of tightly-packed motors. Without breaking my stride I used the bumper of an old classic Capri to give me a leg up, then scaled to the roof and stepped from car to car towards the hall. I climbed down a white Range Rover and approached the entrance to the hall.

The heavy pounding of fists from the other side of the double doors mingled with the distressed screams. There was a metal bar looped into the door handles. I tried to slide it out but the doors were being pushed towards me so hard, straining at the hinges, that it had wedged the metal bar in tightly.

'Move back!' I shouted. 'Move away from the door!'

I pushed the door back with all my might, but I was pushing against fuck knows how many people. Behind those doors, something suddenly changed. The screams of help were now groans of despair. I felt a little slack against the force of the door, the metal bar loosened and rattled against the door handles. I slipped it out and it clanged to the floor. I knew what was coming. I had to get the fuck out of the way. Quickly.

The door flew open with such speed and ferocity that it clipped the side of my head. I stumbled back, just managing to catch myself from falling, but a body came flying out, slamming me onto my backside. Another tripped over my leg and I watched him land on me. His bloody face, inches away from mine, was punctured with nails.

'*The fuck away from me*,' I screamed, as he dripped blood onto my face. I pushed him off me as a flurry of boots blurred by me. I got to my feet and stood with my back against the wall to one side. The footfall lessened and I took a deep breath and peered into the hall.

That same rancid smell from Naaim's house was now mixed with burning flesh, and made me throw up a little in my mouth. I covered my nose and mouth with my arm and took it all in. There remained around a dozen men in the hall, staggering, crawling around like *Night of the Living Dead*. Smoke was coming off them as the acid greedily ate through their punctured skin. All were looking to me for help.

Fuck. Fuck. Fuck. I still didn't have a fucking plan.

I could just about make out the stage at the back, two burning flags and Naaim's small figure in between them. To my left Anthony was curled up in a ball under the drinks table. To my right, Daniel had ducked behind the abandoned DJ booth. He poked his head around and I gestured with my hand to stay the fuck down. He quickly retreated.

Simon was stood at the foot of the stage, the only one not to have scarpered. I ran the length of the hall, still trying to figure out whose fucking side I was on. Naaim registered my arrival with a sweet smile on his face, like his mate had just rocked up. Plastic bottles were neatly lined up by his feet.

I grabbed Simon by the arm. 'Get the fuck out, now.' He didn't even so much as register my presence. Like Naaim, he was ready to go all the way. '*Naaim*,' I screamed, and I didn't know what else to say.

Naaim was no longer that innocent boy who'd sat helplessly on the bus and watched the girl he loved suffer humiliation at the hands of those ignorant thugs. *They*'d turned Naaim into whatever it was that was standing in front of me – a product of his environment. He'd be labelled and treated as a terrorist for the rest of his miserable life, and every mouth would open and form an opinion, and turn this into something that it never was. Pure and simple, Naaim had avenged Layla.

'I did it, Jay,' Naaim shouted, his arms spread to indicate the destruction around him.

Yeah... You did.

It was then that I noticed he had something gripped in his fist, his thumb firmly pressed on the trigger. I'd wondered briefly how one man, one *boy*, had managed to take control of a hall full of men. Men who could have easily ripped off his arm and beaten him with it. Even with the bottled acid, he could easily have been outnumbered and swallowed whole.

I followed the wire trailing from the detonator. It was tucked into his shirt, but with his arms spread victoriously, the wire had popped out of his jeans and was now dangling uselessly by his waist.

Oh, you fucking idiot!

I glanced across at Simon, hoping, *praying* that he hadn't clocked it. The sides of his mouth curled up and he took one long stride forward. Naaim thrust his arm forward, the fake fucking detonator in his hand. Simon grabbed his arm and wrenched him off the stage. Naaim dropped at his feet.

I stepped in between them and put my hands out in a conciliatory manner. Simon also put his hand out, nothing conciliatory about it, and I could do nothing as the brass knuckle duster raced its way into my face.

The last thing I heard before I blacked out was the crack of my nose exploding.

83

Derelict Building Site, South London

From behind the DJ booth, Daniel looked out at the men that he was on his way to becoming. Bleeding, begging and crawling for the exit. Their clothes shred and smoking, their features removed from their faces. The majority had escaped. Daniel could have too. He could have left his spot and run out of the hall. Run all the way home from South to West London, locked his bedroom door and tucked himself up in bed. But he'd had a hand in creating this, now he'd have a hand in ending it all. A chance at redemption that would eat away at the guilt that had been consuming him.

He could see Jay, laid out on the floor, blood streaking from his nose down both sides of his cheeks. Next to him, Simon was on his knees, straddling Naaim, relentlessly raining blows down on his face.

Across the hall was Anthony, curled up under the drinks table in the foetal position. Daniel left his post and carefully negotiated his way around the casualties. Many were not fatal, but probably wished they were. He crouched under the table and shook Anthony by the shoulder.

'Anthony. *Anthony.*'

Anthony slowly turned onto his back. He looked up listlessly at the underside of the table. The side of his face had melted away. The white of his jaw on display.

'Anthony?' Daniel asked, unsure if it was his friend that he was looking at.

'My eyes.' Tears ran freely down Anthony's ruined face as his body shook. 'I can't see anything.'

'I'm going to get help,' Daniel said, and thought *How?* 'It's going to be okay,' he said, and then thought *It's not*. His phone had been knocked out of his hand in the scramble for escape. He ran across the hall, calling Simon's name. Simon had given his fists a rest and was now towering over Naaim, viciously kicking him in the stomach.

'Simon!' Daniel had to raise his voice. The fire had latched onto the curtains and was starting to roar. 'Anthony needs help. It's all over his face.' Simon stopped and looked over at Anthony. From his reaction he'd recognised the horror on his friend's face.

'I need your phone,' Daniel pleaded. 'We have to call for help.'

Simon took his eyes off Anthony and picked up a bottle from the stage. He calmly unscrewed the cap.

'Simon, please. It's gone too far. We have to call for an ambulance?' Daniel cried, but he knew from the fire dancing wildly in Simon's eyes that he had lost his friend to madness.

Daniel stepped away, keeping low as the fire threatened to overwhelm him. He crawled over to Jay, coughing as the smoke filled his lungs. Daniel shook him by the shoulders and noticed rapid movement behind his eyelids.

Jay blinked his eyes open. Looked up at Daniel. And smiled at him.

84
Jay

I was feeling hot, as though someone had turned the thermostat right the way up, and I was in my bed, wearing my winter jacket, a thick duvet wrapped tightly round me. It felt comfortable, but that fucking roar in my ears wouldn't let me sleep. I opened my eyes, determined to seek the offending sound.

Above me Daniel was staring down at me, and I couldn't figure out what he was doing in my bedroom. His face registered deep concern, as though he needed to find solace in a friendly face. So, you know, I smiled at him. Behind him, the roar that wouldn't let me sleep was the sound of the fucking stage burning brightly. Daniel helped me up into a sitting position, but before I could clear my head, I heard a piercing scream. I followed it. Naaim, on the floor, his arms covering his face as Simon rained searing-hot liquid and shrapnel over him.

I shot to my feet and ran hard, building up whatever momentum I could in the short distance between us, and connected head-first with Simon's midriff, knocking him away from Naaim. The plastic bottle dropped from his hand as he fell back, with me in his grip, on top of him. I kept my weight on him and pinned him down.

'*Go!*' I screamed. '*I'm right behind you!*' Daniel helped Naaim to his feet, who was stumbling on the spot, his right arm badly burnt and the side of his face massacred beyond recognition. I noticed his hand shaking as he reached behind the tail of his shirt and gripped something.

Fucking Simon was strong. I kept him down as long as I could, but he reached up and grabbed me by the back of the head, jerking it forward towards him. My already fucked up nose smashed painfully against his forehead, dazzling me. He pushed me away easily and rose to his feet.

I was fucking exhausted, man, I swear to God. On my back, with the fire keeping me warm, I was tempted to stay that way. I silently prayed for the police to make their presence felt right about now, because Simon did not seem like he was going to walk away until he'd killed Naaim. I didn't think I could stop him.

But I had to try. I had to match his determination.

Ignoring the fantastic pain in my face, I got onto my hands and knees, expecting to see Simon launching another attack on Naaim.

But Naaim had gone.

In his place, Daniel was lying on the floor. Eyes peacefully closed. Blood streaming out of a large wound in his stomach.

I scrambled over and grabbed Daniel from under his arms and started to drag him away from the fire. '*Help me*!' I screamed at Simon, but he was already backing away. With whatever I had left in the tank I slowly dragged Daniel across the hall, away from the burning stage. '*Fucking stay with me, Daniel.*'

I could clearly hear the sirens, the blue lights illuminating the hall through a small window. At a safe distance from the fire, I laid Daniel down and applied pressure on the wound with one hand, trying to find his pulse with the other.

Behind me, armed police ran into the hall. I put my hand up to get their attention, but they dismissed me and fanned out, attempting to establish the threat.

'*I need help here!*'

A medic put a hand on my shoulder, and another gently removed Daniel's head from my lap.

'I can't find a pulse,' I said quietly.

85

Imy

I picked up the Glock from my flat and tucked it into the back of my jeans. I slipped the silencer into my inside jacket pocket and drove to Javid's house. His drive was empty.

I parked across the road, the Glock digging into my skin, a constant reminder of my jihad. I didn't need to be reminded. I knew damn well what I had to do. I moved the piece away from my skin and slipped it under an old property newspaper on the passenger seat. As I waited for Javid to return, I called Stephanie.

'Steph. Are you home?' I asked.

'Yes. Where are you?' Hesitancy in her voice, she cleared it away. 'Your uncle is here.'

I gripped the phone so tightly that I could have crushed it in my hands. 'Where?'

'Downstairs. Playing with Jack.' I came down hard against the steering wheel with my fist. 'How well do you know him, Imy?' Steph asked.

'I know him well.' I kept my voice neutral.

'He... he's making me uncomfortable. He keeps leering at me and asking me about my wedding dress.'

'Listen to me carefully, Steph.' I failed to keep the urgency out of my voice. 'Treat him as you would any other guest, I'll be home as soon as I can.'

'When?'

I looked across at the empty drive. I had estimated the hit would take no longer than four minutes, from stepping out to returning to my car. I had covered my shoes in clear plastic bags. Leather gloves tight around my hands. The Glock sitting within my reach. All that was missing was Javid Qasim.

'When, Imran?' Stephanie asked again.

'I have to finish this.'

'Come home soon.'

'I will. Let me speak to him.'

I could hear her padding her way downstairs. Jack's voice, screeching excitedly, as though he was being tickled. Pathaan's hands all over him.

'It's Imy, he wants a word.'

I heard snatches of conversation as I pictured Stephanie talking to him through a forced smile.

'I'll make some tea.'

'Four sugars.'

'Jack come help me.'

'But Mum. I want to play with him.'

'Please, Jack.'

The phone changed hands and there was a moment of silence as they left the room.

'I hear congratulations are in order. I wonder, will I get an invite?'

'Pathaan Bhai.' I hated myself for still calling him *Bhai*, to still afford him that respect. 'It's not what you think.'

'You have no idea what I think, Imran,' he sneered. 'You have become weak. You have surrounded yourself with weak people. *Sinful people.* Fallen in love with the enemy. A great shame you have brought upon yourself... I assume that you received my message.'

'Shaz had nothing to do with this,' I said, quietly.

'I felt that you needed incentive, Imran. It seems like you have forgotten that your parents were raped and killed by the very same Kafirs that you now defend.' There was an edge to his voice, and I didn't respond for fear of unsettling him further. 'Is it done?'

'I'm outside his house, waiting for him to return.'

'Sunday has come, Imran. The Sheikh will not be pleased. *I* won't be pleased.'

'I still have a couple of hours.'

'If you want... I can give you further motivation.'

'*Bhai*, *no*.'

'Maybe I'll play family man for a while. I hear the white woman can be very pleasing.'

*

My hand slipped under the newspaper and gripped the Glock every time a car turned onto the road, Pathaan's final words relentlessly ringing in my ears as I waited. A grey Volkswagen Passat slowed and pulled up behind me. A man wearing a dark suit stepped out, crossed the road, and approached Jay's house. I checked the time on the dash, it had just gone ten. He didn't seem to be in a hurry to leave, giving me the impression that Jay wasn't far away.

A further thirty minutes had passed when a red Vauxhall Nova rattled towards me, black smoke spattering out of the exhaust. It turned into the drive.

The car door opened, and Javid stepped out.

86
Jay

Will this fucking night ever end?

I groaned to myself upon seeing Teddy Lawrence through my windscreen, but I wasn't entirely surprised. I'd just returned from giving a statement at Croydon Nick, and my name would have lit up like a firework back at Thames House.

'I came alone.' Lawrence smiled as I stepped out of the car. 'No helicopters, no police cars, no fanfare. Just me and you, buddy.'

I sighed, opened the front door. Lawrence followed close behind in case I slammed the door in his grinning face. I wanted to. 'Wait here.' I directed him into the living room and headed to the kitchen, noisily opening and slamming cabinet doors until I found what I was looking for. 'Wanna drink?' I called out, my good manners betraying me.

'No,' he said. 'I'm good.'

I walked into the living room, glass tumbler in hand. Chivas Regal. No mixer. No ice. My drink as raw as I was feeling. I slumped down on my armchair and let my body sink into it. I wasn't getting up anytime soon.

'Jesus, Jay.' He stood over me, taking me in.

My face was coloured with blood from my twice-broken nose. My clothes were cold and damp from when Daniel had bled over me. My heart had pounded so hard for so long that I could no longer feel it ticking over. I blinked blankly at him.

'Daniel Lewis,' he said. I shut my eyes. 'He's going to make it.'

As frustrated as I was, I allowed the relief to wash over me.

'Largely down to you, Jay.'

'What do you want?'

'To talk.'

'You're wasting your time,' I said. 'This has nothing to do with MI5. Naaim was not a terrorist.'

'That depends on your definition of the word.'

'That supposed to mean?'

'It means that Naaim Sarker and his accomplice Ira Abdikarim were picked up by police three miles outside of Heathrow Airport. They had on their person passports and flight tickets. To Syria.'

'That's bullshit! It's been planted.'

'Grow up, Jay.'

'Fuck off, you grow up!'

'One fatality tonight, heart attack. Eighteen casualties, burnt, disfigured. One lost his eyesight... What were you doing there, Jay?'

'I thought I could help,' I said. It sounded pathetic out loud. 'He's just a kid. What he did was brutal, I get that! But what he's had to endure was just as fucking brutal. There's no grey area, Lawrence. There's no political or religious agenda. This was nothing but revenge.'

He nodded and flicked his wrist so his Tag slipped out of his sleeve and shone into view. 'It's late. I just wanted to swing by to give you a heads up. We're going to have to speak to you tomorrow morning about what's taken place tonight.'

'It's going to have to wait. I'm going back to work tomorrow,' I said, surprising myself.

'Don't think that's a good idea. Give it a day or two.'

'Yeah, well, *I* think it's a good idea. I think it's the Michael fucking Jordan of ideas. I'm through with all this crap. This world is going to shit with or without my interference. Right now, all I want is my alarm slapping me across the face in the morning. I want a commute, I want a desk, a computer, fucking small talk by the photocopier. I want normality.'

'I'll need to debrief you,' Lawrence said. 'We can do it after.'

'*What?*' I just about summed up the energy to form an incredulous expression. 'Debrief. *De-fucking-brief!* What'd I just say to you about normality? I don't work for you, or your shit-for-brains organisation anymore, Lawrence.'

'Don't be naïve, Jay. You may not work for the Secret Service anymore. But you'll always be an MI5 asset. I'll see you tomorrow.'

'*Fucking leeches*,' I shouted, as he walked out of the room. I put the tumbler to my lips and for the first time in months I let the drink in. I let my eyes close and decided that my armchair would be my bed for the night.

87

Hounslow, West London

Teddy Lawrence walked away, not particularly pleased with himself. It seemed every time Lawrence met with Jay, he just ended up troubling him further. It was not his intention.

Lawrence had already tried once to get Jay back on board, and he wanted to ask again. It was on his lips, but he could see that with the mood Jay was in, he was not going to respond well to being asked. It was disappointing. A waste of a talent. Jay had proved himself greatly in the past, and again tonight. If he hadn't turned up at the old construction site in South London, there was no doubt there would have been more fatalities. Numerous witnesses had reported that Jay had opened the doors, allowing the potential victims to escape; and rather than escaping himself, Jay had tried to calm the situation inside the hall.

A damn good asset, but his tendency to play devil's advocate had made him enemies in high places on both sides of the war. Although no longer an official MI5 asset, Jay would remain on their radar. And Assistant Director of Counter Terrorism, John Robinson, had found a new way of using Jay without his consent.

Lawrence clicked on his seat belt, started the car and switched the radio on. Tapping his fingers on the steering wheel in time to Diana Ross, he manoeuvred out, without so much as a glance at the parked Toyota Prius and the shadowy figure inside.

He reached the end of Jay's road, indicated and turned. As soon as he was out of sight, Lawrence pulled up. He killed the engine and radio as he flipped open his centre console, picked up the Bluetooth ear piece and placed it around his ear. He pressed the dial button and as it rang he stepped out of his car and hurried back, stopping at a neatly trimmed bush at the corner of Jay's road.

'Suze. Teddy Lawrence,' he said, as his colleague from Thames House answered. 'I need you to run a car registration, quick as you can.' Lawrence relayed the number plate. He grimaced as his ear piece signalled call-waiting. He slipped out his phone from his pocket and saw that it was John Robinson. 'Call me back as soon as you get a hit, I have to take this.'

'Sir.' Lawrence took the call as he discreetly peered around the bush. Ten cars down, the Prius was still parked across the road from Jay's house.

'Lawrence, my boy,' Robinson bellowed chirpily, in stark contrast to his recent depressive state. 'Come in. I have news.'

'I'm in the middle of something right now, sir,' Lawrence said anxiously, as he waited for the results of the car registration. 'Can it keep?'

'Bin Jabbar has been sighted.'

Lawrence whipped his head back behind the bush. 'Sir?'

'A Mr and Mrs Hanif sheltered him for one night in Pakistan. It appears that the so-called Teacher, the much respected man of the people, took away their children to ensure silence. They called it in. Chapter and Verse. He then headed to Port Gwadar, where he boarded a cargo ship en-route to Dubai, and we're certain of his destination from there. It's all the confirmation that we need, Lawrence.'

MI5 had known that Bin Jabbar had placed a call from a remote village in Afghanistan before fleeing. Now he had been placed in Pakistan, and the eyes of the security forces were upon him. Lawrence recalled the meeting with Robinson, and how he'd desperately tried to reason with him. It was a high risk and dangerous move, but it seemed that Robinson had been proven right.

The Teacher was on the move and they knew his end game.

It was time to bring Jay in and place him under protection, before it was too late.

'Two teams are in position one mile out from the perimeter of the compound, we estimate his arrival between twelve and twenty-four hours,' Robinson said. 'Now come in and watch it unfold. There's a drink waiting for you.'

'Javid Qasim,' Lawrence started. 'We have –'

'No!' Robinson cut abruptly. 'We don't go anywhere near Qasim. Not until this is over. Is that clear?' he barked, disconnecting the call.

It troubled Lawrence, how far Robinson wanted to go with this. It was only a matter of time before Bin Jabbar was caught, but until then Jay's life was still in danger. Lawrence peered around the corner. He was two minutes away from Jay's house, half that if he ran. Robinson's warning to stay clear rang in his ear.

Lawrence turned the corner and casually strolled. His ear piece signalled another call, he answered it on the first ring. 'Suze?' he answered. 'What've you got?'

'Blue Toyota Prius. Number plate, mike, hotel, six, five, yankee...'

Lawrence watched the car door opened and a figure step out. He looked around uncertainly before crossing the road towards Jay's house.

'The vehicle is registered to an... Imran Siddiqui.'

Lawrence disconnected the call, and started to run.

88
Jay

I'd already knocked back two shots and poured myself a third, but it hadn't helped to dim the madness in my mind. One more shot and then I resolved to get up and get things done. I had to shower. I had to iron my itchy black trousers and pull out my bland tie and novelty Monday socks. I'd meant what I said to Lawrence; I *was* going to work tomorrow.

In one swift motion I necked the third shot. Before I could sink any further into my armchair, I got to my feet quickly. I felt light-headed. I couldn't remember the last time I'd had a bite. I put my hands out to steady myself, took a breath and headed to the kitchen to put the tumbler in the dishwasher. A small act, but one that would put me back on the road to normal – but even that glimpse of normality was snatched away from me.

In the hallway, through the frosted pane of the front door, I clocked a still figure. I marched down the hallway and pulled opened the door, ready to give Lawrence *what's fucking what.*

Instead, a man was pointing a shiny gun in my face.

I looked at the empty glass in my hand. *The fuck was in that drink!*

I'd had my throat sliced. I'd just walked away from an acid attack. Let's not even get started on my involvement with the Oxford Street attack. My world was so violent that I simply shrugged and made my way into the living room with the gun feathering the back of my neck. I slumped back down in my armchair. I took in the plastic bags on his feet. The black leather gloves. The Glock .40 handgun trained on me. The silencer, the cherry on top. A right fucking professional. I met his eyes. I swear to God, nothing surprises me anymore.

'First, you save my life. Now, you want to take it.'

Even in my current predicament, I was quite happy with that line.

'I'm sorry, Javid.' He said, lowering his gaze, giving me an opportunity.

Aiming for his big head, I threw my glass tumbler at him. It flew out of my hands, a country mile away from him and landed harmlessly on the sofa on the other side of the room.

He locked onto my eyes. I gave him a sunny smile. 'Jay,' I said. 'Call me Jay.'

He steadied the Glock and pointed it at my heart.

'You going to tell me your name this time?' I asked.

'Siddiqui,' Lawrence announced, entering the living room. The Glock found itself a new target. Lawrence had his arms up in the air when he should have had an arsenal pointing at this guy's head. Teddy Lawrence to the rescue. *Whoopee fucking doo!* Don't get any blood on your precious fucking suit, will you. He was directed to the armchair next to me. I shook my head at Lawrence in disapproval.

'Imran Siddiqui. Born in Sharana, Afghanistan. An orphan at the age of ten. Moved to London at the age of sixteen. You were my first file, Imran,' Lawrence smiled. 'I must have watched your every move for two months straight. It was redundant; it was always going to be redundant. The only reason your file dropped on my desk was to give me experience. Nothing was ever going to come from it. Every day, I watched you leave for work and pick up your colleague, a Shahzad Naqvi, if I remember correctly. Drinks at lunch time. A joint in the afternoon. I knew your every move and honestly, it bored the living shit out of me.'

'Who do you work for?' Imran asked.

Lawrence hesitated, the gun in the face making the decision for him. 'MI5... Back then I was doing surveillance.'

'There's a file on me. Why?'

'From the age of ten to sixteen, you were housed, educated and trained by members of Ghurfat-al-Mudarris.'

I groaned as I slouched down lower into the armchair and ran both of my hands over my face, then winced in pain as the bone in my broken nose shifted.

'Does my father know you're here?' I said quietly.

'Jay... Not a word,' Lawrence said.

'Your father?' Imran looked bemused. Not as fucking bemused as he was about to look.

'Jay! You've signed The Official –'

'Fuck The Official Secrets Act!' I snapped, and locked eyes with Imran. 'My father. Abdullah Bin Jabbar. The Teacher. Al-*Fucking*-Mudarris himself. Ring any bells?'

89
Imy

'Is that true?' I asked, training my gun back on Jay. He had a mouth on him.

'Yeah, it's true,' Jay snapped. 'Now get that shit out of my face.'

I tried to process the information, but even if it was true that Al-Mudarris was his father, what did that change? He was in hiding, and would be for the remainder of his natural life. The Sheikh was now in command, and he'd issued an order which I had no choice but to carry out. I'd looked into Jay's eyes and hoped he saw in mine the actions of a desperate man. It wasn't personal. It wasn't war. Simply, it was my life or his. I took a step towards him.

Lawrence lifted himself off the armchair. 'Sit back down,' I shouted. Lawrence carefully backed into his seat. The Glock swung in a pendulum motion from one to the other.

It was supposed to be *one kill*. Was it ever going to be that simple?

'It's not personal.' I steadied the Glock on Jay. 'The fatwa must be carried out.'

'Fatwa? On who? *On me?*' He placed a finger to his chest. 'The fuck issued a fatwa on me?'

'It doesn't matter.'

'The fuck it doesn't. Tell me who!'

'Jay, be quiet.' Lawrence said. 'Let me deal with this.'

'Sheikh Ali Ghulam,' I said, gently. He deserved to know.

'Fuck's his problem?' Jay mumbled, digging the heels of his hands into his eyes. It made me desperately want to scratch my scalp.

'That's all I know.' I glanced at the clock behind him, I had just under an hour before Pathaan took his fury out on Stephanie and Jack. My hand tightened around the grip and my finger tensed against the trigger. 'I'm sorry.'

'You don't have to do this,' Lawrence blurted. 'The fatwa is about to be lifted, Imran.'

The sight of the Glock moved to between Lawrence's eyes. 'What do you know about it?' I asked.

'Bin Jabbar has been informed about the fatwa. He's on his way to see the Sheikh. It's over, Imran. Put down the gun.'

I wanted nothing more, but I couldn't. I had no trust in Lawrence. It was because of him and people like him that I'd ended up on this path. Jay dropped his hands from his face, words softly escaped his lips.

'He came out of hiding. For me?'

Lawrence nodded. 'He crossed the Afghanistan border into Pakistan and headed for Port Gwadar. He then boarded a cargo ship headed to Dubai. If he's in Dubai, Imran, it's almost certain that he's making his way to Sheikh Ali Ghulam.'

On my mother's grave, if he was lying to me, the immense guilt that I was feeling would vanish as I emptied the chamber into him.

'Imran, listen to me,' Lawrence continued, as I searched for the truth in his face, 'Two teams are awaiting Bin Jabbar's arrival. We're going to allow him to pass and conduct business with the Sheikh. The fatwa will be lifted.' I glanced across at Jay, his face remained expressionless, as though it couldn't decide what shape to form.

I removed my left hand from the Glock and slowly ran my nails along my scalp. Relief daring to wash over me. Hope tightening in my grasp.

'Where is Al-Mudarris now?' I asked, eyes on the clock.

'Imran...'

'Where is he now?' I repeated.

'We know he's in the Emirates. We know where he's going. We know the fatwa will be lifted,' Lawrence said. 'Twelve hours.'

'It's too late.' I shook my head clear of any hope. 'It's too late...' My left hand joined the other and steadied the Glock. I slipped the safety off. Lawrence flinched but my arm was already swinging away from him with Jay in my sight. The desperation, the unwanted determination drowned my every thought. I blinked rapidly. With each blink I saw Stephanie. I saw Jack. I saw Khala. I saw Shaz. A life and a family that I'd longed for. Lawrence moved quickly to his feet, I swiped him viciously, the barrel of the Glock crashing into his forehead and dropping him to his knees. I did it again, angry at the false hope that he had given me. He fell onto his side at my feet.

It was now. It had to be now. I stepped closer to Javid, raised the gun to his face. He nodded, seemingly accepting his fate. He placed his hands gently on the cold barrel of the Glock and brought it forward so that it was in between his eyes. A trail of blood escaped slowly from his nose.

'Do it,' he said. And I believed him.

I took a breath, it came in ragged bursts. Lawrence was on his hands and knees, scrambling to get up, screaming at me, pleading with me, looking to make a move that wasn't there. I met Jay's eyes, they met mine without fear.

My finger tightened.

'I'm sorry, Jay.'

'*Do it!*'

The Glock popped quietly through the silencer, and tears streamed down my face as I looked at the hole in the armchair, an inch away from Jay's ear.

I'd lost. My life was over.

*

I moved slowly through Jay's hallway, my head weighing me down as nothing but bad thoughts crawled over every inch of my skin. Would Pathaan believe that the fatwa was to be lifted? It didn't matter. Was Al-Mudarris Jay's father?

It didn't matter. All that Pathaan would see was that I had failed him again, and he would react. Pathaan was always quick to react.

He had been, at times, a father to me. At times an older brother. For six years he had raised me, looked out for me and loved me as his own. For six years we had shared the same dream of hope and vengeance, but our paths had crossed again at a time where that dream had long faded and been replaced by all that he despises. I could understand his rage.

But... I had to believe that the love was still there.

'Imran, wait,' Lawrence called out. 'You can't leave. I have to bring you in.' I pulled the front door open, but he caught up with me and palmed it shut.

I turned and faced him and noticed the open cut on his forehead from where I'd twice struck him with the Glock. I almost apologised. *Sorry.* That word forever on my lips. I don't think anybody had ever said that word to me and meant it. He should, *Lawrence* should, be at my feet begging me for forgiveness. It was men like him that made men like me.

'I have to go.'

I turned away from him and reached for the door. His hand gripped my shoulder. 'It's over, Imran.' I spun quickly and pinned him against the wall by his throat.

'*Nothing is over!*' I screamed in his face, tasting the tears that raced down my face and into my mouth. The barrel of the Glock digging again into the cut in his forehead. Above me a light bulb flickered. I released him and took a step back.

'I have to speak with Pathaan,' I said, softly.

'Abassi?' His voice was tight. 'Aba Abassi?'

I nodded weakly. 'He has my family.'

'Abassi is in the *country*?' He slipped out his phone, unlocked it and dialled a number.

'Don't do that?'

'Do you have any idea what this man is capable of?'

Lawrence put the phone to his ear. I snatched it away, disconnected the call and pocketed it. '*Nobody* goes near him.'

'Listen to me, Imran. This is a highly dangerous individual. You cannot do this by yourself. Let me help.'

I shook my head.

'Think this through. He can't be reasoned with.'

'You don't know him like I do,' I said.

'No, Imran. You don't know him like we do.' Lawrence loosened his tie and exhaled. 'An ex-recruiter for Ghurfat-al-Mudarris. The man is a specialist in pain. Responsible for eleven roadside IED attacks, that we know of, solely so that he could collect any official military equipment that he could get his hands on. Radios, guns, vehicles, even stripping our men of their uniforms, leaving our soldiers fighting for their lives without dignity. Have you any idea of his method of recruitment? How Ghurfat-al-Mudarris has over a hundred sleeper agents all over Europe and the US?'

'Don't,' I said, as every one of my senses rocketed.

'Pathaan and his men arrive in small villages in stolen government-issued vehicles, head-to-toe in stolen fatigues and weaponry.'

'It's not true,' I said, my voice barely carrying.

'They'd murder the men and rape the women before killing them. Leaving the villages burning in their wake.'

Maybe I'll play family man for a while.

Pathaan's voice in my head, I shook it hard and tried to clear it. Lawrence was looking at me, his features softening through my tears.

'Only the children were spared.'

'No.'

'Full of hatred and anger and revenge, putting the blame squarely at the feet of the West.'

'*No*,' I screamed. I squeezed my head, my eyes shut tightly, but it was all I could see.

Hiding under my bed.

My father pleading. My mother screaming.

The bed is lifted. A hand reaches out to me.

Pathaan carrying me to safety in his arms.

I opened the front door and ran.

90
Jay

Devil's sat on my shoulder my whole life. Maybe I was born to die young.

At that moment, in that instant, I fucking welcomed it. I wanted him to pull the trigger and feel the bullet rush in between my eyes, deep into my brain so that all my thoughts would turn to nothing. I understood. I understood fucking everything.

I took my eyes off the plant pot that I had been lost in, and turned to Lawrence who'd scampered back into the living room.

'He's taken my phone.' Lawrence had his hand out. 'Give me yours.'

I'd run it over and over in my head until it made nothing but sense. I was just a pawn in their game, for them to move around as they pleased and topple over when they were done.

'Jay! Give me your bloody phone.' His eyes moved around the room, stopping at the landline on the side table. He rushed over and dialled a number. As he waited for it to connect he watched me carefully.

'It's Lawrence. Put an immediate trace on my phone. It's going to come back to a residential address. Dispatch field agents Cooper and Carpenter. Send to their phones the file on Aba Abassi, AKA Pathaan. I want medics and SO19 present and on standby, sirens off and out of sight. We can't have the target spooked; it's imperative that we take him alive.'

Lawrence disconnected the call and ran a finger across the cut on his head. He checked his watch and nodded satisfactorily to himself.

And then... and then he fucking smiled at me.

'You alright, Jay?' He pushed out his cheeks and let out an extended *whoosh*. 'That was close.'

'You knew about the fatwa.'

'Jay,' he frowned, hopping aboard my thought train.

'You knew he'd come out of hiding.'

Lawrence said nothing. I acknowledged it as an admission. I nodded. He glanced at the landline as though it could offer him escape, when it didn't he said, 'We're fighting a war, Jay.'

'Yeah,' I said.

'We had to find a way to entice Bin Jabbar out of hiding. Robinson, he...' Lawrence sighed. 'It doesn't matter.'

'Robinson...?'

'I didn't agree to it.' He walked across the room until he was stood in front of me. 'I offered you an in, Jay, you should have taken it.'

'I've never once told anybody about my involvement with MI5. Dad... Al-Mudarris... The world's most wanted man... He would have known, he would have sussed it out. Maybe he always knew.' I summoned the energy to shrug. 'But he wasn't the one to slap a fatwa on me. In fact, he's risking everything that he's ever worked for to put an end to it. The Sheikh issued it.' I caught his eye.

'Tomorrow, you will be briefed.' He took his time reading the time off his fucking Tag. 'It's late. We'll answer all your questions, tomorrow.'

'I just have the one,' I said. 'How did the Sheikh come by that information? Only me and you knew... And I'm pretty sure I didn't tell him.'

I blinked at him and took in his hand-tailored fucking crumpled suit, his tie loosened at the collar, a shiny sheen across his forehead. His face unable to conceal the truth.

'You. Fucking. Snake... You orchestrated the whole thing.'

373

His lip twitched as if preparing itself for a smile, a charming smile that would explain away everything – but anything he could possibly say would be nothing but noise. I knew the truth.

'You've got him,' I said. 'You've finally caught The Teacher. Pat yourself on the fucking back. But know this: me and you, we're through. There is no reason for our paths to ever cross again.'

'If you just hear me out. Tomorrow, come in and we'll –'

'*We're through!*' I lashed out with a kick. It was petulant, a schoolboy kick, like when somebody nicks your spot in the dinner queue. I barely made contact, just brushing his shin and leaving dirt on his trouser leg from my Jordans.

I straightened up as calmly as I could and told him: 'get the fuck out my house.'

91

Imy

The curtains in Jack's bedroom were drawn. Through the small gap the soft glow of the night light was seeping out. From our bedroom window, Stephanie was staring down at me.

I gripped the Glock tightly in my hand and held it by my side. I inserted the key into the front door and I stepped inside. As I turned to close the door, a black Audi had pulled up across the road. Two men stepped out and paced towards me.

I closed the door.

I glanced into the empty living room. One of Stephanie's pink slippers lay abandoned on its side. I blinked away the picture forming in my head.

I stood at the bottom of the stairs and placed one hand on the bannister. It was loose, as though it had been dearly held onto for solace. I looked up. On the top step was Stephanie's other slipper. I closed my eyes and felt blood boiling inside me, every inch of my skin tingled. I held my breath and climbed one step at a time.

I rounded the corner. Stephanie was standing on the landing. Her feet were bare, her dressing gown wrapped high and tight around her, but not able to conceal the reddening of skin around her neck. Her curled hair, that she'd worn for Sunday lunch at Khala's, was straggled, tangled. She glanced at the gun by my side, revealing the last part of me.

'I didn't make a sound.' There was steel in her voice. 'Jack doesn't know.' She stared absently at the block letters on his bedroom door that made up Jack's name.

I tapped the Glock against my thigh and turned away from her. I gently pushed Jack's door open. The nightlight illuminated his beautiful face as he slept. On the other side of the bed, on the nursing chair where I'd spent many nights reading bedtime stories, Pathaan had his finger to his lips.

'Sshh.' He smiled.

In his other hand he held an ivory-handled curved knife to Jack's neck.

'You couldn't do it.' Pathaan kept his voice low, his gaze on the gun by my side and then back on me. 'It seems that your priorities have changed, Imran. It doesn't matter, there are hundreds waiting to take your place. Better men than you. Men that shun the very *Shaitan* that you now embrace.' He knuckles turned white as he gripped the knife tightly and lifted it under Jack's chin. 'You were warned, Imran. Your failure has come at a price.'

Downstairs there was a loud crash as the front door was forced open. Heavy footsteps climbed the stairs until they were behind me. On the yellow walls of Jack's bedroom the nightlight cast shadows of two men looming, their shadows getting larger as they trained their guns on me, voices overlapping as they shouted for me to drop my weapon.

Pathaan lifted Jack out of bed by his hair and held him in front, like a human shield, the knife point touching the base of his throat. Jack's eyes flew open and locked onto mine. *Dad*, softly escaping from his lips. I heard Stephanie's feral scream as she escaped the grip of the men and ran into the room. She dropped to her knees beside me, her hands clasped together, pleading through tears with the same man who had violated her.

I did this. I had brought this into her home.

A single tear slowly rolled down my face. Pathaan smiled from behind Jack. His face partially visible, taunting me, daring me to risk the shot. The gun twitched in my hand.

'You shed tears for these people?' he said. 'The very same people that killed –'

I couldn't bear to hear that lie again.

I shot him clean between the eyes.

92
Jay

As a child, probably around seven, something like that, Mum would often drag me to the Civic Centre, London Borough of Hounslow. Normally to discuss something mind-numbingly boring, like a council tax query or planning permission. For a hyper seven-year-old it was the most tedious place on the planet. I'd wait for her in the main reception room with people who had no place to live, all their possessions in a black bin liner or two. Beaten by the system, battered by life. The staff were just as depressed, just as stressed. Bearers of bad news. The whole set-up would freak me out.

After the night I had had with Naaim, and Imran, and fucking Teddy Lawrence, I was craving that tedium. Despite my hangover, despite nor having slept, for the first time in my life, a boring day at work was all I wanted.

In the grey light of Monday morning, I stood outside the large, red-brick building. Slowly, I made my way through a cigarette, staring up at the Welcome sign, repeated in ten different languages, and considered the turn of events that saw me working in that very place. I'd hated as a kid.

I tried to look on the bright side.

It was local to me, only a five-minute drive. I didn't have to wake up ridiculously early, like those ambitious types who worked in the City. I wasn't located in Social Services or the Housing Department, or any of those high-stress environments. I was in the ICT Department. I'd sit on my backside on the helpdesk for seven hours and twelve minutes, which suited the lazy in me. Only getting up for a lunch break and the odd cigarette. It wasn't taxing work, answering and logging calls before passing them on to the clever bods in the glamorous Desktop Support Team. I could do the job with my eyes closed, which, on occasion, I did.

It was a soulless job, but what did that matter? MI5 had killed my soul.

I looked at my watch. It had just passed nine-thirty. I shrugged and walked into work. It was a warm morning, but I'd wrapped a lightweight blue and white striped scarf around my neck to cover the scar. I didn't need nor want the attention. But I *was* a little excited at the reception that I would receive on my return. I'd play it cool.

I walked confidently through the lobby. A curt nod to Tim the security guard who stared blankly at me and then asked me for identification. I flashed it at him as I walked towards the pavilion, and used my ID card to enter through the doors and into the ICT department, trying to suppress my smile as the rest of the team noticed me.

Jay's back!

How's it going, matey?

We missed you, Jay. Good to have you back. New trainers?

Yeah, none of that happened.

I made eye contact with Carol; she peered at me over her thick glasses and inclined her head to a desk space.

Not so much as a glance or a nod or any sort of acknowledgement. *Fuck, tough crowd!* I attempted to log into my computer, but just like many of the needy idiots that called in, I'd forgotten my password.

I peered over the desk partition opposite me, at Malcolm, who didn't seem to be on a call. Malcolm was a character. A little aloof, and a bit of a rebel by all accounts. He once changed the London Borough of Hounslow logo on all the templates to London Borough of Howslow. Instant legend status!

I stood up and peered over the partition. He was updating his Facebook status on his phone.

'Malcolm,' I said, brightly. 'Wha's happening?'

'Alright, Jay,' he said, without taking his eyes off his phone. 'You're back then.'

'Yeah, I'm back. I see you've grown a beard while I was away. Suits you.'

Malcolm raised his eyes away from his phone and looked at me, crestfallen. 'I've always had a beard.'

'Ha!' I laughed nervously. 'I know. I know.' My voice reached a Mariah Carey high. 'I'm just playing... Can you change my password, please?'

'Log a call.' Malcolm clearly offended, went back to his phone.

'I'll change your password.' Next to me, ending a call, Kelly flashed me a cute smile and I wondered if she'd consider having a drink with me.

'Nice one,' I said, flashing her what I hoped was an equally cute smile.

To my right, Davey slid his mobile across my desk. I looked at him, a little flickering bogey doing the hokey-cokey from his nostril every time he took a tangerine breath. 'You have to see this,' he enthused. 'It's Wolverine versus Batman. It's amateur, but it'll make you think. Can you imagine if DC and Marvel comics crossed over?'

I looked at the time stamp, the YouTube video was seven minutes long! I settled back in my chair and watched it, making all the appropriate noises.

I spent lunch with my team in the, actually very decent, canteen. Davey was still waxing lyrical about the video, Malcolm at every point finding plot holes in it, and the two of them having a heated debate whilst I made eyes and conversation with Kelly. In the afternoon and on a heavy stomach, I had a return-to-work meeting with Carol. We agreed a gradual return, three days a week, then four, then back full time. She informed me that we had a new call logging system which I'd have to be trained on.

I shrugged. Smiled. It was good to be back.

Normality.

It was a nice enough day. I walked home, as my Nova wasn't talking to me after what I'd put it through. I patted it on the roof by way of apology as I walked to my front door. Behind me I heard heavy rattling. I turned to see a transporter carefully wobbling down my road. It pulled up outside my drive and I smiled so hard at the sight of my Beemer gleaming proudly on top.

I quickly signed the release papers, slapped a fiver in the driver's hands and waved him goodbye. I opened the door carefully, sat in the hot seat and took a breath, but it wouldn't come out properly because of the stupid grin across my face. I ran my fingers over the steering wheel and it felt like home.

I connected my phone via Bluetooth and played the first song on my playlist, created just for this very moment. 'Str8 Ballin'. I turned it up high, let the bass wash over me as 2pac rapped about his life as a street dealer. I slid my seat all the way back, leaned back, kicked off my Jordans and loosened my belt. I wasn't going anywhere for a while.

I was three songs in, when my phone rang.

Without looking at the caller display I accepted the call with the press of a button on the multi-function steering wheel.

'Javid?'

A voice now so familiar came clearly through my speakers, as though my father was here right next to me, calling my name, and it hurt so fucking much.

Before I could stop myself, I said, 'They're coming for you.'

93
Abu Dhabi

When The Teacher met the Sheikh there was only going be one outcome.

The long journey from the rural village in the Maimana region of Afghanistan to Dubai, via Pakistan, was gruelling but without incident.

The shorter journey from Dubai to Abu Dhabi felt as though Bin Jabbar's position had shifted. He had felt eyes on him.

It didn't matter anymore, he thought, as he looked out of the window from the Sheikh's home office. His hands clasped behind his back as his eyes moved around the large, luxurious estate. Bin Jabbar tried to recall the moment his fight, his jihad, had become more important than his son. For all his efforts, really nothing had changed. Muslims were still being mindlessly murdered, at a rate which could never be matched.

'It's done, Al-Mudarris.' Sheikh Ali Ghulam replaced the receiver back in its cradle and straightened his headdress. Bin Jabbar turned away from the window and stood in front of Ghulam's well-kept desk. 'I have informed the appropriate contacts. It shall be communicated to Pathaan. Inshallah. The fatwa on Javid Qasim has been lifted.'

An apology would be an admission that the Sheikh would not dare make. Bin Jabbar did not expect it. The smell of fear that filled the room was admission enough.

Bin Jabbar was a fair man, a man who had always given his people the benefit of the doubt. Ghulam had made a mistake, an error in judgement. But on so many occasions, without question, he had been there when called upon, supporting Bin Jabbar, as a friend, as a financier.

He would be forgiven.

'Al-Mudarris. I will provide you with safe passage to Islamabad. It is all arranged.'

Bin Jabbar rested his eyes and formed his son in his mind.

'You will rest there, Inshallah. It's all taken care of.'

He had his eyes, his heart, his flesh, his blood. Javid had his smile.

'I will personally make sure you live like a king.'

Bin Jabbar opened his eyes and looked at the man who had come so close to taking away the one thing he truly loved.

The weight of the Desert Eagle handgun smashed down with almighty force on Sheikh Ghulam's head.

Dazed, he lifted his head from the desk. A sliver of blood trickled from under his headdress and slowly down his forehead. 'Al-Mudarris, please.' But the handle of the gun was descending again towards his head, and behind it Bin Jabbar's burnt face carried nothing but fury. Ghulam's hands flew to his head for protection. The heavy steel smashed down, *again* and *again* and *again*, cracking first his fingers and then his skull.

Bin Jabbar walked around the desk, past Ghulam's bloody head slumped on his bloody desk. He looked out of the window at the tall telephone mast. It was exactly where he would have placed a man. At the top of the mast was mounted a large satellite dish, behind which he spotted the gleam of a sniper's rifle.

Bin Jabbar turned his back to it. He placed his gun on the desk, beside a barely-breathing Ghulam, and pulled him up by his hair. He picked up the desk phone and wrapped the wire tightly around Ghulam's throat twice over.

The Sheikh finally screamed for forgiveness, as his life slipped away in the hands of The Teacher.

*

Bin Jabbar stepped out of the office as the man he once was. Inzamam Qasim, father of Javid Qasim.

He looked down the long, red-carpeted hallway, checking in both directions. He peered over the balcony. The mansion was empty. Ghulam's security detail, that he had noticed on arrival, had vanished. In his right hand he gripped the blood-splattered Desert Eagle and in his left hand he gripped tightly onto a cell phone that he had removed from Ghulam's thobe.

He dialled a number quickly. It was answered quickly.

'Javid.' Inzamam Qasim gripped the phone and waited to hear his son's voice one last time.

'They're coming for you.'

Qasim smiled. 'Tell me... How are you, Javid?'

'I'm alright.'

'And your mum?' he asked, as though in a dream.

'She's alright... No thanks to you.'

Qasim could feel his son's temper rising. 'You're both better off without me.'

'Yeah?' his son said softly, before he found his voice. 'How the *fuck* would you know?'

Qasim stood at the balcony. On either side of him, two curved sweeping staircases. 'We live in troubled times, Javid. I chose to take on a higher purpose, to help give our people hope. I prayed that one day, you would be standing by my side.'

'*Fuck off.* You disgust me, you hear me? *Higher fucking purpose?* No. I'm not having that. You were a husband and a father. *My father*! That was your fucking purpose.'

With Javid screaming in his ear, Qasim took the staircase to his right, the gun scraping down the gold-plated bannister. He was proud of how his son was tearing him to shreds. As he slowly made his way down the stairs, he saw movement through the downstairs window, three men crouched low. All wearing the pale colours of army fatigues. All holding automatic assault rifles.

'How is your job?' Qasim asked. His gun covered the window as he tried to entice as much information as he could from his son. 'Are you seeing anybody at the moment?'

'You've got no *fucking* right!'

'Please, Javid,' Qasim said. 'I'd like to know.'

'I hope they find you,' Javid said, wearily, the screaming out of his system. 'I want nothing more than for you to suffer and die.'

The window smashed, a gloved hand dropped a canister. Toxic gas quickly filled the room. Qasim refused to cover his face. Desert Eagle handgun in one hand, pointing at the enemy. His son in the other. He wasn't willing to let go of either. A soldier climbed through the window, followed by another and another. Their faces shielded with gas masks. A battering ram pounded against the heavy reinforced front doors three times, before the doors splintered and swung open. Four more men entered the house.

'What's going on?' Javid asked. 'Where are you?'

Keep talking, son. Stay in my ear until the end.

Qasim fired a shot for cover and turned on his heel, bent low and started to climb back up the sweeping staircase. Above him on the balcony, four-gas masked Kafirs were pointing their guns at him as they repeatedly screamed instructions.

'Get down on your knees!'

'Hands in the air!'

'Drop your weapon!'

'Do as they say,' Javid screamed. 'Give up, *please.*'

Qasim did not get on his knees. He didn't put his hands in the air. He didn't drop his weapon.

'Son...' He lifted the gun. 'It was always going to end this way.'

Qasim was quick enough to let off a single shot before his tired body was torn apart, ripped up and pulped by bullets. He tumbled slowly down the staircase. His head connected with the marble floor, his lower body and legs splayed over the last few steps. Heavy footsteps approached him, weapons trained on him. The Desert Eagle had slipped out of his hand, but the phone remained firmly in his grip.

As he lay there, Inzamam Qasim could still hear his son. The one word that he had longed to hear.

'*Dad...?*'

94

Jay

The six-by-nine Blaupunkt speakers beeped to indicate that the call had been disconnected. The music kicked back in. 'Shut 'em down'. Public Enemy. The bass once again took over and trapped me in my Beemer.

I placed my phone in the centre console and tried to get back into it, but I just wasn't feeling it anymore. What I was feeling was a little stupid, sat in my driveway by myself, listening to outdated hip-hop, with my shoes kicked off. I slipped my Jordans back on and turned the volume right the way down on the stereo. The dial came off in my hand. I tried to slot it back in place, but the fitting had a break in it and it sat askew, ruining the whole fucking look of my car stereo. I lifted my leg back and kicked it flush with the sole of my left boot. A large spider crack appeared on the orange digital display. I kicked it again.

Just above my stereo, I kicked the flimsy fucking air vents, too. They broke easily. What wouldn't break so easily was the rear-view mirror, I was pulling at it using my body weight, almost hanging off the fucking thing. I could see my reflection in it, my teeth clamped tight as I put every effort into snapping it away from its neck. It eventually came away with a satisfying crack. I threw it hard and watched it satisfyingly smash through the passenger side window.

I opened the car door and stepped out.

Holding my house key tightly in my hand, I scraped the length of my Beemer as I walked to my front door. Refusing to allow time to curb my temper, I ran up the stairs to my bedroom to retrieve what I was looking for. I emerged from the house with a baseball bat.

What was it that he asked me?

How is your job? Are you seeing anybody at the moment?

I swiped down and cleanly beheaded the wing mirror. '*Yeah, job's alright. I just got back today after some time off. Forgot my fucking password, didn't I?*' The sound of my baseball bat swinging clean through the driver's side window was glorious. '*My Team Leader wants to put me on some training for the call logging system. I'll find a way out of it.*' I popped both headlights and then I went to town on the front grill. '*There is this girl, actually. Kelly. Thinking about asking her out for a drink. I think you'd like her, you narcissist motherfucker! Out to save the fucking world, when you couldn't save your son.*'

The windscreen put up some resistance and the baseball bat vibrated in my hands on impact, the welcome pain ran through my arm and up my shoulder.

Panting hard, I got down on my haunches and dropped the bat. It rolled gently away from me. I could hardly blame it. I looked at my beautiful car. Instant fucking regret. My Beemer was as broken as I was.

Not giving a fuck that my neighbours were out in force, I got to my feet and pressed the fob key. It efficiently chirped and locked my car as I entered my home and shut the front fucking door on the whole fucking world.

I switched the TV on and waited for the inevitable news to confirm reports that The Teacher had been killed. It'd be front page on every newspaper. Talking heads, so called fucking experts, chatting shit well into the night. A victory for the West. A victory for those who I'd sided with. The world would briefly rejoice. The world would believe whatever was fed to them...

Me? I won't believe it until I see my father's body with my own eyes.

95

Eight months later...

Finally, the moment he had been waiting for had arrived.

Eight months ago, Rafi Kabir had entered his parents' bedroom as they slept soundly. He'd kissed his mother and father gently on the cheek and, with a rucksack full of clothes and football trading cards, he quietly backed out of his parents' bedroom and walked out of his home into the early hours of the morning. He'd walked to the end of his street where Pathaan had been waiting.

He had handed Rafi a motorcycle helmet.

Rafi had clung on to Pathaan, his skinny arms around his waist, his face resting on the cool back of the leather jacket. All the way out of Blackburn and into London.

Rafi had never been to London before, it was as dirty as he'd been told it'd be. They stayed in a cramped flat in the backstreets of Hammersmith. The flat belonged to Yousuf Ejaz, a British Muslim and member of Ghurfat-al-Mudarris. Yousuf had been recovering from a broken leg. In the day, Rafi helped to look after him, in the evening, Rafi listened intently as Pathaan re-educated them on jihad, a far cry from the teachings of al-Mudarris.

Never fear the afterlife. Give yourself wholly to The Cause.

Never fear the afterlife. Show to the world that we are not afraid to look the Kafir in the eye before we take our last breath.

Never fear the afterlife. Allah will grant you the highest place in Jannah.

Pathaan had died without fear of the afterlife.

Rafi, who had just turned eleven, would never forget his words.

'How does it feel?' Yousuf met Rafi's eye through the full length mirror.

'Like it's a part of me, Bruv.' Rafi smiled at his reflection, a vision that he had dreamt about many times.

'Okay. So let's get you dressed.' Yousuf helped Rafi put on the jacket of the decorative sherwani that they had bought one size too big. A rich cream in colour, with maroon piping around the sleeves and neck line which matched the drainpipe maroon shalwar. Yousuf got to his knees as he carefully buttoned up the jacket. He looked up at Rafi and laughed. 'You look like the groom.'

'Shut up,' Rafi said. 'I ain't never getting married.'

Yousuf cleared his throat and looked away.

'Come on. Let us pray.'

*

It took a lot of will for Rafi not to tear into the school kids who ripped the piss out of his appearance on the H91 bus. He had dealt with little shits like that his whole life, before his father had uprooted his family to a predominantly Muslim part of Blackburn. He kept his breathing even, as Pathaan Bhai had taught him, and let the filth serve as motivation.

Not familiar with Hounslow, Rafi stepped off the bus one stop too early. He walked the last mile towards Osterley Park Hotel with his head down, acutely aware that the police or some do-gooder could recognise him. Even eight months on, he was still a missing child.

Rafi weaved through the parked cars within the hotel car park, the music blaring in his ears as he approached the function hall. To his right, a handful of screeching kids were kicking a can around the car park as an improvised football. A very small part of him wanted to abandon everything and join in.

One of them, a little white kid, red in the face from kicking the can around, approached him.

'Are you on my dad's side?' he asked, taking in Rafi's outfit.

Rafi nodded.

'This way.' The boy walked into the hotel and past reception. He picked up one red rose from many red and white roses laid out neatly on a table outside the function hall, and handed it to Rafi. 'You have to wear this.' The boy had to raise his voice over the music. 'Red for my dad's side. White for my mum's side.' Rafi accepted the rose and pin and struggled to attach it to the jacket of his sherwani. 'I can help.' The boy smiled. Rafi handed him the rose and the boy held it against his chest. Rafi, careful not to nick the boy's hand with the pin, secured the rose in place. 'Teamwork!' the boy happily exclaimed. 'My name is Jack. What's yours?'

'Rafi.'

Together, Rafi and Jack pushed open the double doors to the hall and stepped in just as a classic Bollywood song, from a classic Bollywood movie starring Amitabh Bachan, Rafi's favourite actor, filled the hall. So many occasions, Rafi had danced and showed off and re-enacted the lines to that movie, in his living room, in front of his family.

'Where are your Mum and Dad?' Jack asked.

'Parking the car,' Rafi said,

'I have to go.' Jack said, something catching his attention. 'My mum's calling me. You want to say hello?'

Rafi followed his gaze towards the back of the hall, to the bride and groom's table. The bride was gesturing for Jack to join him. Rafi nodded. 'I have a gift.'

Rafi followed the boy through the guests. It made him sick as he noticed the difference in colour and culture. Revealing dresses side by side with traditional lenga's. Masala chai sharing the same table space as bottles of beer. White and brown easily mixing, talking, smiling, laughing, *dancing*, as though they didn't hate each other. Rafi's eyes searched the hall for the man who had killed Pathaan. The man who'd given away all their secrets to the Kafir in exchange for freedom.

'That's my Nana and Granddad next to my mum.' Jack pointed at the sour-faced elderly couple sat next to the bride, as they approached. 'That's my Khala on the other side. I don't know where my Dad is.' Jack ran around the back of the long table and stood by his mother. 'Where's Dad?' Jack asked.

'He's around somewhere,' his mother replied. 'Mingling, I should guess. Who's this?'

'This is Rafi. He's bought you a gift.'

She turned to smile at Rafi, just as Rafi turned away to see Imran Siddiqui across the other side of the hall. He was walking slowly towards them, stopping only to shake hands with guests, his smile so wide, as though every fucking thing that had come before had been forgotten about.

'Dad,' Jack called across, before turning to Rafi. 'That's my Dad,' Jack smiled proudly.

Rafi waited for Imran to fucking acknowledge him. He watched Imran smile adoringly at his wife, his son, his white family, before his eyes found Rafi. That wiped the smile off his face and replaced it with pure fear. Imran took a purposeful stride forward towards the table, then another, and then he broke into a run.

Rafi slipped his hand into the side pocket of the decorative jacket of his sherwani, and it emerged gripping a small detonator. It was time to show Imran what it truly meant to be a soldier of Ghurfat-al-Mudarris.

Rafi closed his eyes and visualised the white light flashing across the guests, gathered to celebrate the coming together of cultures. He visualised the devastation on Imran's face, helpless, unable to help those he loved the most, as the deafening blast tore through them.

He opened his eyes and smiled at Imran.
Allahu Akbar.

Acknowledgements

They say the second book is the hardest to write. They know what they're talking about. I couldn't have done it, not on my own.

The biggest thanks to my amazing family. My wife, for always finding me when I feel lost. My eldest for making it clear that the writing had to revolve around his time. My youngest, well, he didn't know what was going on, but just his smile and babbling advice made me want to be a better version of myself. My mum, dad and brother, you don't realise how much you inspire me.

A huge thanks to my agent, Julian Alexander, of LAW Literary Agency. Right at the beginning he made it clear that I could approach him with anything that was on my mind. A decision which I think he now regrets. Thanks for being patient with me, Julian.

A massive gratitude to my publisher, HQ/HarperCollins, for believing in me. My editor, the wise and wonderful Clio Cornish, who sees things that I never see and finds solutions when all I see is problems. My publicist, the always-smiling Lily Capewell, who does not take no for an answer. Thank you Team HQ – you make me feel like an Author.

Finally, and most importantly, I want to Thank God. I know I don't always play ball, but me and you? I think we're cool.

ONE PLACE. MANY STORIES

Bold, innovative and
empowering publishing.

FOLLOW US ON:

@HQStories